P9-CRV-974

Smoke

Also by Lisa Miscione

Angel Fire
The Darkness Gathers
Twice

Smoke

Lisa Miscione

 St. Martin's Minotaur ❧ New York

www.minotaurbooks.com

Library of Congress Cataloging-in-Publication Data

Miscione, Lisa.
    Smoke / Lisa Miscione.— 1st St. Martin's Minotaur ed.
        p. cm.
    ISBN 0-312-34185-7
    EAN 978-0-312-34185-5
    1. Strong, Lydia (Fictitious character)—Fiction. 2. Suicide
victims—Family relationships—Fiction. 3. Brothers and
sisters—Fiction. 4. Women journalists—Fiction. 5. Missing
persons—Fiction. I. Title.

PS3613.I83S66 2005
813'.6—dc22

                                        2005049405

First Edition: December 2005

10 9 8 7 6 5 4 3 2 1

For Lucy

Acknowledgments

I am most thankful to (and for) my husband, **Jeffrey Unger**, whose tremendous talents as my publicist, webmaster, editor, reader, and fan are only surpassed by his being the most wonderful husband and my very best friend.

As always, thanks to my fabulous agent, **Elaine Markson**, and her indispensable assistant, **Gary Johnson**. Their faith, advice, guidance, and enthusiasm are all priceless.

I am so grateful to **Kelley Ragland** for her wonderful editing. Every book I have written has been enriched by her talent and guidance.

I have been blessed with an amazingly loving and supportive network of family and friends who have each offered their own special brand of encouragement and support in my career and in my life. I am eternally grateful for each and every one of them.

And very special thanks to **Master Nick Scrima** of the Chinese Martial Arts Center in Dunedin, Florida. He knows why.

Part One

The Lost Girl

Until you've smoked out the bees,
You can't eat the honey.
                    —Russian proverb

One

Lydia Strong wanted a cigarette to celebrate the defeat of her enemy. She leaned back in her chair and looked at the manuscript that sat fat and neat on her desk beside her computer. She felt like a prizefighter who had finally, after a brutal showdown, sent her opponent to the mat. *The Lost Girl* had taken her nearly a year to write and every page had been a battle. It was a first for her. Words were her tools, sometimes her weapons. Either way, she'd always wielded them with ease. But this book didn't want to be written. Every day the blank page had seemed like a taunt, a dare, a bully on the playground looking for her lunch money.

Maybe it was because in the writing of it, she had to let go of things she'd been clinging to for years. Maybe because, as painful as those things were, they were comfortable, familiar, and a part of her didn't really want to see them exorcised. But now they were safely incarcerated in the pages of her manuscript. Soon they'd be edited and revised, edited and revised again. Then they'd be exposed to the light of the world. And, like all demons, in the sun they'd turn to piles of dust.

She laughed a little, just because of the lightness of her relief. She got up from her desk and tossed around the idea of going out for a pack of cigarettes. Maybe if Jeffrey wasn't lying on the couch reading the Sunday *Times,* she'd go down to the bodega on the corner of Lafayette and Great Jones, smoke a cigarette on the street and then throw away the rest of the pack. But he'd be able to tell and then he'd give her a hard time. It wasn't worth it.

"I'm done," she called, walking out of her office and through the loft. But he wasn't on the couch; he was standing at the counter that divided the kitchen from the living room, talking on the phone.

"Oops, sorry," she said when she saw him.

He looked at her strangely when she walked in. She hadn't heard the phone ring. She took a frosty bottle of Ketel One vodka from the freezer and poured herself a lowball, trying and failing to be quiet as she put some ice in the glass and squirted some lime juice from one of those little plastic bottles shaped cutely like a lime.

"I see," he said, lowering his eyes to the floor beneath his feet, tapping a pen on the countertop. "No, I'd rather tell her, David, if you don't mind."

"Is that my grandfather?" Lydia asked, looking at him now. She could tell there was something wrong, but she sipped at the drink in her hand and pretended she couldn't. She needed a few minutes to enjoy the completion of her manuscript before life leaked in and started demanding attention.

Jeffrey put the phone back in the cradle and didn't look at her right away.

"Did you hear me? I'm finished. I finished *The Lost Girl.*"

"That's fantastic. Congratulations," he said softly, moving toward her and taking her into his arms.

"Want a drink?" she asked.

"Not right now," he said. She pulled away from him after a second and then walked over to the living room. The fire they'd made earlier in the afternoon was low, just a few flames danced. Outside, a light snow tapped against the windows and their view of lower Manhattan was obscured by frost.

She sat on the couch and curled her legs up beneath her. Something in her chest was thumping. She didn't like the look on Jeffrey's face or the careful way he was moving toward her.

"There's some news," he said, sitting beside her.

"Are they all right?" she asked, bracing herself. Her maternal grandparents, David and Eleanor Strong, were the only living family members to whom she had any connection. She thought of them, both hearty, young-minded, still traveling, enjoying their lives and each other. It seemed like they would always be there. But with both of them in their early seventies, she knew she'd have to deal with their mortality at some point. But she hadn't done that yet. And she wasn't ready.

"Oh, yeah," he said quickly. "Yeah, they're both fine."

She felt a wash of relief. "Okay," she said, releasing a breath she'd been holding.

"Then what?" she said, sitting up, leaning into him as he sat beside her. He took her hand in his and cast his eyes down.

"Your father . . ." he said, letting the sentence trail.

The phrase sounded so strange. She never thought of herself as having a father. Most times she forgot he even existed.

"What about him?" she asked, frowning.

"He's dead, Lydia," he said. "I'm sorry."

Something shifted inside of her. "Dead?" she said, like it was a word that didn't have any meaning to her.

"I'm sorry," he said again, releasing her hand and taking hold of her shoulder. She looked at his face, saw worry there, sadness for her.

"How?" she asked after a moment where she searched herself for feeling and came up with nothing. She *wanted* to feel something, but there was only a cool numbness.

"Your grandfather didn't have the details."

She'd met her father only once, when she was fifteen years old, on the day after her mother's funeral. It was a lifetime ago, and she found that she remembered everything about that time like a lucid dream. Some details were vivid but a strange fog seemed to hang over the events.

She remembered the door ajar on the day she discovered her mother's body, the blaring stereo that greeted her as she arrived home. But the terrible discovery of her mother's body and the grim investigation that followed was a jumble of isolated events with no real timeline in her memory. She remembered the crowded funeral service and the hushed sobbing and the somber voice of the priest, the burial on a day that was too bright and sunny, too beautiful. She remembered identifying Jed McIntyre as the man who'd been following her and her mother for days. She remembered the single garnet earring missing from her mother's jewelry box. And she remembered her father's visit. The one and only time she'd seen him in the flesh.

She had sat alone in the living room staring out the bay window at the woods behind her house. The leaves were turning, a riot of orange, red, and gold. The day was cool and sun washed, and she remembered wishing for rain. She wanted thunder and gale-force winds, hail and lightning.

She'd heard the doorbell but paid no attention, sure it was another neighbor come to offer their condolences. She pulled herself into a tight ball and closed her eyes, dreading having to smile politely, having to say she would be all right. Then she heard her grandfather's voice as he opened the door, then a soft murmuring, then silence. Her grandfather's voice sounded angry, but she thought she must be mistaken. Then she saw him at the door, his face tight and ashen.

Hovering behind her grandfather, there was a stranger with her storm-cloud gray eyes. Tall and slouching, poorly dressed, he held flowers and had a hangdog look about him, an aura of shame. He shifted uncomfortably from foot to foot. He was a tall, lean man, blondish, faded looking, like a bad copy of himself. Even though she'd never met him, she knew him immediately.

"You're my father?" she asked, getting up.

"You don't have to see him, Lydia," her grandfather said.

But her curiosity had been great. It was the first feeling she'd had other than grief and horror since her mother died.

"No," she said. "It's okay, Grandpa."

She stood up and her father walked toward her. He held the flowers out to her. She took them, her eyes fixed on him. Struggling in her relationship with her mother, she'd thought about her missing father often. None of the fantasies she'd had about him in her life had even come close to predicting the ordinary man who stood before her. She had imagined him as a great lover, dark and handsome; a motorcycle daredevil, reckless and brave; an international spy, suave and sophisticated. What other kind of man, she concluded, could have stolen her strong, beautiful mother's heart and then left her broken and forever sad? Surely, some great danger or some irresistible intrigue had lured him from his family. In spite of what her mother said.

"Don't fantasize about your father, Lydia," her mother had told her numerous times. "He was just an irresponsible man, living for get-rich-quick schemes, always looking for something more than he had."

She had never believed her mother, until the moment he stood before her, eyes begging, hands quivering. It had felt like another death for her.

She let the flowers drop to the floor, turned her back on him, and walked back to her perch by the window. She might have forgiven him for leaving them, for breaking her mother's heart, but she could never forgive him for being so unremarkable. She could never forgive that he had obviously left them for nothing.

"It's time for you to go," her grandfather had said. He'd stood like a sentry in the corner of the room. He had always been a big man, with strong, imposing shoulders and hands as big as oven mitts, a strong, angular face that looked like it should be carved in a mountain somewhere.

"You've made her a cold bitch, just like her mother," her father said then. For all this size, David Strong moved on him like a cat.

Up until the day they moved from the house where Lydia's mother had been murdered, the stain left by her father bleeding into the carpet after her grandfather had belted him remained, a faint reminder of a small man. She remembered thinking that the house was full of her parents' blood, and the thought made her stomach turn. That was the only memory she had of her father.

"Lydia," said Jeffrey.

"I'm okay," she said, snapping back to the present. And she was. She was shocked and there was something churning in her stomach. But she felt strong, stable. She could hardly be grief stricken for a man she'd barely known.

"I guess I'm not sure how to feel."

Jeffrey shook his head slowly, looked at her as if he were wondering if she would cry. He didn't say anything.

"Is there a funeral?" she asked, leaning back on the couch.

"There was. Last week. Your grandfather only found out because an old buddy of his who still lives in Nyack saw the obit."

Lydia's grandparents had recently moved from Nyack to a two-bedroom apartment on the Upper West Side, partly to be closer to Lydia and partly because they were unable to sleep in a house where Jed McIntyre, the man who'd murdered their daughter, had come for them as well.

Lydia nodded, placed her drink on the coffee table, and laid her head in Jeffrey's lap.

"I'm sorry, Lydia," he said quietly, putting a hand on her head.

"It's a strange feeling," she said after a few minutes of quiet. "To lose something you never had. I don't know how to explain it. I don't know how to *feel* it."

But she knew she didn't have to explain herself to him. He understood her; he always did. She turned around, took his hand in hers, played absently with the thick platinum band he wore on his left hand. Inscribed on the underside of it were her name and the date of their wedding. She wore a matching band, studded randomly with tiny star-cut sapphires.

They'd been married in a simple ceremony on Hanalei Bay in Kauai nearly a year ago. She'd worn a simple white linen shift and traditional plumeria lei and stood barefoot with him on the sand at sunset. Their ceremony, officiated by an old Hawaiian priestess, had been witnessed by David and Eleanor Strong and Dax Chicago, a man who'd become their closest friend.

"I can't believe you'd have the nerve to wear white," Dax had whispered to her after she and Jeffrey had exchanged rings. She'd laughed out loud. In all her life, she'd never felt as light and happy as she had that day. The long and treacherous journey they'd taken to the altar had ended well and she was grateful.

"What do we need to do?" Jeffrey asked her now. "You know—to observe this?"

She closed her eyes. "I don't know. I'll get back to you."

It was after ten when the phone rang. Jeff was still reading and Lydia was half asleep, her head still in his lap. She'd managed to push thoughts of her father away enough to doze but not enough to actually fall asleep; a kind of low-grade sadness and uneasiness had taken hold of her. She hopped up to get the phone.

"Who'd call so late?" asked Jeff, not looking up from his book on New York State gun law. He had his glasses on, which Lydia thought made him look sexy and intellectual. He thought they just made him look old but he couldn't read without them so he endured.

"Must be more good news," said Lydia. She was thinking to herself that it was probably Dax, king of trampling boundaries.

The caller ID read "unavailable."

"Hello?"

"This is Detective Matt Stenopolis, NYPD Missing Persons Unit. I need to speak to Lydia Strong."

His voice sounded youngish but there was a gravity and deep timbre to it that told Lydia he took himself seriously and expected others to do the same.

"This is."

"Ms. Strong, you left a message for Lily Samuels about two weeks ago indicating that you were returning a call she made to you." She could hear street noise on the other end of the phone.

"That's right," she said, concern and curiosity aroused.

He cleared his throat. "Ms. Samuels has been missing now for over two weeks and I'm wondering if we can talk."

"Sure," she said. "Of course."

"I'm calling from my car. I know it's late but would it be inconvenient if I came by?"

"Um, no," she said glancing at the clock. "Come on by."

She gave him the address and hung up the phone.

"Who was that?" said Jeffrey, putting down his book and looking at her.

"A detective. Lily Samuels is missing," she said leaning against the counter.

"Who?"

"Remember that journalism class I taught at NYU as a visiting professor a couple of years ago? She was one of my students. She started at the *Post* last year on the crime desk."

Lydia had felt a special affinity for Lily from the day she had walked into the large, over-warm classroom and sat in the front row. There was an earnestness, an honesty to her that Lydia could see in her deep brown eyes. And she had a belly full of fire. Lydia could always recognize it, that love of the hunt, that drive for the heart of a story. Lily's talent had set her apart from the rest of the class; the kindness and compassion in her interview style and in her writing put her head and shoulders above most of the professional writers Lydia knew. In the past two years, Lydia had given her advice on pursuing stories she was working on for her degree, and eventually a reference that got her a foot in the door at the *Post*.

It wasn't long before the buzzer rang. She checked the video monitor. A very tall, well-dressed, youngish man in a leather coat lifted his shield to the video monitor. Lydia pressed the button that allowed entry to the elevator bank downstairs. She watched as he stepped out of view and into the elevator that would lift directly into the apartment.

It was the little things like this which reminded her that she was free; she didn't have to feel the cold fingers of fear tugging at her every time the buzzer rang late, didn't have to wonder if the person she saw at the door was a threat. It was like a grip had been released from her heart. Jed McIntyre, the man who murdered her mother and then last year came for her after his erroneous release from a maximum-security mental hospital, was dead. Unlike incarceration, death was a securely permanent condition. And Lydia found she could breathe again.

As she waited by the elevator door, she heard Jeffrey in the kitchen making coffee.

"How long has she been missing?" he called from the kitchen.

"Two weeks," said Lydia grimly. In a missing persons investigation it was the first thirty-six hours that were critical. After that time period had passed, the odds of anyone being found alive decreased exponentially. For Lily, that window had closed.

"And the guy is still working into the night," said Jeffrey. "Must have its hooks in him."

Lydia nodded to herself. They both knew what that was like.

Detective Matt Stenopolis was, simply put, gigantic. He ducked his head slightly as he stepped from the elevator and Lydia's hand disappeared into his when he took it in greeting. He had pale white skin, a chaos of blue-black hair and a dark shadow of stubble to match. He smelled like snow and cigarettes.

He's bigger than Dax, thought Lydia, as he and Jeffrey introduced themselves. It was a different kind of big, though. Dax was big by design. The detective was big by genetics. His shoulders, wide as a refrigerator, slouched the way the shoulders of all extremely tall people seem to, as if protecting themselves against the jeers and taunts that have been hurled at them all their lives.

"Thanks for letting me stop by so late, Ms. Strong."

"No problem. Lily's a friend," she said. "Anything I can do."

He followed her into the living room and she encouraged him to have a seat on the couch. When he sat on it, the large sofa looked as if it had been made for Barbie Dolls. She thought she heard it groan in protest.

"Coffee?" she asked.

"Please," he answered gratefully.

"Three weeks ago today," began the detective, as Lydia handed him a cup of coffee, "Lily Samuels' brother Mickey committed suicide in his car in an Office Depot parking lot in Riverdale."

"Oh, no," said Lydia. She remembered thinking that Lily had sounded strained and worried in her message. But she hadn't mentioned Mickey's suicide. Not that anyone would leave that kind of news on someone's voicemail.

The detective nodded slowly, took a sip of his coffee, and continued.

"The police ruled it a suicide right away. The guy was alone in his car with all the doors locked. He had a half-finished bottle of Jack Daniels between his legs. There was gunshot residue on his right hand. He left a note for his sister. He put his gun in his mouth and pulled the trigger."

They were all silent for a second, as if out of respect.

"What did the note say?" asked Lydia.

"It said: 'Dear Lily, I'm so sorry to leave you all alone here. But I just can't do it anymore. You're the strong one. It's too much for me."

He said it like he'd played the note over and over in his mind and the words had ceased to have meaning for him. But Lydia could hear the crushing sadness in them.

"Lily was totally devastated, of course. And apparently she refused to believe he would kill himself. I mean, she wasn't just doubtful. She was positive that he couldn't have done it."

"That's pretty common with family members of a suicide," said Jeffrey.

"An initial phase of denial is common. But, according to friends she was *certain,* and after the funeral she set out to prove it. She took a week off from her job and went up to Riverdale." Detective Stenopolis took a sip of his coffee.

"I remember her telling me that she and her brother were close, more like best friends than siblings," said Lydia. "She didn't have any indication that he was depressed or in some kind of trouble?"

"Apparently not. Friends got the sense that there had been some kind of conflict between them. But she never said what specifically, just that he was 'acting like a jerk.' He had moved from the city up to Riverdale about six months ago, apparently wanting to open some kind of café and performance space, leaving a mega-money job in banking. Sounded to me like he was burned out."

He was quiet a second, then he went on.

"Lily Samuels went up to Riverdale on October 15th. She was in touch with her friends for the first week. Then nothing. Her cell phone voicemail, which we accessed with the help of her mobile service provider, was full of worried messages from her friends. One of those messages was from you. Do you remember what she said on her message to you?"

"I can do better than that, Detective. I'm sure I saved it because I didn't hear back from her. I tend to save email messages and phone messages until I connect with the person involved, otherwise I just forget."

"There are messages on there from 1995," said Jeffrey with a small smile. He considered her system of keeping track of messages somewhat disorganized. Ever since he'd read *Clear Your Clutter with Feng Shui,* he'd been nearly impossible to live with on such matters. She ignored him as she grabbed the cordless phone. She entered her codes and after she skipped about twelve messages, she put the phone on its speaker setting.

"This message was left on October 22nd at 7:04 P.M.," said the electronic voice.

Then, "Ms. Strong, it's Lily Samuels." She released a heavy sigh. "I *really* need your help. I am out of my league. Big time. I—I just really need to talk to you. Can you call me back? As soon as possible? Thanks. Bye."

Lydia felt a twist of guilt in her stomach. Listening to the message now she heard the fear, the anxiety in Lily's voice. When she'd heard it the first time, Lily had just seemed really stressed to her. It had taken Lydia until the next day to return the call because she'd been stressed out herself, wrestling with her own work.

"I've never heard her voice before," said Detective Stenopolis, an expression on his face that Lydia couldn't read. "She sounds so young."

"She *is* young," said Lydia. "Twenty-five or twenty-six, I think."

"Twenty-six," he said. "Under what circumstances did she generally contact you? Did you talk often? Would you say you were friends?"

"It was really more of mentoring relationship. She was a student of mine when I taught a journalism class at NYU. She was special, really talented. At the end of the class, I encouraged her to keep in touch if she needed anything. She'd call for advice on stories, references, stuff like that."

"So when you got the call you thought she was probably calling about work?"

"Yes. That was generally what we talked about. Sometimes we chatted about personal things briefly but mainly not."

"When was the last time you saw her?"

"I think we had drinks about a year and a half ago. She wanted to thank me for getting her in for her interview at the *Post*."

Detective Stenopolis was scribbling notes as she spoke and continued writing for a minute after she'd gone silent.

She remembered that Lily was radiant that night with excitement. The interview had gone well and she felt like she was on her way to fulfilling the only dream she'd ever had, to be a journalist. She was dating someone new—a banker, if Lydia remembered right—and Lily seemed smitten with him. At the time, things in Lydia's life had been pretty hairy, so her time with Lily had seemed like a little oasis of cocktails and girl talk in a sea of madness.

"Who reported her missing?" asked Lydia. Curiosity was tapping her on the shoulder.

"Her mother. When Lily missed her mother's fiftieth birthday everyone knew there was something wrong. Apparently, it was not unlike Lily to be incommunicado for a week or so when she was working on something. But she was a loving daughter and a good friend. No matter how busy she was, she wouldn't miss her mother's birthday, especially knowing what a hard time it would be for her on the heels of Mickey's death."

"Her mother must be a wreck," said Lydia. What a nightmare it must be to lose a child to suicide and then for the other to go missing. It was hard to imagine.

"She's heavily medicated right now. Major valium just to get through the day, the husband says."

"Lily's father?" asked Lydia, reaching for something Lily had told her about her family.

"Her stepfather. Raised both kids from the time Lily was two and Mickey was four."

"What happened to their father?" asked Lydia.

Detective Stenopolis paused for a second, seemed to consider whether he should say. "Suicide," he said, finally. "Shot himself in a car, drunk on JD. Just like his son Mickey."

Lydia felt her heart thump. It was strange to be having this conversation after just hearing about her father's own death. It seemed surreal and Lydia felt a familiar nervousness, a slight anxiety.

"That's pretty odd," said Jeffrey, narrowing his eyes.

The detective rubbed his hands together as if he were warming them, seemed to consider it for a moment, whether it was odd or not. Then, "Depression runs in families often. I'm not sure how uncommon it is. Suicide. I don't know . . . maybe it's easier to do it if you know someone who has."

Lydia wouldn't have thought of it that way but it made an odd kind of sense to her. As if the idea of suicide was a contagion; the more closely exposed to it you were, the easier it was to catch.

"So you said you've been working on the case for two weeks?" said Lydia.

The detective nodded. "Today is the fourteenth day. I think she's been missing since October 23rd, though, because no one who called her on or after that day heard back from her. Which means that the thirty-six hours where it would be most likely for us to find her passed before we ever knew she was gone."

Lydia looked down at the floor. If I'd called her back on the 22nd, could I have helped her? Lydia thought. It wasn't a healthy way to think but that was the way her mind worked. There was little point in considering the answer.

"So what have you got so far?" asked Jeffrey.

Detective Stenopolis gave him a look. "Thanks so much for your time," he said, politely. "Ms. Strong, would you mind if I sent a tech over to record that message from your voicemail?"

"We can take care of that, if you want, Detective," said Jeffrey.

"One of the communication techs from my firm can do it tomorrow and we'll email you the digital file."

"That would be great," he said, rising and handing Jeffrey his card. "It could take a week to get someone from the department over here on such a low priority."

"Low priority?" said Lydia with a frown. "I'd think something like this would be big news. A pretty young reporter goes missing while trying to prove her brother didn't kill himself. In fact, I'm surprised I haven't heard anything about this earlier in the media."

Lydia was usually a news junkie, but admittedly she had been a bit of a hermit in the last few weeks while she struggled to finish her manuscript. She had tried to keep outside input at a bare minimum.

"The *Post* did a piece. And there's been some coverage in Riverdale. But there's absolutely no evidence of foul play. She had clothes and a good deal of cash with her; we know that. Her car is gone. She easily could have just taken off."

"But you don't think she did."

"No. I don't."

"What do you think happened?" Lydia said, knowing she was pushing.

"All due respect, Ms. Strong, but I'm not going to discuss this with you."

She nodded to indicate she understood. They'd been fortunate with access in the past because of Jeffrey's connections to the FBI and the NYPD. But cops generally didn't like writers *or* private investigators. Since she was a true crime writer and a partner in Jeffrey's private detective firm, Mark, Striker and Strong, she was a little of both.

"I understand," she said, following him toward the elevator.

"I appreciate your cooperation, both of you," he said, shaking each of their hands. "If you think of anything else, call anytime."

He stooped back into the elevator and gave them a little wave as the door closed in front of him.

"Lydia," said Jeffrey, his voice a warning and a question.

"What?" she said defensively. The buzz was so intense that her hands were shaking a little.

Two

Detective Matt Stenopolis contorted himself into the unmarked Caprice. The whole car bounced with his weight when he got in and his partner Jesamyn Breslow was tossed around like she was in a ship on stormy seas.

"Jesus," she said when he was finally settled, his knees fanned out around the steering column.

"Put on some weight. We won't have this problem."

She was small. Too small, he'd thought at first, to be a cop at not even five-four, barely a hundred and fifteen. Everybody knew that it was the smaller men and women who were more likely to use deadly force because they couldn't handle themselves in a hand-to-hand struggle. But over the last two years, she had proven herself to be tougher than any man he'd ever known without ever drawing her weapon. He felt *sorry* for some of the perps who'd tangled with her. There was a skell they'd picked up in the Bronx for killing his girlfriend and their three-month-old son. He resisted and before Matt even realized what was going on, the guy was on the ground screaming like a little girl, his arm twisted unnaturally behind him.

"I know kung fu," she liked to joke, imitating Keanu Reeves' line in *The Matrix*. But it was no joke; she *did* know kung fu, had studied it for nearly ten years.

"How'd it go?" she asked him.

"They still have the original message," he told her. "They're going to have one of the techs from their firm email us the digital file."

She nodded. "You didn't give them anything, did you?"

"No. But they were definitely curious. Soon as they started asking questions I was out of there."

"Good. Because that's the last thing we need right now."

They'd been warned about Lydia Strong. She had a national reputation as a major pain in the ass. And Jeffrey Mark, a former FBI agent turned private investigator, had a lot of connections, not just with the Feds but in the department as well. Enough so that it was hard to get rid of them once they got their teeth into your investigation.

"They're like pit bulls," warned their supervisor, Captain John Kepler. "Once they get their jaws around your leg, you'll have to shoot 'em to get them to let go. And even then it won't be easy."

Matt wouldn't have gone to see them at all except that he was desperate. Out of leads and out of time. Kepler wouldn't allow them to focus on Lily Samuels full time for very much longer, he knew. It was the bank records that really did them in. They'd subpoenaed her banking records the first day and it had taken about a week and half to get the information. Just this past Thursday, they'd learned that on October 22nd, Lily Samuels closed her checking, savings, and money market accounts at Chase Manhattan bank, withdrawing close to $40,000. As far as they could tell, it was all the money she had in the world.

"Okay," said Kepler, Friday morning. "That's it. She took off."

"No," said Jesamyn. "Not necessarily. What if someone forced her to withdraw that money?"

Kepler sighed, looked back and forth between them.

"Did you get the security tape from the branch where she withdrew the funds?" he asked.

"We're still waiting for it," said Matt.

"Well, what the fuck is taking so long?"

Matt looked down at the floor. "They promised by Monday."

As soon as he'd seen the withdrawal he'd asked the bank contact for the security video from the branch. They'd been promising it for two days.

"Get that tape," said Kepler. "If she's on it and it doesn't look as if she's under duress, we're going to close the case. I need you two on other things."

They'd left his office. Jesamyn had her head down; he could see her jaw working the way it did when she was angry or frustrated. He was a little of both. Over the last two weeks they'd gotten to know Lily through her friends and family, through spending time in her West Village apartment. She was not the type of girl to close her bank accounts and take off for parts unknown. Something had happened to her; they were both sure of that. And sure if they couldn't figure it out, they'd be failing someone who needed help. Big time.

He drove up toward the Ninth Precinct, which was just a few blocks away. It was freezing, blustery outside but an oven in the Caprice. He could feel beads of sweat popping up on his brow. Breslow always had to have the heater going full blast; she was always too cold. He let her have her way because in the summer, she let him keep the AC on full blast since he was always too hot because of his size. All summer, she kept a fleece pullover in the car. But in the winter, for whatever reason, she couldn't stand to be cold. It made her cranky.

"What did the message say?" asked Jesamyn as they rolled up First Avenue toward the station house on Fifth Street.

"She said that she needed some advice, that she was out of her league 'big time.' "

"What kind of advice?"

"Lydia Strong said Lily was her student at one point and that they talked now and then about stories she was working on. Strong was like her mentor."

"Don't do that," she said.

"What?"

"Don't talk about her in the past tense. Not yet."

"Sorry," he said.

Jesamyn always, without fail, got personally wrapped up in their cases. It made her an incredibly determined and highly effective investigator but it was emotionally draining for her. He'd warned her about it, about the burnout that would eventually take her over. Like he was one to talk.

"But she's also a private investigator, right?"

"Strong? I think she's more like a consultant than an actual PI. But I don't know. Why?"

"Maybe that's why Lily called her. You know, she's out there trying to prove that Mickey didn't kill himself. She wasn't working on a story. What she was doing was really more like an investigation. Maybe she called Lydia Strong for advice on that. Maybe that's what she meant when she said she was out of her league."

"Maybe," said Matt, not sure where she was going.

They pulled into a spot in front of the precinct. The midnight guys were on their way out. Matt sometimes wished he were still in uniform. It wasn't easy but there was something simple about patrolling the streets, answering calls. The midnight shift. That was the real job. Especially in a place like the Ninth, affectionately referred to as the Ninth Street Shithouse, because of its reputation as a place you were sent if you were a discipline case or a fuck-up. Its borders were Broadway to

Avenue D, Houston to Fourteenth Street. They called it a "B" house because it was a healthy mix between the haves and the have-nots. The projects in Alphabet City were hot enough to keep you busy, but there were a lot of nice, law-abiding New Yorkers, too, living in the gentrified buildings around Tompkins Square, cool lofts on First and Second, the NYU dorms on Ninth and Eleventh. It was a good balance, not too crazy, not too slow. Not like the South Bronx, which was an "A" house where every night was like downtown Baghdad. Or Midtown North, a "C" house, which was basically Mr. Roger's Neighborhood; you could go months without a decent collar.

"Man," said Jesamyn, waving to a good-looking young Latino guy getting into his squad car. "I am so glad I'm not in uniform anymore. I was freezing my ass off for years out there."

"Yeah, but at least patrol, you leave it behind at the end of your shift. Investigations come home with you, get into bed and keep you up all night busting your chops."

Jesamyn looked at her watch. "Shit," she said. "I have to pick up the rug rat from my mother's place."

"It's late. Why don't you let him sleep there?" She did that some nights when they'd made a collar and had a mountain of paperwork to file.

She shook her head, her neat blonde bob shimmering prettily in the light from the streetlamp coming in through the windshield. "No. I need him home with me at night. And I like to get him off to school in the morning when I can, have breakfast together. It's important, you know."

He nodded. He knew it was hard on her, being a single mother. But he admired her and envied her a little for it. In a way, it couldn't be all bad to be needed so much by someone. And Benjamin was a sweet, cute little kid. With a button nose, deep, warm brown eyes, and a pouty little mouth, he looked just like his mom. And he wasn't much shorter.

"Meet you back here at nine? We'll head over to the bank offices. See about that security video," he said.

She looked at him. "I'm not sure what to hope for, you know. If she's on it and looks okay, we have to drop the case, but maybe she *did* take off. If not, then—" She stopped. She didn't have to finish; he was thinking the same thing.

The gentleman his mother had raised compelled Matt to watch as Jesamyn climbed into her Ford Explorer and took off up Fifth Street tooting her horn good-night. It used to make her mad, like he was implying that she couldn't take care of herself. And it *was* silly since if it came down to it, she'd probably wind up protecting him as he tripped over his own big clumsy feet. But he didn't think she minded anymore; they understood each other better after working together for two years.

"How's it going, Mount?" called the desk sergeant as Matt entered the precinct through the heavy wood doors.

The other cops at the Ninth called him Mount, short for Mount Stenopolis. Very creative bunch of guys. Real geniuses.

"Pretty good. How 'bout you, Sarge? Case of the clap clearing up?"

"Under control," he said with a smile. "Hear your mother's still on meds, though."

He smiled, even as he felt his chest constrict with anger. You don't insult a Greek guy's mother. His big secret was that he was sensitive about his mother. That he was sensitive in general. Matt could banter with the best of them, but he knew it got to him in a way it didn't get to the other guys. He did a good job of hiding it, though.

"You're killin' me," he said.

He lumbered up the three flights to his office, taking two steps at a time with ease. At his desk, he checked for messages on his voicemail, found none, and pulled out Lily's file. He looked up at the picture he had pinned to the corkboard over the desk in his cube. Whoever had taken the picture had captured her essence. There was a sweetness to her, but also a kind of wisdom in her black eyes. Her smile was warm, her heart-shaped face open and friendly. A storm cloud of jet-black curls framed her face. He felt an ache looking at her, knowing that the clock was ticking.

Maybe, if he was honest with himself, that was why he'd finally gone to see Lydia Strong. Maybe part of him was hoping that she'd take an interest, so if tomorrow turned out to be the last day they'd be able to devote any real time to Lily, someone else would pick up the trail. If there was a trail to pick up.

Somewhere on another floor a phone rang and rang. He could hear Marilyn Manson music coming from the gym on the floor above him and the heavy clink of someone doing reps. There was an unpleasant smell in the air like someone had burned popcorn in the microwave oven again. He looked at his watch. It was nearly midnight.

He'd spend a couple of hours going over the file again, see if they missed anything. Then he'd grab a few hours on one of the bunks, shower and change here in the morning. He always kept a clean set of clothes in his locker because he spent a lot of nights at the precinct. After all, it wasn't like he had anyone to go home to.

Three

The day dawned bright and cold but Lydia barely noticed as she surfed the web looking for information on Lily and Mickey Samuels. She'd been up half the night thinking about it, keeping Jeffrey awake with her nervous energy. Around four, she gave up on the idea that she might go back to sleep, headed to her office, and booted her computer. She logged onto LexisNexis and plugged in the name Mickey Samuels and came back with nothing. She tried "Michael Samuels" and got three listings. Scrolling through them, she discovered that only one of them related to Lily's brother.

The *Riverdale Press* ran a brief piece on Mickey's suicide, which basically confirmed the details Matt Stenopolis had given her the night before, without adding much more.

Local Café Owner Ends Life

The body of Michael James Samuels, 28, was discovered yesterday by a local resident as he arrived to work at the Walmart on Broadway. Police have ruled the death a suicide, Samuels having died from a self-inflicted gunshot wound to the head. Jessup Irving, 65, noticed a car parked at the far reaches of the empty lot and went to investigate.

"I saw someone sitting there so still. It just seemed odd to me, early as it was. Not yet seven."

As he approached the car, he made a gruesome discovery.

"I just started praying," said Irving. "Then I took my cell phone and called 911."

The discovery of gunshot residue on Samuels' right hand and

powder burns at his temple confirmed what police had surmised at the scene, that the death was a suicide. Police say there is no evidence of foul play. Friends reported that Samuels had lately been depressed and acting erratically due to a recent breakup and the fact that business was slow at his recently opened coffee shop and performance space called No Doze. Neither Samuels' family nor ex-girlfriend could be reached for comment.

"It just goes to show that guns and alcohol don't mix well," said Irving, commenting on the discovery of a half-consumed bottle of whiskey in Samuels' car.

"Words to live by," said Lydia out loud as she read, lingering on the photograph of Mickey Samuels. He was a good-looking guy with high cheekbones, bright blue eyes, and an expansive smile he had in common with his sister. There was that same brightness to him, the same wide-open, happily expectant look to his face that she had always liked about Lily. It was hard to imagine him sitting alone in a dark car with a gun and a bottle of JD, thinking that the barrel looked brighter than the rest of his life. Lydia made a note on a pad of paper by her keyboard: *Girlfriend?*

She tried searches on Google and Yahoo as well, but came up with nothing. She wasn't *that* surprised. People had strange attitudes about suicide and it wasn't covered much in the media, unless the deceased was a celebrity or the case could be tied into a larger story on, for example, the failure of a controversial anti-depressant or something like that. Otherwise people seemed to want to avoid the topic. Maybe because there was so much guilt and anger involved for the people left behind, such a sense of disconnect from the loved one who'd chosen death instead of life with them.

There was a larger piece on Lily in the *Post*. It talked some about her education, her career, her grief over her brother's death. The article reported that she had packed a bag on October 15th after taking a week off from work and headed up to Riverdale. Local residents reported her asking questions of residents and business owners, spending time in her brother's apartment, at his coffee house that had been closed since his death. And like Detective Stenopolis had said, no one had seen her after October 22nd. Residents of Riverdale who had contact with her just assumed she had given up and gone home. It was October 30th, her mother's birthday, before anyone reported her missing. The article ended with a mention of a ten-thousand-dollar reward offered by the family for any information leading to Lily.

There was a sidebar about missing persons statistics in the United States. Apparently, in California alone in 2003, more than thirty thousand people had disappeared from their lives voluntarily. Meaning that they packed some things, cashed out their accounts, and without a word to anyone in their lives, just left. Five hundred eighty-five disappeared under suspicious circumstances with significant evidence of a stranger abduction. And 247 were missing, the circumstances of their disappearance totally unknown. Nationally, in 2001 more than eight hundred thousand adults and children were counted as missing by the FBI's National Crime Information Center. Nearly a million people gone by accident, foul play, or design. Just gone.

There was also a single-page website someone had set up, probably the parents, with a picture of Lily and the word MISSING emblazoned across the top and a number to call. There was the offer of a $10,000 reward. The paragraph gave a brief description of Lily, mentioning how she was last seen by her family three days after her brother's funeral. She left their house, supposedly to go back to her life and her job. She returned to the city, only to pack a bag and ask for some time off work. No one who loved her had seen her since that day.

Lydia leaned back in her chair and took a deep breath. She reached for her coffee cup and drank from it even though it was stone cold now. The milky gray light of morning was coming in through the tall windows and she could hear the street noise starting to rise as the city woke up for business. She liked it here in her little cocoon surrounded by floor-to-ceiling shelves of books, her leather couches and warm chenille throws. She *liked* the writing life; it was safe.

Her work as a true crime writer had led her to consult with Jeffrey's firm long before he made her a partner. And though she sometimes felt more like an investigator than a writer, the word was her first love. That was the place she could put order to the chaos she found in the world. That was the place she *tried* to do so, anyway. But her book was finished. She would turn it in today and it would be *months* before her editor took a scalpel to it. She would have a little time on her hands.

A low-level anxiety started to bubble beneath the surface of her skin as she looked around her office. Over the years, Jeffrey had dubbed this feeling "The Buzz." The feeling she got when something needed investigating or was not quite what it seemed. She had that feeling now about Lily. And then, of course, there was her thing about lost girls.

Shawna Fox, Tatiana Quinn, even Wanda Jane Felix, who was lost in another way. She carried little pieces of all of them with her, the cases from her past, the girls she couldn't help in spite of her best efforts.

When she thought of them, which was more often than she would admit, she had the feeling you might have if you dropped a diamond down a sewer. As if through your own clumsiness you lost something so precious to someplace so dark and labyrinthine that it could never be found. Of course, intellectually, Lydia knew she was in no way responsible for what had happened to her lost girls. But that didn't help her to manage her sadness over their fate and the vague *if onlys* that occasionally haunted her.

Of course, Lily was not a girl. She was a woman and a writer, not so unlike Lydia. And she was a friend.

"I guess I don't have to ask what you're doing," said Jeffrey, walking into her office. He placed a hot cup of coffee on her desk and took his own cup over to the couch where he reclined, throwing his feet up onto the coffee table and looking at Lydia with an expression that reminded her that he knew her better than anyone. The mystery was gone. She was an open book.

"You don't know *everything*," she said.

"Hmm."

She raised her coffee to him. "Thanks," she said with a smile.

"My pleasure." Then, "The detective said that Lily Samuels had quite a bit of cash on her."

She *knew* he'd been thinking about it, too. "Yeah," she answered with a shrug.

"So maybe she's just taking some time out to get her head together. Her brother just killed himself, you know. Maybe she doesn't want to be found at the moment."

"Do you think she'd really do that to her mother, who was still reeling from Mickey's death?"

"People do weird things when they're grieving . . . especially after a suicide. It's a painful, solitary time."

"Still. My experience with Lily is that she is a remarkably sweet and compassionate person. It seems out of character."

"But you really don't know her *that* well, right? I mean you said yourself that it was more of a mentoring relationship than a friendship, which means that she looked up to you and probably wanted to impress you. Maybe you only saw what you wanted to see."

"I don't think so, Jeffrey. I really don't."

He stood up. "Well, I'll have Craig copy that voicemail message and email it over to Detective Stenopolis. I'll give Craig our login and password; he can dial in from the office."

"Actually, can you just have him copy it onto a CD?"

He gave her a look. "Then we'd have to deliver it to the Ninth Precinct."

She smiled sweetly. "I can take care of that."

He shook his head and couldn't keep himself from returning her smile. "Well, Lydia, that's awfully considerate of you."

"You know me. Always happy to help."

"He's not going to tell you anything," warned Jeffrey.

"We'll see."

No matter how stressful her life became, the smell of her son's hair could soothe her. Baby fine, silky blond, and infused with the aroma of the Johnson's Baby Shampoo she'd washed it with all his life. Of course, sometimes it smelled like spaghetti or Play-Doh but those were just variations on a theme.

Jesamyn Breslow tried not to stare at Benjamin as he ate his Cheerios with bananas, because she didn't want to be one of *those* mothers who was always mooning, stroking, adjusting. But she just loved to watch him, his peaches-and-cream skin, his cute little feet. He wasn't quite at the point where he was squirming away from her hugs and kisses. He still threw his arms around her and told her he loved her. But she'd seen the little boys at school, just a year or two older than Benjamin, endure their mother's affections with stoic misery. She knew those days weren't far away. Her nephew, her brother's son, had been the most loving child until the third grade. Now his parents were looking around for the pod that contained their real child, eager to be rid of the alien that refused good-bye kisses and suddenly insisted that the bathroom door be closed *and* locked.

"What's the matter, Mom?" Benjamin asked. She'd been zoning out, staring into her own bowl of Cheerios.

"Nothing. I'm just tired, babe," she said, touching his head. She looked into his face. Even she knew it was a tiny mirror of her own face, with shades of his father in his mischievous eyes and irresistible smile.

"How can you be tired? You just woke up," he said, spreading out his hands.

"Good question," she said.

She looked at the clock on the wall. "Okay, champ, time to brush your teeth and get your coat on. We gotta get you to school."

She cleared his bowl and her own off the round beechwood table and brought them over to the sink, rinsed them and stuck them in the dishwasher. The sky outside was a sad gray, contemplating snow.

She placed the milk in the refrigerator, which was so totally papered with Benji's drawings and cards and reports that she could almost forget its hideous avocado color. With her toe, she pressed down a piece of one of the Formica tiles that was peeling up. The place needed serious work but she lacked the time and the inclination to take care of it. That was the only thing she missed about her marriage to Dylan: a live-in handyman who didn't charge. Well, that and the regular sex.

"Mom? Are you going to let me take the bus ever?" asked Benji, draining the last of his orange juice. "Dad says I should start taking the bus."

"We'll see. Let's just get through today."

"That's what you *always* say."

She patted him on the butt. "Teeth. Coat. Five minutes." He marched off like a good little soldier.

That was the big battle. The school bus. She wasn't ready for that. The bullies, the unsupervised time at the bus stop. The fact that he'd have to take a different bus to get to her mother's place on the days she couldn't be home for him. She liked to drive him, have those last twenty minutes with him in the car and the peace of mind of seeing him enter the double wooden doors. She knew he was safe for the day, or at least as safe as *she* could make him. If he took the bus, all day she'd have to wonder. After all, they lived in New York City, lots of variables. Too many for the mind of a mother and a cop. Paranoid, that's what Dylan called it. He could think what he wanted.

From their apartment on the Upper West Side, it only took about fifteen minutes without traffic to get to Riverdale where Benjamin attended a private academy that cost Jesamyn a small fortune. But because of her grandfathered apartment, a three-bedroom that cost only an unheard of $850 a month, some help from her mother, and child support from Dylan, she was able to swing it. It was the one thing on which she and Dylan were able to agree, that Benjamin should have the very best education no matter what other sacrifices they all had to make. And he was thriving there; he loved it. That was priceless to her.

She wound up Riverside Drive and eventually merged onto the Henry Hudson, getting off at the Fieldston exit. She passed through oak-lined streets with multi-million-dollar homes nestled on perfectly manicured lawns. The leaves were turning and the sun, which had decided to shine on Riverdale at least, created a brilliant light show of amber, rust, and green.

"My friend Stone lives in that house," said Benji. "He has a pool *and* a hot tub."

"Wow," said Jesamyn. *Stone,* she thought. What kind of name was that for a kid? The house looked like a monastery to her with a stone façade and a large varnished wooden door with a wrought iron knocker in its center, a barrel-tiled roof. Two million, at least. At least.

"Is he nice?" she asked, having a hard time imagining that Stone was not a spoiled brat. But that was just her bias. "That's more important than the things he *has,* I think."

"I know, Mom," said Ben, rolling his eyes. He'd heard the lecture a hundred times before. "Yes, he's nice. Very nice. He also has a bed shaped like a race car."

When she pulled up the winding drive toward the large brick buildings, through the expansive grounds, past the soccer field and the giant library, she was, as always, washed with gratitude that she had been able to give that to her son. She felt like he could go on to be anything he wanted from this place.

"Okay, see ya," said Ben, undoing his seat belt and grabbing his Lord of the Rings backpack from the floor in front of him.

"Don't forget, Grandma will pick you up after soccer and I'll see you for dinner."

"I won't forget," he said as she hugged him and kissed his face.

"I love you, Benji," she said.

"I love you," he said with a wide smile.

She watched as he met up with a couple of other kids on the steps and ran into the school. She caught sight of another mom, standing on the sidewalk gazing after a little girl wistfully. They exchanged a look and knew each other's hearts too well.

The traffic was bumper to bumper down the Henry Hudson and it took her nearly an hour to make it to the precinct where Mount was waiting for her by the Caprice. She parked her car in the lot. Some of the guys were playing a pick-up game of basketball in the playground next door. They mock catcalled and whistled at her as she waited to cross the street. She gave them the finger, smiled at their whooping response, and jogged over to Mount. He looked annoyed, like he'd been waiting.

"What?" she said. "Did you sleep here?"

"Actually, I did."

She shook her head and patted him on the elbow. "You really need to get a life," she said. "Or at least a date every now and then. You live like a monk."

"Tell me about it."

Mount was kind of cute in spite of his size. He had thick dark hair, with equally dark eyes that communicated his kindness and depth. But there was sadness there, too. She would call him intense, smoldering even. But he was just so awkward; she figured women might find it kind of a turn-off. Maybe if he were a basketball player making millions, he'd have more luck with women. But he was a cop. A really big cop.

"You just need to find the right kind of woman," she advised as he bounced her around the Caprice trying to get himself in.

"And what kind of woman is that precisely? Someone who can see beyond my physical deformities? Is that what you mean?"

"Oh, stop feeling sorry for yourself. You're not deformed. You're tall. There's a difference. You should go on the Internet. Maybe there's a website, like 'I dig tall guys dot com.'"

"That's very funny. And I mean hilarious."

"Can we stop at Starbucks?"

He sighed heavily. "This is New York City and you want to stop at a *chain*. Support the independents. Resist the homogenization of America."

"Can you pull over, please?"

He pulled in front of Veselka, a neighborhood Ukrainian restaurant that had become an East Village institution, and she popped in for coffee for both of them, as was their ritual when they worked mornings. She had only brought up Starbucks to aggravate him.

The downtown offices of Lily's bank were all oak paneling and navy blue carpets, ecru walls. Everything about it said staid, reliable, and discreet. The phones rang constantly in a low electronic hum, the receptionist answering in a mellow, barely audible voice. The lighting was pleasant, having a slightly pinkish hue—not the harsh white typical of fluorescents.

"I should have been a banker," said Jesamyn, flipping through the pages of *Money* magazine. She sat on a soft leather chair so deep her feet barely touched the floor. Matt sat on a love seat near her, taking up the entire thing.

"Why's that?"

"I don't know. Less stress. More money."

"Yeah, but you'd have to be nice."

"Hmm. That would be hard."

They both looked up as they heard a door push open and a fit-looking young man entered the room.

"Detectives Breslow and Stenopolis?" he said. "I'm Brian Davis, head of branch security."

Jesamyn smiled to see the young man's eyes go wide as Matt stood to his full height.

"Whoa," Davis said. "Wow. I hope you play basketball."

Matt shook his hand. "Only when I'm not rescuing kittens from trees."

"Sorry," he answered with an embarrassed smile. "You must get stupid comments like that all the time."

Davis shook Jesamyn's hand and held onto it a second longer than he needed to. Jesamyn found herself forced to look into a set of warm blue eyes set in relief against ink black hair and paper pale skin. In a millisecond, she'd processed the expensive cut of his charcoal suit, the lack of a wedding ring on his left hand, the scent of his cologne. *Cute,* she thought, and smiled.

"No offense," said Matt, which was usually what he said right before he offended someone. "You look a little young to be the head of branch security."

"Well, thanks, I guess," he said, seemingly unperturbed. "I came to the bank after a few years in the FBI small-business investigation division. So I guess I skipped some rungs on the ladder."

Jesamyn found herself wondering how old that meant he was but couldn't ask without it sounding like she was flirting so she kept her mouth shut. Davis escorted them through a door, down a long gray hallway, and finally to a conference room. More oak wainscoting and navy carpets. The lights in the room were a dim orange. A flat-screen monitor hung on the far wall and the highly varnished table was surrounded by very ergonomic-looking black chairs. Very posh and high tech at the same time.

"Have a seat," he said. "Can I get you anything?"

"No, thanks," said Matt. "We just really need to look at that tape. The information is going to be vital to our investigation."

He nodded quickly and moved over to the screen without another word. He punched a few buttons on a remote and the monitor came to life.

The bank was crowded that day, a Friday afternoon. People depositing checks and getting cash for the weekend were dressed for a coldish October afternoon with light jackets, some with hats. Jesamyn was scanning the faces in the crown for the face that had become so familiar to her that she was seeing it in her dreams. A youngish face— pretty, sweet, an open honesty to it.

"Right here," said Davis, hitting the pause button. "Naturally, our fraud department was very concerned about your suspicions."

A young girl stepped up to the counter wearing a navy blue coat and a red beret-type hat. Her silky hair fanned out around her shoulders. They both recognized her right away. It was Lily.

"Is that why it took you so long to get us the video?" asked Matt, leaning in closer to the screen.

Davis cleared his throat. "We have very strict security protocols. Our customers expect that, of course."

When neither Jesamyn nor Matt said anything, he continued. "This teller, Thelma Baker," said Davis, pointing to a woman on the screen, "said that Lily entered this branch in Riverdale at about noon and requested all the cash from her accounts. She had valid ID. Any of our customers are within their rights to cash out any of their accounts at any branch, at any time. The officer who helped her tried to discourage her from closing the money market account because of penalties. But she said—and I'm quoting—'It's an emergency. I need it for my brother.' Which seems strange since you mentioned over the phone, Detective Stenopolis, that her brother had recently died."

"It is strange," said Jesamyn. She looked at the girl on the tape. There was nothing about her to suggest she was under any pressure. She looked grave, serious, no trace of the smile Jesamyn had seen in every photograph of her. But she appeared to be alone and acting of her own free will.

He let the tape play and they watched Lily being greeted by a young man. Brian paused the video. "That's the bank officer," he said.

He let the tape go again. Lily shook the man's hand and smiled politely. Then he escorted her out of the range of the camera.

"What was the amount of the withdrawal?" asked Jesamyn.

"Thirty-eight thousand, nine hundred fifty-six dollars and eighty-three cents."

It was a significant amount but certainly not enough to disappear on for very long, not these days. She looked over at Matt who was just staring at the screen. He had a kind of moony expression on his face. It was an expression she'd seen on him a number of times when she'd caught him looking at photographs of Lily. She worried about him. No grown man should be that lonely.

"Can we have a copy of this video?" asked Matt.

Davis handed him a CD jewel case, obviously a copy of the one in the DVD player. A sticker on it read: Lily Samuels, account closing, October 22.

"Does this help you at all, Detectives?" asked Brian.

"I'm not sure yet, Mr. Davis. But we appreciate your time," said Jesamyn, rising.

"Brian," he said, handing her a card. "Don't hesitate to call if there's *anything* I can do for you."

She couldn't keep from smiling at him as he took her hand. "If you or anyone at the branch thinks of anything else, please let us know," she said.

"In fact," said Matt, "can we have the names of the teller and the bank officer as well as the address of the branch?"

"Sure," said Brian, slipping another card from his shirt. "The teller I mentioned was Thelma Baker. And the bank officer was a man named Angel Rodriquez."

He scribbled on the back of his card. "Here you go."

"Thanks," said Matt, shaking his hand.

Back in the car, both of them sat for a minute in silence, parked illegally by St. Patrick's on Fifty-First Street. Fifth Avenue was a thick, noisy river of cars and the sky was still threatening snow. New Yorkers walked briskly carrying bags from Saks and Bendel, Tiffany, or briefcases, or backpacks. Tourists walked slowly, their eyes inevitably cast upward toward the tops of buildings, pausing to gawk at the cathedral. In a few more weeks, when the tree was up at Rockefeller Plaza, it would be nearly impossible to walk down the street in this neighborhood. Jesamyn reminded herself, as she did every year, to get her shopping for Benji done early. But she never did.

"Now what?" said Matt, looking dejected.

"I don't know, Mount. Maybe we have to face facts. If we'd had this video a week and a half ago, there wouldn't even have been much of an investigation."

She, for one, felt a little lighter for having seen the tape. For the past two weeks, Lily Samuels was never far from her thoughts, invading her dreams. She'd imagined in detail all the thousand things that might have happened to her: stranger abduction, murder, suicide, or accident—all the myriad nightmarish things that happen to people every day. The possibility that she'd just taken her money and driven off somewhere for some time alone or maybe to make a fresh start on her life . . . well, it was a relief to Jesamyn.

"Maybe she walked away from her life," she said. "Maybe temporarily. Maybe not."

Mount just shook his head like he couldn't accept it. "It doesn't feel right."

He started the engine and rolled into traffic.

"Where are we going?" she asked, though she didn't really have to.

"Riverdale. I want to talk to the people Lily talked to."

At first she'd been "the vic," toward the end of the first week she was "Samuels," now she was "Lily." He was always lecturing Jesamyn about getting too involved, too personally invested in the outcome of a case. And here he was. She knew a schoolboy crush when she saw one.

"Mount—," she started. He raised a hand.

"Humor me this one time will ya', Jez," he said a little testily. "We go up there, ask a few questions. If there's nothing, we're back in front of the captain by noon. We'll tell him we're ready to declare her voluntary missing."

"Okay, okay," she said, raising her palms. "Let's go to Riverdale."

Four

Lydia sat on the edge of the bed with the phone to her ear, zoning out as it rang. She'd noticed recently that it took her grandparents longer to get to the phone than it used to. Sometimes it rang five or six times before one of them picked it up. If anyone picked it up at all. They didn't have an answering machine, though Lydia had purchased one for them as a Christmas gift a couple of years ago.

"It's a trick," said her grandfather. "A way for the phone company to make more money."

"How's that, Grandpa?" she'd asked.

"If people call and I don't pick up, they know I'm not home, they don't get charged. If it's important, they'll call back. If a machine answers, they get charged for the call. *And* I get charged when I call them back. They get to charge for *two* calls instead of just one."

Lydia had laughed. She had to give it to him; he was right.

"Oh, David. Join the living, will you?" said her grandmother. "All my life, this Depression Era thinking. It's—well, it's *depressing*. Hook up the machine."

Lydia was thinking it was a battle that her grandmother had apparently lost or given up on as she listened to the fifth ring. She was about to hang up when she heard her grandfather's voice.

"Hey, Grandpa," she said.

"What's up, kid?"

She could see his silver hair, his broad shoulders and ruddy skin. She knew he was probably wearing jeans and a flannel shirt, probably Rockports or maybe sneakers.

"Jeffrey told me about my father," she said, pulling up her feet so that she was sitting cross-legged on the bed. She looked at the clock.

9:36 A.M. The shower was running in the bathroom, the hot water steaming it up the way she liked it. She knew the conversation with her grandparents would be short; it always was. Can't let the phone company get too much of anyone's money.

He was silent for a second. "So how did that hit you?"

"I don't know," she said, putting her hands in front of her eyes to block the bright morning sun that was streaming in the east-facing window. She got up and pulled the blind. "I'm not sure it has yet."

"Well, the world's a better place without him, if you ask me." David Strong held a grudge; there was no doubt about it.

"Don't hold back, Grandpa. Tell me how you really feel," Lydia said.

He chuckled a little. "Well, don't lose any sleep over it. I'll put your grandmother on."

She smiled to herself. What was it about that generation? They really hated the telephone; not that her grandfather was much of a communicator. Her grandmother always did most of the talking.

"How are you taking the news, dear?" asked her grandmother. Her grandmother's voice still sounded young to Lydia's ears. It was strong and vital, reminding her so much of her mother's voice. It had the same pitch and cadence; their laughter was identical.

"I'm okay, Grandma."

"Of course you are," she said. "You've been through worse."

That was definitely true. Much, much worse.

"Will we see you this weekend?" her grandmother asked. Since their wedding, Lydia and Jeffrey had made it a point to see her grandparents every couple of weeks. She'd been guilty of not appreciating them enough in the past, of getting so wrapped up in her work that months would go by. These days she tried to take better care of the relationships in her life. Now that they were in the city on the Upper West Side, it was easier. For a lot of reasons.

"On Sunday, around three?"

"Good. I have something for you," she said.

"What?"

Lydia heard her grandmother take a breath, and then pause. "I'd rather just show it to you when you get here. Can I say one thing? About your father?"

"Sure."

"You know, most of us do our best in this world. Even if that turns out to be pretty crappy. There's no use to holding onto anger like your grandfather does. It'll give you indigestion. Or worse."

Lydia thought her grandmother might be watching too much Dr. Phil.

"I hear you, Grandma," she said. "Thanks."

In the shower, she let the hot pulsing streams of water beat thoughts of her father away. A lifetime ago she hadn't allowed herself hot showers in the morning, only cold. Morning, she used to reason, was the time to get moving, not the time for lingering in a hot shower. Hot showers were for bedtime. Her perspective on lots of things had changed over the last few years. She was gentler with herself these days, and hence she found she was gentler with others. Well, some people anyway.

She washed her hair with a sage-mint aromatherapy shampoo and lathered her body with a shower gel containing the same two ingredients. The scent was heavenly, reminding her of New Mexico and easing some of the tension in her shoulders that had settled there while she hunched over her computer.

As she rinsed, she thought about Lily. She wondered how Detective Stenopolis had gone about his investigation into finding out what had happened to her. She'd gotten the sense that he was pragmatic, competent, dogged. That he'd probably started up in Riverdale, talking to the people who saw her last. He'd probably checked her banking and credit card records. She knew he'd checked Lily's cell phone records. Worked his way to her friends and family from there. That's the way Jeffrey would have done it; following the hard chain of facts that would hopefully lead him to a conclusion as to what had happened, if not to the girl herself.

Lydia's style was a little different. She knew that sometimes the truth only left a footprint in the sand, a scent on the wind, a whisper in your ear. You had to be present, use all your senses to find it, not just your eyes. Sometimes the path you see can lead you away from the truth. If it were my investigation, my story to write, where would I start? Lydia wondered. With Lily's apartment and her closest friends. That was the place to begin looking for the true heart of a woman. And only in knowing that, can you know where she might have gone or to whom she was vulnerable.

She heard the phone ringing as she toweled off. Wrapping herself in a plush terry robe, she dove over the bed to catch the phone before the voicemail did.

"I'm looking for Ms. Lydia Strong?" said an officious sounding female voice when Lydia answered. Older. Stern.

"This is."

"My name is Patricia O'Connell. I am the lawyer representing the estate of Arthur James Tavernier."

It took a second for the name to register; when it did, her stomach bottomed out. Her father. "His estate?"

"Yes. Your father has left a number of things for you and I am charged with making sure you receive them."

Part of her wanted to tell this lawyer that she had no interest in anything belonging to her father. But curiosity got the better of her. What kind of an estate could he have had? From what she knew of him he had no education, he couldn't hold down a job. At least these were the things her mother had told her. And what would you leave to a daughter you'd only met once?

"What kind of things?"

"Those items are sealed and for your eyes only, Ms. Strong."

Lydia was silent; she wasn't quite sure what to say.

"Unfortunately," said the lawyer, "your father died with considerable debt but it will be satisfied with the sale of his home. There's no money."

Lydia didn't waste her time being offended at the stupidity and insensitivity of that statement. "Can you send me the items?"

"We'd appreciate it if you could pick them up at our offices. We're located at three-thirty-three West Fifty-Seventh Street. Will that be a problem?"

The offices of Mark, Striker and Strong were just a few blocks from that address. It wouldn't be much trouble to go by or to send a messenger.

"It's just that Mr. Tavernier's estate, because of the amount of his debt, does not cover our fee," O'Connell went on, Lydia guessed by way of explanation for the tackiness of her request.

"So you're trying to save on postage?"

Sarcasm was obviously lost on O'Connell. "That's right."

"Okay," said Lydia. "I'll come by as soon as possible."

"When can we expect you?"

"I don't know," she said. "Soon."

She hung up the phone then, thinking that it was going to be an extremely weird day.

Angel Rodriquez had a fresh, open face, with café au lait skin and a shy smile. He was handsome in a boyish way; Detective Stenopolis could see that his body was well defined, muscular beneath his white button-down shirt and navy blue tie. Matt found that he always noticed men like Angel with a kind of envy. The guy was *easy* with himself, knew he was attractive. There probably wasn't a woman in the world that didn't respond to him when he turned on the charm. His partner included. The stern expression she usually wore on her face softened just slightly at the sight of him. He'd never had that effect on women. In fact, he imagined that they literally shrank away from him, repulsed by his size.

But Angel seemed a little nervous to Matt. A tiny bit edgy. The charm he'd displayed when he thought they were bank customers wavered just a tad when he'd learned they were cops asking about Lily Samuels.

The same had been true of Thelma Baker. She was an older woman with rich chocolate skin and a close-cropped head of hair. She had a remarkable face with high cheekbones and almond-shaped eyes. Gold hoop earrings and a deep shade of plum on her lips accented her striking features. She'd smiled warmly as they approached. But when Jesamyn introduced them and flashed her shield, Ms. Baker became flustered. She didn't look like the kind of woman to fluster easily. She had the bearing of a school principal or a Supreme Court justice, stern, unflappable.

"Corporate didn't say you'd be coming," she said.

"They didn't know," answered Jesamyn politely.

"Well, let me just give them a call," she said, reaching for the phone.

"Ms. Baker," said Matt gently, "that won't be necessary. We just have a few questions about Lily Samuels. We're not going to take up too much of your time. Or ask about bank policy. I just want to know how she *seemed* to you."

"How she seemed?" she asked, with a cock of her head, taking her hand back from the receiver.

"Yes," said Jesamyn. "Her manner. Did she seem nervous, anxious, happy, excited?"

Thelma Baker looked back and forth between their faces. "You know," she said finally. "She didn't seem any of those things. She seemed flat. Empty."

The way she said it made Matt think that she'd given it some thought, that Lily had made an impression on her.

"What do you mean?"

"She was a pretty girl, you know. Young, with a sweet face. It was a face you'd expect to see smiling. But she didn't smile or seem to even be seeing anything around her. I felt like she just looked right through me. I tried to catch her eyes, but she just had this *stare*."

Jesamyn was looking out the window at the busy street that ran past the bank. There were parking spaces on both sides of the two-way street and traffic was brisk.

"Did you see how she came in?" Jesamyn asked looking back from the window.

"What do you mean?" asked Ms. Baker, looking down at the counter in front of her. She's stalling, thought Matt.

"Did you see her park a car, or did she get out of a vehicle, or walk up the street."

"I'm sorry. I didn't notice."

"Take a minute, Ms. Baker. Think about it," said Matt.

"No, I'm sorry. It was very busy that day and I was helping customers, not staring out the window. I only talked to her for a second before Angel Rodriquez came and took her to his office. Let me call him for you."

Matt looked at her with an expression he'd cultivated to communicate compassion and the knowledge that she wasn't telling him everything she knew. He slid a card over the counter. "Just think about it," he said solemnly.

She looked at him and he thought he saw worry there.

"I'll call Mr. Rodriquez," she said, picking up the phone.

On his desk, Angel had a picture of a pretty Latina woman, holding a boy that looked like a miniature of Angel. It was a small office with glass walls. He moved immediately behind the desk and held out a hand to indicate that they should sit in the facing chairs. Matt stood. The chair beside Jesamyn didn't look like it would be very comfortable for him, if he could squeeze himself into it at all. He saw Angel slide his chair back a bit and realized that his standing like that might seem intimidating. Oh, well.

Angel picked up one of those pink rubber stress balls and started to squeeze. The screen saver on his computer was an image of a young Arnold Schwarzenegger, straining with a dumbbell. A caption read, *No pain, no gain.*

"I had to make a couple of calls," said Angel. "This wasn't the branch where she opened her account. But because she said it was an emergency, we were able to make special arrangements."

"She took the money in cash?"

"Yes, she wanted cash and we were able to provide that."

"How did she seem to you? How would you describe her manner?" asked Jesamyn.

Angel thought about it a second. "I guess I would say tired. She said her brother had an emergency. She didn't specify the emergency and I didn't ask. But she didn't really seem anxious or upset; just tired."

Matt thought about the words Angel and Thelma had used to describe Lily. Tired. Flat. Empty. Words that were strikingly different from the words family and friends had used to describe her. Bright. Energetic. Happy. What could have caused her personality to change so dramatically in just a short time?

"Tired," repeated Jesamyn. He could tell that she was thinking the same thing. "Did it seem like—and I know it's not easy to speculate about things like this—but did it seem like she was on something? That she might be high?"

"No," said Angel quickly. "Ms. Samuels appeared to have her faculties about her at all times."

Jesamyn and Matt exchanged a look. The sentence had the quality of a company line, assigned and rehearsed.

"Angel," said Jesamyn leaning forward and speaking softly. "A young woman is missing. We're not investigating fraud. We don't care about the thirty-eight thousand dollars. If we leave here today with the impression that Lily Samuels was fine that day and withdrew her funds of her own free will, we're going to have to drop this case. Are you comfortable with giving us that impression?"

While she spoke, Matt noticed that Angel's eyes had drifted to the picture on his desk. He sat like that for a second after Jesamyn had stopped talking.

"I had no indication that Ms. Samuels was not acting of her own accord," he said, raising his eyes to hers.

Jesamyn leaned back and nodded, but her expression communicated her skepticism.

"Just think about it," said Matt for the third time since they'd entered the bank, sliding a card over the desk toward Angel.

"I will," he said with nod, rising. "If I think of anything else, I'll be in contact."

"Shit," said Jesamyn, once they were back outside in front of the bank. They stood in the cold air, gold, orange, and red leaves from a maple tree above them fluttering around them like butterflies. He knew she was thinking that they shouldn't have come here, that they should have taken the video at face value, gone back to the precinct and moved on. Because now they had the strong impression that there was something seriously wrong with Lily that day but no way to prove it. They'd have to live with that now. Matt was feeling pretty bleak about it, too, until he raised his eyes from the concrete.

"Well, well," said Matt, looking across the street. Thelma Baker stood opposite them wearing a long brown coat that flowed around her elegantly. She gave them a little wave and then ducked into a coffee shop. They followed.

The Java Hut smelled of freshly ground beans and decadent baked goods. A glass case displayed a devastating assortment of cakes, donuts, danishes, and gooey cinnamon buns. Thelma had grabbed a booth all the way in the back. Matt and Jesamyn made their way through the small, crowded space toward her. They slid in across from her.

"That day," she said, without looking up at them. "It has stayed with me."

"Why's that?" asked Jesamyn, noticing Thelma's beautiful dark hands, perfectly manicured nails, a collection of expensive-looking rings.

"Because I have good instincts about people. And I knew that something wasn't right with that girl. I mean—it was just a feeling. Nothing that you'd really act on. But when I saw her picture in the paper, I just thought, what if I'd said something or done something different?"

"What could you have done?" asked Matt.

She looked at him before she answered, giving him a light smile. "You asked me before how she'd gotten into the bank and I told you I didn't know. But I saw her get out of the passenger side of a car across the street. It was a black car, one of those monster SUVs. After she was inside, it pulled around and waited in front of the entrance to the bank. I noticed it because its windows were all tinted black as pitch. That's illegal in New York now. You can't have tinted windows like that anymore. She kept looking back at that car. Three or four times while she was standing in front of me. Not frantic, not like she was afraid. But she just kept checking. But it was very busy that day, and once Angel came to take her in back, I got caught up with other things."

She sighed lightly, tapped her gold wedding band on the table. "I remembered all that when I saw her picture in the *Post*. I called corporate and told them that she'd been in our branch that day and closed her accounts. They told me I was right to call and that they'd handle the call to the police. I never heard from the cops until today. But a day or so later, I got a visit from the head of fraud security."

The waitress came then and all three ordered regular cups of coffee.

"He wanted to make sure that we hadn't had any indication she wasn't acting of her own accord. We're trained to look for that kind of thing. I mentioned her demeanor and the vehicle I'd seen but said that it didn't seem like she was acting under duress of any kind. And that was true. It was all just a vibe, just a feeling on my part."

"Then they provided you and Mr. Rodriquez with the things you needed to say to protect the bank from liability, should Lily or her family ever claim that the money was obtained fraudulently and that the bank failed to protect her accounts," said Jesamyn.

"That's right," she answered with a nod.

"When I heard from my manager that the security video and Ms. Samuels' banking records had been requested by branch security, I was relieved. I figured the bank was working with the police and that the things I'd observed had been passed along. But then I 'accidentally' saw the statement the bank had given to the police and it made no mention of the SUV."

"Accidentally?"

"I accidentally came across it while I was looking to file something away in the branch manager's cabinet," she said with a small smile.

"Why didn't you go to the police?" Matt asked, though he figured he knew the answer.

"I called corporate and asked to speak to the head of branch security."

"Brian Davis?" asked Jesamyn.

She nodded.

"What did he say?"

"He very gently suggested that the information wasn't relevant since we were *certain* that she wasn't acting under duress. He said some shit about being a team player and how the bank couldn't afford disloyalty. Let's just say the message was clear."

She put her head in her hand for a second and then rubbed at her temples with a long graceful hand. She looked up at them again.

"I've been with this bank twenty years; I'm fully vested. I've got two sons in college."

The waitress placed the coffee in front of them, asked if they wanted anything else, and walked off when no one answered.

"I'm sorry," Thelma said. "I'm so sorry for that girl."

Jesamyn put a hand on her arm. "We all have to make choices, Ms. Baker. We don't judge you. Coming forward now is very brave."

She looked up at them then and nodded. "Thanks," she said, gently withdrawing her arm. "I appreciate that. But I really hope it's not too late to help her."

"We do, too," said Matt. He didn't judge Thelma Baker either. It was easy for a person to get squashed by a corporate giant; it happened every day, all over the world. They used people up, controlled them by threatening their livelihood. But he couldn't quash the rising tide of frustration and anger he felt swelling in his chest. If they'd had this information two weeks ago, where would it have led them?

"I saw part of the license plate," she said, pulling a pen from her purse and scribbling on a napkin. "My eyes are not great but I think the first three digits were H57. That's all I know."

She got up then, quickly, as if she'd woken from a trance and realized she was in a strange place. She looked around her, Matt guessed for other bank employees. She took five dollars and threw it on the table.

"I'm sorry," she said again as she left.

Jesamyn looked at the napkin in front of her. "A partial license plate and a vehicle description," she said, almost incredulous, as if someone had just told her she won the lottery. It was literally the first substantial clue they'd found in two weeks. Matt's excitement was only tempered by the thought that it was probably way too late.

"Too little, too late," said Kepler back at the Ninth. His office reeked of cigarette smoke and hamburgers. There was no smoking allowed anywhere indoors. But that didn't seem to bother their captain. Everyone knew Kepler smoked with the door closed, leaning out over his windowsill when he was feeling considerate. No one tried to stop him. He was an even bigger bastard when he couldn't smoke.

"You're joking," said Jesamyn. "This is huge."

She stood at the edge of his faux wood and aluminum desk, as Kepler leaned back in his gray vinyl swivel chair. Mount stood by the door, leaning against the jamb. Kepler looked at Jesamyn and gave her a small nod.

"The fact that you think it's huge just underscores how little you have. *Two weeks ago*, it might have been huge."

Matt and Jesamyn both stared at him. Jesamyn had a brief but vivid fantasy of throwing herself over the desk at his throat. Kepler stood and walked around his desk. There was a ketchup stain on his tie. His gray hair looked as if he'd been running his fingers through it all day. A shadow of stubble darkened his jaw.

"So she got herself messed up on drugs, hooked up with some dealer, and she cashed in her bank account to buy crack," said Kepler. "In a few weeks, she'll show up in the system after a crack house sweep. Stranger things have happened."

"No—" began Matt.

Kepler cut him off. "It doesn't mean anything, Stenopolis. Except that someone gave her a ride to the bank."

Mount looked like he was about to have a brain aneurysm; his neck was turning red.

"Okay," said Jesamyn, trying to diffuse the tension that was rising in the room. "You have to let us run the plate at least."

"It's a partial plate and a vague description, which means you'll get multiple hits. And then who'll follow up on those?"

"We'll put it on the back burner," she bargained.

Kepler took a thick, heavy file from beside him and handed it to her with a sigh. "The way back burner," he said.

She took the file from him. "Rosario Mendez," she read.

"Missing woman from the projects on Avenue A. She's eight months pregnant. Girlfriend, or ex, to hear him tell it, of Jorge Alonzo."

"Latin Kings," said Matt, recognizing the name. "He's one of the big guys."

"That's right. The case belongs to Rosa and Wong, but they need all the help they can get. Go see one of them and make yourselves useful." He nodded toward the file. "Those are some of the statements— family, friends, Kings."

"How long has she been gone?"

"Three days. The boyfriend has been cleared as a suspect. They're looking at rival gangs."

Kepler walked back behind his desk. "That's it. Why are you still here?"

Back in the cube that contained both of their desks, Matt and Jesamyn sat silent. Jesamyn flipped though the file on Mendez. Matt stared at his laptop screen. He'd plugged in the partial description and plate number and was waiting for a hit. The system was slow for whatever reason and as he waited, Jesamyn saw his eyes drift up to the picture of Lily he kept over his desk. He looked sad; she felt for him.

"You don't need to look at me like that," he said, without turning to look at her.

"Like what?" she said, putting her eyes back on the page in front of her.

"Like I'm pathetic, pitiable."

"Grow up, Mount. Seriously."

The phone on his desk rang and he picked up while giving her a dirty look.

"Stenopolis," he said gruffly. A pause. "You're kidding. What does she want?" Another longer pause, then, "Uh, no. I'll come down." He hung up the phone.

"Guess who's here?" he asked her.

"Who?"

"Lydia Strong," he said, walking out the door. Jesamyn followed him with her eyes and listened to the thunder of his big feet on the stairs.

"Oh, brother," she said out loud to no one.

Five

"You really didn't need to go out of your way like this, Ms. Strong," Detective Stenopolis said, taking the CD from her. The precinct was busy for a Monday afternoon. Two uniformed officers were bringing in a couple of transvestite hookers, commonly known as she-males, dressed in platforms and micro-minis. They were making a point of being loud and belligerent, male voices coming out of smooth and heavily made-up faces. An older man was yelling at the young female officer at the desk about how his building on Avenue B, where he'd lived for nearly twenty years, was turning into a crack house. The phones never stopped ringing.

"Please, call me Lydia," she said. "It was no trouble. Our email is down and I had to be in the area."

Detective Stenopolis gave her a look that told Lydia he didn't believe her. And she couldn't really be offended by that because it was, of course, a bald-faced lie.

"Well, thanks. I appreciate your help," he said, turning from her.

"Detective," she said, placing a hand on his arm. "I was hoping we could talk a second."

He turned back to her and she saw something funny in his face. She could swear that underneath those severe, dark features, there was a smile hiding. She sized him up: six-foot-six maybe, 250 pounds at least. He wore a pair of khaki pants, a denim shirt under a leather jacket—calfskin by the feel of it. His shoes were dark brown Timberland hiking boots; they were the approximate size of Volkswagens. Most guys his size wouldn't know how to dress, but he'd put himself together respectably enough.

"What do you want to talk about, Ms. Strong?" he said, sounding strained.

"Just wondering how much longer your supervisor is going to let you keep this case active," she said softly, narrowing her eyes. "It has been two weeks. And it sounds to me like you have very little."

Bull's-eye, she thought when she saw his expression shift to surprise for a millisecond and then back to stern. But he didn't say anything else, just stood there looking at her. She lifted her shoulders a little and held his eyes.

"I have the luxury of time and resources. And Lily is someone I care about," she said. "I *will* be looking into what happened to her."

"I can't stop you," he said. She saw it again, that smile in his eyes. Was he playing her?

"No, you can't," she said. "But you can *use* me." He didn't say anything so she pushed through for what she wanted. "Let me see your file."

He laughed a little. "Due respect? I know *all* about you, Ms. Strong. This is a police matter. I'm not giving my file to a *writer*. If you're interested in becoming a cop, there are some applications for the academy over by the door. You can pick one up on your way out."

She smiled. He *was* playing her. "I don't think so," she said, moving a little closer to him. "Because then I'd be more worried about following rules and protecting my turf than finding out what happened to a missing young woman who needs all the help she can get."

Though she didn't see it on his face, she sensed that she'd hit him hard.

He held up the CD. "Thanks again for this," he said, moving through the door, ducking just slightly to avoid hitting his head. Through the small glass window in the wood, he turned and looked at her with an expression she couldn't read, and then disappeared.

She walked out of the precinct wondering how long it would be before he called her. She hoped it was soon; she'd decided that she liked Detective Stenopolis. But she didn't really need him, she thought, as she slid into her black Mercedes SLK Kompressor and pulled up Fifth Street.

Jeffrey was already working on banking and credit card records, as well as cell phone activity, thanks to the agency's many contacts cultivated over the years. And she was already getting in touch with the people who knew Lily best. They were well on their way to peeling back the layers of her life, with or without Matt Stenopolis to help them.

Hardly anyone ever used directory assistance anymore. But Lydia had learned over the years that many more people than one might expect had listed telephone numbers. Especially young single people; they didn't want to pay for unlisted service and they wanted to be easily found in case Miss or Mr. Right should come looking for them. Lydia remembered Lily's best friend's name only because she thought it was funny that they had both been named after flowers. Jasmine Karr was a first-year resident at NYU Medical Center. Lydia had left a message for Jasmine at her apartment as she headed toward the precinct and was surprised when Jasmine called back less than fifteen minutes later.

"She respects and admires you so much, Ms. Strong," said Jasmine, her voice sounding far too young to belong to someone nearly thirty. "I'm so thankful that you're taking an interest in this. I know she will be, too."

"I was hoping you and I could get together. Talk a little bit about Lily and how things were with her before she disappeared."

"Sure. Of course," Jasmine said. "But I told the police everything I know."

"I'm sure you did. But it would help me, if you don't mind. I was also wondering if you have access to her apartment."

"Actually, I do," she said. "Her mother asked if I'd take care of her plants until she gets back. So I've been doing that and keeping things clean. I just want things to be nice when she comes home."

They both knew that her statement was hopeful instead of certain. "I'm still at the hospital. I just called in for my messages. But my shift ends here at noon," she said. "I could meet you at Lily's around one if that works. Do you know the address?"

Lydia made her way through crosstown traffic, thinking she should have taken the subway or walked instead of driving. But she'd been feeling lazy. And the subways held some very bad memories that hadn't faded much in the past year. Eventually, she parked in a lot on Jane Street and walked down Eighth toward Bank. The sidewalks were bustling with the usual mix of businesspeople breaking for lunch, mommies or nannies pushing prams, punks, homeless people, and peanut vendors. The day was cool, the air filled with city music and the smell of honey roasted nuts.

In the marble and oak pre-war lobby a young woman in a navy blue fleece pullover on top of green scrubs and a worn pair of Nikes was sitting on a plush leather chair, looking zoned out and exhausted.

"Jasmine?" asked Lydia.

"Yes, Ms. Strong. I recognize you from television."

They shook hands and Jasmine told the doorman in his green

uniform with gold piping on the sleeves that they wouldn't be long. He looked up from a magazine and nodded as though he couldn't care less.

"This is a nice building," said Lydia, doing the calculations in her head. Depending on the size of the apartment she couldn't imagine Lily paying any less than $1500 a month, even for a studio in a building like this one in such an astronomically high-rent district. She knew what a young newspaper reporter made. It wasn't enough to live here.

"Yeah," said Jasmine. "I'm still living with my parents up in Queens. I used to spend the night here with her a lot."

"You haven't been staying here recently?"

"Since she's been missing? No. I—I just can't." She shook her head and Lydia saw tears gather in her eyes. "I can't be here without her. It doesn't seem right."

Lydia nodded her understanding as the elevator reached the sixth floor and they stepped out into the hallway. There was tasteful burgundy carpeting and cream walls lined with sconce lighting.

"Did she have trouble affording this place?" asked Lydia as they walked into a spacious, sunlit one-bedroom apartment.

Jasmine shrugged. "I think her parents helped her out a little. Her mom was worried about her living in the city after college; they wanted her to be someplace safe. She was living in a railroad apartment on Avenue B after she moved out of the NYU dorms—until her parents came to visit. A month later she moved in here."

Lydia sat on the futon while Jasmine sank onto an enormous blue velvet pillow lying on the varnished hardwood floor. A counter separated the living space from a state-of-the-art kitchen with granite countertops and stainless steel appliances not unlike Lydia's own. From where she sat, Lydia could see into a bedroom. There was a large king bed and a dresser that looked like the kind of stuff you buy at Ikea when you're young and have no money. It comes in a box: a pile of wood, a bag of bolts and a set of indecipherable instructions.

"Detective Stenopolis said that Mickey and Lily weren't getting along before he died," said Lydia.

Jasmine pulled her legs into a full lotus position and nodded. "No, they weren't. And it was weird because she worshiped him. But after he quit his job and moved up to Riverdale, things started to change. He became hard to reach, started being really short and distant with her. I don't think she was mad as much as she was hurt. She thought it was the new girlfriend. Lily didn't like her very much."

"Maybe she was jealous?"

"Maybe a little—because she and Mickey had such a bond. He'd never really had a serious, serious girlfriend before. But she's not really like that. Lily likes nice people, kind people, people with passion. She has good taste. I've always kind of felt that if Lily doesn't like someone, then there's usually a reason."

Lydia nodded. "So why did Mickey move up there in the first place?"

"He was burned out. He'd made a killing, put a lot of money away. He had always had this dream of owning a coffee shop that was like a performance space at night, you know, small bands, poetry readings. He wanted to hang a different artist's work on the walls every month. Something really artsy and cool, totally different from the insanity of his Wall Street job. So he went for it."

"But it didn't go well?"

"It seemed to, at first. We went up there after he opened. The space was beautiful, there seemed to be a good crowd. He was talking about applying for a liquor license." She moved away a wisp of hair that had fallen into her eyes. "He seemed like the same old Mickey but happier. Less than six months later, he was dead."

"It doesn't make a lot of sense," said Lydia, leaning forward.

"You know," said Jasmine, looking down. "Since my residency started I have been so busy, so exhausted all the time, that I really didn't pay the kind of attention that I should have, I guess. I knew Lily was upset about the way Mickey was acting. She kept saying, 'There's something really weird going on with him.' We talked about it but I guess I was only half-listening. Now when I think about those months, trying to figure things out, I feel like I only have small pieces."

"What are some of the things you remember her mentioning?"

"She was talking about how he was hanging around with a weird group of people, friends of this girl he was seeing."

"Do you remember her name?"

She closed her eyes for a second, as if trying to recall. Lydia noticed for the first time how pretty Jasmine was. With her hair back and her baggy scrubs, her beauty hadn't been obvious at first. But in the bright sun coming in from the window, Lydia admired her fair golden skin and inky black hair, the delicate lashes on her wide eyes. When Jasmine opened her eyes again, Lydia saw that they were light hazel, with the slightest tease of green.

"I met her when we went up to visit over the summer," she said slowly. "I think it was Mariah. I don't think I ever got her last name. She was beautiful, with this really long blonde hair, bombshell body. There was something cold about her, something sneaky. But Mickey was smitten. Big time."

Lydia flashed on Lily's message. *"I'm out of my league. Big time,"* she'd said.

"He was always looking to throw himself into something. When he was a trader on Wall Street, it was his religion. He lived and breathed the *Journal*. When he got into the martial arts, it was his obsession. Then it was Buddhism. Lily always called him a 'seeker.' She said he was always looking to belong somewhere but that he always felt like he was on the outside looking in. Lily always thought that it was the death of their father that made him like that. Lily was only two when their dad died, but Mickey was seven. Old enough to feel the loss. Mr. Samuels, their stepdad, loves them both; he was always good to them. But Lily never remembered her biological father; Mickey did. I think there were some challenges for Mr. Samuels in taking on the role of father for Mickey." She shook her head, chewed on the cuticle of her thumb. "I hate myself for not being more present. I should have listened better."

Lydia saw the tears start again before Jasmine put her head in her hands. She felt a familiar, helpless sadness opening within her. It was a terrible empathy she'd always had for the people who'd lost loved ones. She saw their pain, their fear, that slick-walled abyss of grief within them, and it connected with the space inside her that still grieved the murder of her own mother.

"Go easy on yourself, Jasmine," she said softly. "It's too easy to blame ourselves. And it doesn't help anyone."

She nodded but didn't look up from her hands. Lydia gave her a minute. She got up to find a tissue for Jasmine and looked around the apartment. It was the apartment of a person who worked a lot, didn't have much money and spent most of her time in the space sleeping. It was neat, tasteful, but didn't have the charisma and energy of a more home-centered person. The fixtures were generic; even the simply framed posters on the wall—Van Gogh's *Starry Night*, some erotic bloom by Georgia O'Keeffe, the inevitable Robert Doisneau print of *The Kiss* where a couple are lip locked in a crowded Paris train station—were on the walls of a thousand other apartments all over the city.

She found some tissues in the bathroom and brought them to Jasmine, who thanked her.

"I'm sorry," she said, blowing her nose. "I still can't believe this is happening. When I'm working I can almost forget about it; I'm on my ER rotation and there are so many people hurt and in pain. It's so frenetic. I can forget about Lily, about what has happened. Isn't that awful?"

"No. I think it's normal," said Lydia, sitting back down. After all, she'd been doing it all her adult life, using her work to avoid her pain and problems. Better than heroin, she thought. "The brain can only handle so much worry and grief at a time. It needs a way to shift off for a while."

Jasmine nodded doubtfully.

"When the news came about Mickey," she said with a sniffle, "Lily was just destroyed. I'll never forget her face or the way she screamed. I was here when her stepfather called. The next few days were kind of this miserable blur. The viewing, the service, the burial."

"Was Mariah at the funeral?"

Jasmine shook her head. "No. I never saw her again after meeting her. I think she left him; that was supposedly one of the reasons he was in so much despair."

Lydia nodded.

"The police said that Lily was sure he hadn't killed himself."

Jasmine nodded, stretched out her legs. "Absolutely positive. In spite of the physical evidence, she refused to believe it."

"Was your impression that she was in denial?"

"I didn't know what to think," she said, looking down at her sneakers. "It was all just so stunning. She stayed a couple of days with her parents. She took family leave from the paper and then asked for her vacation to extend her time off. She left for Riverdale about a week after he died."

"Did you talk to her while she was up there?"

"We traded a couple of messages. But we never actually had a conversation."

Lydia looked at the young woman in front of her. Her eyes were rimmed red from crying and smudged beneath with blue fatigue from what Lydia was sure was at least a fifteen-hour shift. Something within Lydia wanted to comfort her, to give her a hug and tuck her in someplace. It wasn't a new feeling, but it was new that she didn't press it down and become colder to defend herself against the vulnerability it opened inside her. But she didn't really know how to be like that—even after so many years of interviews like this one, so many weeping, broken people. It cost so much to comfort someone; you had to take on a little of their sadness. Lydia stood up from the couch.

"Do you mind if I take a look around?" Lydia asked.

Jasmine shook her head. "Please," she said, wiping her eyes.

The hallway from the living area to the bedroom was a gallery of family photos. Lydia flipped on the light and observed a collection of faces captured in the joyous moments of their lives. Lily and Mickey rode on the back of an elephant in a jungle. Lily wrapped her arms around an older woman who had to be her mother; the resemblance was striking as they stood before a birthday cake with many candles. Lily and Jasmine danced in a crowded bar or club with a couple of other sexy young girls decked out for the evening. Mickey's graduation. Mickey at Machu Picchu. Lily playing soccer, a gangly adolescent with a foalish prettiness to her.

Lydia walked the brief length of the hall, her boot heels clicking on the hard wood, and gazed at the faces. Near the end of the wall, there was a picture of Mickey holding a professionally painted sign that read NO DOZE. The O's were little coffee cups and the steam coming from them was comprised of wispy musical notes. Beside him was a strikingly beautiful blonde; her arms snaked around his neck possessively. Mickey's smile was broad, his eyes crinkled warmly. He was, unmistakably, a happy man. The woman with him had a look to her that Lydia immediately disliked; there was something coquettish, something falsely sweet to her smile. Her eyes were as flat and as dull as a cat's. Just from the photograph, it was easy to see why Lily had disliked her. Lydia wondered if they'd fought about Mariah, if that had been the rift that had grown between them at the end. Try to convince a young man in love that the gorgeous girl throwing herself at him isn't the sweet thing he imagines her to be. See how well it goes. He'd have been angry with Lily for it, especially since on some level he would have known she was right. He might have accused her of being jealous, which might also have been partly true.

"That's her," said Jasmine coming up behind Lydia. "Funny, though. I don't remember that photo on the wall."

Lydia looked at it; it did seem out of symmetry with the placement of the others.

"How long ago was that?"

"More than six months ago now."

Lydia pointed to a black-and-white shot of a man who looked a lot like Mickey holding a baby. "Who's that?" Lydia asked.

"That's their biological father; I think his name was Graves. Simon Graves."

There was an air of melancholy to the photo, an expression of sadness on his face though he gazed into the eyes of his child. Lydia wrapped her arms around herself, as if the mood of the photo could leak into her own heart if she allowed it, and bring memories of the loss—if she even had a right to call it that—she had recently suffered.

"And this," said Jasmine, "is their stepfather, Tim Samuels." He was a big man, with an infectious smile and laughing green eyes. He had strawberry blond hair, with light brows and lashes to match. He held a young Lily on his hip and had his arm around Mickey, who barely reached his elbow. Lily smiled, staring at Tim Samuels with unabashed adoration. Mickey sulked, his arms folded, the very picture of sullen adolescence.

"What does he do?" Lydia asked.

"He owned a private security firm. But he sold it about a year and half ago, made so much money that he decided to retire."

"Private security?"

"Yeah, you know, like bodyguards."

"Hmm," said Lydia. She didn't remember Lily mentioning anything like that, but they had only had brief discussions about her family.

In the bedroom, Jasmine sat on the king-sized bed while Lydia sifted through Lily's drawers. There was a Tibetan prayer flag hanging on the wall but few other decorative touches. A small wooden Buddha wobbled on the dresser top as Lydia opened and closed drawers, finding only tee-shirts, socks, lingerie. Lydia walked over to the closet, opened it, and saw a neat row of clothes ordered by color, mainly black, charcoal, and navy. An equally orderly row of shoes sat at attention.

"I wish she was messier," said Lydia, looking around the Spartan space. She was hoping for piles of papers and notebooks, journals.

Jasmine laughed. "The girl is *anal.*"

"Where's her computer?" asked Lydia suddenly.

"Her laptop would be with her. She never went anywhere without that thing. All her notes were on that, or her Palm Pilot. Any journal she kept, anything like that, would be on that. I told the police; they asked the same question."

"Shit," said Lydia, disappointed.

"She had this black laptop bag that was her, like, portable office," said Jasmine, holding up her hands to indicate its size. "She had a desk at the *Post* but she kept everything in that bag because she didn't like to write there. She liked to write at home or at the NYU library—you can still go there if you're an alum. Pens, notebooks, Palm Pilot, laptop, *everything* was in there."

Lydia took another loop around the apartment but didn't find anything that helped her. She walked back over to the photo wall and pointed to the picture of Mariah and Mickey.

"Can I take this?" she asked.

"Sure," said Jasmine.

Lydia removed the picture from the frame and slid it into her bag.

"Are you going to find her?" Jasmine asked softly.

"Yes," said Lydia, sounding more certain that she felt. "I am."

"He killed her. What the fuck you think happened?" asked the young man with the braids and the oversized Knicks tee-shirt.

He was acting tough, moving around, waving his arms, making a show of his anger for their benefit, but he was barely holding back his tears. Jesamyn and Matt stood quietly in the living room, letting him blow off steam. He was Rosario Mendez's younger brother. She'd more or less raised him since their mother was addicted to crack and died some years earlier. The apartment was clean, with furniture that looked like it had seen a lot of years, walls that needed some paint, but there was a flat-screen television hanging on the wall, a Sony PlayStation and at least fifty games on the shelves, a stereo and speaker system that looked like it cost more than either one of them made in half a year.

On the table there was a picture of the young man before them in a cap and gown, standing next to Rosario; both of them wore bright smiles as she reached playfully for his cap. A bassinet sat in the corner, filled with colorful toys.

"She knew he would kill her one day. She told me, 'He's gonna kill me, Baby. Make sure he doesn't get away with it.' "

His name was Baby Boy Mendez, legally. Rumor was that his mother hadn't given him a name when he was born and never reported any other name she might have come up with before the city deadline. So Baby Boy stuck. Something about it made Jesamyn sad for him . . . that and the fact that he was just eighteen years old. He seemed much younger. But he wouldn't be going into the child services system. And, if he wasn't careful, the street would get him.

He moved in close to them, arms outstretched. He had a desperate energy to him, which caused Jesamyn to put her pad and pen down on the table behind her to keep her hands free.

"So what are you going to do it about it?" he said, getting in their faces a little. "Just walk around asking a lot of stupid fucking questions, right."

Mount put up his hand to move Baby Boy back a step. "You're going to need to calm down, son. And step back. You're in my space."

Mount's size intimidated even the toughest thugs they ran into. And Baby Boy just sank into the couch like someone had let the air out of him.

"No one's going to help her," he said, his voice catching. "You'll nose around for a few days, then disappear. She was *pregnant,* man."

"Mr. Mendez, Alonzo was beating your sister?" asked Matt.

"Hell, *yes,* he was beating her. How many times I have to tell you guys the same shit. Pregnant with his baby and he was still smacking her around. She just kept going back to him."

"Is there any chance she took off to get away from him? That she went into hiding?" asked Matt.

Baby Boy looked at him angrily. "Not without me," he said, his voice going shrill. "She wouldn't leave here without *me.*"

"Okay," said Jesamyn, holding up her hand in a calming gesture. "I'm sure that's true. But if she *had* taken off, can you think of anyplace else she might have gone? Was there another boyfriend, close friend, a relative out of state?"

He put his head in his hands and shook his head. "We never had no one else, just each other and the little guy on the way, you know?"

Jesamyn noticed that he shifted between referring to his sister in the past and present tense, as if he were struggling with hope and despair.

"When was the last time you saw her?" asked Matt.

"Saturday night. I was heading out with my boys. She was staying home. The baby was making her tired. Alonzo kept calling, wanted her to go to the clubs. She kept telling him no, she didn't want to. He kept calling. After a while, she stopped answering the phone. As I was leaving, I heard him say on the answering machine, 'I'm bringing the Escalade to come get you, bitch. You *best* be ready.' That's how he talked to her, man. And she just *took* it."

"No signs of struggle here at the apartment?"

"*Shit,*" he said, drawing the word out. "I already told the police all of this."

"As I mentioned, in the absence of any solid leads on Rosario, we're reinterviewing people to see if there's something we missed the first time around," said Matt.

The kid sighed heavily, frustration and anger coming off of him in waves. He leaned back on the couch.

"No, it was neat and clean the way she liked it. All the lights were out. The clothes she was wearing when I left were folded on her bed. I figured she just changed and went out to avoid a fight."

"What was she wearing when you left?" asked Jesamyn.

"Some, like, gray baggy nightgown thing. Ugly as shit but she said it was comfortable."

"Okay," said Jesamyn, jotting it down. "Is there anything else about that night that you remember?"

"I remember thinking I should stay home with her. That's what I remember," he said, the tears rolling now. "I should have stayed home with her."

He started to sob and Matt moved over to him, placed a hand on his shoulder. It was kind of a risky thing to do but the kid had no visible reaction. After a minute, he looked up at Matt.

"I haven't seen anything on television about her, you know that? That pregnant white girl in California? You couldn't turn on the television without seeing her face. I haven't seen one picture of my sister anywhere. A Latina girl from the projects goes missing, no one cares."

Matt and Jesamyn stood silent for a second. There was no use arguing about it; they all knew the truth.

"We care," said Matt finally. And Jesamyn knew how deeply he meant it. She loved him a little bit for that.

"You were good with him," she said in the car, as they pulled out of their space. They'd come back to the Caprice, surprised to see that it hadn't been vandalized in any way. Often when you parked a patrol car, marked or unmarked, in the projects you came back to find it covered with eggs or spray paint, maybe vegetables, whatever was handy.

"He's a kid. She was basically his mother," he said. "I feel for him."

Baby Boy was the last of three reinterviews they'd done that afternoon and Mount was consistently kind and respectful, in spite of the abuse that was hurled at them. The next-door neighbor called them 'pigs' under his stinking breath when they'd come to the door. A lot of cops would have reacted, but Mount kept calling him sir, speaking in that mellow way he had. Rosario's best friend Angelica had taunted Mount about his height, wondering out loud if everything about him was so big. Mount had turned bright red but kept his respectful, easy manner. Jesamyn wondered, did it roll off of him or did he hold it inside?

"You're a big softie," she said, patting him on the knee.

The sun was hanging low in the sky, painting it a light pink and orange visible above the building tops.

"I gotta get moving," she said, looking at her watch. "I told Ben we'd have dinner together tonight. Want to join us?"

"I'd love to, but I think I'm going to see what came back on that partial plate."

She nodded. She knew Lily Samuels had never left his mind the whole afternoon. The case was with her, too, but not in the same way. It was weighing on Mount's heart.

"Don't sleep here again tonight, okay?

He nodded. "I won't."

She didn't believe him.

The search Matt ran on the partial plate and description came back with twenty-eight hits. Twenty-eight black SUVs with license plates beginning with H57 in the New York area. He made a quick scan of the list, plugged a couple of the names into VICAP, the Violent Criminal Apprehension Program database administered by the FBI, and through the New York system. None of the owners came back with any warrants or criminal records. Nothing else obvious popped. The only thing that caught his attention was a black Navigator belonging to a Michele LaForge that had a couple of outstanding parking tickets. He pulled up her license photo, didn't recognize her, but printed it anyway for the file. It was nothing; he knew that. He had nothing. Two weeks ago he could have followed up with every one of these people. Just poked around, saw what shook loose. Now, he'd be lucky if he could get to one or two a day over the next few weeks.

He rubbed his eyes when the computer screen started to swim. His frustration, the lack of sleep from the night before, and a totally shit day were taking their toll. It was time to go home.

"Sorry, Lily," he said to her picture. He was wiped, no good to her or anyone. That was the thing about this job; you could just go and go until you dropped. You never felt right about going home to bed when someone was missing. You could never feel okay about just relaxing, chilling in front of the television, letting your mom cook you some dinner. You did it, you just never felt good about it. At least that's how *he* felt. Jesamyn had something important in her life, Benjamin. Something that was equally important, more important than the job. She went home at the end of the day without guilt. He envied her that.

Last year he'd been diagnosed with a bleeding ulcer. His doctor, who'd been treating him since he was fourteen years old, had issued a stern warning about stress and its effects on the body, short and long term. So he'd quit smoking, stopped eating fast food, and took the medication his doctor prescribed. For a while, he'd even worked out, but that hadn't lasted. He had started to feel that burn in his stomach again two nights ago. It was like an existential alarm. When he was pushing himself too hard, he got a painful warning.

He slid the file under his arm and lumbered down the stairs.

"Go home will ya', Mount," said Ray Labriola, a narcotics guy who passed him on the stairs. "You're making the rest of us look bad."

"I'm taking off," said Mount, looking at his watch. Nearly nine. "Have a good one."

"You too, brother," said Ray.

The night was cold as he stepped outside, the street strangely quiet. A wind blew the fallen leaves around him as he walked to his brand new Dodge Ram pickup. He slid into the comfortable leather interior with ease. It was the first vehicle he'd ever owned that didn't feel like a ridiculously small clown car to him. He felt almost normal in it. He turned the car on and all the dials and digital readouts glowed a nifty red and blue. Tiny ram heads lit up in various places. He loved his new car. He let the engine warm up as he took the cellular phone from his pocket.

"Mom?"

"Mateo! So late," said his mother, her Greek accent still thick even after thirty-five years in New York. "Where are you?"

"Working, Ma. Whaddaya think?"

"I worry," she said with a dramatic sigh. He knew she watched New York One News all night until she knew he was off duty. She waited to hear if any police officers had been hurt or killed. It had been worse for her when he was on patrol. She thought of detective work as "white shirt" police work, safe and intellectual. She meant "white collar."

"I keep a plate for you."

"Thanks, Ma. I'll be a while still. Don't wait."

"We haven't seen you in two days," she said. "Remember your ulcer."

"I know," he said gently. "I'll see you in the morning."

He heard his father's voice and could picture him lying beside her in bed, the television on. "Tell him not to forget alternate side of the street parking tomorrow."

"You hear, Mateo?"

"Yeah, Ma. I heard. Good night."

Every night, his father felt compelled to remind him to move the car from one side of the street to the other lest he should get a parking ticket. Every night since he got his first car.

He lived beside his parents in a two-family house in Brooklyn. So while he wasn't *exactly* a thirty-six-year-old man who lived with his parents, he kind of was. They had separate living spaces but his mother still did his laundry, cleaned his place, and cooked most of his meals. This, he perceived, was yet another mark against him in the dating arena. His younger brother, Theo, lived two row houses down on the same block with his pretty wife, Anne, and his two fantastic kids Maura and little Mateo, named after his uncle.

He dialed another number and then rolled out of the lot.

"Ms. Strong," he said when she answered.

"Detective, good to hear from you," she said amiably. He heard victory in her voice. He liked her in spite of her smug attitude. He liked her confidence and determination, qualities he knew most men found unattractive.

"I have something for you," he said. "Can I drop it by? Will you meet me on the street?"

"Sure," she said. "Are you on your way?"

"I'll be there in two minutes."

She was waiting in front of her door on Great Jones Street when he pulled up, shivering in her leather jacket and jeans. He pushed the door open for her and she climbed inside.

"Big car," she said. He figured her for one of those liberals who thought no one should be driving an SUV.

"I'm a big guy," he said. She smiled.

He handed her the folder and told her what he'd learned from Thelma Baker that morning. Over the next five minutes, he related the salient features of the case, which wasn't much.

"Why are you doing this?" she asked when he was finished.

Lydia Strong had burned him earlier. What she'd said about him caring more about his ego and protecting his turf than about Lily. He didn't know why, but he didn't want her to believe that.

"I'm out of time. And so is Lily. Like you said, you have better resources than I do. I can't give you my case file; besides, there's nothing of much use to you there." He nodded toward the folder. "Those are the first real leads I've had in two weeks and I don't have time to follow up on them. Lily deserves someone to look into who was driving that car."

Lydia looked at him. "She does. And I will. Do you want me to keep you informed?"

"Please," he said with a nod. "Please do. I wrote my cell phone number in there. Don't call me at the station. And I have a copy of that list. I'll be following up on my own time, as well."

"Just one question," she said. "How much time did you spend looking into Mickey's life?"

He shook his head slightly. "Her brother. Not much, really. Why?"

"Just wondering. There was a girlfriend. She and Lily didn't get along."

He shook his head. "I've been looking at Lily's life, retracing her steps, talking to the people that knew her best. I did some cursory looking into Mickey's life up there but I never met a girlfriend. Never came across anything that led me to believe his suicide and Lily's disappearance were connected."

She was quiet for a second but turned her gray eyes on him. She said slowly, "Other than that's the reason she went up there in the first place."

He thought about it a second. Then, "Right. But if I got hit by a car on my way to the grocery store, you wouldn't go to the grocery store looking for the driver of the car that hit me."

"Unless the driver was trying to stop you from getting what you were looking for at the store," said Lydia.

He'd never thought about it that way. "Well," he said, for lack of anything better coming to mind.

After a second: "Well, thanks, Detective. You're doing the right thing for Lily."

Something about the way the light from the streetlamp hit her then made her look very young—too young to be who she was. The light glinted off her blue-black hair and made her pale skin luminous. There was a simmering intensity to her that he recognized, a fierce desire to put the pieces together. He saw those things in her and he respected her for it. He didn't know enough about her to know what put the fire in her. He'd heard rumors about a murdered mother but he didn't know whether that was the truth or not.

She got out of the car then without another word, tucking the folder under her arm. He watched her cross the street. She was about five-six, five-seven with strong, straight shoulders. She walked with the confidence of a woman who knew how to take care of herself. She was lean but with a fabulous fullness about her hips and breasts. She looked strong, fit but he knew her body would be soft, womanly. So many women seemed emaciated to him lately, as if they were being strangled by this terrible need to be thin. His mother had always said,

"A woman who can't feed herself, can't love herself. And if she can't love herself, she can't love you." He'd always thought it was kind of this funny mix of old and new world values; but that was his mother. Meanwhile, his cousins with their lusty Mediterranean bodies were forever battling their natural shape and curves, trying to fit into a society that wanted women to be as small and quiet as possible. He loved them for their big personalities, their passions, and their full bodies. They were some of the most beautiful women he knew.

He waited until Lydia was inside the door and then he pulled out into traffic.

He took the phone from his pocket and dialed. He listened as the phone on the other end rang, praying he wouldn't get voicemail.

"Hello," purred a warm female voice.

"Katrina," he said, and the taste of her name on his tongue aroused him.

"Is that you, Mateo?" She sounded breathlessly glad to hear from him. But that was all part of the show, wasn't it?

"Are you busy?" he asked.

"Never too busy for you," she said softly. "When can I expect you?"

"What did he want?" asked Jeffrey as she walked back into her office. He was sitting on her couch, sifting though articles Lily had written in the last year pulled from LexisNexis. He leaned back and rubbed his eyes. They'd been reading for hours. They weren't sure what they were looking for exactly. They just wanted to know where Lily's head had been at before her brother had died. Lydia sat back down beside him and he dropped his arm around her shoulder. She rested against his body.

"He wanted to give me this," she said holding up the manila folder.

"What is it?"

"Apparently, the woman who greeted Lily at the bank the day she closed her accounts noticed a black SUV waiting outside for her. She said that Lily seemed concerned about it, kept looking behind her at the vehicle. The woman got a partial plate. These are the results of the search he did."

"Anything interesting?"

"I'm not sure," she said, opening the folder and settling in. She flipped through the pages, reading the listings of the twenty-eight drivers who owned black SUVs.

"It's a pretty straight and narrow crew," said Lydia after a second, her eyes still on the file. "No criminal records, no DUIs, no warrants. A couple of parking tickets—" She stopped talking abruptly and held up one of the driver's license photos Detective Stenopolis had printed.

"What is it?"

The woman in the photo had short-cropped black hair and a full face. It was a black-and-white photograph so Lydia couldn't determine the color of her eyes, but they looked dark. Something about the expression on her face jolted Lydia. She got up quickly and went over to her bag and sifted out the photograph she'd taken from Lily's apartment.

She sat back down and held the photograph up next to the printout and compared the two.

"It's the same person," said Jeffrey, staring over her shoulder.

"Are you sure?" she said. The printout was poor quality and the light in the office was low.

"Yeah, look at the cheekbones, the shape of her eyes. She was younger and heavier when the driver's license photo was taken, but look at the nose. It's definitely the same woman."

Lydia examined the features of her face and saw that he was right. The license photo was taken nearly two years earlier. Either she'd altered her appearance since then for some purpose or she was just one of those people who constantly wanted a new look.

"Jasmine said that Lily and Mickey knew her as Mariah."

"Well, the DMV knows her as Michele LaForge."

"This address is in Riverdale," she said, turning her eyes to him.

He looked at her a minute, and she waited for him to say something. She saw a kind of resignation in his eyes and she knew what he was thinking. After a year of relative peace following a period of terrible fear and chaos, their quiet life was about to get a shake-up again. They both knew it was inevitable; it was what they did. It was how they lived. And small, or maybe not so small, parts of each of them wouldn't have it any other way. He put a hand to her face and kissed her lightly on the mouth.

"We'll go up there in the morning," he said.

"Jeffrey, what if—," she said, letting the sentence trail. There was a parade of what ifs in her mind; their march would keep her up all night. *What if Lily's somewhere against her will, afraid, hurt? What if Mariah knows something? What if there's crucial information at that address that could lead them to Lily? What if tomorrow morning is too late?*

He nodded solemnly. She didn't have to tell him what she was thinking.

"Call Dax," he said. "I'll get our coats. It's not like we're going to get any sleep anyway."

She watched him leave the office and then picked up the phone.

"It's late," he answered, but she could hear the television in the background. He sounded cranky.

"Sorry to interrupt your late-night television viewing," she said. "But I think we're going to come by and get you. There's something in your neighborhood we want to check out."

She heard him turn off the set and sit up. "Oh, yeah," he said, sounding happier, his Australian accent drawing out his syllables.

Dax had had kind of a tough year, recovering from two severed Achilles' tendons, an injury he sustained while trying to help Lydia and Jeffrey. She knew that since then, he hadn't been working as much as usual. Although exactly *who* Dax worked for when he wasn't working for Mark, Striker and Strong was apparently a confidential matter. Lydia had gone to every possible length to find out, from snooping to begging. But he was like the sphinx, stony and inscrutably silent about his life.

"What's going on?" he asked.

"We'll be up there in an hour; we'll explain it all then."

"Sweet," he said and hung up.

Six

Benjamin was in bed, safe between his *Lord of the Rings* sheets. This was her favorite time, when they were both under the same roof. They'd ordered in from the diner across the street and watched *Monsters, Inc.* for the one hundred and fiftieth time. What was it about kids? Why did they want to watch the same things over and over? It must be a comfort thing.

With him sound asleep, she opened a bottle of chardonnay and curled up on the couch, listening to her child breathe on the baby monitor, which she still kept in his room though he was way too old for it. It relaxed her, the sound of him and the glass of wine. The television was on but the sound was down, and she zoned out on the images from the ten o'clock news. She pushed away any thoughts about Lily Samuels and Rosario Mendez; she'd done all she could for them today and thinking about them all night wasn't going to help anyone. She'd almost succeeded when something on the screen caught her attention.

The words "Bizarre Halloween 'Shooting'" popped red in the corner of the screen and Jesamyn reached quickly for the remote, turned the volume up.

"—when a young woman was shot three times in the back during the parade," said a plastic-looking male newscaster. "Onlookers thought it was part of the show or a prank of some kind when a white van came to a stop on a side street off the parade route, pursuing a young woman running toward Main Street. When two men emerged from the van chasing her and shots were fired, the crowd dispersed in a panic. Spectators saw the two men lift the lifeless body, place it back in the van, and drive away. In the melee, no one was able to identify a license-plate number.

"Was it a Halloween prank? Police still don't know. There was no blood found at the scene, leading police to believe that the shooting could have been staged. They are asking if anyone has any photographs or videotape of the evening, to please call the crime stoppers tip line." He gave the number and the newscast went on to another story.

Jesamyn was about to pick up the phone to call Mount to tell him about the story, even though it probably didn't mean anything. It could have easily been a prank, although a very sick prank. They could call the Riverdale precinct tomorrow and see what they had and get a description of the girl, at the very least.

But before she could dial, she heard a key in her front door. She got to her feet quickly and moved toward the front hall, cursing herself for not putting the dead bolt on yet. She *had* to get that key back from him. The chain kept the door from opening all the way.

"We both know that chain is useless. I could easily ram my way in there if I wanted to," he said with a smile. She leaned against the wall and looked at him. He pressed his face up against the opening between the door and the jamb. Those ice blue eyes had caused her to betray herself too many times. He'd shaved his black hair down to the skull as he sometimes did when he wanted to look tough, and he had about two days of stubble on his face.

"But then I'd be within my legal rights to kill you," she said pleasantly. He reached his hand through the door and playfully grabbed for her tee-shirt. She moved just out of his reach.

"The father of your child. I don't think so."

"He's young. He'll get over it."

He gave her the smile. The smile that said, "I'm so sexy, so loveable, and you can't resist me no matter what I've done."

"Come on, Jez. I haven't seen the kid in three days. I know he's sleeping; I just want to poke my head in."

She stared at him. Over the years, the effect that his smile once had on her had greatly diminished. But she'd just be lying to herself if she said it didn't still ignite something within her. She considered her visceral sexual attraction to him a mutinous physical impulse to be quashed at all costs.

"I'll let you in," she said. "But I want that key before you leave. Otherwise, I'm changing the locks. I also want your word that you won't come again without calling."

"What about when I pick up Ben and bring him home from school?" he said.

"I'll give the key to Ben. He's old enough now."

His smile faded a little bit and she thought she saw genuine sadness in his eyes. But with Dylan it was impossible to tell the difference between sincere feeling and calculated manipulation.

"Okay," he said, softly. "Okay."

She unlatched the door and he gave her a quick, hard embrace and a kiss on the cheek. "You're the best," he told her. "You really are."

She followed him through the apartment and stood in the doorway and watched him watch Ben. She didn't trust him not to wake Ben up. And once he was awake and knew that his dad was here, forget it. They'd all be up all night. But Dylan was good; he was quiet as he sat in the small wooden chair beside Ben's bed. A nightlight that looked like an aquarium rotated, casting the shadows of fish in a dim blue light on the walls. For a second she remembered what it was like when they all lived here together, when they were a family. There had been plenty of quiet, happy times that looked just like this moment.

Dylan turned to her and pointed at the baby monitor beside Ben's bed, gave her a disapproving shake of his head. She crossed her arms and raised her eyebrows in a dare: *What are you going to do about it?* She didn't stalk out of the room, which was her impulse. He was antagonizing her to get her to leave so that he could "accidentally" wake up Ben. She knew most of his techniques and had developed countertechniques to block them.

After another moment, he rose and walked past her and out of the room. She closed the door behind her. In the kitchen, she noticed that he looked tired. He'd taken off his leather jacket and hung it over one of the chairs. He reached into the refrigerator and grabbed a Corona.

"Make yourself at home," she said, sitting down at the table.

"It used to *be* my home," he said without heat.

It was an invitation to rumble. But she didn't have it in her tonight. Besides arguing was a kind of intimacy for them, like if they could make each other mad it meant they still cared. She didn't want to give him the satisfaction. In the light the refrigerator cast on him, she could see that he looked tense and strained. She hadn't noticed at the door.

"What's up, Dylan? What's going on?"

She *did* care about him. He had been her husband for four years. He was the father of her child. And in the three years since their divorce, they'd been slowly and haltingly approaching friendship. They'd both done a lot of growing up.

He took the opener from the drawer by the sink and popped the top off his bottle.

"I killed someone last night," he said, his jaw tensing. He closed the refrigerator and they were in semi-darkness with only the light from the living room shining.

"Our buyer got made and we had to go in fast. I killed a sixteen-year-old kid. He turned a MAC M10 on us, I guess thinking he'd shoot his way out; he could have killed us all."

"I didn't hear about it," she said, standing and moving toward him. She could see the weight of it on him.

"It was a good shooting," he said, taking a long draw on the beer and leaning against the counter. She moved near him and put a hand on his arm.

"I'm being investigated, of course," he said with a slow shrug. "But I know I had no choice. Still . . . when I fired, I only saw that gun. When he was down, all I could see was this skinny kid lying there, bleeding out. He didn't even have any hair on his face."

She didn't say anything, just waited for him to go on.

"He knew he was going to die," said Dylan quietly. "He was scared."

He stared at the kitchen wall as if it were all playing out for him there. His face was expressionless and pale but she could see the hand that held his beer shaking just slightly. In her years on the job, Jesamyn had only drawn her weapon twice and never fired it in the line of duty. Dylan worked buy-and-bust up in the South Bronx. It was one of the riskiest possible details. A cop goes undercover to buy drugs from dealers and once the purchase is made, a team moves in and makes the collar. Two cops had died last year in his precinct. But if you did your time, it was two years to a gold shield, something Dylan wanted badly. He envied Jesamyn's quick rise to detective and it was one of the things that had contributed to the end of their marriage.

"I just thought about Ben and you all night last night," he said, lowering his eyes to her face. "While I was in the station, waiting for my PBA rep—I just had a lot of time to think. I watched the life *drain* from someone. It just left him so easily and when he was dead, there was like this shuddering and he was just gone. There was no mistaking it, you know, that life had left."

He rubbed his eyes like he was trying to wipe the memory from them. Jesamyn stayed silent; she was stunned. She'd never heard him talk the way he was talking or look the way he looked. So sad and lost.

"I looked around and there were all these drugs on the table. And this gun in his hand. He had all this jewelry on and these expensive sneakers and leather coat. And it all just seemed so pointless. Like I'd taken this life because of all this *stuff*."

He didn't say anything else but searched her face like he was look-ing for something he needed there. She moved into him, wrapped her arms around him. He put the beer down and held onto her as tightly as he ever had in their years together. She felt the magnetic draw of their sexual chemistry and the pull of his connection to her heart.

"I'm sorry," she said, looking up at him. "Are you okay?"

"I will be. I just needed to see him, you know? And you. I needed to remember what was real."

She pulled away from him and walked into the living room. She needed to get away from him. She wanted to comfort him but it was too easy to get pulled into his universe, to let that familiarity and desire draw her back into his thrall. She sat on the couch and curled her legs up. He sat across from her.

"Don't worry," he said. "I'm not going to put the moves on you to-night, Jez. I just need to be here awhile, okay."

She nodded and felt a wash of relief laced with disappointment.

"Okay," she said, getting up with a nod. She walked to the hall closet and withdrew a blanket and pillows, brought them back to the couch. She stood beside Dylan and put a hand on his strong shoulder, touched the back of his neck. The urge to care for him was as strong as it had ever been.

"You can stay here tonight if you want, Dylan," she said. "On the couch. Just be gone when he gets up, okay? I don't want him to get confused."

"Thanks, Jez," he said looking up to her and taking her hand. "I never deserved you. Don't think I don't know that."

She smiled, kissed him on the top of the head. "We've both made mistakes."

Beware the man who thinks he doesn't deserve you, her mother had fa-mously warned. *He knows himself better than you do.*

It wasn't even an hour before she saw him standing in her doorway. She didn't stop him as he entered her room and closed the door.

"I'm sorry," he said, sitting beside her. She moved easily into his arms and in the next moment, his lips were on her. There was some-thing desperate about the way he kissed her and something primal within her responded to him the way she always had. *Stupid, stupid, stupid,* she chastised herself. But he felt too damn good to turn away. His soft, warm skin, the strong, defined muscles in his chest, her loneliness, her love for the man who had given her Benjamin, all of these elements formed a powerful alchemy that she could never resist.

He'd drifted off after making love to Katrina; it wasn't like him. He didn't like to linger at her place, but she'd let him sleep awhile. When he opened his eyes, she lay beside him on her side, propped up on her elbow. A blue light glowed in her window from the sign for an all-night livery cab company across the street. Her perfectly round breasts with rosebud nipples defied gravity, her thick, honey-colored hair draped over her slender shoulder and neck. The shadows from outside, the swaying branches of a tree, a passing car, drifted over her face and body, the wall behind her. She was so beautiful he could almost imagine loving her.

"You want to stay?" she asked.

"No," he said, sitting up. "Thanks." He smiled at her and touched her arm.

"You can, you know," she said, holding onto his hand for a second. "I don't have anyone else tonight."

He looked at her; the expression on her face was open, sincere. She was young; he wasn't sure how young. He'd never asked. He guessed in her early twenties. He wondered for a moment what it would be like to stay in her arms, to wake up beside her.

"I should go," he said and rose, pulling on his boxers.

He saw her nod and get up, wrap herself in a purple silk robe. "I like it when you're here, Mateo. I feel safe," she said. "I know you're a good man."

He thought her standards must be pretty low, but he was not cruel enough to say it even as a joke. "No one has the right to hurt you, Katrina," he said, turning to look at her. "If anyone does, or even threatens, you let me know."

She smiled at him. "See what I mean," she said. She walked over to the mirror and took a brush from the vanity there. She ran it through her hair.

"No one hurts me." She gazed at him in the mirror with heavy-lidded eyes. "Don't worry, Mateo."

He watched her ass. It was perfect. Heart-shaped and soft as a down pillow. The sight of it beneath the purple silk made him go hard again. He turned away as he buttoned his shirt so she wouldn't see.

When he was dressed, he walked over to her with two hundred-dollar bills folded in half.

"It's too much, Mateo," she said with a pout and a shake of her head. Her hair flipped prettily as her tiny hands, soft and carefully manicured, reached for the cash.

"Take it. Please," he said, giving her a soft kiss on the mouth. It was a dance that they did. Somehow she knew he needed her to act like he didn't have to pay. Maybe all men who came to see her needed that. But she had a way of making him feel like she *wanted* him there. He spent a lot of time wondering if she was sincere or not. He'd never been with a woman in this way before. He'd never paid for it. There were things about it that he liked. There were things about it that he hated. But he kept coming back.

At the door, she kissed him again and they both pretended that they didn't hear her cell phone ring in her purse. On the stairs, he heard the tinkle of her laughter like ice cubes in a glass at a party to which he hadn't been invited. He pretended it didn't bother him as he got into his car where his own cell phone was ringing.

"What are you doing up?" he answered, seeing Jez's number on the caller ID. It was nearly one in the morning.

"I wanted to tell you about something I saw on the news before I forgot. Did you hear about a weird shooting in Riverdale on Halloween?"

"Sounds vaguely familiar. It was a hoax though, wasn't it?"

"I guess. Maybe," she said, her voice little more than a whisper. "But I saw this item on the news that the police are looking for information. I thought we could at least get some info, a description of the woman who was supposedly shot."

"Good idea. I'll check it out tomorrow. Why are you whispering?" he asked. He knew the layout of her apartment. Even with Ben asleep, she wouldn't have to whisper to avoid waking him. She didn't answer him.

"Oh, Jez. For Christ's sake," he said with a groan.

"He shot someone last night. He wanted to see Ben."

Matt had heard a cop shot some kid in the Bronx last night but he hadn't made the connection. He wasn't surprised. Dylan always was a cocked fist looking for a jaw, a drawn gun waiting for an excuse. It had only been a matter of time before he killed someone.

"Was it good?"

"Yeah, he says it was good. But he'll have some time on his hands while they investigate."

"And he'll be looking to spend it with you."

"With Ben," she said firmly.

He bit his tongue. There was no point in lecturing. Dylan Breslow was a habit Jesamyn couldn't break. It never ceased to amaze him when good, smart, beautiful women fell for the men who were guaranteed to hurt them again and again. At least she'd gotten as far as divorcing him. Now it seemed it was just a matter of learning not to sleep with him every time he showed up at her place.

"I gotta go," she said. "See you tomorrow."

"Good-night, Jez."

Seven

"I don't know the address," said Dax, looking at the photocopy of Michele LaForge's driver's license under the bright track lighting in his kitchen. "But that doesn't mean anything."

He hefted his weight onto one of the barstools that stood in front of the counter. Lydia could tell by the way he had been standing that his injury was hurting him. She didn't say anything. It made him mad when she did. But it was hard to see Dax struggling physically, like watching a dog with three legs. It just seemed so wrong; especially since Lydia blamed herself and knew Jeffrey felt a similar burden of guilt.

"Everything's always about the two of you," Dax had said when they'd tried to apologize. "The *Lydia and Jeffrey Show*, twenty-four-hour drama and mayhem. It's not your fault. It's my fault. It's not even my fault. It's Jed McIntyre's fault. And that goddamn midget."

She realized she was staring at him and averted her eyes when he raised his eyes from the paper in his hand. "She looks a little freaky, if you ask me," said Dax.

"That was her two years ago," said Lydia. "This is her now." She handed him the picture she'd taken from Lily's wall.

"Big improvement," said Dax. "Wow. What did she *do* anyway? Why are you so interested in her?"

They told him about Lily and Mickey Samuels, about Mariah, a.k.a. Michele LaForge. Dax glanced at the photograph of Mickey and Mariah.

"You can't trust a woman who looks that good," said Dax with a shake of his head, handing the picture back to Lydia.

"That is insulting on so many levels, I can't even begin to address them," she said, snapping the photo from his hand.

"What?" he said, pulling wide innocent eyes. "Why?"

"Well, what are you saying?" she asked, leaning toward him on the counter. "That I'm ugly or that I'm not trustworthy?"

He smiled at her in the obnoxious way he had when he was baiting her. "Why do you have to take everything so personally?"

She rolled her eyes and moved over toward Jeffrey, looked over his shoulder at the screen.

"*Anyway,*" said Dax, "my point is: did she have anything to gain from Mickey's death or Lily's disappearance?"

Lydia shrugged. "She'd only been dating Mickey for a short time, so I doubt he wrote her into his will. It's my sense that she and Lily didn't get along but I don't see where she'd have anything to gain by Lily disappearing."

Jeffrey was looking at her. "Maybe it's possible that they put their differences aside and were working together to try to find out what happened to Mickey. Maybe neither of them believed he'd killed himself. That would explain her giving Lily a lift to the bank. Maybe they've gone off together, following some kind of lead."

"But Jasmine mentioned that Mariah didn't even come to Mickey's funeral. They'd broken up."

Jeffrey nodded. She could see him shifting the pieces around in his mind.

"Maybe," said Dax, "she was taking advantage of Lily's vulnerable state, manipulating her in some way."

"What? To take her money?" asked Lydia. She answered her own question. "Maybe."

The world was full of all kinds of predators. Lydia looked at the picture of Mickey and Mariah. Where before Mariah had just seemed somewhat off-putting with her coquettish smile and knowing eyes, now Lydia saw malice in her.

"Well, let's see if we can't find Ms. LaForge and see what she has to say," said Jeffrey, turning around the screen and showing the map to her last known address.

"Give it to me," whispered Lydia. It had been her habit for most of the fifteen years they'd known each other to lean over his shoulder and give him advice on whatever it was he was doing and then try to take over. Tonight it was picking a lock on a wooden gate. Jeffrey found this simultaneously annoying and loveable, like so many of her personality quirks.

"I got it," said Jeffrey, working at the lock with the tools he'd brought in the inside pocket of his coat.

The night was cold and dark with no moonlight, no stars visible in the sky; a streetlamp above them was browned out, glowing an eerie orange but casting no light.

"Can you even see?" she asked, trying to nudge him out of the way.

"Excuse me," he said, nudging her back. "I was doing this when you were still in grade school." The lock to the wooden gate snapped open as if to emphasize his point. Behind it was a high, narrow set of stairs that led into a deeper darkness.

Jeffrey led the way up the stairs as Lydia closed the gate behind them. The night was hushed, only the distant rush of cars on the Henry Hudson to the west of them and Broadway to the east was audible, just barely. And the occasional squeal of the 1/9 train coming to a stop in the railroad yards below them.

The steep stone staircase was overrun with weeds and in terrible disrepair, making their progress upwards difficult and treacherous. At the top there was another door. The wood was decayed, looked as if it might have been painted red at one point. A notice had been pasted there. It read menacingly: CONDEMNED: THIS STRUCTURE HAS BEEN DECLARED UNSAFE AND UNINHABITABLE BY THE CITY OF NEW YORK. TRESPASSING IS STRICTLY PROHIBITED. VIOLATORS WILL BE PROSECUTED.

"You don't think that means us, do you?" asked Lydia.

"Nah," answered Jeffrey. He was about to go to work on the lock when Lydia pushed on the door and it opened slowly, emitting a high pitched squeak.

They stepped onto a floor that felt soft beneath their feet; a smell of mold and rot was strong. Lydia pulled a small flashlight from her pocket and shone the powerful beam into the darkness. Some small dark forms skittered away from the light and she shuddered. The room was narrow and bare, wood floors, stone walls, a fireplace centered on the supporting wall. Two large windows at the back of the narrow space looked out into a thick of trees. They walked the space and found a narrow staircase toward the back of the building leading up to a second level. It looked old. It smelled old. It *felt* old.

"What is this place?" Jeffrey asked. The layer of dust, the sheer aura of abandonment told Jeffrey that no one had lived there for years.

"She used a fake address for her driver's license?" said Lydia.

They walked up the narrow flight of stairs, Jeffrey leading the way and testing his weight carefully on each step as they wound into the darkness of the upper level. At the top they entered an almost identical room to the one downstairs. It was empty as well, clean and Spartan. From the window, he could see the Range Rover on the street where Dax was sitting, waiting for them and keeping watch on the entrance. He'd looked dejected when they'd left him behind in the car, like the last kid to get picked for the stickball game. But they all knew he wasn't in any condition to come along.

Jeffrey could feel Lydia's disappointment as she swung the beam of the flashlight around the barren room. They both smelled a dead end.

"Is this all there is to this place?" she said. He didn't really think she was expecting an answer so he didn't give one. Her voice echoed against the stone, sounding hollow and sad.

The phone in his pocket vibrated. He withdrew it and answered.

"Someone's coming. He parked down the street and came up on foot; I didn't see him at first," said Dax. "Shit. He's in the gate. Scary-looking dude."

Jeff hung up and killed the flashlight. A second later, they heard footsteps downstairs. Firm and purposeful, they crossed the span of the downstairs room. Male, medium build, Jeffrey surmised. Expecting to hear someone climb the stairs, he drew the Glock he carried at his waist. He and Lydia retreated quickly and quietly to the separate far dark corners of the space, and waited. He felt the adrenaline start to pump.

But instead of feet on the stairs they heard a door open and then close hard. Then there was silence. They waited a second, two, then met in the middle of the room.

"I didn't see a door downstairs," whispered Lydia.

"Neither did I," he said, moving close to her.

At the bottom of the stairwell, they crouched in the cover of the pitch darkness, waiting. They didn't see the door that had slammed. There was no back exit, no closet, no other rooms.

"Maybe—" Lydia started to say in the darkness. But then a panel in the floor lifted and a rectangle of light slid across the wood surface. A large man in jeans and a long leather coat emerged from the floor. Before he closed the trapdoor behind him, Jeffrey saw his face in stark impressions. A hard, white face with a granite ridge for a brow, heavy dark eyebrows, a wide, stern mouth. His head was shaved, scalp shining in the yellow light from below.

He let the door drop loudly and he started toward the exit and then stopped, seemed to lift his nose to the air. He turned toward them. They were not ten feet from him, but in the pitch-black corner where they crouched, Jeffrey was relatively sure they could not be seen. Jeffrey heard rather than saw him take a step in their direction and he felt Lydia's body tense behind him. She was wearing perfume, a light floral scent. He could smell it and he wondered if the man in leather could smell it, too. They both stopped breathing and the air felt electric with bad possibilities.

But the man turned suddenly, as if he'd heard something, and moved quickly toward the front door. They caught sight of him once more in the relative light of the outside and then he was gone, shoes knocking loudly on the stone stairs outside. Jeff took the phone from his pocket and dialed Dax.

"He's coming back out. Follow him," he said and hung up without waiting for a response. Lydia was already on her way to the trapdoor they'd seen. She dropped to a crouch and felt the floor with her hands, searching for a seam in the wood. It took them a few seconds to find the latch, sunken into the wood. Lydia tugged at it, but it proved too heavy.

"I can't get it," she said, breathless. She moved to the side and he took her place. It took all of Jeffrey's strength to heave the door open, heavy as it was on stiff hinges, though the other man had seemed to manage it with little effort. When it was open, they peered over the edge. A bare bulb on the wall cast light on a narrow stone passageway surrounding a wooden staircase. They exchanged a look, both remembering what had happened the last time they dipped below the surface into tunnels beneath. Then they headed down anyway.

Lydia felt the adrenaline of discovery flooding her system, as well as the exuberance of hope. Perhaps finding Lily would be as easy as opening this door. But a dark current of fear ran beneath her optimism. Perhaps finding Lily *would* be as easy as opening this door. Jeffrey worked the lock as she shone the flashlight beam, and after what seemed like an hour—but was really just a few minutes—they both heard a solid click and the door swung open.

Her heart sank with disappointment as they stepped through the door into an empty room containing a cot and what looked like hospital equipment—a heart monitor, a metal tray empty of instruments, and a ventilator. The room was windowless. Drywall had been erected to make the room seem more like a hospital room and there was an odor of antibacterial cleanser, but beneath it all Lydia could smell the decay and rot of old wood. The place made her nervous; nothing good could happen in a room like this. She was sure of that, if nothing else.

"What are we looking at here?" asked Jeffrey, walking around the room inspecting the machines, the space under the bed.

Lydia shook her head slowly. "I have no idea. But I don't like it."

"And what was he doing in here?" asked Jeff.

She took her cell phone out of her pocket and thought about taking a few pictures of the room, the hallway leading to the room. But then she realized that they were in the dark except for the beam of their flashlight and didn't have a flash.

"Let's get out of here," said Jeffrey after a minute of looking around and seeing nothing further. "I wouldn't want to be trapped in here if that guy comes back. And I'm feeling claustrophobic."

Jeffrey was a tough guy, but in small spaces and airplanes he had to be medicated. Vodka usually did the trick. She stood and walked toward the door. She made a last sweep of the room with her flashlight. Something glinted beneath its beam.

"What was that?" she said, having just caught it out of the corner of her eye as she turned to leave the room.

"What?"

He took the light from her and walked over to the corner of the room. He shone the beam and saw only piles of dust and dirt that had been swept to the edge of the room with a broom and left there. He could see the tracks of the broom bristles, the straight edge to the dust piles. He reached down into the dirt and came back with something delicate and pink. A heart-shaped gem, small in his palm but big enough to be expensive as far as jewels went. He handed it to Lydia and shone the light on it; the gem glittered brilliantly in her hand.

"Wow," said Lydia, her eyes widening.

"What?"

"It's a pink diamond," she said, turning the stone in her hand. "Do you know how much this is worth?"

"It could just be glass or crystal," he said.

"Look at the brilliance, the fire inside of it. It's a diamond, trust me," she said. "This is one of the rarest stones in the world. Less than one tenth of one percent of diamonds can truly be classified as pink."

He stared at her. "For someone who doesn't like diamonds, you seem to know a lot about them."

"Just because I didn't *want* a big diamond, doesn't mean I don't *like* them," she said. She turned those gray eyes on him. "Do you know how many people die in those mines every year? Whole cultures are oppressed and enslaved by the diamond mining industry."

"I know, I know," he said, trying not to roll his eyes. "You mentioned it."

He'd been disappointed when she said she didn't want a diamond for their engagement last year. She'd lost so much, been ravaged by so much pain and loss; he'd just wanted to give her something that promised a brighter future for them both, something glittering and precious, something only he could give to her.

But it was hard to give Lydia anything; she was intensely independent, had her own money and managed most of his money besides. What she needed or wanted, she generally got for herself. Though she loved beautiful things, he knew they didn't mean anything to her. They were just objects.

"You've been manipulated by the media to think that all women need a diamond as proof of their husband's love and devotion," she'd told him. "All I need is to look into your face and I *know*. Besides, the fact that you put up with all my crap is proof enough."

So they'd settled on matching wedding bands, sapphires in hers being the only flourish she wanted. He'd thought of surprising her with a diamond, but in the end he couldn't decide if that was just his impulse to control her, to give her what he thought she should have rather than what she wanted and needed.

"What's it doing here?" she said, gazing at it. "Who would just leave this here?"

"Do you recognize it as something Lily wore?"

She shook her head. "Not that I noticed. And I think I would have noticed."

He took it in his hand. "It doesn't have any hardware on it that indicates it was part of a piece of jewelry."

"No," she said. "It has to be more than a carat. Unbelievable." She took it from him, wrapped it in a tissue she took from her pocket, and placed it in her coat. She took a long look around the room.

"Do you think she was down here?" she asked, not really expecting an answer.

"I really hope not."

They didn't realize how bad the air had been inside until they were outside again, drawing the crisp cold night into their lungs. They hustled down the stairs and Dax was waiting in the Rover. They piled in, Jeffrey in the front, Lydia in back.

"Did you follow him?" asked Jeffrey, when Dax started the car.

"Yeah, I did," he said, moving around the corner. "He was parked over here."

Dax pointed as they passed a spot about a tenth of a mile from the empty house.

"He got into a large white van. It had a logo on it that I didn't recognize, it looked like a sun with some kind of geometric design in its center. I followed him up this way."

They wound up a dark road that edged the subway yard, where sleeping trains reflected the light from streetlamps off their silver roofs. A thin moon revealed itself as dark clouds drifted slowly in the night sky. They wound past opulent homes behind stone gates, through a small town center, and eventually to streets that bordered the Henry Hudson Parkway. Dax slowed down but didn't stop as they passed a building that looked like a church. It was a brown clay structure with a vaulted roof and short stout bell tower containing no bell. Within the center of the triangular roof was a stained glass version of the logo Dax had described. Lydia could just make out the sign that hung above the door. It read: THE NEW DAY. Something about it sent a cold finger tracing down her spine.

"We could just walk up and knock on the door," suggested Jeffrey. "Start asking questions about Lily and Mariah."

"Or try to get in the back?" said Lydia, itching a little to get inside the brown building that tried hard to look like a church. Something about it felt like a dare to her.

Jeffrey shook his head. "Breaking and entering an abandoned building is one thing."

"Breaking into an inhabited one takes research," said Dax. They pulled away slowly, Lydia looking at the building until it was out of sight.

They'd headed back to Dax's place. From the outside, Dax's Riverdale home looked like a hundred other big Victorian houses in the tony suburb. But the inside was mostly bare of furniture, except for a big leather recliner parked in front of a giant flat-screen television that received about five million channels and a DVD player in the den. There was a giant wrought-iron four-poster bed in an upstairs room, with another flat-screen hanging on the wall.

His basement was a maze of rooms—one a weapons armory filled with enough fire power to equip an army; one with a cruel metal table, complete with five-point restraints; yet another adjacent to a second room connected by a two-way mirror. Lydia never tired of questioning him about these things, but he never gave her a straight answer. But she wasn't interested in the mystery that was Dax tonight. She Googled.

"Welcome to The New Day," said Lydia out loud. Dax and Jeffrey came to stand behind her where she stood at the kitchen counter tapping away on Dax's laptop.

"Damn. I love the Internet," said Dax.

The screen flashed with the icon they'd seen on the stained glass window of the church. Another image flashed, this one of smiling people, one white, one black, Arab, Asian, dressed in white tunic shirts and blue jeans, arms linked, feet bare. That faded and was replaced with an image of two men holding hands, then two women with their heads together and laughing eyes. A young Latina girl held a baby in her arms and wore an expression of joy. The gallery of images kept fading into one another.

"When did churches start acting like country clubs where only the elite among us are welcome?" Lydia read. "Jesus didn't judge, nor did Buddha, nor did Allah. So why do our major religions today seem to create so much pain, so much violence? The Middle East, abortion clinic bombings, Catholic priests violating our children: these are all symptoms of institutions that are diseased at their core, institutions created to control, to alienate, to steal, and to ultimately divorce us from God rather than bring us home.

"But there is another way. A New Day has dawned."

"I'm convinced," said Dax. "Sign me up."

"Me, too," said Jeffrey.

"Don't you find," Lydia went on reading, "that no matter how much you accomplish, it always feels like something is missing? That you're always looking on to the next thing you think will *finally* make you happy."

"Well, no, not really," said Dax.

"Yeah, no, not so much," said Jeffrey.

"As you accrue your wealth, amass possessions, spend endless hours pursuing your career, obsessing over your physical appearance, isn't there something deep within that nags at you? Isn't there a voice that whispers: *Is this all there is?*"

"Wow. Other people are hearing voices?" said Dax. "I'm so relieved."

"Dax, will you shut it? This is serious," asked Lydia without turning to look at him. He made a face at her behind her back. Jeffrey rolled his eyes.

"Do you find that you hold onto grudges and pain year after year? Perhaps you've suffered a tragedy, a terrible loss, and you find you just can't move on. Or do you find that your inner life is a broken record of angry and hateful thoughts, not just about others but about *yourself*. It's not your fault. You have been programmed to think that way. From the day you were born, you have been socialized to be dissatisfied. Why? Because as long as you are dissatisfied with your life and yourself, divorced from your spiritual center, you will continue to *consume*. Because in this society, happiness is always one Mercedes, one face-lift, one diamond ring away.

"But there is another way. A New Day has dawned."

The website gave the address of the building they'd visited and a phone number to call.

"We have open gatherings every Sunday at five in the evening. Come and listen. You may hear the first truthful words of your life."

Lydia fell silent and they all stared at the screen for a minute.

"Sounds like we have ourselves a date," said Dax, clapping his hands together.

"We can't wait until Sunday," said Lydia. "We have to find out what goes on there sooner."

She turned to look at Dax. "Jeffrey and I are too high profile to just go strolling in there looking for our New Day."

"That's right. The duo that took 'private' out of private investigations," said Dax. "What are you suggesting then?"

"Dax, darling," she said, slipping an arm around his waist and looking up at him. "Isn't there a voice that whispers: *Is this all there is?*"

Eight

The Samuels family lived well. They weren't rich, exactly, not in the chauffeur-driven-car, private-jet kind of way. But they were clearly more than comfortable. A late model black Audi TT and a navy Acura MDV nestled in the neatest and most organized three-car garage Lydia had ever seen. Beside the two vehicles a beautiful Harley Davidson Low Rider preened, parked at a three-quarter angle, so all the world could see its specialty paint job. Delicate white flames on a red gas tank and wheel fenders, polished chrome works and suicide grips.

"Nice hog," said Lydia as they pulled the Kompressor around the circular drive. It was a gorgeous beach house with weathered gray clapboard, a steep, charcoal-colored shingle roof and white trim. A wrap-around porch and a widow's walk added an air of romance. Lydia could smell the salt from the Atlantic, hear the cry of gulls and the lapping of the ocean on the shore. It almost made the two-hour drive on the Long Island Expressway worth it.

A man she recognized as Tim Samuels from the photographs on Lily's walls appeared at a picture window. He was even bigger than he'd appeared in the photo, with an aura of warmth and geniality. She imagined he might even seem joyful at other points in his life. But not today. Today he wore his sadness like a cloak. The sun passed behind the clouds as if out of respect for his grief, as he emerged from the front door.

"You must be Lydia and Jeff," he said, reaching for Lydia's hand as he approached them.

They could hear the halyard of a sailboat mast clinking in the wind that seemed to pick up.

"That's right," said Lydia, shaking his hand. Jeffrey did the same.

"We've heard a lot about you from Lily. She's a big fan of yours," he said with a smile. He seemed to be searching Lydia with his eyes for a hint of what his daughter had seen in her to so impress her.

"Well, I'm a big fan of Lily's," said Lydia. "That's why I want to see what I can do for her."

"We appreciate it. Let's head inside."

They sat on a plush, champagne-colored couch that was angled to look out onto the expansive view of the Atlantic Ocean. A series of French doors without window treatments looked out onto another wrap-around veranda. The outdoor furniture had been stripped of its cushions, looked barren and lonely as if dreaming of summer. The moody sea churned dark with bright whitecaps. A fireplace burned to their right.

The room, decorated in shades of gold, cream, and pale blue, was a gallery dedicated to Mickey and Lily; there was no available space that didn't contain a framed picture of one or both of their faces. The walls contained floor-to-ceiling shelves of books. A coffee table fashioned of varnished beach wood beneath a piece of beveled glass sat on a plush white area rug between them. Tim Samuels offered them some coffee, which they declined. Then he sat in one of the plush, floral-printed chairs across from them. Lydia could picture the family gathered there, beautiful and happy, playing Scrabble, opening Christmas gifts, swapping stories—doing whatever it was beautiful, happy families did in front of the fire.

"My wife," he said when he sat, "won't join us." He looked into his teacup. "I mean, she can't really. She's upstairs, sleeping. It's the drugs, you know. Seems like she's either catatonic or hysterical. These are the choices lately."

"I won't pretend to know what either of you are going through," said Lydia gently. "All I can say is that we want to help however we can."

He closed his eyes and nodded gratefully.

"I can't tell you how happy I was to get your call. The police warned us about that reward, the freaks and weirdos it would draw from the woodwork. I thought they were exaggerating. The phone literally rang day and night . . . liars, pranksters, psychics, but not one real lead. At first we had the police and volunteers here twenty-four seven. Then people started going back to their lives. I tried to answer it myself for a while, then I just started letting it go to voicemail and I was checking it every hour or so. Then it stopped ringing altogether. And that was worse. The silence. There's been nothing but silence for days now. Until your call.

"It's weird," he said, putting his cup down on the table. "Everybody just kind of moves on. Except for us. We're stuck in this place, this black hole of loss. We can't crawl out."

He had the haunted look of a man who'd used up all his tears and had no way left to express his sadness. Lydia let a moment pass and then asked him to share with them the days just before Lily disappeared and they listened as he talked about the call regarding Mickey's suicide, the parade of friends and relatives, the service. He talked about Lily's grief, and her denial over the way he died.

"So it didn't strike you as impossible that Mickey could have killed himself?" Lily asked.

He shook his head slowly. "The evidence was conclusive. The police had no doubt whatsoever that Mickey ended his own life. The doors to his car were all locked, there were no other fingerprints in the vehicle, on the gun, or on the bottle between his legs. He had gunshot residue on his right hand. He had a blood alcohol level nearly three times the legal limit."

"Without the physical evidence, though, would you have considered Mickey capable of ending his own life?"

He looked over her head, as if the answer was above her somewhere. "Mickey wrestled with depression all his life. This is what we couldn't make Lily understand."

"She didn't know?" asked Lydia, with a frown.

"She didn't know the *extent* of his depression. No," he said with a shake of his head. "She knew he was moody, had a tendency to go through depressive phases. But she didn't know that he was on and off anti-depressants since he was an adolescent. And that his depression seemed to be getting harder to deal with as he got older. It was part of the reason he quit his job on Wall Street. He thought maybe the stress was making his depression worse. He thought if he could do something he really loved, it might help."

"But they were very close," said Jeffrey. "It seems strange that she didn't know."

"Yes, they were close. But Mickey was adamant that she never be told. She adored him. Like, hero-worshipped him. I think part of him was afraid he might lose that if she knew. So we respected his wishes and kept his condition private." He released a sigh. "Maybe we were wrong to do that. But it's too late now."

"So you weren't unable to accept it in the same way Lily was when you learned how Mickey died," said Lydia.

"Well, I wouldn't say that. We were shocked, of course. It's not as if Mickey had made attempts on his life before. And honestly, in the months before he died, he was happier than we'd ever seen him. But I guess it had always been a fear in the back of our minds, because of his depression and because of his father's suicide. So in the way that it was our worst fear realized, I guess it was easier for us to believe."

Lydia knew what it was like to have your worst nightmare become reality. The horror and the disbelief were almost too much to bear; she saw that it was crushing him. His stepson was dead. Lily was missing. His wife had retreated to a drug-induced catatonia.

"You said he was happier than you'd ever seen him in the months before he died. Why was that?" she asked.

Samuels smiled a little, remembering. "He loved the coffee shop. He'd made some new friends. He had a nice place, plenty of money. He just seemed—I don't know," he said, searching for the right words, "*at peace,* I guess. For the first time in his life."

His brow wrinkled then, his face dissolving into a grimace of sadness and confusion. He put his head in his hands. Lydia and Jeffrey were quiet while the gulls cried outside and the wind began to howl. After a moment, Samuels looked back up, seemed more composed.

"They say, I guess, that once someone has decided to kill themselves they experience a time of peace and euphoria, like they see a light at the end of the tunnel they've been trudging through so long," said Samuels with a sigh. "I don't want to think that was the reason for Mickey's new happiness. But maybe it was." He shook his head.

"Maybe it was," he said again.

His eyes glazed over in the thousand-yard stare Lydia had seen often. It made her uncomfortable; she looked away. She let a few moments pass before speaking again.

"Did Mickey ever say anything to you about something called The New Day?"

It happened quickly and maybe someone less observant wouldn't have noticed, but Samuels flinched. He shook his head slowly then.

"The New Day?" he asked, cocking his head. "What's that?"

"Neither Mickey or Lily ever mentioned it to you, Mr. Samuels?" asked Lydia. "They never mentioned being involved or knowing anyone who was involved?"

"No," he said, shaking his head again. "What is it?"

"As far as we can tell, it's some kind of New Age church," said Jeffrey. "Kind of a pan-spirituality thing."

Samuels gave a skeptical frown. "And you think my kids were involved with them?"

"We don't know. We have reason to believe that there might be a connection through the woman Mickey was dating. Did you or your wife ever meet Mariah?"

A slight smile tentatively turned up the corners of Samuel's mouth.

"Mickey had more girls in a month than I've had in my life," he said with a male admiration Lydia found slightly distasteful. "But Monica and I have never met anyone more than once. I don't remember anyone by that name."

"What about a 'Michele'? A very pretty blonde," said Lydia.

"Ms. Strong, they were *all* very pretty blondes. That was his type. Tall, willowy blondes; that's what he liked."

She took the picture from her pocket, as well as the license photo, and handed them both to Samuels. Something on his face seemed to freeze, but a second later he pulled his forehead into a frown.

"These are the same girl?" he said, holding one in each hand and making a point of looking back and forth.

"Yes," said Lydia.

He pursed his lips and shook his head again. He handed both of the photographs back to Lydia. "I've never seen her before. I'm sure of it."

Lydia nodded and replaced the pictures in her jacket. She was having a hard time getting a real vibe off of Tim Samuels.

"According to Jasmine, Lily wasn't too thrilled with Mariah. She and Mickey were at odds about it."

He rubbed his eyes. "That's news to me. Neither of them mentioned a problem."

He looked at them with eyes that were a little too wide for Lydia, eyebrows raised a little too high. She held his gaze and, after a second, he looked to the floor.

"I'll tell you one thing, though," he said. "We raised the kids to be *very* skeptical about religion. We didn't raise them in the church. We taught them about God and about our spiritual beliefs, about our faith in a benevolent universe. But we were pretty down on organized religion. I'm fairly certain neither one of them would have joined up with one—even a 'New Age' one."

"I'm sure you're right," said Lydia, though she wasn't sure of anything. She removed the pink diamond from her pocket and held it out to him on a piece of velvet she'd wrapped it in. It glittered in her palm, shimmering with a deep fire in the light from the window.

"Did you ever see Lily wear anything like this?" asked Lydia. He glanced at it quickly and shook his head. He didn't seem to recognize its value or to be impressed by it in any way.

"Lily isn't much into jewelry," he said absently. She expected him to ask where they'd found the stone but he didn't and for some reason, she didn't offer. Because she had the sense that he was not being entirely open with them, Lydia felt it best not to be entirely open with him. She wrapped the stone back up and put it back in her pocket. She felt disappointed and vaguely dissatisfied, as if there was something obvious she was missing or a question she needed to ask but hadn't thought of yet.

Samuels let out a long deep breath and shifted in his seat. He seemed suddenly uncomfortable and frustrated.

"Anyway, how does any of this help you find Lily?" he said, rubbing his eyes.

"The police have done a thorough job of tracing Lily's steps," said Lydia. "But I think that she was tracing *Mickey's* steps. So that's what I'm trying to do."

He looked at her skeptically. "So are you saying that you don't think Mickey killed himself?"

"No. I'm not saying that. But I know that Lily didn't believe that; so I'm just doing what I would do if I were in her place. Do you see?"

"I see," he said, leaning back and looking at her. There was something on his face now that she couldn't read, a slight narrowing of his eyes.

"Okay. What can I do to help you?" he asked, after examining her a moment.

"You don't by chance have records of those hotline calls, do you?"

"As a matter of fact, I do. Turns out there's a service you can hire to monitor all the calls that come in to a particular hotline established for these purposes and provide reports that include transcripts, telephone numbers, even names and addresses if the caller dials in from a listed number. I was turning them over to the police every day but I kept copies. I'll warn you, there are two boxes of printouts. Nothing has come of them so far."

"You've been turning them over to Detective Stenopolis?"

"Yes, at first. But, like I said, nothing really came of it. They got a couple of calls on the Crime Stoppers Hotline, too. As far as I know, those turned out to be dead ends, as well. And, you know, once they got those banking records indicating that Lily had cleaned out her accounts, there was a definite falling off of urgency. I was just considering looking into hiring a private investigator when you called."

He stood and motioned for Lydia and Jeffrey to follow. He took them into a home office, which might have been neat and organized at one point but was now cluttered with piles of postcards and fliers. A long folding table had been placed along the far wall, opposite a large oak desk that had the look of an antique. Several chairs, which looked as if they'd been taken from a dining room set, sat empty facing the phones. Two large boxes filled with files sat under the phone. There was a big blow-up of Lily's face on a poster on the wall. Lydia could imagine the place bustling with urgency, volunteers working hard, family and friends still hopeful, phones ringing, excitement rising following a tip and then dropping lower with each disappointment. The silence in the room was the sound of despair.

"Lily Central," he said solemnly. "For all the good it did."

"It's not over yet, Mr. Samuels," said Lydia, putting a hand on his arm.

"No," he said. *It might never be over.* That was what he was thinking but didn't say. She could see it on his face.

"Did anybody you didn't recognize come to Mickey's funeral?" Jeffrey asked.

Samuels let out a little laugh.

"The queen of England could have showed up at Mickey's funeral and I wouldn't have noticed. It was a very bad day and to be honest I hardly remember it. I think, in fact, I tapped into Rebecca's tranquilizers. I just didn't see how else you were supposed to get through something like that. We were zombies, I'm sure. Not very present for Lily. Not as present as we clearly should have been."

Samuels' words echoed Jasmine's words. Not *present* enough, not there for her. Lydia wondered if anybody *had* been present for Lily. How vulnerable she must have been, grief-stricken and alone. Any predator could have smelled the sadness on her, used it to lure her into danger. The copy from the New Day website came back to her. *Perhaps you've suffered a tragedy, a terrible loss, and you find you just can't move on.*

"I'd like to contribute to your investigation," said Samuels, taking a checkbook from the drawer in his desk and sinking into the leather chair behind it.

"That's not necessary," said Lydia, holding up a hand. "Lily's a friend. We want to do this for her."

Money didn't motivate Lydia. She was drawn into investigations by something other than financial gain. She'd only had one case where there was an actual client involved and the truth of it was that she didn't like answering to people. These days, she had the luxury of answering only to herself and her instincts. The other cases they took at the firm she'd helped to build allowed Lydia the freedom and the resources to follow her gut, her buzz, with little concern about cost.

"Thank you," he said with that same unreadable expression she'd seen in the living room. "And I know Monica will thank you, too, when she can."

They talked some about the lead Detective Stenopolis had discovered during his interview at the bank. Samuels didn't recognize the vehicle description but seemed heartened by the news.

"I don't understand why he didn't call to let me know this," said Samuels. "He's been pretty good about keeping me in the loop."

"Maybe he didn't want to get your hopes up. There may not be anything to it," said Lydia with a shrug.

"It's our impression that he has pressure from above to move on," said Jeffrey. "From a police perspective, it looks a lot like Lily just took off. They're not going to devote resources to her disappearance much longer. He might be embarrassed. Not looking forward to giving you that news."

Samuels nodded his understanding and looked at him eagerly. "Are you going to follow up on those hits?" he asked.

"Yes," said Jeffrey. "We already have someone on it."

"I wish there was something more I could do," said Samuels as he helped Jeffrey load the boxes into the Kompressor. In the gray light of the outdoors, he looked older, more tired than he had inside. Lydia saw lines on his face she hadn't noticed in the house. She saw dark circles, two days of pale stubble on a strong jaw.

"I'm going a little crazy with my own uselessness. Mickey's gone. I don't know how to help Lily, or her mother. You spend your whole life thinking you have some control and then in a matter of weeks . . ." He let the sentence trail.

"Just know that we are going to do everything in our power to bring Lily home to you," said Lydia. "And if you think of anything, no matter how inconsequential you think it is, anything strange, anything off, anything that made you wonder even for a moment, please call me."

He looked down at the gravel on the drive. "Do you think she's alive?"

It was a hard question to ask, she knew. It was harder to answer. His whole body seemed to brace for the response. Part of her wanted to reassure him, give him some hope. But she couldn't do that, it wasn't right.

"I don't know," she said putting a hand on her arm. "But have faith, Mr. Samuels. We do."

They watched him in the rearview mirror as they pulled up the drive. He followed them with his eyes and then turned his back, walked with slouching shoulders, hands in his pockets, back into the house. Lydia would have paid money to see his face when he thought no one was looking.

"He held something back from us," said Jeffrey when the house was out of sight.

Lydia nodded. "Definitely."

"What's your sense of him?"

She thought about it a second. "It's hard to say. I didn't get a good read on him."

He looked at her out of the corner of his eye. "That's never a good sign."

"I know," she said. Usually a person's essence was clear to Lydia within seconds of the first greeting. People emitted an energy that either meshed or clashed, that attracted or repelled. They'd both learned over the years that Lydia's impressions, more often than not, would be proved correct over time. In the few instances when she'd had trouble getting a read on someone, they'd later discovered that the person in question was deeply veiled, guarded, or hiding vital parts of himself.

"I just didn't buy that Lily and Mickey could be so close and she not know that he'd been on and off anti-depressants all his life," she said.

"Why would Samuels lie about that?"

"I'm not sure," she said with a quick shake of her head. "But it kind of makes Lily sound like she didn't know her brother as well as she thought she did. And it makes her certainty that he didn't kill himself seem based on ignorance of key facts."

He nodded his agreement.

"You know how he seemed to me?" said Jeff. "He seemed *insincere*. That little breakdown he had?"

"No tears," she said. "I noticed that, too."

They pulled onto the Long Island Expressway and Lydia was glad to see that traffic into the city was lighter than it had been on the way out. But still they came to a stop as the traffic thickened. The sky outside was hopeful, with patches of blue straining through the gray cloud cover.

"I got a call yesterday," she said, looking out the window at the trees and the sea of cars.

"From who?" he answered, glancing at her.

"A law firm on Fifty-Seventh Street, representing my father's estate," she said. "They say they have a box for me. Things he left me supposedly. They want me to pick it up."

He was quiet a second, then put a hand on the back of her neck. "How do you feel about that?"

She looked into his face. Warm hazel eyes in a landscape of strong, defined features. Strong cheekbones and full, wide lips, clean-shaven jaw. There was a vein on his temple that appeared when he was angry, a muscle that worked in his jaw when he was worried or thinking hard. She knew every line and feature of his face and just the sight of it could give her comfort.

"I don't know. I think I hate it a little. I mean, what could he possibly have wanted me to have? It seems kind of cowardly to try to make a connection *after* he died."

"So what are you going to do?"

"I don't know. I guess I'm curious enough to go get the goddamn box."

He smiled at her and it ignited her smile. "Of course you are," he said, squeezing her shoulder.

"You know what's weird? I just have this sense that I should feel more than I do about his passing. I mean, when Samuels was talking about Mickey, I could imagine that kid, sitting there in a dark car with a bottle of Jack in one hand and a gun in the other. I could feel despair so total that the barrel of a gun looked better than the future. I *felt* for him, *felt* the terrible sadness of it. But I don't have any of that compassion or empathy for Arthur Tavernier. When I think of my father, I just feel empty."

Jeffrey was quiet for a second, considering her words. She had always loved about him that he was a careful listener, always present for what she was saying, not just waiting to say what he wanted to say.

After a while: "Maybe the box will help you get in touch with that. Maybe you'll find the place where your father should be is not as empty as you think."

She let go of a little laugh. "That's what I'm afraid of."

"Let's stop and get it on the way to the office?"

She nodded and gave him a smile, took his hand and held it for a while as they crawled back toward the city.

"It's hard to say what happened, Detective Stenopolis," said the voice on the other end of the line. "Witnesses say a van approached the parade from a side street. A young woman ran into the crowd, wearing only a tee-shirt and underpants. Two men gave chase. When shots were fired, the crowd panicked and dispersed. Witnesses say that the men then lifted her body and carried it back to the van and reversed back down the street it had arrived from."

Mount liked the sound of her voice; it was smoky, sexy. It belonged to a Detective Margie Swann from the Fiftieth Precinct in Riverdale.

"Did you get a description of the girl?"

"Thin, nearly emaciated. Short cropped black hair, like a buzz cut. That's about it. I'm emailing you a jpeg right now. Are you at your computer?"

"I am," he said, clicking on the SEND/RECEIVE button. "Nothing yet."

"This photograph was just given to us this morning, Detective. It's very fuzzy, hard to see anything, but we've sent it on to State to see what their techs can do for it."

"You'd think a lot of people would have had cameras and video equipment that night since it was Halloween."

"You'd think. But I guess people were too busy running away to be taking pictures. People freak these days when there's a public disturbance, run for the hills."

"No area businesses with outside surveillance cams?"

"None. It's kind of a small main street area with lots of mom-and-pop type businesses still. Locals try to keep it that way. It's pretty low tech around here."

He pressed SEND/RECEIVE again and nothing popped up.

"Still nothing?" she asked.

"No. Sometimes things are a little slow around here."

"Here, too," she said with a smile in her voice.

"My partner said that there was no blood found at the scene?"

"That's right. There was a squad car there right after the shooting. But they didn't see anything. It might mean that she was shot in the back with small caliber bullets or from a far enough distance that there were no exit wounds to bleed out. Or it might mean that there were blanks in the gun and it was some kind of prank. I don't know. It was Halloween after all. It could be someone's idea of a joke."

"A joke?" he said with a laugh. "I don't get it."

"There are lots of things I don't get, Detective. I'm sure you feel the same way."

He sighed into the phone as his answer. "Can we stay in touch?" he asked. "Let me know if you get any more images?"

"Yeah, definitely. And if you identify her as your missing girl, please let me know right away. Maybe we can help each other."

"It's a deal."

He hung up and waited a few more seconds, then checked for the email again. This time a little bell sounded and a message from Margie Swann appeared in his inbox. He clicked on the attachment and waited while the image filled his screen. It was very blurry, as if the shutter speed had been set too slow. Colorful costumes, streetlights, bizarre masks pulled like taffy, colors ran into one another. In the center, he could see the back of a painfully thin girl, running away from a white van. One leg stuck out of the door, a black pant leg ending in a black boot, obviously connected to someone who was about to give chase. The woman's face was turned just slightly so that he caught the edge of her profile. Her head was shaved. There was no way to tell if it was Lily or not. Lily had long, dark curly hair. In the photographs he had of her, she was busty, very lush looking. Not heavy but certainly not emaciated the way the girl in the photograph was. If it was Lily, something had caused her appearance to alter dramatically. There was a frightening chaos to the photo, the masked faces adding a surreal quality to the image.

"What's that?" asked Jesamyn, arriving at her desk.

"It's an image from the Fiftieth Precinct in Riverdale. That shooting you called about."

"Man, you are *fast*," she said.

He tried not to notice the happy glow that seemed to be coming off of her. He knew that in a matter of days, that glow would turn to a pall. That was the way it was with her and Dylan. Euphoria to misery and back again. She came behind him, rested her weight on the back of his chair, and looked over his shoulder.

"It's not her," she said.

"How can you be sure?"

"That girl is twenty pounds thinner at least than Lily was in the bank on the 22nd. And no one with hair like Lily's would ever shave it down to the skull. Lily's a pretty girl. Pretty girls don't make themselves ugly on purpose."

"What if someone else made her ugly?"

"Kidnapped her, starved her, and shaved her head?"

The phrase was meant, he thought, to sound unlikely. But it hit him hard. Mount turned to look at her, feeling his stomach hollow out. He could tell by the look on her face that she had freaked herself out, too.

"Shit," she said.

"What are you two doing?" Kepler. "I know for a fact that you have at least three more people on your reinterview list."

"We're on our way out right now," said Jesamyn, turning to look at Kepler and blocking the screen from his view. Matt didn't turn from the screen while Jesamyn gave Kepler a rundown of the reinterviews they had conducted the day before. Matt very quickly forwarded the email to Lydia Strong; she had left a business card in the jewel case of the CD she'd given him yesterday with her email address.

"Forwarded from the five-oh," he wrote in the dialog box. "Click this link for the story attached to this photo." He inserted a link he'd found to an article in the *Journal-News*.

"If this is our girl," he wrote, "she really needs you. I don't know what else I can do for her."

Or what else can be done for her, he thought. Since the girl in this photo was supposedly shot three times in the back just moments after the picture was taken.

"I'm coming back in five minutes. Don't let me find you here," Kepler was saying to Jesamyn as Matt pressed SEND. He deleted the file from his sent-mail box and hoped it wouldn't come down to having to worry about what the IT guys could take off the server. He stood quickly then to his full height and was happy to see Kepler take a step back. He took some satisfaction in knowing that Captain Kepler could be a piece of gum beneath his shoe if Matt were that kind of guy.

Lydia pushed the glass doors open, and Jeffrey carried the box in. The offices of Mark, Striker and Strong had the quiet hum of a busy space with good acoustics. The sound of it, the muffled voices, the muted ringing of the phone, still gave Jeffrey pleasure. It amazed him how it had grown since he started the agency in his one-bedroom apartment in the East Village. He and the firm's two original partners, Jacob Hanley and Christian Striker, had started their private investigation firm nearly eight years ago, now. All former FBI men, they had become tired for their own reasons of the politics of the bureau, sick of the paranoia about the public perception of the organization, and they'd decided they'd be more effective investigators on their own.

They'd started out with small cases—insurance fraud, husbands checking up on wives, some employee screening. Then, through their connections, they'd started working with the FBI and NYPD on cold cases, or cases where the police felt their hands were tied . . . in those cases, the firm's involvement was strictly confidential.

It was Lydia and Jeffrey's first official case together, the infamous Cheerleader Murders, which put Mark, Hanley and Striker on their way to real success. He'd run into a dead end in his investigation into the disappearance of five cheerleaders at a suburban high school. He'd come to a place where all the evidence led into a black hole. He knew he needed a fresh perspective. Desperate, he called the most intuitive person he knew, a young writer named Lydia Strong. Her observations broke the case, and the publicity surrounding the book she later wrote brought them recognition they might never have had. The phone started ringing and never stopped.

The Cheerleader Murders was their first *official* case together. Before that, he'd consulted on her work as a writer for the *Washington Post* and then as a true crime writer. And it had been her observations, when she was just fifteen years old and he was a young FBI agent, that led him to find her mother's killer. He'd kept in touch with Lydia's grandparents after he solved Marion Strong's murder and captured her killer, partly because Lydia's sadness had touched him. And mostly because he felt some kind of connection to her, though she was just a young girl then.

When she came to Washington, D.C., where he was still with the FBI, to do her undergraduate work at Georgetown, he'd become her friend, then her mentor. Around the same time he quit the bureau, she quit the *Post* to write her first true crime novel. *With a Vengeance* was the story of the serial killer who murdered her mother. With that project, they became colleagues. Somewhere along the line, he'd wanted more. But it was a difficult road to that place; not until just a few years ago had they surrendered to their feelings for each other.

When Jacob Hanley died, Jeffrey and Christian Striker asked Lydia to come on as a partner. Now, they were partners in every sense of the word; it was a thought that gave Jeffrey tremendous satisfaction.

Jeffrey carried the box into her office and put it on the floor. She stood in the doorway, keeping her eyes on the box, looking at it as if she didn't want to enter while it was in her office.

"What do you want to do?" he asked.

"I don't know. Can we put it in *your* office until I decide? I don't want to look at it right now."

"Sure," he said, picking it up. She moved out of his way and he carried the box back toward his office. She followed. It was musty and it smelled of mold, and he sneezed loudly as he set it down by the door. He, for one, was dying to know what was inside, but he wouldn't push her, knowing if he did, she'd just dig her heels in and maybe *never* open it . . . just to be stubborn.

"What are you, her beast of burden?" said Dax from a reclining position on the couch.

"Comfortable, Dax?" said Jeffrey, sliding the box into the corner over by the windows facing downtown Manhattan.

"Very. What is this—chenille?"

"It *is* chenille," said Lydia, stripping off her black cashmere coat and throwing it over one of the leather chairs facing Jeffrey's desk. "Very impressive knowledge of textiles."

"So what happened?" she said, sitting across from him in one of the matching gold chenille chairs opposite the brushed chrome and frosted glass coffee table.

Jeffrey came and sat on the arm of her chair. He caught sight of their reflection in the glass wall that separated his office from the reception area. For a second, he watched them, these three clad mostly in black. A beautiful woman with blue-black hair and fair skin . . . the expensive drape of her designer clothes, the easy way she crossed her legs, communicating wealth and confidence. A man, older than she but fit and equally well dressed, hovering protectively. Another man, the approximate size of a refrigerator, leaning into them, forearms on his thighs, fingers laced. There was an aura of intensity to the group and, yes, excitement. Jeffrey knew it felt good to all of them to be back in the chase. The quiet of the last year had been a necessary time of healing. Jed McIntyre had taken something from all of them, and left part of himself behind in each of them. They'd needed time to process the events that had changed and scarred them. He felt vaguely guilty that it took someone else's tragedy to move them toward the next stages of their recovery, but that, it seemed, was the way their lives were constructed, for better or worse.

"What happened?" repeated Dax. "I went to The New Day and told them I needed to be saved."

Lydia looked at him. "You did?"

"Yeah," he said. "They said it was too late for me."

"Seriously, Dax. What happened?"

He stood up and stripped off his three-quarter-length leather jacket, exposing his muscular shoulders and huge biceps straining against a black tee-shirt.

"You might think about laying off the weight training," said Lydia. "Pretty soon, you're not going to be able to put your arms down at your sides anymore."

He ignored her and reached into his lapel pocket and withdrew some brochures, handed them to Lydia, and sat back down.

She read the titles off of each of them. "Grief Counseling, Addiction Recovery, Moving on From a Painful Childhood, Ending an Abusive Relationship, Stop the Cycle of Child Abuse, The Legacy of Sexual Abuse, The Weight of Your Pain." They were all simple tri-fold pamphlets, with the same images of culturally diverse faces that they'd seen on the Internet.

"Sounds like The New Day has it covered in the self-improvement department," said Jeffrey.

"I went there this morning and walked in through the front door," Dax said, leaning back on the couch. "I didn't see anyone at first but there was like this kiosk beside a reception desk that held all these pamphlets."

Dax was taking some, shoving them in his pocket when a woman appeared at the door. She wore a white tunic and faded blue jeans over a slender body; her short blonde hair was slicked back from her face. A slight smile turned up the corners of her mouth. She had a kind of peaceful, ageless face . . . like she could have been thirty or fifty and would have been beautiful either way.

"Can I help you?" she said, leaning against the doorway.

"I found your church on the Internet," said Dax. "I thought I'd see what you had to offer."

There was something catlike about her, aloof and knowing. She nodded.

"I've been feeling . . . depressed," he said.

She looked at him, cocked her head slightly. "I noticed you limping when you came in," she said, pointing to a surveillance camera in the corner of the room. Dax had noticed it on arriving. He'd also noticed a keypad by the door for what looked like a component in a very expensive, very sophisticated alarm system. There was no brand on the keypad or on any of the exterior windows.

The blonde woman motioned for him to follow her and they

moved to a comfortable sitting room, off a much larger room with a stage and rows of chairs that looked more like a movie theater than the chapel he'd expected.

"I told her, you know, that I'd been in a car accident over a year ago. That a friend of mine had died and some of my other friends had also been hurt. My injuries are not healing the way I expected they would and I can't work the way I used to, at least not yet. That this period of convalescence has caused me to look at some of the choices I've made in my life and I'm not as happy with things as I thought. I've been feeling hopeless, depressed. But I don't know how to change things."

He was looking at his feet as he spoke, and his voice had gone really soft, almost throaty, and Lydia and Jeffrey exchanged a look. He put his head in his hands and Lydia saw his big shoulders shake. She felt like someone had punched her in the stomach. She moved quickly over beside him on the couch and put both her arms around him, or tried to.

"Oh, no, Dax," she said, all her guilt rearing up in her heart. "Do you really feel that way?" I'm so sorry."

He looked up at her with a broad smile. "Pretty convincing, huh?"

"Oh, my God," she said, punching him as hard as she could in the side. He let out a groan as she connected right below his ribcage. "You asshole."

She moved back to the chair and glared at him while he laughed. She really hated him in that moment. Then she felt laughter and a smile threaten. She quashed them. She wouldn't give him the satisfaction.

"Lydia, I never knew you cared," he said when he'd stopped laughing. He cracked himself up again.

"I don't," she said stonily.

"You're such a hardass all the time," he said. "But you just have a big marshmallow center, don't you?"

She narrowed her eyes at him. "Can we get on with this?"

Jeffrey could see the flush in her cheeks that told him she was really angry. Only he knew that beneath her stone façade was a cauldron of emotions so strong that she was swept away by them sometimes. And that was the reason for the façade in the first place. He'd heard journalists and reviewers call her cold, unfeeling in her treatment of some of her subject matter. But he knew the truth. He put a hand on her shoulder.

"Okay," said Dax, wiping his eyes. "So, she was not quite as loving as you, Lydia, but she was very sympathetic."

The room she'd taken him to was gently lit with pink lightbulbs, painted a soothing pale blue. Again he saw cameras, but they were small, recessed into the wall. He kept his face turned from them as best he could without being conspicuous; he had done this since approaching the building out of habit.

"So many people feel that way," she said. "More than you'd ever imagine."

He actually managed to get himself a little teary while talking to the pretty woman, who'd introduced herself as Vivian. And after a few minutes of comforting platitudes, a young man walked in, wearing the same outfit: white tunic and blue jeans. He handed Dax a cup of something hot. It smelled like some kind of herbal tea. Dax took it and thanked the kid, put it on the low coffee table in front of him. Vivian made no explanation for the kid or the tea. She slid a box of tissues across the table toward him. He took one and blew his nose loudly.

"The kid had a really glazed-over look to him. Not like drugged but more—" he said now to Lydia and Jeffrey, and paused as if searching for the right word. "Vacant."

Lydia thought about what Matt Stenopolis had told her. Thelma Baker had used the words *hollow* and *empty* to describe Lily. Nothing could be further from the girl Lydia knew. Lily was a bright light, a firecracker. Anybody who met her, no matter how casual the encounter, would have seen that about her.

Dax said that Vivian had nodded to the young man and he left quietly.

"My mother always said that everything looks better after a good cup of tea," said Vivian, leaning into him and smiling.

"My mother always said you're a worthless piece of meat that will never amount to anything," Dax had said, leaning away from the cup.

Vivian nodded solemnly. "Sometimes our parents, acting from their own place of pain, don't realize how powerful their words can be. How we carry them with us for the rest of our lives."

Dax asked if he could use the bathroom then, pretending that the conversation was making him so uncomfortable that he needed a break. He took the tea with him. Vivian rose to escort him.

"Just point me in the right direction," he said as she exited the room with him.

"First door on the left," she said. "Shall I hold that for you until you return?" She nodded to the cup in his hand.

"No. I'll hold onto it."

She looked at him strangely but couldn't really insist without changing the texture of their encounter. She didn't return to the room but stood and watched him as he made his way to the bathroom. A quick glance revealed a white hallway of closed doors.

Inside, he dumped the tea down the drain and folded the Styrofoam cup and put it in the back pocket of his pants.

"You were right," Dax said to Vivian when he returned to her from the bathroom. "I *do* feel better after that cup of tea."

She looked at him skeptically. He extended his hand and she placed hers in his. Her grip was steely, her kind eyes were searing into him now.

"I'm going to think about the things you said, Vivian. You've really made me feel a lot better. Thank you so much."

"I'm glad," she said quietly. "Are you sure you wouldn't like to sit a while longer?"

"No, thanks," he said, giving her his best sad smile. "I have a lot to think about."

"I just had the feeling she was watching me for the effects of whatever was in that cup," he told them. "I washed my face and hung out in the washroom awhile," he told Lydia and Jeffrey. "She was waiting outside for me when I exited. I just didn't have the opportunity to dig around. I did notice one thing, though. That high-rise that stands behind the church? It's connected by a walkway."

"Do you have the cup?" Lydia asked eagerly.

"I already gave it to Striker when I came in. He said he'd get it to the lab, get a tox and fingerprint analysis."

"Good," said Jeffrey.

"What you said about the alarm system not having a brand name. Why is that relevant?" asked Lydia.

"Because the commercial alarm systems are about being a deterrent as much as about alerting a home owner that someone has succeeded in invading their house. They're actually somewhat useless because, think about it, once you've *heard* that alarm, the system has already failed you. Like, someone is *in* your house, man; get your gun. But people like them because it gives them a false sense of security. People who actually need and want to keep people off the premises are going to find someone to install a real security system. On my way in I saw motion detectors, three exterior cameras that I could count without being conspicuous. Inside I saw laser sensors, and noticed that there were security shutters over the windows and doors that probably come down at night when the security system is activated. All very discreet, though. You'd not notice any of it unless you were looking and even then you'd have to know what you were looking for. Anyway, there are only a few companies that do that kind of work in the U.S. for the private sector. I'll make some calls."

"Do you think they'll follow up with you? Did you give them a way to get in touch with you?" asked Lydia.

"She asked for my number so that she could call and check in with me but I told her I didn't feel comfortable with that. I told her maybe I'd come back for that open meeting I read about on the Internet. I left then. She didn't look happy.

"You should have given them a number," said Lydia.

"Oh, they'll find me. Ignatius Bond is listed. I guarantee we hear from them within twenty-four hours. Vivian looked to be a bit of a diehard."

"You told her your name was Ignatius Bond?" said Lydia.

"Yes, you can call me Iggy."

"That's a pretty conspicuous cover name, Dax," said Jeff.

"Exactly. So conspicuous that no one would ever suspect you'd make it up, yeah? Not like John Doe or some shit. I have a social for Iggy, the whole nine, so if they run a background check on me, I'm covered."

"What does Iggy do?" asked Lydia, just out of curiosity.

"He's a construction worker."

It fit with his whole not-being-able-to-work-because-of-his-injuries thing.

"She'll be calling, trust me. I think she was hot for me."

"Naturally," said Lydia. Dax leaned back again into the couch and stretched out his legs painfully.

"We need to get back in there," said Lydia, looking at Jeffrey.

Jeffrey nodded and looked at Dax. "What do you think?"

"I'm going to make some calls to the security companies I know, find out what I can about that alarm system. When I know what we're dealing with, we'll try to get a look without Vivian breathing down my neck."

Dax let a moment pass, then looked at Lydia sheepishly.

"Forgiven?" he asked, maybe feeling a little bad for jerking her around.

"We'll see," she said, rising. "I'm going to go check my email."

"I have to go to physical therapy," he said in a clear bid for sympathy as she walked past him.

"I hope it hurts," she tossed back at him. "A lot."

Dax looked at Jeffrey with a mischievous smile. Jeffrey didn't return the grin. He'd been Dax's partner in torturing Lydia in the past but he felt like Dax had stepped over the line and he didn't like it.

"You need to be gentler with her," said Jeffrey after Lydia had left the room. "She's fragile these days."

"She's as fragile as a bag of nails," said Dax.

Jeffrey looked at Dax sternly. Part of the love between Lydia and Dax, he knew, was antagonism . . . and most of the time it was pretty funny. But he was feeling protective of his wife. He walked over and shut the door.

"She just learned that her father, a man she barely knew, has died. And that," he said, nodding toward the box that sat in the corner of his office, "is a box of things he left her. She's not ready to deal with it—which means she's not ready to deal with a lot of things regarding her father. Furthermore, it hasn't been a year since we killed Jed McIntyre and she had the miscarriage. She's just getting her feet under her and now she has to deal with this. So . . . just go easy on her."

Dax looked down at his feet. "All right already," he said, getting up. "It's been a hard year for you two, huh?"

Jeff looked at him. "For all of us, man."

Dax nodded. "I'll call you after I find out about the security system. A couple hours tops."

Lydia came back through the door without knocking, holding a photo printout in her hand.

"Take a look at this," she said. They came and stood behind her, gazing at the blurry photograph of a girl running through a crowd of people wearing costumes.

"What's this?" Jeff asked.

"It's a witness photograph from Halloween night in Riverdale. Apparently, a girl was shot in the middle of this parade. Police were unsure whether it was a Halloween prank or not, since there was no blood found at the scene. But look at this," said Lydia, pointing to the white van. There was a logo they could just barely make out on the side of the van, the image of a sun with some geometric shapes inside.

"The New Day," said Dax slowly.

"Is that the van you saw last night?" she asked, looking up at him.

"Yeah, or very similar," said Dax. "I think I'd better skip that PT appointment and make those calls now."

"Sounds like a good idea," said Lydia.

"Does that look like Lily Samuels to you?" asked Jeff.

"At first glance, I'd say no. Too thin and her head is shaved," said Lydia.

"You better hope that's not her," said Dax, looking closely at the photograph. Lydia could tell he was noticing the things she had noticed, the way her shoulder blades were visible straining through her flesh, the way she was clad only in panties and a thin tee, the way her arms were pumping in a dead heat. The woman in the photograph was running for her life and Lydia was sure if they could see her face that it would be a mask of terror. She prayed it wasn't Lily. Because if it was, they might be too late.

"Pink diamonds are for the very wealthy," said Christian Striker, holding the gem in his hand. "This stone is just more than a carat. Very pricey."

"Strange thing to find in the dirt at an abandoned house," said Jeffrey.

"Is that where you found it?" he asked with a shake of his head. He pulled a loop from his desk and examined the diamond.

"When you talk about diamonds, you talk about four things: cut, carat, clarity, and color. This is a brilliant stone, heart-shaped cut, nearly flawless. I can see one minuscule imperfection in the stone, making the clarity like a VVS1 or 2, meaning that the inclusion is not visible to the naked eye. And then there's the color. White diamonds are measured by the colorlessness. Colored stones, called 'fancy' diamonds, are more valuable the richer their hue. Many colored stones are irradiated these days, meaning that the color was created in a lab. This is just because they're in style but exist so rarely in nature. But to me this looks like a natural pink diamond, only because the pink tint is so subtle."

Christian Striker knew more than anyone Lydia had ever met. He had an encyclopedic knowledge of facts—history, science, geology, mathematics—which is to say he knew a little bit about many things. Lydia liked hanging out with him because she always learned something. And he was cute, with sandy blond hair and a boyish face but searing dark eyes, so brown they were nearly black, that missed nothing. He was a few years younger than Jeffrey, who had just turned forty-three.

"Where would you get one of these?" asked Jeffrey.

"I imagine most diamond dealers can get their hands on one. The largest diamond mine in the world is the Argyle mine in Kimberly,

Australia . . . of course there's Sierra Leone, Russia, and since 1991 Canada has become a major player on the scene. They have two diamond mines in the Northwest Territories, and two others expected to be operating by 2006. There's been a bit of a diamond rush up there in recent years. What people like about the Canadian diamonds is they're 'clean.'"

"What do you mean?" asked Jeffrey.

"They're not what people call 'blood' diamonds or 'dirty' diamonds. They're not used to finance terror, war, and weapons the way they are in Sierra Leone and Angola. You know in Sierra Leone, for example, the Revolutionary United Front controls the mines and uses the proceeds to buy weapons. They also provide untraceable diamonds to other terrorist organizations to launder money. The people *doing* the mining are dying in slave-labor conditions; they're imprisoned by the rebels and forced to work until they die. Meanwhile, said rebels randomly amputate the hands of children as a warning to their parents not to support the civilian government. These rebels are just children themselves, children high on drugs, carrying AK47s and machetes. It's pretty fucked."

"See?" Lydia said to Jeffrey. He nodded.

"Anyway," said Christian. "This is a nice one. Most dealers don't sell gems without settings. So, it's possible that this was purchased on the black market, which makes it even more likely that it's a blood diamond."

He handed the gem back to Lydia and she gazed at it. It *was* stunning. She considered it a terrible irony that something so naturally gorgeous could be surrounded by so much ugliness. Was it greed or a lust for beauty that led people to kill and die for these stones? Maybe both.

"Who would know where this might have come from?" asked Jeffrey.

"I know a guy in the diamond district," said Christian, flipping through his Rolodex. He wrote a name and number on a pad by his phone and handed it to Jeff. "Tell him I sent you. He'll tell you what he can."

Nine

Jorge Alonzo thought he was king of the jungle. To show he was not intimidated by Matt Stenopolis's size or the presence of detectives in his apartment, he slumped in his leather recliner, scrolling through channels on his digital cable. When he did finally turn his eyes to them, he stared at them like he was hard. Matt could feel his chest constricting, the guy was pissing him off so bad.

"Rosario's brother told us that you were calling her all night, trying to get her to go the club with you," Jesamyn was saying. Matt was looking around the apartment: large flat-screen television with surround-sound speakers, a Blaupunkt audio system, leather furniture as soft to the touch as velvet. Matt counted four framed posters of naked or nearly naked women in a variety of evocative poses. There were some Japanese anime prints that looked pretty expensive, featuring scantily clad Asian women with gravity-defying breasts and bulbous asses, long thin legs and tiny waists.

"I know what that punk *thinks* he heard. But I was finished with that bitch," he said lazily. "We were done. She was getting fat." He held out his hands to express her expanding girth.

"She was pregnant. With your child," said Jesamyn slowly, looking at him like he was a curiosity better seen on the Discovery Channel than right in front of her face.

"So she said. I asked for a paternity test," he said, scratching his crotch and looking at Jesamyn with a smile. "Fat bitch. Not like you, girl. Your shit is *tight*."

Matt was on him then. He knocked the remote out of Alonzo's hand and lifted him off the recliner like he was made out of gauze.

"What the fuck—" Jorge protested shrilly.

"You'll have some fucking respect for my partner, you piece of shit," Matt said, the anger in his chest threatening to split him in two. His disrespect for Jez, his general attitude, and the fact that if Matt worked OT for the rest of his life he'd never be able to afford an audio-visual system like that without going into debt was making him crazy.

"Man, you can *not* put your hands on me like that," Jorge yelled. "That's police brutality." He straightened out his shirt and the baggy jeans that were threatening a trip to his knees.

Matt hovered over him, a good two heads taller and about twice as wide.

"Do something about it, bitch," he said quietly. Jesamyn strolled over to the window and looked outside as if the view of the brick wall was the most interesting thing in the world. Jorge looked up at Matt and then down at the floor.

"Now, sit down, punk, and answer our questions like you have a clue how to conduct yourself in polite society." Matt stepped back and hoped, *hoped,* that he would make a move. But unarmed and with none of the other Kings around, Jorge dropped his attitude. He sank into the couch. Matt was disappointed.

"I told the other cops everything I know," he whined. "They cleared me. Isn't this like double jeopardy or some shit to question me again?"

"No. It's not double jeopardy, you moron," said Matt. He was about to explain what double jeopardy was but he stopped himself. What was the point?

"When was the last time you saw Rosario?" asked Jesamyn.

"I don't remember," he said sullenly, leaning down and picking up the pieces of the remote at his feet.

"You don't remember," Jesamyn repeated. "You don't remember when you last saw her? Or what you told the police the last time they questioned you?"

They danced around with Jorge awhile longer. They asked him a question; he gave a vague answer or pretended he didn't remember. Finally, he said he wouldn't talk anymore without his lawyer.

"Who's going to pay for this?" he asked, holding up the broken remote as they walked out of his Riverside Drive apartment. Neither one of them responded and he yelled the question again as the elevator doors closed on them.

"No one's going to pay for it," said Jesamyn grimly in the quiet of the elevator. "That girl and the baby inside her are dead somewhere and no one is going to pay for it."

"Notice how he talked about her in the past tense?" Matt asked.

She nodded and didn't say anything else. Sometimes the darkness of the job closed in on both of them. The glow she had earlier in the day was gone. Now she just looked tired. He wanted to put his hand on her arm but he didn't.

Out on the street, Matt's cell phone rang.

"Stenopolis," he answered.

"It's Lydia Strong."

"Hey."

"Thanks for the photo. I think it helped us."

"Yeah?" he said, the brightening of his tone attracting attention from Jesamyn.

"It connects to something we found. Have you ever heard of an organization called The New Day?"

"Doesn't ring a bell," he said, unlocking the doors of the Caprice for his partner. Jesamyn climbed inside to get out of the cold and shut the door, peering at him through the glass. He walked over to the driver's side and leaned on the roof and watched the traffic roll on Riverside. He listened as she told him what they'd learned since he saw her last night and how the logo on the van in the photograph was the same as the building in the Bronx.

"There's nothing in those hotline transcripts," he said, feeling slightly defensive suddenly. Was she going to start trying to tell him he hadn't done a thorough job with the leads they had? "We've been following up."

"Yeah," said Lydia. "I know you have. We've got some trainees going over them too. So far we don't have anything there, either. We're moving forward with The New Day."

"Sounds like vapor to me, Ms. Strong," he said. It had taken her less than twenty-four hours to go off in a direction he'd never even considered and come up with a more substantial lead than he'd approached in two weeks. It pissed him off a little.

"Call me Lydia," she said. "And I think you're wrong. If you have something better to go on, please share it."

He smiled at her though she couldn't see him. What had Kepler said? Pit bulls. They were like pit bulls.

"Okay," he said with a sigh. "I'll see what I can find out about The New Day. Maybe they have some complaints against them, something in the system." It's not about me, he reminded himself. It's about Lily. That's why I hooked Lydia Strong in the first place.

"I was hoping you'd say that, Detective. Call me back?"

"As soon as I get back to the station."

He hung up and contorted himself into the Caprice.

"Who was that?" Jesamyn wanted to know.

"None of your business," he said. His bad mood had turned foul.

"Girlfriend?" she teased, punching him on the arm.

"Let's talk about *your* love life," he said, starting the car.

"Let's not," she said. He nodded and raised his eyebrows at her.

She frowned at him. "Man," she said when he stared blackly ahead and pulled out into traffic too quickly. "Who dropped your ice cream cone on the sidewalk?"

She walked through the elevator doors and stepped onto the hardwood floor. Before entering the giant loft space she bowed. The hours Jesamyn had to herself were precious and few. And she used them well at her kung fu temple. This was the place she cleansed herself with sweat and hard work. She'd come to the martial arts while attending John Jay College of Criminal Justice, to learn how to defend herself and to develop skills that would help her compensate for her size when she joined the New York City police department, really the only thing she had ever wanted to do with her life. What she'd learned there had taught her valuable lessons about herself, what she was capable of, what she could endure. When she first arrived, young, a little out of shape, lacking confidence, she found a group of people, her Shifu and his black-belt students, who taught her, then gently pushed and cajoled her with respect and faith, into doing things she never would have thought herself able. Her Shifu had a way of believing she could do the things she didn't believe she could do, and then demanding them out of her with a hard, knowing stare. All her life she'd been told she wasn't athletic, she wasn't physical, by a mother who wasn't those things herself. Her controlling and critical father had considered her a failure for choosing to go into law enforcement, but his disdain for her and for women in general had communicated itself to her in a thousand different ways all her life. She had been in the endgame of a relationship characterized by terrible infidelity and emotional abuse. She came to the temple on Twenty-Seventh Street feeling bad about herself in ways she didn't even realize. But forced to look at herself in the long wall of floor-to-ceiling windows for two hours, three days a week, she met a whole new woman, one who was defined by her accomplishments and through her actions, not through the negative messages of others who were acting out of their own misery. At the temple she found her strength and speed, she found her center, she found her power.

"Detective Breslow, you look tense," her Shifu said from his office behind glass walls. He wasn't even looking at her.

"It's been a long day, Shifu," she said with a bow. "Difficult."

"Leave it at the door."

"Yes, Shifu." Passing him and going into the women's locker room to change. Her Shifu was a badass, the indisputable king of the world he had created. All the black-belt students respected and revered him, the boys wanted to *be* him. Jesamyn was just profoundly grateful for the things he'd taught her about kung fu and about herself, for his endless patience and the way he'd helped her to hone her techniques. It was the way a father should be: patient, knowing, and understanding. Pushing without insulting, correcting without humiliating, demanding more and better while praising the effort and small successes. She'd never had that kind of instruction growing up, and the little girl inside her worshipped him just a tiny bit for it.

In the locker room she changed into black baggy pants, wrestling shoes, and the school tee-shirt. She was one of three women at the school, which could be annoying. Sometimes it felt like she was fighting her way through a jungle of adrenaline and testosterone, with everyone several inches taller and many pounds heavier than she was. But she figured if she could hold her own with these guys, highly trained fighters with the boundless energy of people in extraordinary shape, she could handle herself with most of the out-of-shape street fighters she ran into on the job . . . and the criminals, too.

On the floor, they did forty minutes of killer calisthenics, endless push-ups, sit-ups, jumping jacks. It could be longer or shorter depending on what kind of mood whoever was teaching the class was in that day. Then there was a half an hour of drilling and stances. Once you learned a technique, the philosophy was you had to throw it a thousand times before you would begin to get it right. Drilling forced your head and your muscles to remember the techniques, and eventually they became more instinct than thought. By the end of the first hour, most of what she was wearing was soaked through with sweat. Then it was time to spar.

They fought without guards, avoiding shots to the head, the groin, and the breasts. The principle was that a fighter had to learn how to take a hit. You had to condition your body to endure blows and understand what it feels like to be hit. Someone who had never been hit would be shocked if on the street a blow was delivered. It's painful, it's shocking, and it's very upsetting. So for the rest of the class, they basically just beat the crap out of each other . . . but with discipline, technique, and control. So pumped with adrenaline, they never felt a thing while sparring. It was hard play, fun in a way she could never explain to someone who hadn't experienced it. It was only after that all the aches and pains would set in, the bruises would bloom.

When she left, she was clean. All the stress and negativity of her day had drained from her. She felt light and relaxed, happy and confident. Even though she would be two hours later getting to Benjamin, she was a better person when she got to him; not wound up from the job, not tense and snappish.

"Hey, ass-kicker." A sexy male voice she didn't expect surprised her when she stepped onto the sidewalk.

"Mom. You're a *bad*ass."

She turned to see Dylan put a hand on Benjamin's head. "Hey, little dude, I told you no swearing around your mom."

"No swearing, period," she said, kneeling down and taking Benjamin into her arms. His little body always felt so good.

"But you swear all the time," he said into her hair. He wrapped his arms around her neck and squeezed.

"Never mind that," she said, standing and taking his hand. She smiled at Dylan, hating herself for how happy she was to see him. "What are you guys doing here? I thought you were going to the movies."

"We saw *Spy Kids*. Benj was so impressed that I thought he might like to see his mom in action. I can't believe you never brought him here."

"You were like, pow! And like, wham!" said Benjamin, imitating her techniques. He was pretty good.

"I figured I'd start him up next year. I thought he might get scared seeing me fight."

"No way, Mom! You're like Jackie Chan."

Dylan shook his head but gave her a smile. *You baby him too much.* That's what he was thinking but he didn't say it. "How 'bout some pizza?" he asked.

"Sounds good. I'm starved. There's a place around the corner on Broadway."

They walked up the street together, Benjamin just a few feet ahead of them throwing kicks and punches with sound effects. Dylan took her hand and she didn't pull away. Normally she didn't like Benjamin to see them holding hands or being affectionate with each other. She'd quashed the hopes he harbored that they'd be together again, live under the same roof. She didn't want him to be confused. But there was something about the three of them together, walking on the street. It just felt right. It didn't mean anything, she told herself. Just that their relationship was easier; they could be together with Benjamin, be kind to each other and not fight, not get ugly with each other. It was progress. That's all it was.

Ten

Jeffrey had taken off to go talk to Christian's jeweler and Dax sat in a spare office among the trainees trying to find out what he could about the specialized security system installed at The New Day. Lydia did something she thought she wouldn't do. She went into her office and closed the door, got on her computer, and entered a name into Lexis-Nexis. Arthur James Tavernier.

Most of the listings were not related to her father. But one of the early entries was his obituary. Short and simple, it said only that he had died and when the services would be. Would she have gone if she knew? Maybe. Out of curiosity. Maybe not. It did lead her to wonder however who had held the services. She didn't have to read far.

The next entry was a brief article on her father's death that had run in a small local Nyack paper. He died of an apparent heart attack in his small two-bedroom home. He was found three days after the incident when neighbors complained of the smell. At the bottom of the article, which she almost skipped, there was a single sentence that felt like a blow to the solar plexus. *"Arthur Tavernier is survived by his wife of fifteen years, Jaynie, and their daughter, Este, from whom he was estranged."*

She put her head in her hand and exhaled deeply. She'd always imagined him as alone in a single-room apartment, with no one in his life. But he'd had another family. And unless Este was his stepdaughter by marriage, Lydia had a sister she never knew about. She wasn't sure what to do with that information. She searched for some kind of feeling about it, about the way her father died, about the fact that she might have a half-sister somewhere, and came up with a kind of emptiness, a numbness that she was afraid wasn't normal. What kind of person felt nothing when faced with these types of things?

From the leather bag at her feet she fished out the business card that Patricia O'Connell had given her when she and Jeffrey picked up the box.

"Ms. O'Connell," said Lydia when she finally got the woman on the line.

"Yes, Ms. Strong, what can I do for you?"

"I need to know, is there a way for me to get in touch with Mr. Tavernier's wife or his daughter?"

There was a pause on the other end of the line and Lydia heard her moving papers around.

"Well," she said. "I'm not sure it's my place to give you their contact information. There was nothing in his final instructions to that effect." She hesitated, then added, "As I understand it, they were *also* estranged from Mr. Tavernier." She said it like a woman who had made judgments about things she didn't understand.

"All right," said Lydia. "Well, did they all share my father's last name?"

Another pause. "Ms. Strong, there was nothing about them in your box?"

Now it was Lydia's turn to go silent. She looked across the hall through the glass wall that separated her office from the hallway; she could see the entrance to Jeffrey's office. The box was in there waiting for her to get up the courage to open it.

"I haven't had the opportunity to go through it yet," she said.

"Well, perhaps there's something in there to help you find out what you want to know."

Lydia sighed. She hated people who didn't easily give things that were easy to give, people for whom rules and procedures were more important than other people.

"Can you do this for me?" she said, trying to keep patience in her tone. "If you have their contact information, can you please call one or both of them and tell them I'm interested in speaking with them? And then give them my name and number."

"I'll see what I can do, Ms. Strong," she said vaguely. "I'll get back to you."

Lydia said her thanks but the lawyer had already hung up.

She felt a swell of emotion now, some combination of anger, resentment, and sadness. She didn't want this. She didn't want a box from her dead father waiting for her in Jeffrey's office. She didn't want to learn that she might have a sister somewhere. But like with all the mysteries of her life, there was this eternal flame inside of her, this burning to *know*. She could take that box to the Dumpster, call Patricia O'Connell back and tell her not to bother. And that would be the end of it. But she *couldn't*. She just wasn't hardwired to walk away from a question mark.

"Shit," she said out loud to no one.

"What's up?" Dax filled the doorway. She hated him at the moment. He had hurt her feelings. And since her feelings were so rarely exposed for the hurting, vulnerable to so few people, they were still smarting.

"Nothing," she said flatly. "What do you want?"

He walked in and sat down, unperturbed by her mood.

"Well," he said. "I've got some good news and some bad news."

She looked at him with an expression that she hoped would encourage him to just spit it out.

"It looks to me like the security system installed at The New Day is a custom job. We're talking motion detectors on the exterior, roving security cameras, infrared beams in entrance hallways, security shutters over doors and windows. Retina and palm scan entries on certain areas, heat sensors on door knobs, serious stuff. A system like the one they have would cost a hundred grand, at least. It would be nearly impossible to get in—or out—once the system is activated."

"And the building behind was connected by an interior walkway?"

"There are two connections. One on the first floor and one in the basement of the building."

Lydia cocked her head at him. "You didn't mention that before."

"That's because I just found out."

"How?"

"I know the guy who designed and installed the system."

"I guess that would be the good news?" she asked.

He nodded and gave her a smile.

"Doesn't seem very secure," she said. "You pay someone a hundred grand to secure a building and then he runs around telling people how to subvert the system."

"That's the problem with mercenaries," he said with a shrug. "Loyalties shift."

"So he told you how to get in?"

"Not exactly. He gave me the specs of the system. But he's so good at building these things that even *he* couldn't get in. I'll have to figure it out."

"When the alarm goes off, who gets alerted?"

"It's not connected to the police department or to any outside security agency."

"So presumably there's a security staff on the premises."

"My guy didn't know anything about that, said that the client was highly secretive and that when his people were installing the system, there was no one around. But presumably, yes, I imagine there's a security staff. We'll have to assume."

"Why would a church, especially one concerned with abandoning materialism, be so concerned with security?"

"It's a good question. Another question would be how they found out about the guy that designed this system. I mean, it's not like he's in the phone book or anything. You need to *know* people to get in touch with him."

"What kind of people?"

"People you don't want to know. Like, bad guys . . . gangsters, mobsters, guerillas, the CIA. Really bad."

Lydia looked at him. "And where do *you* know this guy from?"

"We served together. He's former British Special Forces. Now he's freelance."

"Like you."

He nodded. "Yes, like me."

He'd gotten a serious tone to his voice and the stony expression to his face that he always got when she asked too many questions. He'd give her a little bit of information, stuff she already knew like the bit about his having served with the British Special Forces, then he'd shut down.

"So does that mean *your* loyalties are prone to shifting?"

He gave her a look. "That hurts."

"Hmm. How long will it take you to figure out a way in to The New Day?"

"A couple hours," he said. "We'll go tonight if you want."

"I want. I haven't been able to find anything about them on the Internet other than their own website. Detective Stenopolis said he'd check to see if there was anything in the system about them but I haven't heard back from him.

"So we go find out for ourselves," said Dax, standing. "I just need to find a way in."

Jeffrey walked down Broadway to Forty-Seventh Street, New York City's diamond district. The street was mobbed with people, as it generally was. They walked slowly, stopped suddenly to stare at the glittering gems on display. He made his way through as quickly as he could, dodging and weaving between window shoppers. He came to the address Christian had given him and walked inside and stood at the door.

He could see in the shop a young man, a Hasidic Jew dressed in traditional garb, sitting behind a cash register. Jeffrey noticed wires coming from behind the long curls that hung at each of his temples. There was an Apple iPod sitting on the glass counter in front of him. It took the kid a minute to notice him standing there. He quickly took the headphones from his ears. He reached beneath the counter and the door in front of Jeffrey buzzed open.

He stepped inside. The place smelled of cheap cologne and something meaty cooking.

"Can I help you?" the kid said. He had an open, earnest face, a slight New York accent. The whole Hasidic thing was weird to Jeffrey. The older guys, he understood traipsing around in their traditional garb. But the young men, modern Americans with iPods, didn't they want a more up-to-date look? Something that didn't alienate them so totally from the present? It had always seemed to him that a religion that didn't stay with the times was doomed to plenty of conflict between younger and older generations within, and eventually extinction.

"I'm here to see Chiam," he said resting a hand on the glass counter.

"I'm Chiam," the kid said. "But maybe you mean my dad."

"Christian Striker said he might be able to answer some questions for me."

The kid nodded and walked through a door toward the back of the small space. It was a small rectangle of a room, barely two hundred square feet, with bare white walls. There was nothing to distract from the glass cases lining the three interior walls and their magnificent contents. Diamonds. Earrings, necklaces, stunning solitaires. He noticed a case containing a small sign that read "Fancy Diamonds." In here, the gems were red and blue, pink and yellow. They were beautiful, certainly, but to Jeffrey nothing compared to a colorless white diamond with its cold fire.

An older version of the man he'd spoken to emerged from the back. He extended a hand.

"Christian called and said to expect you," he said. "I am Chiam Bechim."

Jeffrey shook his hand. "Jeffrey Mark. Good to meet you."

Chiam opened a small door between the cases and Jeffrey walked through, followed him into a back room. Chiam senior barked something in Yiddish to his son, who reddened. Jeffrey saw him put the iPod in a drawer by the register, muttering something under his breath.

It looked like a laboratory, with clean well-lit work stations that were empty at the present. Large magnifying glasses were mounted on moveable arms over tables lined with delicate tools, Jeffrey imagined for mounting gems in their settings. They walked into an office with glass walls. The space had an unobstructed view of the work stations. Chiam, he guessed, liked to keep an eye on things. In the back of his office, there was a large safe that looked like it recessed into the wall when it wasn't in use.

Chiam motioned for Jeffrey to sit in a chair opposite a small wooden desk as the older man sat heavily into a wooden banker's chair. The desk was meticulously organized, files neatly arranged, ten blue Bic pens in a leather cup. A computer sat neat and white on small metal desk to the side. Jeffrey removed the gem from his pocket and handed the little velvet pouch to Chiam. He took a jeweler's loop from his drawer, unwrapped the stone, and examined it.

"Lovely," he said. "Quite nearly flawless. A tiny, tiny imperfection deep in the stone but invisible to the naked eye. Pink diamonds like this are very, very rare. Though recently there's been a huge demand for them. So some jewelers started buying irradiated stones, real diamonds that have been colored. Most people don't know the difference. But this one is real."

"How can you tell?"

"Trust me," he said looking at Jeff with eyes that had examined a million stones. "I can tell."

He had deep, knowing brown eyes set in a landscape of soft and wrinkled skin. A full gray beard hung nearly to the middle of his chest.

"Where did you get this?" Chiam asked when Jeffrey nodded. He'd narrowed his eyes just slightly.

"It came into my possession by accident," said Jeffrey, wanting to be vague without being rude.

"That's a lucky accident," said Chiam, leaning back.

"I guess that depends on where you think this stone might have come from."

Chiam stared at Jeff for a second and then nodded, as if deciding with himself to talk.

"Last week a dealer came to New York City from South Africa. He supposedly had in his possession a collection of rare diamonds. Flawless, colorless stones . . . some pink and yellow. He traveled here on a private jet with three heavily armed bodyguards, carrying more than five million dollars in precious gems. Somewhere between the airport and his first appointment, he, the driver of his limo, and his three bodyguards were all killed. The diamonds, quite obviously, are gone."

Jeffrey remembered hearing something about a South African

businessman being killed, his limo found on a service road near the Westchester Airport. The implication of the report, if Jeffrey remembered, was that it was some kind of an organized crime hit. But he didn't remember hearing anything else about it.

"And you think that this might be one of those diamonds?"

He picked up the diamond and looked at it again. "Like I said, they're very, very rare. Last week a dealer is killed, his gems stolen, among which there was supposedly a cache of nearly flawless pink diamonds. This week you come to my shop with an extraordinary stone that you say came into your possession 'by accident.' If you weren't a friend of Striker's, I might be calling some of *my* friends," said Chiam with a flat smile.

Few people realized that the Jews had a pretty nasty mob themselves. Jeffrey had noticed another exit door toward the back when he'd followed Chiam to the office and noticed a set of keys hanging in the dead bolt. He found himself wondering whether he could get to the back or the front exit faster, and where the back exit would leave him off.

"Has there been any speculation as to who might have killed the dealer and taken the stones?" asked Jeffrey.

"There's always speculation," he said with a sigh. "Maybe the Albanians, maybe the Italians, maybe the Russians."

"Maybe the Jews," said Jeffrey.

"No," said Chiam with a short, mirthless laugh. "Not the Jews."

Jeff nodded and guessed that if it had been the Jews they probably wouldn't be having this conversation.

"Anyway," said the old man. "There's been no movement. At least not locally. Whoever took the diamonds will want to sell them eventually. That's when *maybe* we hear who is responsible."

"Then what?"

He turned up the corners of his mouth, but Jeffrey wouldn't have called it a smile. "Too many variables. No way to know."

"When you hear something, I'd like to know," said Jeffrey, sliding his card over the desk toward Chiam. He nodded, taking the card.

"Are you pursuing this through your own avenues?" asked Chiam.

"I am," he answered.

Chiam seemed to consider his response. "Well, then. I'll promise to tell you what I learn, if you promise to tell me what you learn."

"It's a deal," said Jeffrey.

"Now," said Chiam, looking satisfied. "How much do you want for this stone?"

———

When Matt Stenopolis called, Lydia was sitting in Jeffrey's office staring at the box. A couple of times, she moved toward it but had wound up sinking back into the couch. She knew all about opening boxes. Once the lid was off, it could never be closed again. She considered herself a pretty tough chick, but that box scared her. She couldn't quite say why.

The buzzer on Jeffrey's desk sounded and a voice came over the speaker. "Lydia," said Jessa, one of the trainees, "are you in there? There's a Matt Stenopolis on line two."

She jumped up, glad for the distraction. "Got it," she said and picked up the call.

"Detective," she said.

"Yeah, Ms. Strong. Can we get together?"

She was surprised he wanted to meet rather than talk on the phone. She got the feeling that he didn't like her very much, considered her a necessary evil as far as Lily Samuels was concerned.

"Sure," she said. "Where and when?"

"The New Day achieved tax-exempt status in 1997. They claim to have over two hundred and fifty thousand members worldwide, growing steadily since their origination in 1977," Matt told Lydia over strong coffee and a scratched Formica table at a Greek restaurant in midtown. It was bustling with the dinner crowd, loud voices, clinking silverware, and the occasional cry of "Opa!" as a waiter lit the *saganaki* on fire. The place itself was a dive, looking more like your average New York diner than anything else, but it had the best Greek food outside of his mother's kitchen and he had a craving for *pastitso* that would not be denied.

"So The New Day is a religion?" she said, sounding skeptical, tracing the rim of her coffee cup with a delicate finger.

"Yeah, I guess that's what they call themselves," he said. Matt was not of the belief that you could just start a religion in the same way that you could start a company. It seemed a little backwards to him and he was suspicious of any so-called religion that had just popped up in the last twenty or thirty or even fifty years. Some backwoods bumpkin or science fiction writer declares himself a prophet, gets a few weak-willed souls to agree, and all of sudden he's talking to God. Maybe he was just being picky but frankly he would need some parting of the seas, water into wine, or something along those lines to be convinced.

"What are their precepts? I mean are we talking a Heaven's Gate kind of thing . . . hitch a ride to God on the Hale Bopp Comet? Or what?"

"Well, from what I can determine, there aren't any deities involved. They claim to be compatible with any religious belief, kind of a direct line to whatever God you believe in. Their whole concept is that through a kind of spiritual cleansing they can help people overcome addictions, reach their full potential as human beings and in so doing get closer to God."

"And what do they get from their members in return?"

"The members of The New Day turn over everything to the church when they join. It's not that they *give* it to The New Day, though. My understanding is that The New Day creates an account for the member and manages all his or her money and assets. They get an allowance or a dividend from their invested money to meet living expenses. Supposedly, the member can cash out that account and leave whenever he or she wants."

She nodded thoughtfully and he wondered if she was thinking what he had when he heard that. He'd thought about Lily Samuels cashing out all of her accounts while someone waited for her in a black SUV.

"What if you want to join The New Day and you don't have any money?" said Lydia.

"I don't know," he said. He only had limited information.

After he and Jesamyn met with the other detectives working on the Rosario Mendez case, and Jesamyn had left for the evening, Matt had called a friend of his, a guy he went to high school with out in Queens who was now an agent with the FBI. Special Agent John Starks was part of a unit whose task it was to track and observe the activities of domestic groups, such as the Michigan Militia or the Branch Davidians, with political or religious agendas that might pose a threat to homeland security. To Matt's surprise, his friend, Starkey to everyone from the neighborhood, knew a lot about The New Day.

"Basically, when you sign up, it's like going to rehab," Starkey had told him. "They separate you from your life and your family. You can have no other club affiliations, like not even a gym membership. And you have to quit your job. Apparently, there's a period they call 'cleansing' which can last from six months to a year. After this time, you're allowed to return to your life if you want, while remaining a member of The New Day the way you would belong to any church. Or you can go to work for the church."

Lydia had pulled a notepad from her pocket and was scribbling notes.

"I'm just taking some notes," she said when she saw him watching her. Then, "How did the FBI learn about The New Day?"

"They've been investigated by federal agencies three times in the last twenty-five years."

"What for?" she asked. Her phone beeped in her jacket and he waited while she fished it out, glanced at the screen, and returned it to her pocket. She smiled briefly, thoughtfully, and turned back to Matt. He continued.

"They started calling attention to themselves when they bought up a whole bunch of property in this small town in Florida. It was this kind of sleepy beach town with lots of undeveloped land and struggling businesses. They bought up some historic buildings and started renovating, really giving the area a face-lift. They brought a bunch of members in and helped them buy small businesses. But people were suspicious of them and wanted to know what they were doing there. The FBI investigated but they weren't doing anything illegal and nothing came of it. That was back in 1980. They continued to grow their presence in that community and now they own more than fifty percent of the commercial property."

The waitress brought Matt's *pastitso,* a kind of meat, cheese, and noodle dish that resembled lasagna. Lydia, who claimed she wasn't hungry, had ordered *baklava*. The serving of the sweet pastry dish was bigger than Lydia's head and she dug right in, apparently unconcerned with caloric content. He liked that about her, too.

"In 2000," he went on, "a man named George Benchly claimed that he had 'escaped' The New Day. He said that at a very low point in his life, he had been laid off from his job at a dot com and his wife had left him, he had attended an open meeting, having heard about the organization from a friend. He turned over his assets and signed on for a cleansing. They told him that he could leave at any point. But when, about three weeks into it, he decided it wasn't for him, they wouldn't let him go. He managed to escape and went to the authorities. When confronted, a New Day official claimed that it was their policy to 'discourage' people from leaving a cleansing, much in the way someone who wanted to leave a drug or alcohol treatment center would be discouraged. They returned Mr. Benchly's assets to his control, claiming that he had a serious substance abuse problem and needed help. Three weeks later, Mr. Benchly was found dead in a motel room. He'd shot himself in the head. Tox reports showed crack cocaine. The thing was, prior to his joining The New Day, Mr. Benchly had never had a substance abuse problem at all, at least not according to his ex-wife, former employers, and friends.

"This incident caused the FBI to investigate The New Day again. But again, they found nothing illegal in their activities."

"But they were taking people's money and holding them against their will."

"Well, no. Those people were willingly signing over their assets to be managed by accountants who were also New Day members. And in the contract people sign when they are accepted for a cleansing, it states clearly that they will be 'discouraged' from leaving before the cleansing is complete."

"You have to wonder," said Lydia, taking a sip from her coffee. "Where do you have to be in your life to turn over your autonomy like that? Your assets, your freedom."

She shuddered slightly as if she couldn't imagine anything worse.

"Maybe you just have to be really desperate," said Matt, finishing off his food and thinking about another order. "Or clinically depressed or hopeless, vulnerable to anyone who promises to make you feel better."

Lydia looked at him then and he couldn't tell what she was thinking. She had a very still face, beautiful in the way that precious metals were beautiful, cool, and distant. The gray of her eyes was impenetrable; there was no way to know what was going on behind them unless she told you.

"Did you sense that Lily was that kind of person?" she asked.

"No," he said without hesitation. "I didn't."

"But her brother might have been."

"Did Tim Samuels tell you that?"

"Yeah. He said Mickey had been depressed on and off most of his life."

Matt was starting to see where she might be going with this. Lily's mother had told him early on in the investigation that where Mickey went, Lily followed. She was hysterical at the time and he thought she was communicating her fear that Lily had also killed herself and that it was a corpse for which they were searching. He told Lydia what he was thinking and she just nodded as if it didn't surprise her.

When she didn't say anything, he went on with what Starkey had told him.

"The most recent investigation was back in 2002," he said, "conducted by the ATF. Another New Day escapee, Rusty Klautz, claimed that they were stockpiling weapons. Supposedly there's a farm called New Day Produce out in Florida near the Gulf Coast. They grow organic fruit and vegetables, raise free range chickens, hormone- and antibiotic-free dairy, make fresh juices and then sell it all at farmers' markets in the area. The escapee claimed that this farm, nearly a hundred acres in the middle of nowhere, is actually a front. He said that there were weapons everywhere, buried in bunkers beneath the ground, hidden in barns. But aerial photographs showed nothing suspect. There was no intelligence to confirm that the types of weapons Klautz claimed were there had been bought or sold here. And Klautz had a history of being a conspiracy theorist, even had a newsletter back in the seventies. He was a Vietnam vet with a history of mental illness."

"Let me guess," said Lydia.

"Wrapped his Harley around a tree," said Matt.

Lydia just nodded, looked down at her empty coffee cup.

Matt shrugged, slaked down his last bit of coffee. "The FBI keeps tabs on them now, supposedly. The New Day is definitely on their radar."

"Did they ever go in to see if Klautz's claims were true? Are they currently under surveillance?"

"Starkey wouldn't say. But that would be my guess. At least they're monitoring chatter. Three allegations in thirty years are not really *that* many. Hell, the Catholic church probably has more allegations against them that."

"It's enough to interest the Feds."

"The Feds are paranoid about stuff like this these days for obvious reasons." He nodded in the general direction of the altered skyline. "Any organizing group with a political or religious agenda is interesting to them."

Lydia leaned back in her chair and looked beyond him out the window. She let out a long sigh. "So what's the hierarchy like?"

"Since the late nineties, the head of The New Day is a guy named Trevor Rhames. Starkey says they know amazingly little about him and what they do know, he wouldn't tell me. As for the rest of the structure of the organization, again, he wouldn't say."

"What about a member list? Names of people who belong to The New Day."

Matt shook his head. "If the FBI has one, they're not sharing. At least not with me."

"Well," she said with a sigh. She leaned away from the table and cracked the tension out of her neck. "We've had trainees working on those transcripts and the list of vehicles. So far they haven't found anything that warrants following up. Other than, of course, the link to Mickey's girlfriend, which led us to The New Day. So from here—" she said and then stopped herself. "Maybe you don't want to know."

He looked at her and felt the full weight of his conflict. Of course he wanted to know, wanted to be a part of finding Lily Samuels. But he couldn't do that without risking his job. He stayed silent, looked down at the check, took his wallet from his jacket. Lydia snagged the bill from him.

"It's on me, Detective," she said. "Please."

She took some cash from her bag and placed it with the check under the sugar container.

"She's clean," he said, wanting to offer something. "Michele LaForge. Other than those parking tickets, she has no criminal record. None of the other drivers have criminal records either. I've been following up after hours. If I had the time, I'd be visiting each of those people. You know, just to see. You never know."

That was the real bones of detective work, slowly looking at every possibility. Quietly visiting, observing, asking careful questions, sometimes the same question over and over. The old dogs, the guys that had fifteen, twenty years on said they used to be able to do their jobs like that. Today, it was all political, high tech. Get the DNA, the fingerprint, run it through the system, find your man. Clear the case; bring the crime stats down so the mayor looks good. Fast was key. Careful was not so important. In the Missing Persons Division, the first thirty-six hours was the panic, the rush when all resources were available to you. After that, they figured you were looking for a corpse. The bosses started to get impatient for you to clear or move on. But Lily never got her thirty-six hours; they were long past before anyone realized she was gone. He felt that crush in his chest again.

They were out on the street before either of them spoke again.

"Thank you, Detective," she said. "I know this isn't easy or comfortable for you."

He nodded. "I want you to find her. I'll check my ego and break a few rules to help you to do that," he said.

She looked at him thoughtfully.

"You know my husband left the FBI because he felt like the politics and policies, the rules and procedures put the Bureau before the victims. He left so that he could be a better investigator."

Matt nodded. He knew what she was getting at. But he was a cop; it was the only thing he had ever wanted to be.

"Anyway, all I'm saying is call me if you decide the same thing about the NYPD. There's something to be said for the private sector."

"I'll keep that in mind," he said with a smile as she slid into her Mercedes. He stood and watched her as she pulled into traffic and sped off with a gunning of the engine.

At the first traffic light, Lydia checked her cell phone. She'd had the ringer off in the restaurant but it had still signaled her when messages came in; she'd felt it vibrating in her pocket. Jeff had called and Dax, too, within a minute of each other. While she'd still been with the detective, she'd received a text message from Jeffrey. "With DS?" it read. "Mt @ D's 2100. 5683U. J." His shorthand translated to: "Are you with Detective Stenopolis? Meet me at Dax's at 9 P.M. Love you, Jeff."

The glowing red light from the dashboard clock read 7:08. She had some time. There was a stop she wanted to make before meeting the boys.

She turned on the radio and flipped through stations, finally settling on some old-school house music. It lifted the pall that was settling over her a little, bringing to mind heaving dance floors and disco lights. Then she remembered the last time she'd been in a place like that and watched a young girl die there. She turned off the radio and drove in silence.

There was a personality profile for people who joined cults. That's what The New Day sounded like to Lydia—a cult. Lily didn't fit that profile. But maybe Mickey did. Tim Samuels claimed that his stepson struggled with depression all his life. She well knew that the death of a parent was traumatic enough to leave scars that last a lifetime. But the *suicide* of a parent must be even more devastating. It might have left him with a lifelong terror of abandonment or deep sense of unworthiness that would account for what she remembered Lily saying and what Jasmine had confirmed: that Mickey was a seeker. He might have been vulnerable to a place like The New Day. Of course, Lily had had the same experiences but she was younger and she had accepted Tim Samuels as her father. She didn't remember Simon Graves and so maybe avoided his terrible legacy.

In her class at NYU, Lydia had taught that the art of investigation was much like the art of method acting. The investigator had to develop an empathy for the person for whom she was looking, reach inside for the true heart and mind of the subject to find their motivations. Otherwise the search would be hollow, superficial, and ultimately unsuccessful, unless they got lucky. She didn't mention, and she probably should have, how terribly dangerous this could be. How it could lead an investigator to become personally involved with his or her subject. How it could lead to burnout, at best. Or at worst the kind of haunting Lydia experienced. The lost girls were always with her, always waiting to be found.

She wondered about Lily, grieving, feeling alone, convinced that her brother had not killed himself and being the only one who felt that way. She was vulnerable to begin with; she began her investigation with a tremendous love and empathy for her subject. If she'd followed Lydia's investigative techniques and philosophies, she could have easily been sucked into the same black hole that took Mickey.

She pressed a button on the dash. "Call Jeffrey," she said to the voice-activated phone in her car.

"Where have you been?" he said when he answered.

She told him about Detective Stenopolis and all he had shared about The New Day, then told him her thoughts about Lily.

"I was wondering how long it would be before you found a way to blame yourself for this," said Jeffrey.

"I'm not blaming myself," she said defensively. "I'm just following my own advice. I'm getting inside her head."

"Uh-huh," he said, letting the subject drop. "Well, Dax thinks he found a way inside The New Day."

"He thinks?" She had a brief but vivid imagining of them all being captured by The New Day, strapped into five-point restraints on gurneys, forced to watch some kind of religious videos with their eyes pried open in a hideous *Clockwork Orange* scenario.

"Well, it's not an exact science, breaking and entering," said Jeffrey. "There are a lot of variables, as you well know."

"Great," she said.

"I'm with Dax now in Riverdale," he said. "We're going over the details. When can you get here?"

"I have to make a stop first and then I'll be there."

"Where are you stopping?" he said, sounding suspicious. She had a bad reputation for doing reckless things on her own and paid for it by having to answer a lot of annoying questions from her husband.

"I have to pick something up from my grandmother."

"What?"

"I'm not sure."

She was so glad her grandparents had moved into the city. The house they'd had in Nyack and then later the one they'd had in Sleepy Hollow had each been uncomfortable for her in different ways. The house in Nyack was so like the house in which she had lived with her mother, the house in which her mother had been murdered. Same clapboard, white trim, same shingled roof.

When her grandparents moved to Nyack to take care of Lydia after the death of her mother, they thought it was important that she stay in the same neighborhood, attend the same school so that her life as she knew it wasn't totally obliterated. Looking back, Lydia wondered if it had been the best idea. It might have been harder initially but in the long run, moving to another area, starting at a new school might have helped her to reinvent herself. Instead, in school she would forever be "the girl whose mother was murdered." Living less than a mile from the house where her mother had been killed, she always had to consciously avoid that street and notice neighbors and the parents of her classmates avoiding that street during car pools. There were always small reminders that seemed to keep the wound forever fresh.

The house in Sleepy Hollow had been different, quaint and Victorian. But Jed McIntyre had been there, too. The move to the city had been good for everyone.

She walked into the lobby of the luxury high-rise and nodded to the doorman, who recognized her and let her through without buzzing up to her grandparents. The heels of her boots clicked loudly on the marble floors and echoed off the high ceiling. She looked at her reflection in the polished metal doors of the elevator and thought she might try wearing some other color than black one day, but doubted it.

She rode the elevator to the fifteenth floor. Her grandmother was waiting for her at the door in a navy velvet dressing gown and slippers Lydia had given her for Christmas the previous year. The doorman must have called up to say she was on her way.

"This is a surprise, Lydia," said her grandmother, embracing her. She smelled of ivory soap and talcum powder, her hands felt soft and papery. She stepped aside so Lydia could enter, and Lydia walked through the entranceway and into the living room.

"Grandpa's sleeping."

"It's only eight o'clock," she said, looking at the clock on the VCR. "If it were summer, it would still be light out."

"Well, if he didn't get up at four in the morning he might not go to bed so early. But try to tell your grandfather anything and see where you get with it."

The television was on with the sound down. Lydia could smell garlic from something her grandmother had cooked earlier.

"What are you watching?" she asked, sitting on the chintz sofa her grandparents had had since she was child.

"One of those crime scene investigation shows," she said, waving a hand at the screen. "I don't know which one; they're all the same to me."

The low oak coffee table before her, the Tiffany standing lamp, the china cabinet were all items Lydia remembered from her childhood. Most everything else in the apartment was new, the building completed just months before they took residence. The apartment was modern, with every amenity: a brand-new, state-of-the-art gourmet kitchen, washer and dryer, parquet floors. Large windows provided sweeping views of the city. The old items looked out of place, antiquated, in the space, but Lydia couldn't imagine her grandparents without them.

When Lydia and Jeffrey had bought their apartment in the Village, both of them had sold off most of their old belongings, keeping only their clothes, some meaningful pieces of art and jewelry. But they had chosen most of the items in their apartment together. New beginnings demanded new objects. Her grandparents didn't share that philosophy. Don't replace anything that isn't broken beyond repair and change as little as possible. That was more of their approach to things.

Lydia watched as her grandmother lowered herself gingerly into her chair. She was going to ask if the arthritis was getting worse, but she knew her grandmother wouldn't tell her anyway. Stoicism was highly prized in the Strong family; complaining was considered a weakness. Despite the rigidity of her movements, Eleanor Strong's fabulous bone structure, her innate sense of style, and a great hairdresser kept her looking far younger that her nearly seventy-five years.

"Grandma—" Lydia began.

"I knew I shouldn't have said anything," she said. "I should have just waited until you came. Ever since you were a little girl, you've always been so impatient."

Lydia couldn't argue. Her grandmother seemed about to get up again but Lydia stopped her. "Just tell me where it is, Grandma. I'll get it."

She pointed over to a roll-top desk at the other end of the large living room and Lydia walked toward it.

"In the bottom drawer," she said. "I suppose you're going to be angry."

Lydia opened the drawer and withdrew a stack of unopened letters, maybe ten or fifteen of them, grouped together with a rubber band. They were addressed to her at her grandparents' house in Nyack. The name on the return address of the letter at the top of the stack read, "Arthur James Tavernier." She flipped through and read the postmarks: 1985, 1987, 1988—all sent around the date of her May 7th birthday. She turned to look at her grandmother, who was looking at her slippers.

"Why, Grandma?" she said, quietly. "Why did you keep these from me? Why are you giving them to me now?"

She sighed. "At the time, it seemed like the right thing. You were so fragile, your grandfather hated him so much. Over the years, when you were older, stronger, it just seemed like a secret I had kept so long that it had turned into a lie, a deception. At a point, the letters stopped. You never asked about him. I told myself that I'd give them to you if you ever showed a curiosity about him. But you didn't. So." She ended with a shrug.

The women in the Strong family had always been unapologetic for the decisions they made. Marion Strong had been a strict, severe mother, not unloving but exacting. And Eleanor was the same. Lydia had never known either of them to regret a decision. But she saw something that might have been self-doubt glittering in her grandmother's eyes.

"But why now?" said Lydia, walking back to the couch and sitting down.

"I figured now or never," she said pragmatically. "I couldn't very well just leave them for when I died. That would be pretty chicken of me."

She remembered another stack of letters she used to have. Letters Jed McIntyre had sent her. She'd kept them in a drawer unopened to remind herself that he was just a man, incarcerated and only able to reach her through the US Postal Service. Not a demon who could reach down from the sky and destroy the people and things she loved; though that turned out to be closer to the truth.

She felt a rush of emotion, a childish mix of anger and sadness. Then a familiar numbness washed over her. The letters felt awkward and heavy in her hand. She wished there was a fire she could throw them into.

"I don't know what to say, Grandma," said Lydia.

"You don't have to say anything. Just read them or throw them away. It's your choice now."

Lydia got up and walked over to the window, looked at the glowing windows in the building across the street. She did a quick pace of the width of the room.

"It should have been my choice all along," she said finally.

Lydia walked back over to the couch and sat down. She looked at her grandmother, who looked at the floor. Lydia released a long, slow breath, zoning out on the muted television screen where an older man held a young girl in an embrace while the girl wept.

"Well," said Eleanor. "It's like I said. We all do our best in this life, Lydia. I know I did my best."

When she'd said that over the phone, Lydia had thought Eleanor was talking about her father, but she'd been talking about herself. She knew her grandmother well enough to know that this was as close to an apology as she would come.

Out on the street, the night seemed to have gone from chilly to bitter and Lydia pulled the cashmere of her coat tight around her as she walked down Riverside Drive toward the parking lot where she'd left her car. She could smell the scent of burning wood from someone's fireplace.

She felt as if someone had smacked her in the head. All these years, she'd thought her father had abandoned her and never looked back. She'd been cold to him when he came to see her that day and she'd thought he'd never reached out to her again. And over the years her feelings on the matter had shifted from guilt and self-blame to anger, to disdain and back again. It had never occurred to her that he might have made attempts to contact her that her grandparents had blocked. She didn't know how to feel about it. The wind picked up as she walked and she walked a little faster, clutching her bag with the letters tucked inside. She came to a wire garbage can and considered it a moment, just throwing them in and walking away. But, of course, she couldn't do that.

She was so deep in thought that it took her longer than it might have to sense that she was being followed. Standing by the garbage can, she caught movement out of the corner of her eye. When she started walking again, she heard footfalls behind her.

Lydia ducked into a bodega and walked toward the back, not totally sure of her plan but keeping her eyes on the plate-glass windows that looked out on the street. She opened one of the cases and took out a Pepsi, watching through the glass.

He walked slowly and didn't try to hide himself. A tall thin man with a shaved head, dressed in a long black leather coat, a black shirt beneath opened to the chest. His strides were so long and smooth that he seemed to be floating when observed from the waist up, as Lydia saw him out the window. He came to a stop and looked in the store. Lydia moved out of sight instinctively, letting the glass case close. But it was too late. Obviously, he'd seen her come in there. He'd seen her move into the aisle. She felt her heart start to dance in her chest as a wide smile spread across his face. He lifted a hand and then wagged a finger at her, in a gesture of reprimand. There was a terrible menace in his smile, a strange vacancy in his eyes. *Where have I seen him before?* she thought. And then she remembered, the abandoned building in the Bronx. Was it the same man? She couldn't be sure. The man she'd seen in Riverdale had seemed stockier, not as tall. But it was the same leather coat. She was sure of that.

She reached into her bag and felt the cool metal of the Beretta she carried. She saw the skinny Arab guy at the counter look at the man on the street and then look at her uneasily. He quickly got down on the floor and she heard a cell phone dialing, then some rapid-fire Arabic or some other language she didn't understand at all.

By now she'd wrapped her fingers around the grip of her gun, her breathing came faster, her lungs felt like they couldn't get enough air. He started to move. She drew her gun from the bag and heard the clerk issue a little scream. He must have been watching her on a surveillance camera somewhere. She took cover, her body pressed against the metal end cap of the shelves, and watched the door from the mirror mounted near the ceiling at the far corner of the small shop. She saw his large form darken the doorway. She waited for the jingle of the bell announcing that he was coming in but there was silence. And more silence. Then a little whimper, a sniffle. The clerk behind the counter was crying. Then she heard sirens off in the distance. She saw the man in the door turn his head and then run off.

She moved out after him. On the street, she watched him run up Ninety-Fifth toward Broadway and then disappear around the corner. She turned and ran in the opposite direction toward her car.

Eleven

"You're looking a little frayed, Lydia," said Dax over the speaker at the end of his drive. "And you're late. *And* your phone is off."

She gave the finger to the camera near the speaker box.

"That's a vulgar gesture, quite unladylike," Dax said.

"Dax, will you just open the gate?" she heard Jeffrey say in the background.

The tall wrought-iron gate hanging between two huge stone ballasts opened slowly and Lydia drove up the circular drive. She was glad to hear the heavy metal clang behind her, not looking over her shoulder for the first time since she left the city. She was still shaky with the residual effects of adrenaline; she felt exhausted.

Jeffrey walked out the front door and approached, opened the door of her car for her.

"What's up?" he said, as she sank into his arms.

"I've had a really bad night," she said.

"Was it the same guy?" Dax wanted to know, when they were all gathered in his kitchen after she told them what had happened. She ate a peanut butter and raspberry jelly sandwich Dax provided, an offer that represented the pinnacle of his culinary skills. But Lydia was starving and it tasted fantastic.

"I'm not sure," she said between gooey bites. "It could have been."

"Sounds like it," said Jeff.

"Yeah," she said. "But it could have been any bald-headed guy wearing a black leather coat. I mean this *is* New York after all."

"But how many of them would be following you around?"

She shrugged. "No shortage of freaks in this city."

"But it wasn't random," said Jeffrey, looking at her seriously. She could see that his shoulders were tense. "That wasn't your vibe."

"No, that wasn't my vibe," she said, shaking her head. "He shook his finger at me, like a warning." She shuddered a little, remembering his smile, the empty, flat look in his eyes.

"Anybody who knows anything about you knows that a warning has the same effect as a dare," said Dax. The only indication that he was worried or concerned at all was the slight thickening of his accent. He drew out *dare* to about three syllables: *de-a-ear.* Lydia had noticed that excitement, anger, and alcohol often caused him to become nearly unintelligible.

"Okay, so what were they warning you about?" asked Jeffrey.

"Maybe someone doesn't want you looking into Lily's disappearance," offered Dax.

"Or Mickey's suicide," said Lydia.

"Or The New Day," said Jeffrey, eating the crust of the sandwich Lydia had left on her plate.

"Well, you know my philosophy," said Lydia. "The more people don't want you looking into something, the more reason there generally is to look."

"That philosophy has *not* worked well for us in the past," said Jeffrey.

"True," said Lydia, nodding and meeting his eyes. "Let's go home then."

They were all quiet for a second. Dax was the first to laugh.

"So how do we get in there?" asked Lydia after a minute.

"Well, there's good news and bad news," said Dax. "The bad news is that there is no way into The New Day once it has been locked down. Not without setting off alarms. If I had six weeks for recon to gain passwords and a trained team, maybe. But since all I had was six hours and the two of you, we'll need to get in while the place is still open."

"What's the good news?"

"There's a door in the kitchen that supposedly opens only from the inside and is not attached to any alarm system *before* the place locks down at night. The plan is for one of you to get to that door and let the other one in. You use the same door to exit. It's the only door in the building that doesn't have a security shutter coming down over it at night. You should be able to push it open from the inside, no problem. Just remember, if you're in there after the place locks down an alarm will sound. I'll be on the street waiting in the Rover. But you'll have to run. Fast."

Lydia sighed, rubbed her head that was starting to ache. "So what? We're just going to walk in the front door?"

"There's a meeting tonight," said Jeffrey, looking at his watch. "In forty-five minutes."

"Okay," said Lydia, standing. "I'll go in and meet you at the door, Jeffrey."

He shook his head. "No way. *I* go in and meet *you* at the door."

"I want to see Trevor Rhames," she said, pulling her coat back on.

He looked at her. "You've been followed. They know who you are."

"Not necessarily," she said weakly, regretting having said anything. "It could have been a coincidence. Some random freak."

"Give me a break," he said. She could tell he was getting mad because she saw the small vein on his temple pop out.

"Look. If they know who I am, then they know who you are and we both have an equal chance of being made. I'll wear a hat and some glasses. I'll be inconspicuous."

"We'll talk about it in the car," said Dax, moving toward the door.

"There's nothing to talk about," said Jeffrey, following him.

"You're right about that," said Lydia, closing the door behind them.

Matt thought, not for the first time, that Missing Persons might not be the right place for him. He pulled into the driveway of his house and looked over at his parents' bedroom window. It was dark, but he knew his mother had heard his car pull up, seen the lights in the drive. He took the extra-large pizza, six-pack of Coronas and Lily Samuels' file off the passenger seat and went into his house.

When he'd stopped back by the precinct, he'd seen Rosa there at her cube, poring over the Mendez file. She had a desperate, angry look to her that he recognized from the mirror. He knew what she was thinking. *How can a flesh and blood person just disappear? It's not right.*

He had walked over toward her and leaned on a desk nearby.

"Any developments?" he'd asked pointlessly.

She shook her head and looked up at him. Evelyn Rosa was a café au lait–skinned woman, with fifteen years on and a bad attitude. She would have been beautiful but she was hard as granite, tough from growing up on the streets of the Bronx, tougher still from her years on the street as a cop. For all that steel in her, every once in a while, she'd come in with a bruise on her arm or the shadow of shiner. Rumor was her live-in boyfriend of over ten years sometimes had too much to drink and they went at it. Apparently she gave as good as she got—most of the time.

"I hear you gave Alonzo a hard time today," she said.

"Yeah, sorry. He got to me," said Matt. "He *really* got to me."

"He has that effect on people. I really hate that motherfucker."

"You think he killed her?"

She nodded. "I think he killed her and doesn't give a shit about it. But I've got no evidence. Nothing. And he's all lawyered up now."

"Where's your partner?"

"He went home. He figures we're looking for a corpse. No rush."

She shrugged and couldn't meet his eyes. He felt for her.

In his living room, he saw Rosa's face again. Haunted, she'd looked haunted. He imagined that they were all getting that look about them, all of them that were carrying around the ultimate unanswered question. *Where have they gone?*

How are you supposed to live with this job? he wondered, as he flipped open the lid of the pizza box and scrolled through the channel guide on his digital cable with his other hand. He had the sound down and flashed through the images quickly: a guy pulling a huge marlin from crystal green waters, a woman crying by a fireplace looking beautiful and sad; a couple kissing.

Homicide, okay. The deed was done; your job was to find the perpetrator and bring justice. But Missing Persons, you had to find people who have dropped away from their lives. There was a terrible urgency at first and then when those intense thirty-six hours passed, slowly people moved away from it. When people started to get the sense that a person has fallen through one of the cracks in the universe, that when news does come, it will be bad, they start to distance themselves. Even cops did this, the good ones anyway, the effective ones. The sane ones. It probably helped if you had kids or something else important going on in your life. Those guys were able to keep the ones that never got found off the list of things that they thought about in bed at night. He hadn't been able to do that. Not with Lily. He thought about her all the time, even when he was thinking about Rosario Mendez.

He flipped off the television and walked to the kitchen where he popped the lid off a Corona. There were two plates of dinner in the refrigerator for him and a note on the Formica table in the kitchen. "Eat!"

it read. "Love, Mom!" He felt guilty for bringing home the pizza. She'd see the box when she came in to clean and her feelings would be hurt. He'd have to remember to take it out to the garbage can on the side of the house before he left in the morning.

He walked through his house and upstairs without turning on the lights. His row house was spotlessly clean, not a speck of dust on the used furniture collected from his brother, his parents, his cousins. The only things he'd bought himself were the big-screen television in the living room that sat in front of a blue velour couch that had once belonged to one of his aunts, and the new desktop computer that sat on the old wood desk in the spare room upstairs, the desk on which, as a kid, he'd done his math homework. Up in his bedroom, he knew he'd find his laundry in neat piles on his bed, his shirts pressed and hanging in the closet.

Upstairs, he set the Corona on the desk, booted up the computer, and opened Lily's file again. Maybe it was the fiftieth or the one-hundredth time he'd been through it. But he had new information now, information about The New Day, thanks to Lydia Strong. Maybe there was something he'd missed before. Maybe.

It took Jesamyn exactly one evening with Dylan to remember why they weren't married anymore.

The three of them had shared a pepperoni pizza and then piled into Jesamyn's Explorer, heading up to her apartment. They were all light, laughing, joking around like a normal, happy family. Once strapped into the backseat, Benjamin was asleep in under ten, emitting a funny little snore that had Dylan and Jesamyn giggling quietly.

"You wore him out," she said with a smile, pulling onto the West Side Highway. There was a lot of traffic for the time of night and it was slow going as the river of traffic tried to squeeze past the construction she would swear had been going on for about fifteen years.

"He wore *me* out," Dylan said with a light laugh. "The kid just has this boundless energy, a million questions." He was quiet for a second, smiling to himself. Then, "I don't know how you do it, Jez. On your own, full time. I know it's hard."

There was a heavy silence between them, populated by their regrets and all that had passed between them.

"I'm sorry it turned out like this," he said finally.

She glanced over at him and quickly put her eyes back on the road. He was staring down at his fingernails, looking sad. *A little too sad,* something inside her whispered. *He's playing you.* She didn't say anything, just stared ahead of her. In their marriage together, she had always rushed to fill the silences. There was always too much talking, not enough listening. She sensed that he hadn't said what he really wanted to say so she just kept quiet.

"Do you ever think about us? About if we could make it right again?" he asked her softly, putting a hand on her knee. She cursed her mutinous heart for fluttering.

"Don't, Dylan," she said. "Not now. Not with him in the car."

Dylan's cell phone rang and he pulled it from his pocket. She saw him glance at the caller ID and stuff it back in his pocket without answering.

"I'm sorry," he said with a sigh. "You're right. I just wanted you to know that I've been thinking about it."

She couldn't even look at him. Her heart was thumping and tears threatened but she held them back. She didn't know what to think of him or how he was acting. He was kind, mature, thoughtful—all the things she'd wanted from him when they were together, all the things that had seemed so impossible for him. It just felt too good to be true. On the other hand, maybe the scare he'd had was a wake-up call for him.

She thought about this and they rode in silence the rest of the way back to the Upper West Side. Miraculously, she found a spot on the street and didn't have to spring for a night in the garage. While she grabbed her bags and Ben's from the trunk, Dylan was able to extract Ben from the backseat without waking him and carried him up the street.

"Did you talk to your PBA rep today?" she said quietly.

"Yeah, I did," said Dylan, shifting Ben up a little. "He thinks it's going to be okay. The shooting was good. I know it and everyone who was there that night knows it. I just have to go in and answer questions, so do the other guys. It's still going to be a week without my weapon, at least."

She put a hand on his arm. "It's going to be fine," she said. They both knew there weren't any guarantees. If there was unrest in the community over the incident, or if there was some unspoken agenda to come down on white cops that shot black kids, or if he just got an unsympathetic investigator, things could go badly for him.

"It's good to be with you, Jez. Thanks for being here for me."

In the elevator, the cell phone rang again but he made no move for it. Benjamin stirred at the noise but didn't quite wake up.

"Don't you need to get that?" she asked.

"Nah. It's probably just Barnes again. The guys are getting together tonight but I told him I needed to spend some time with my family."

I would have been crazy to divorce this guy, thought Jesamyn. But who the hell is he?

Ben woke up long enough to brush his teeth and put on his pajamas. She knelt down on the floor beside him as she tucked him into bed and kissed him on the head.

"Mom?" he said as she turned off his big light and flipped on the aquarium nightlight. "Do you like Dad again?"

She quashed the rise of guilt and smiled. "I've always liked your dad. He gave me you. And I love *you* more than anything."

He looked into her eyes and gave her that smile, a carbon copy of his father's. Irresistible.

"I love you, too," he said, turning over.

She closed the door mostly, leaving it slightly ajar the way Ben liked it, and moved quietly down the hall. She heard the tone in his voice before she saw him leaning in the doorjamb to the kitchen, talking into his cell phone like he was making out with it. That tone, that sweet, coaxing tone she knew so well.

"Not tonight, baby," he said, his voice low. "I'm working. I'll make it up to you tomorrow. Hey, and honey, don't call anymore tonight. You'll get me in trouble with my boss."

She felt her stomach bottom out and she remembered . . . a dozen other overheard phone calls, the nights he said he'd made a collar but there was no overtime in his paycheck, once an earring in her couch. Each time it had hit like a blow to the solar plexus. Tonight was no different. She put a hand against the wall. She couldn't believe he could still do it to her, run her through a gamut of emotions in just a few hours. Was she really this weak, this *stupid*?

In a way she was relieved, because it meant she was right about him all along. She had come to believe that he was pathologically unfaithful, that it wasn't part of his makeup to be present for her and Ben. He wanted to play; he wanted to party. He didn't really want to be a husband and a father, not full time anyway. This was why she'd decided to end their marriage. She hadn't been wrong. Small comfort, but she'd take it.

She picked up his coat off the couch and stood behind him, waiting for him to feel her there. After another sickening few seconds of him cooing on the phone to whomever it was he was cooing to, he flipped the phone shut and turned around.

"Uh—" he said. He looked stricken. "That was Barnes. We were just fooling around."

"Oh, spare me, Dylan," she said, handing him his coat. "Just go."

"Jez, please," he said, taking her by the shoulders. "I *really* need you guys right now."

"Key," she said.

"What?"

"Give me that goddamn key before I take it from you. And you know I can."

He looked at her and his eyes went from pleading to angry.

"This is why we're not married anymore, Jesamyn," he said, reaching into his pocket and fishing out the keys. "No understanding, no compromise."

She let go of a little laugh. "There are some points on which people are not expected to compromise," she said.

He fumbled with the keys, his jacket over his arm, took one of them off the ring and handed it to her. His face had flushed red and she could see a vein pumping in his temple.

"Both of them," she said forcing herself to keep her voice down. "The apartment door, too."

He sighed and took another one off the ring. She tested it in the door; the lock turned.

"I'll follow you down and check the other one, too. If you don't mind."

"You don't trust me?"

She gave him a smile. She locked the door behind her and they rode the elevator down together in a cool silence.

"I can't believe I thought—" she started and then clamped her mouth shut.

"You and I haven't been together in a long time, Jez," he said softly. "I have every right to be involved with someone else. I didn't know things were going to heat up between us again."

She shook her head and didn't respond further. The doors slid open and she walked quickly to the outside entrance and tried the key. When the lock turned, she stepped aside and held it for him.

"Jez, let's talk about this." He spoke softly, reaching for her hand. She folded her arms across her chest.

"Dylan, everything that needs saying between us, we said a long time ago. I was just suffering from some kind of temporary insanity. Clearly."

He walked onto the street and stood looking at her through the glass. He was so handsome and the girl in her loved him so much, she could imagine herself throwing the door open and running into his arms. She *wanted* to, even now. Instead, she turned and walked coolly for the elevator door though she wanted to run, catching it just before it closed again. She rode up, staring at her reflection in the mirrored doors, her body tense, her mouth pressed into a straight, hard line. She looked hard at the woman glaring back at her. Only her eyes betrayed the terrible sadness and disappointment she felt. She just made it into the apartment before she started to cry. She cried quietly, her head against the door, careful not to wake her son.

Twelve

Maybe fifty people had gathered in front of The New Day building. They stood in the cold, smoking cigarettes, drinking from paper coffee cups. A thin girl, very young with bad acne, stood with shoulders stooped, shivering against the cold. A woman wearing a three-quarter-length wool coat over a business suit clutched a soft briefcase to her side and looked around with a frown on her face, like she was somewhere she didn't want to be. A smallish man with slicked-back hair, wearing creased jeans, a faux leather jacket and matching loafers, laughed nervously as he tried to make conversation with a pretty black woman.

Lydia stood off to the side, leaning against a maple tree and listening to the quiet conversations that cropped up between strangers waiting for a common event. People seemed nervous, excited, tentative. She had to wonder why they'd come here. What were they seeking? Her eyes fell on the thin girl with the bad skin. The girl hunched her shoulders in, stood away from the crowd. She seemed sad and tired. It was contagious; Lydia started to feel that way, too.

After a while, a willowy woman in the white tunic and blue jeans Lydia had seen on the website opened the large wooden doors and people filed inside. Lydia lingered outside awhile, moving behind the tree. She wanted to be among the last to enter and sit toward the back. She hoped that her baseball hat and wire-rimmed glasses would keep anyone from recognizing her, though Jeffrey had been skeptical. He'd given up the argument and they'd parted angry with each other.

She hung back with the smokers and entered with the last of the people to walk through the door. They walked through the foyer and Lydia chose a seat as close to the door as possible, gratified that no one seemed to notice her. She had a row to herself and watched as people took tea from an urn on a table off to the side, dumping packs of sugar and creamer into their paper cups. People chattered a little at first, then grew silent. A definite tension built as people waited, started to get impatient.

"You're here because you want to change your life," said Trevor Rhames loudly as he entered the room from an unseen door to the side. "But you don't know how.

"People always think it's the things they *don't* have that are making them unhappy. 'If I can just get this, or buy that, or have that, then finally I'll achieve real peace and joy.' What they don't realize is that it's leaving things behind, wanting *less* that is the secret to true happiness."

Trevor Rhames spoke quietly but his voice resonated with authority. He was short and stocky, his hair just a shadow on his shaved head, but there was a powerful bearing to him. His eyes were ice blue, pale and dramatic. They demanded. He wore black jeans and a black cotton shirt open at the chest, heavy leather boots. An unlikely getup for a preacher. He paced the front of the room slowly, picking a pair of eyes from the crowd and then focusing on that person for a while, as if he were speaking directly to him.

"It is when we *abandon* materialism and vanity, worry less about what kind of car we drive and how much we weigh, that we open our minds to the Universe, to the thing religion calls God. God is everywhere, all around us; he *is* the ground beneath our feet, the sky above us, and the trees around us. He *is* us. All we have to do is recognize him."

He was a supernova. His energy filled the room and sucked everything else out. Even Lydia, who'd come for very different reasons than the other people gathered, felt his power. How powerful would he seem if you were lost, in pain, not sure of anything about yourself and your life? she wondered. How powerful had he seemed to Mickey? To Lily?

He was not a handsome man. His jaw was too big, his nose crooked. The stubble on his face made him look unkempt instead of rugged. A scar ran from behind his ear down the side of his neck and disappeared into the collar of his shirt. His boots added about an inch of height and he was still short. And yet Lydia could see how women might find him attractive. There was a pull to him, like the riptide in a violent sea. She was not immune to it; she felt the tug in spite of her intellectual perspective on it.

He went on and she settled into her seat in the back of the room.

The people around her seemed rapt, hanging on his every word. She noticed something then, that many of them were holding and were sipping from or had placed beside them a paper cup. She scanned the large room, an auditorium with a brightly lit stage and rows of soft, large, comfortable seats. The construction was new, she could smell the leather of the seats around her, the paint on the walls. On a table to the side of the room was a stack of paper cups, an urn with a sign: TEA. She remembered what Dax had said about the woman he met earlier handing him a cup and his instinct not to drink from it.

"What they don't want you to know," he said loudly, startling her from her thoughts, "is that the media purposely, perpetually keeps you in a state of self-hatred so that you will continue to *consume.*"

He raised his hands and came to stop in front of a woman in the front row. Lydia was too far back to see her; she could only see a head of dyed blonde hair.

" 'I'm too fat,' you think to yourself," he said, looking down at her. " 'Yes, you are,' says the media. 'Buy this and you'll look better, feel better, *be* better. But then have this cheeseburger; you deserve it!' " He shook his head in disdain, and then gave the audience a warm, sympathetic smile. He walked up and down the aisle in front of the seats.

"You have wrinkles or your breasts are too small or you're losing your hair or whatever it is someone *else* has told you is wrong with you. But don't worry. They have a remedy for everything—for the right price." He paused here, looking around at the crowd. Lydia found herself shrinking down in her seat. She didn't want Rhames to see her face.

"What they don't want you to know is that you are *exactly* the way God intended you and any value or devaluing associated with your appearance or your station in life is man-made. It's not organic, not real. It's an illusion created to keep you buying into a system that wants to enslave you, keep you working at a job you hate, hating yourself, buying what they say will make it all better over and over again until you die."

He paused again, again looking from face to face.

"There's another way," he said. He'd lowered his voice to a whisper and Lydia watched as people unconsciously leaned forward. "I am offering you a New Day."

He put his hand out to a woman in the audience and when she took it, he gently pulled her in front of the crowd. She was an average-looking woman, her dry, curly hair clearly color damaged. She wore the formless clothing of someone insecure about her body, a cardigan sweater, a long, full skirt. She wore a heavy mask of makeup. In the bright spotlight that shone on the front of the room it looked pink and cakey. She looked around the room, obviously wishing she could sink into the ground.

"When I look at you," he said, "I see what they've sold you. This color in your hair, these clothes to hide a body you think is substandard, this paint to hide a face you don't want to see when you look in the mirror. But I also see *you*."

The woman started to tear, put a hand to her mouth. "You're beautiful," he told her. "You don't need to hide from me."

He embraced her then and she started to sob. She could hear other women in the audience start to sniffle. One man got up and left. No one tried to stop him; he was shaking his head skeptically as he stalked past Lydia. She noticed that he didn't have a cup.

All the people in here had come because they were in pain; there was no other reason to join a group like this, no reason to come here. Lydia would bet that on the meta tags of the New Day website, they'd listed words like "depression," "despair," "loneliness," . . . maybe even things like "weight loss" or "hair loss." So that anyone searching for those words on the Internet might find a link to The New Day. She glanced at her watch and wondered whether Dax and Jeffrey were in place.

"In this New Day," Rhames went on, "you work for the betterment of yourself and for the world around you, not for the profit of some corporate giant. You spend your free time getting to know God by getting to know yourself, cleansing yourself of the poisons you've been fed since before you were old enough to even know what was happening to you. Imagine a life free from addiction, anxiety, depression, bad relationships, dead-end jobs, and financial worry.

"Imagine," he said, a wide smile splitting his face. "Imagine a New Day."

As Rhames continued his spiel, Lydia waited for him to turn his back for a second, then slipped from the darkened room into the hallway. She stood there for a moment, looked around her as if lost and trying to orient herself. She looked for cameras, waited for some tunic-clad hippie to arrive and escort her from the building. But if there were cameras in the long hallway, she couldn't see them. And when no one came, she made her way deeper into the building, toward the kitchen. Dax had managed to obtain an old building layout from his contact, so she had an idea which way to go, though she'd never really been good with maps.

Doors were closed; lights were dim. There was a palpable hush. The building had an air of desertion to it, like a school empty for the summer, its hallways echoing with the memory of footfalls and voices. Lydia walked quickly, trying to keep her boot heels from clicking on the tile floors.

When she came to the place she thought the door should be, she realized that she must have turned right where she should have turned left. She doubled back, feeling a little stupid, butterflies in her stomach. She couldn't shake the feeling that it was too easy to move around a building that had such tight security. It *would* have been more logical for Jeffrey to come in with the meeting group, she knew that. But she'd had a strong desire to see Trevor Rhames, to understand more about The New Day. Now she wondered, as she usually wound up doing at some point, if she should have listened to Jeffrey. Maybe they knew who she was, were watching her, giving her just enough rope to hang herself. Then again, maybe she was just being paranoid. Maybe the cameras Dax had mentioned didn't come on until the building locked down.

At the end of a long hallway, she came to an institutional-sized kitchen. She pushed through one of the doors marked NEW DAY STAFF ONLY. In the dark, she felt her way though a maze of large ovens and grills, metal sinks and cabinets, shelves of canned goods. It was a kitchen that served a lot of people, maybe hundreds. For some reason the place gave her the chills.

At the back of kitchen, she found the door and took a deep breath before opening it, bracing herself for an alarm if Dax's intel was wrong and preparing herself for a sprint. But the door pushed open quietly and standing there was her favorite sight. Jeffrey. He stepped inside and took a roll of electrical tape from his pocket and taped the latch of the door down so that it appeared closed but remained unlocked. When the place shut down, they'd still have a way out, unless the system read that a door wasn't closed properly. She let the door shut behind him.

"I told you it would be all right," she said.

"We'll see," he said. "Anyway, what are we looking for in here?"

"Lily Samuels for one. Or any evidence that she might have been here," she said, shrugging. "I don't know exactly. I guess we'll know it when we see it."

"Hello?" The voice was groggy, as if its owner had been sleeping. Matt looked at the clock. It was just after ten . . . not that late.

"I'm looking for Randall Holmes."

There was a pause on the line, a drawing in of breath, a rustling of sheets.

"Who's calling?" It was hard to tell if he was talking to a man or a woman, the voice was hoarse, sounded old.

"This is Detective Stenopolis from the NYPD. Mr. Holmes made a call to a tip line. I'm following up, sir. Sorry for the late hour."

The voice heaved a sigh. "Son, that was two weeks ago."

"You're Randall Holmes?"

"Well, who the hell else would I be? You called me."

Matt smiled. "You're right, sir. I'm sorry."

The man grunted on the other end of the line.

"You told the tip line operator that you saw Lily Samuels in church. Is that right, sir?"

"No, that's not what I said," he said. "That place is no church, I'll tell you that. Bunch of Moonies, if you ask me."

"Which place?"

He heard the man breathing heavily on the other line. "How do I know you're not one of them?"

Matt put his head into his hand. After going through Lily's file and finding nothing, he'd started sifting through some copies of the tip line transcripts he'd brought home with him. About halfway through the stack, he'd come across Randall Holmes, who'd claimed that he'd seen Lily at church. The notation from whoever took the call was that Holmes was "unstable, ranting." A note indicated that Jesamyn had made a follow-up call the next day and came to the same conclusion, that the guy was nuts. But now, knowing about The New Day, this call about a church from a man who lived in Riverdale held more potential. At least that's what Matt had hoped.

"Sir, I'm a Missing Persons detective with the NYPD. I'm one of the good guys. I promise."

The old man snorted. "I've heard that one before."

Matt sighed, feeling disappointment and frustration squeeze at the back of his neck, tense the muscles on his shoulders. Another dead end.

"Okay, Mr. Holmes, thanks for your time," he said, getting ready to hang up and go to sleep.

"Anyway, you're too late," he whispered.

"Too late for what?"

"Too late to help that girl."

Matt felt his stomach do a little flip. "What do you mean?"

"I *mean* I watch them go in. Some of them come out. Some of them don't. I sit on the porch after most of the others have gone to sleep. I like to go outside still, like to breathe the clean air. The rest of the people in this place are already dead, they're just waiting to stop breathing. Not me. I want to suck every last breath of air out of this world."

"Where are you, sir?"

There was a pause. "At the home here, the Sunnyvale Home for the Elderly. Boy, you don't know much of anything, do you?"

He was calling from almost directly across the street from The New Day.

"No, sir, not really. Maybe you could help me out."

"I sit in the dark corner of the porch so I can see without being seen, you know. It's always so much better not to be seen."

"I agree," said Matt solemnly. "What can you see from your porch?"

"I can see the brown building with the stained glass window. They try to make it look like a church. But there's no God in there. I know that for a fact."

"You said you watch people go in?"

"Some nights they gather outside, groups of people. They look nervous and hungry like they're waiting for a meal or a handout. A thin girl with bony shoulders and no tits opens the door for them after a while. They go inside; a few usually come out in the first half hour or so. Some come out a couple hours later. Others don't come out at all."

"You saw Lily Samuels there one night?"

"The girl on the news. I saw her. I told the nurse. She said it was dark and my eyes aren't what they used to be. So I called the number they gave on the television. I have a phone in my room, my son makes sure I have a good television and my own phone number here."

"He must be a very good son," said Matt.

He made some kind of grunting noise that might have been assent or disdain. Hard to tell.

"So you saw her standing and waiting with the others?"

"That's right. She looked lost," he said. "Very sad. Sadder than the others, somehow."

"Did you see her come out?"

"No. She didn't come out that night."

"That night? You saw her come out another night?"

The old man laughed. "No, son, haven't you been listening? What I'm trying to tell you is that if they don't come out the same night they go in, they don't come out at all."

"What are you doing over here, miss?"

"I'm sorry," said Lydia with an embarrassed smile. "I got a little lost on my way from the bathroom."

The woman looked at her stonily. She had hard, angular features and creamy white skin. "You'll have to return to the meeting now."

"I was just heading back."

The blonde woman who'd led the group gathered outside into the meeting walked her back to the auditorium. Lydia slipped back into the dark and noticed that the crowd had thinned considerably. Trevor Rhames was booming now, his voice resonating; he was pacing wildly; something about society trapping people in a prison of self-hatred and materialism. But she wasn't listening anymore. She was looking for a way out. She scanned the room for other doors and saw one down by the stage. But heavy and metal, with a glowing red exit sign over it, it looked like an exterior door. Shit, she thought. It was always a bad idea to split up. Always.

They'd decided that to save time, Jeffrey would take the corridor to the adjacent building to see what was over there and she'd look for an administrative office with computers or files, maybe even a list of members. He jogged off down the hallway and disappeared while she watched. As soon as she turned the corner, the bony woman had been there, looking at her with hard, suspicious eyes.

Lydia took a seat near the back and turned to see the woman standing by the door, her arms folded like a sentry. Lydia glanced around her. There had been about thirty people in the room, now there were maybe ten. In the dark, all she could see were the backs of their heads. They seemed to be nodding just slightly, almost in unison.

If she got up to leave, they'd probably escort her out of the building. Jeffrey would be alone, not knowing she was out. Then she remembered the door leading to the kitchen. She could leave the building and then sneak back in that way. She got up and walked toward the door.

"Leaving so soon?" asked the woman.

"Yeah," said Lydia. "I don't think this is my cup of tea. No pun intended."

The woman offered a wan smile. There was something so cold about her, something so stiff.

"We all find our way," she said.

Lydia wondered briefly if that was true. Did everyone find their way in this world? Didn't some people get crushed, or left behind? Or was *that* the way they found, *their* way, if not the way they wanted.

Two large men in the New Day uniform of blue jeans and white tunics were waiting outside the door. They wore the same cool, smug expressions. But all of them had those vacant eyes. They and the woman stayed close as she walked to the door. She felt their eyes on the back of her neck and she fought the urge to run or turn and punch one of them in their empty faces to see if they were really flesh-and-blood people. Out in the cold, they stood on the top stair leading to the church.

"Good-night," Lydia said and walked up the street. The blonde lifted a hand in farewell.

Lydia pulled her coat tight around her and walked quickly north. She passed Dax sitting in the Rover but didn't look at him. She could still feel their eyes on her. Dax didn't look at her either; obviously he sensed something was wrong or saw the three standing in the doorway, watching her leave.

Jeffrey crossed from the church building through the breezeway with glass walls into the taller condo building. He pushed through a light-colored wooden door and entered an empty foyer where the only sound was the buzzing of fluorescent lights. The floors and walls were crisp white, the high ceilings a robin's egg blue. The empty reception desk that stood in front of the entrance was a white lacquer semicircle. The space was antiseptic, meant, he thought, to communicate purity, cleanliness. Then he remembered what Matt Stenopolis had told Lydia about the "cleansing" period new members were required to undergo. The place gave him the creeps and an uneasy instinct whispered that they should get out as fast as possible. He paused for a second, glancing around for cameras, but didn't see any. He walked over to the reception desk, on which sat a multi-line phone, a clipboard, and a cup of pens printed with the New Day logo.

Jeffrey realized when he held the pen in his hand that he'd seen the logo often on items like coffee cups, notepads. It hadn't really clicked for him when he'd seen the logo on the van. But now he recalled seeing it on advertisements on the subway for things like depression counseling, addiction recovery, breaking the cycle of child abuse. The light blue line drawing of sunbeams reaching through cloud cover on a white background. He thought of the website and the brochures Dax had taken. It was outreach. Like the pedophile who picks the child with the lowest self-esteem, or the rapist who picks the smallest, most defenseless woman, they were trawling for people in the most pain, people who'd give almost anything to feel better.

The list of visitors was blank. But Jeffrey could see that heavy handwriting on the page above had left an impression on the blank sheet that must have been below it. He held it up to the light and tilted it, hoping to make something out. But his eyes were not great to begin with, so he gave up quickly. He took the sheet, folded it, and put it in his pocket.

The sounding of a soft bell startled him. He turned to see an elevator bank to his right. The lighted display above one of the doors indicated that the car was in a downward descent. He looked around for a place to hide.

Lydia walked nearly two blocks as quickly as she could without looking as if she were afraid or in any kind of a rush. She passed some shops that were closed for the evening, a small café, a copy and mailing center, a pet store. The neighborhood was an awkward mix of businesses, private homes, and condo buildings. Some of the homes were old and regal, adding a quaintness to the area which otherwise would have been like any other modern city block. They stood proudly beside the larger, newer apartment buildings that had cropped up, looking a bit out of place but refusing to give ground.

When she was out of sight of the church, she made a quick right and dashed between two condo buildings and followed an alley that ran parallel to the way she had come. She turned off the alley and cut through someone's lawn and set off a motion detector as she passed, a floodlight lighting up the yard, revealing a rusted swing set and a sandbox filled with weeds. She moved quickly through a side yard and crossed a small dark street, underneath a canopy of towering elms. The night was dark and once she was off the main street, the streetlights there gave off little more than an orange glow. The neighborhood was quiet. She could see the blue flash of television screens and orange lamplight in bay windows.

She came up behind the New Day building and crossed the yard quickly, edging the bushes on the perimeter and cutting across where the distance from the bushes to the building was shortest. She saw a door without handles and hoped it was the same door she'd opened for Jeffrey. She couldn't be sure, she felt turned around and disoriented. She put her fingers between the frame and the door and tried to pull, but it was stuck fast. She couldn't budge it. Either someone had found the tape and locked the door, or it was too heavy for her small fingertips— or it was the wrong door.

She moved along the wall looking for another door in the same general area, feeling along the masonry. She was sure now, seeing the front of the building, that the door she was at was the right one. She went back and tried it again. She couldn't move it. She felt her heart start to race as she realized she wasn't going to be able to get back into the building. That Jeff was in there alone, thinking she was in there, too. She looked around for something to try to pry into the space between the frame and the door but there was nothing except some large rocks and a few thin branches.

Jeffrey picked the lock on an inside door and slipped into a room just as he heard the elevator doors slide open behind him. Leaning against the wall, he listened to the sound of feet approaching. But whoever it was passed by the door, their shadows flashing on the thin white strip of light that came in under the door. Then there was silence.

When he could breathe again, he looked around to find himself in what looked like a security nerve center. The lights were dim and the room was cool. There was a wall of locked glass cabinets housing rows of computer servers. He walked around the wall and came to an alcove containing twenty closed-circuit monitors in five rows of four. An empty seat that was still warm and a half-consumed bottle of water told him he wouldn't be alone for long.

Images of long empty hallways lined with closed doors, elevator banks, wide shots of the building's exterior, the auditorium where Trevor Rhames was doing his preaching, flashed in intervals on the black-and-white screens. As he watched he saw Lydia being escorted from the building by a blonde woman and two big men. He watched until she was off camera. He knew she'd try to come back through the door they'd left open and that he'd have to hurry if he was going to meet her there.

He sat at the computer monitor beside the security screens and moved the mouse. The dark screen came to life and a menu of options popped up in front of him. He clicked on the file that said "Camera Views" and found a list of subcategories. "Hallways and Exterior Views" was already highlighted. He chose a folder named "Interior Rooms" and the images on the screens changed.

He let out a long breath. "Oh my God," he said, just as he heard the shutters begin to come down and the alarms start to sound. Then the knob to the door started to turn.

The night erupted with the thunderous sound of moving metal. Lydia took an unconscious step back and brought her hand to her chest. The security shutters were coming down over the doors and windows. Dax had been wrong. There *was* a security shutter over the door to the kitchen. She fought a rising tide of panic as she looked around on the ground and found a large rock. She pried it from the earth and raced to the door. She placed the rock at the base, holding it there, hoping to keep the door from coming down all the way.

When the door hit the rock it made a terrible grinding sound and stopped, moved halfway back up then came to a final crunching halt, as if the rock had knocked it off its track. She sighed with relief. Jeffrey could still get out, *if* he would leave believing she was still inside. The lawn flooded with light then and Lydia was exposed.

She heard the sound of footsteps and voices and saw two large forms turn the corner. They stood for a second, looking in her direction. The way the floods were shining, she could only make them out as tall and menacing shadows. One of them pointed. And then they both began running toward her.

Lydia ran. She peered behind her once and caught the impression of bald heads and leather. She thought of the man they'd seen last night and the one who had followed her from her grandmother's apartment. She felt the icy cold finger of fear on her spine, though her heart was a steam engine, working hard and burning hot. She could hear them gaining on her. They were bigger, had longer legs. There was no way she could outrun them.

Then the Land Rover was pulling in front of her and coming to a squealing stop. The door flew open.

"What the fuck happened? Where's Jeff?" yelled Dax, starting to drive before she'd closed the door.

"He's still in there," she said, breathless, slamming the door. "Loop around. We have to go back."

Dax gunned the engine and the Rover launched forward. Lydia looked behind to see the two men who'd been chasing her come to a stop in the middle of the street. Dax turned a corner fast and the rubber squealed against the concrete.

"I knocked one of the security doors off its track," she said, still trying to catch her breath. "The door to the kitchen where he came in . . . he can still get out that way."

"I thought . . ."

"Your guy was wrong or he lied. There *was* a security door."

Dax issued a string of expletives that embarrassed even Lydia, who swore like a truck driver without even thinking about it most of the time.

"What do we do?" asked Lydia.

"They won't expect us to come back," he said. "I'm going to make a long loop and then we'll come back around."

He started talking then about what they would do next, how she shouldn't worry and how Jeffrey could take care of himself. But she wasn't listening. All she could hear was a ringing in her ears and the pounding of her heart. She looked at the brown building as they approached again from the opposite direction. It was locked down like a fortress. All she could think was, *Jeffrey's in there. I left him in there.*

Thirteen

Some memories don't fade with time and distance. Some grow more vivid, while the people, events, and places around them, just before or just after, become faint and vague. Like colorized black-and-white films, they remain eerily bright, something just off about them, something that glows. They take on a special cast and over time become mythic in their scope and impact.

Lydia met Jeffrey Mark on the worst day of her life. She was fifteen years old and she had just discovered the murdered body of her mother. She'd sat rigid on the front stoop of her home, unable to respond to the people who tried to help her. She had gotten the idea in her mind that if she didn't speak, if she sat very still on the stoop and didn't react to the horror she had just witnessed, that she would wake up to discover she was dreaming. She clung to this idea. It made sense to her.

Lydia remembered sitting on the stoop with a female police officer who had tried her best to console her and to convince her to go inside the house, but Lydia would not move. She could remember clearly the scent of the woman's shampoo, the feel of her hand on her arm. But her words were just a soothing mumble that Lydia couldn't understand. She sat there for hours, stone-faced and shivering, while police officers walked to and from the house.

It was sitting on that stoop that she first saw Jeffrey. He pulled up with another man in a black car. She saw him looking at her as the sedan came to a stop, gravel crunching under its wheels. He walked toward her, his eyes on her the whole time. He looked strong and important to her, like someone who would have rescued her mother if he could have. He knelt before her and asked the female officer to leave.

"Lydia," he said. "I know how afraid and sad you are right now. But

I need you to be tough. I need you to help me find the man that hurt your mom."

He held out his hand to her then. There was something about the way he spoke to her that brought her back to herself, something about his eyes that made her trust him right away. He seemed like a superhero to her, ten feet tall and bulletproof. She took his hand without a word and allowed him to lead her back into the house.

Part of her, even now, nearly twenty years later, still thought of him as a superhero. If anyone could fix the wrong things, it was Jeffrey. For a long time, when she realized that she had fallen in love with him and he with her along the way, she kept him at a distance. To love him like that would be to acknowledge him as human, that his heart could stop beating, that the boundaries of his flesh were weak. It was an idea she could barely stand; her fear of losing him had almost caused her to never allow herself to love him at all.

"Are you with me, Lydia? Are you listening?" Dax had taken a large gun from the glove compartment and was handing it to her. "Pull it together, woman. We have to go get your husband out of there."

He had pulled the Rover onto a side street and was leaning over her to get another gun from beneath her seat. It was his big Magnum Desert Eagle, the nasty Israeli gun he favored. It was as big and as loud as a cannon.

"He'll come back to that door," she said.

"But he won't leave without you," Dax said, opening the car door and easing himself onto the street. He looked stiff and as if he was in pain. He went around to the trunk and Lydia saw him take out a crowbar. He stuck the gun in his jacket, kept the crowbar in his hand.

"He'll know I'm out," she said as he came around to her side of the car. "Because we agreed to meet back there when we were done or if something went wrong."

"What if he thinks you got caught?"

"I don't know," she said as they started moving quickly to the alleyway she had used before. She noticed how badly Dax was limping.

"Dax—" she started. He put up a hand.

"No arguments. Let's go."

"I thought you said there was no way in once the gates were down," she said.

"No," he said, giving her an uneasy glance. "I said there was no way to get in *quietly*."

———

Jeffrey wondered if he'd hit the guy too hard, if maybe he'd killed him. He looked young, lying at Jeffrey's feet, a river of blood flowing from his nose. Jeffrey leaned down and put a finger to his neck. He was relieved to feel the blood pumping through his artery. The kid would have a headache, likely a couple of shiners and broken nose. That's what happened when you took the butt of a Glock between the eyes. Jeffrey heard the Nextel beep, and a voice said, "Charley, are you clear? Are you clear?"

Jeffrey took the phone from the kid's waistband. "I'm clear," he said into the mike.

"Good. We need you down at the auditorium. It's possible that there was a second intruder, still on the premises. We need to organize."

"Okay," said Jeffrey.

"How many times do I have to tell you, man?" said the voice snottily. "Ten-four, okay? Ten-four."

"Ten-four," said Jeffrey. What an asshole, he thought. What difference did it make really?

He looked down at Charley. Was he one of the "cleansed" members of The New Day? Was he here of his own free will? Or did he come here for help with his drinking or gambling or depression and get sucked in? He was clean shaven with silky blonde hair that hung in wispy bangs over his eyes. He was skinny to the point of being emaciated with a pouty mouth and long, girlish lashes. Jeffrey put him at nineteen, possibly twenty years old, about a hundred and fifty pounds. He bent down and took the kid by both of his hands and pulled him into a sitting position. With effort he hoisted him over his shoulder. The dead weight was almost too much for him, but something within him wouldn't allow him to leave Charley behind. Not after what he'd seen on those security monitors.

The hallway outside was deserted and he ran as fast as he could with the kid on his back through the foyer. He saw that the front door was barred with security shutters now, likewise the glass walls of the breezeway. They weren't just trying to keep people out, he understood now. They were trying to keep people *in*.

They were waiting for him on the other side, the two large men he'd seen escort Lydia from the building. He pulled the gun from the holster and stuck it into Charley's side.

"I'll kill him," he said as the two men approached. "I've got Black Talon bullets in this gun, they'll rip him apart inside like a circular saw blade."

The men came to a stop. "The bullet goes in, spins around like a

Tasmanian Devil, shredding whatever it comes in contact with until it bounces off a bone and exits like a cannonball. You never know where it's going to come out."

They didn't know if he was telling the truth or not. He widened his eyes to make himself look a little unstable, and started shifting from foot to foot. People didn't like when someone holding a big semi-automatic seemed jittery. They usually wanted him to go away. But these guys were different; they weren't reacting to him. They stood stone-faced, vacant, like they were robots waiting for orders. They weren't afraid for themselves or their friend; they weren't angry. They stood apart to watch him pass, their arms at their sides. Jeffrey passed between them quickly and turned back to face them, backing away. They hadn't moved.

"Leave the boy," one of them said. "And you can leave here without interference."

Jeffrey kept backing away; now he held the gun in their general direction. No reaction whatsoever. He heard footsteps behind him, big people moving quickly. When he turned he saw the man from the abandoned building and his ugly twin, the one Lydia must have seen at the convenience store. They were both bald, clad in leather. They didn't look vacant; they looked disturbed, both of them with these weird half smiles and staring eyes.

"Stop right there, or the kid dies," he said. But they kept coming. So Jeff turned and ran down an empty hallway behind him; all four of the men gave chase. He was heading toward the kitchen, praying that the door was as they had left it, open and waiting for a quick exit. He stopped and fired behind him, the sound exploding off the walls. He heard one round hit flesh and a man started to scream; one of the tunic-clad goons fell to his knees and clutched his arm. The other men took cover but they didn't return fire. Jeffrey kept running, his heart and his lungs on fire. The kid seemed to get heavier and he still hadn't stirred at all.

He saw the double doors of the kitchen ahead of him and heard the pounding feet of the men behind him. He heard an explosion of gunfire in front of him—the hallways reverberated with it. He could see a muzzle flash through the windows in the double doors. Only one gun in the world sounded like that, and he only knew one person who carried it.

The door opened slowly and Dax stepped out, the gun in his hand as big as his forearm. Jeffrey moved to the side as Dax aimed his weapon and started to fire. *Boom. Boom. Boom.* It was deafening and Jeffrey's ears were ringing as he made his way though the maze of industrial-sized appliances. He saw Lydia ahead of him, holding open

the door that looked as though they'd blasted through it. He put the
kid on the floor and together they dragged him under the half-closed
security shutter.

"Go, go, go," yelled Dax, backing toward them quickly, still firing.
They were firing back now but badly, like their hearts weren't it. They
were missing Dax though he was a damn big target.

Outside, Jeffrey hoisted the kid back onto his shoulders as Dax slid
out the door with less grace than he once might have. He got up stiffly
and took what looked like a grenade out of his pocket.

"What are you going to do with that?" Lydia asked as he pulled the
pin. He let it go and rolled it through the door.

"Holy shit," she said, and they all started to move quickly toward
the Rover, Lydia taking up the rear with her gun drawn. Dax was limping badly; Jeffrey was carrying a body. Someone had to keep an eye on
what was coming up behind them. And then the blast rang out. Lydia
felt the vibration in her chest, in her bones.

"Don't worry," said Dax. "It wasn't a grenade, exactly. Not exactly.
More like a flash bomb. More sound than fury, if you know what I
mean."

Nobody came out the door after them. And they made their way
back to the car with no one behind them. Dax unlocked the hatch and
they put Charley in the back of the Rover.

"Who the hell's this?" asked Dax.

"I don't know. His name's Charley. I couldn't leave him there. I
think he's just a kid." They all looked at him for a second; he was still
out but starting to stir.

"Looks like you hit him pretty hard," observed Lydia.

The blood had traveled from his nose and soaked the front of his
white tunic. It looked like spilt tar in the darkness.

"Yeah, I guess I don't know my own strength."

Dax shrugged. "Maybe he knows something."

They got in the car, Lydia and Dax up front, Jeffrey in back with his
gun on the kid. Who knew how he'd behave once he came around; he
was already shifting and groaning softly in pain. Dax gunned the engine and spun the car around, driving fast up the empty street. They
heard the wail of approaching sirens.

"I think we have to call the police," said Jeffrey after a second.

"The people who do the breaking in, shooting, and bombing aren't
usually the ones to call the police, Jeff," said Dax sensibly.

"What did you see in there, Jeffrey?" asked Lydia, looking back at
him.

"On the video monitors, I saw people with shaved heads lying in hospital beds. They were connected to feeding tubes, heart monitors. They were in five-point restraints. They were conscious, Lydia. Wide awake."

For a second they all flashed on the image of the emaciated woman with the shaved head, running for her life through a gathering of witches, dinosaurs, and clowns. Lydia's heart started to race as she imagined the girl's terror, knowing what awaited her if she was caught.

"Did you see Lily?" asked Lydia.

He shook his head. "No."

Lydia took the cell phone out of her pocket and called Matt Stenopolis.

"Stenopolis, I know you didn't just call me at home at nearly eleven o'clock at night to tell me about a conversation you had with some old freak in a nursing home."

Kepler had something in his mouth and he was crunching on it loudly.

"Sir, he says that people are going into that place and not coming out."

"Has it occurred to you, Detective, that they are exiting another door, one the old man can't see from the porch?"

Here's where it got tough. He couldn't tell Kepler what Jeffrey Mark had found while breaking and entering, then shooting his way out of The New Day. That was fruit from a poisonous tree. He couldn't admit to involving them in the case he had been told to walk away from. He had to stick with the Randall Holmes tip, which on its own was pretty weak.

Matt sighed. "It's enough to call in for a warrant, isn't it?"

"Hell, no, it's not enough," said Kepler. "The statement of an old man who, by your admission, is one hammer short of a toolbox is not enough to call a judge at midnight and ask for a warrant."

"Is it enough to call him at nine in the morning?"

"Good-night, Detective."

"Sir, let me ask you, if it turns out that Lily Samuels is in there and we knew that The New Day was already under investigation by the FBI for various other allegations and did nothing to follow up on this lead, do you want to be the one responsible? Because I'm not going to twist for it, Captain."

He could see Kepler turning that shade of red he turned whenever anyone dared to step up to him. Generally a tiny, almost imperceptible twitch would develop just under the lashes of his right lower eyelid.

"And are you prepared to turn in your shield if she's not in there?" he asked, his voice quiet but white hot with anger.

Matt let out a long breath; it was so unfair and stupid. "No, I'm not. It shouldn't come down to that. I'm just trying to do my job, sir."

There was silence on the other line. Matt put his head in his hand. This conversation was not good for his career.

"Go get your warrant, Stenopolis. And you know what? If she's not in there, you're going to be in uniform doing the shittiest, most demeaning details I can find in this city until you die or I do."

Matt felt something loosen inside. "Thank you, sir."

The line went dead.

He just didn't get Kepler sometimes. It seemed to annoy him when people were trying to do their jobs; he always seemed to be hindering rather than facilitating. Unless it was a big, high-profile case that brought positive attention to the precinct. But the Lily Samuels case had been that, two weeks ago. Then everyone started getting the vibe that she had taken off on her own, and Kepler had put it on the back burner. Maybe he just didn't like admitting through his actions that he might have been wrong to give up so fast. Whatever. Matt speed-dialed Jez.

"What's up," she answered. That's all it took. He could tell in her tone, strained and tired, that she was upset. That didn't take long, he thought. When she was on her own, she was very even tempered most of the time. When Dylan was back in the picture, she was up and down . . . always elated or depressive.

"Hey, I think we have a lead on where Lily Samuels might be," he said.

"You're kidding," she answered, her tone brightening.

"No, can you get your mother to stay with Ben? Meet me at the Fiftieth Precinct."

He could hear the covers rustling as she got out of bed. "It might take me an hour or so."

"No problem. I gotta call in for a warrant."

"What happened?"

"I'll tell you all about it."

Fourteen

"This is a direct violation of my client's first amendment rights," said Jude Templar. He was a tall, svelte young man with a drawn, pale face and an unsettling pair of jet-black eyes. Matt was used to seeing him in thousand-dollar suits but tonight he wore baggy jeans with calfskin loafers and a soft fleece jersey, zipped at the neck. Even so he had that easy air, the polished and pressed look of the very rich. A pair of wire-rimmed glasses made him look older, more intellectual than maybe he was. He wore them low on his long, thin nose and looked at Matt over their edge.

"Tonight, three people broke into this facility. They damaged property, shot at security guards. And now you have the nerve to show up here with a warrant as if *these* people are the criminals."

He'd arrived with two squad cars from the Fiftieth Precinct. Two of the cops who accompanied him had been there an hour earlier investigating a report of a break-in and shooting. But since The New Day had a reputation in the neighborhood as being freaks and weirdos, it had been kind of a half-assed visit. They basically just took a report and returned to the precinct to make fun of the Moonies. What interested Matt the most was that there was no mention made of the kid Jeffrey Mark had carried from the church.

"Mr. Templar, we have information that leads us to believe that Lily Samuels is being held here against her will. And that she's not the only one."

"That's preposterous," Templar said with a disdainful laugh. "Detective, I'd like your shield number."

"Mr. Templar, I'm not a rookie," he said slowly. "Please do not try to intimidate me."

Jude Templar was a well-known New York lawyer, famed for his associations with the dregs of high society. Basketball player accused of rape? Rock star with a gun shooting up a downtown club? Supermodel caught with crack? Jude Templar was your man. As long as you were rich, he could get you off. Question was, what was he doing representing Trevor Rhames?

Matt had been standing on the walkway leading up to the church, Templar three steps above him on the stoop. Matt walked up the stairs and towered over the lawyer.

"Now who's using intimidation tactics?" he asked, taking a step back to look up at Matt.

"Mr. Templar, I don't *need* to use intimidation tactics. I have a legal right to be here and if you get in my way, I'll be arresting you for interfering with an investigation."

Templar turned a steely gaze on Matt, then stepped away from the door he'd been blocking with his body. Matt walked inside and found an empty foyer.

"I'd like to speak with Trevor Rhames," he said.

"I am afraid that's not possible. My client is out of town."

"Since when?"

Templar looked at his watch, a platinum job blinding Matt with diamonds. "Since about an hour ago. After the break-in, which the police seemed to care very little about, he felt that his personal security was in jeopardy."

"Where did he go?"

"My client is a citizen of the United States. He is entitled to go where he wishes and he is entitled to his privacy. In other words, Detective, it's none of your goddamned business."

"Interesting choice of words," said Matt. He could find out where Rhames was later. He heard a car pull up, a door slam, and the quick, important stride of his partner on the walkway.

"Oh, lookie here," she said as she entered. Jesamyn had had run-ins with Templar in the past. Ugly ones. She hated his guts.

"Detective Breslow," he said with a solemn nod.

"Hey, Templar. Why are pharmaceutical companies using lawyers now instead of rats in their laboratories?"

He gave her a look.

"Because some people actually *like* rats."

Jude Templar rolled his eyes. He pulled his face into a mask of disdain and annoyance and kept it that way as he sat in a chair behind the reception desk and made himself comfortable. He held out his hand

and Matt handed him the warrant to search the premises. He glanced at it and put it down on the desk, gave Matt a small nod.

"Let's do this," said Matt. He motioned for the uniformed officers and the two other detectives who had driven up with Jesamyn to enter the building.

Templar pulled a pack of Dunhill cigarettes from the pocket of his jeans, extracted one and lit it with a lighter.

"That'll kill you," said Matt.

"Not fast enough," said Jesamyn sweetly.

"Well, we all seem hell-bent on behavior that's going to hurt us tonight, don't we?" said Templar.

An hour later, his smile had widened as the search turned up nothing. The computers had been wiped clean. File cabinets had been emptied. There was no garbage in the wastebaskets or in the Dumpsters outside. The security nerve center Jeffrey Mark had described seemed to consist of only a few outdoor cameras broadcasting on four of the twenty monitors. The other monitors seemed not to be in operation. The computer that controlled them had no operating system. When it was turned on, there was just a black screen with a thin cursor blinking on the upper left-hand side, waiting for a prompt no one on the premises knew how to give.

Matt called in for some computer experts but he wasn't all that interested in The New Day. He was interested in finding Lily. And he didn't think what they had found on those systems would bring them any closer to her. But he could be wrong. He hoped he was.

Templar identified the building across the breezeway as a dormitory for church members and employees, where members could *choose* to live with a small stipend in exchange for work on behalf of The New Day but were certainly not *forced* to live. Only about 20 percent of the rooms were occupied. The rest of the rooms were clean and empty, beds and desks awaiting tenants.

Most of the members on the premises were young, in their twenties and thirties. Some were disturbed from their sleep, others were playing cards in a rec center. None of them seemed under duress. Jesamyn and one of the other detectives set about rounding them up in a single room and one by one taking them into another space to ask questions. Who were they? How did they come to be living there? Where were the rest of the New Day members? Had anyone seen Lily Samuels?

"What exactly did you expect to find here, Detective?" said Templar with flat eyes and a mirthless smile. Matt had returned to the foyer, frustration and disappointment lodged in his throat like a chicken bone.

He turned on Templar quickly. "We have computer experts on their way. They have ways of retrieving deleted data."

It sounded weak and desperate even to his own ears.

"This is an organization that *helps* people, Detective. You'll find no evidence to the contrary."

Matt was just barely holding onto his temper. He looked the lawyer over and figured he could lift the little ferret off the ground by the collar of his shirt, shake him until all the money fell out of his pockets.

"Really," he said instead. "Helps people by keeping them in five-point restraints, hooked up to feeding tubes and stealing all their money."

Templar's smile turned to granite. "Is that what Randall Holmes told you, Detective Stenopolis?"

Matt didn't say anything.

"It wasn't *his* tip that led you to come here in the middle of the night, was it?"

Matt took a long, slow breath. "Listen to me," he said, his voice little more than a whisper. "You tell Trevor Rhames that I want Lily Samuels back or I'm going to tear the roof off of The New Day. I'll use every resource I have at my disposal."

Templar rose from his seat and leaned on the desk in front of him.

"I wouldn't advise you to start issuing threats to Trevor Rhames. It's not healthy."

"I know that I didn't just hear you threaten a New York City police officer," said Jesamyn, coming up behind them. "I know you're not that stupid. Are you, Templar?"

He gave her a cold, assessing look and Jesamyn squared off, stuck her chin out at him in a dare.

"The New Day has no knowledge of Lily Samuels or her whereabouts," he said. "You have no evidence otherwise. So, you'll desist from harassing my client."

"That's not exactly true. Because we have an eyewitness who places Lily at this church just days before she was reported missing."

"An old man in a nursing home with poor eyesight and documented dementia." Matt glanced at the cellular phone sitting on the desk where Templar had been sitting. The boy had been busy.

"We have a photograph of Lily running from a van bearing the emblem of The New Day on Halloween night."

Jude Templar blinked at that but said nothing.

"We have reports of a black SUV waiting for Lily as she withdrew all of her money from Chase Manhattan bank and we've linked its license plate to the owner. I think it will only be a matter of time before we can connect her to The New Day."

Another reptilian blink from the lawyer.

"I'm also aware of the allegations leveled against Rhames and The New Day since its inception in 1977."

"Allegations which were never substantiated," Templar said, looking at his cuticles.

"I want Lily Samuels and I'm going to do whatever it takes to get her back," Matt said, leaning into Templar, putting his face so close to the lawyer that he could smell his cologne. He felt Jesamyn's hand on his arm.

"Mount—" she started, looking uneasily at Templar and then back at him, but he lifted a hand.

"Be careful, Detective," said Templar. "Be very careful."

Templar reached for the phone he'd left on the desk, never taking his eyes off Matt. "I'll wait outside until you're done with your pointless, fruitless search. But our conversation is officially over. And, if you don't stay away from me, so is your pathetic career."

Matt pointed to the ceiling. "The roof," he said. "Right the fuck off."

Templar turned his back and left.

"Take it easy, Mount," whispered Jez. "You coming unglued or what?"

He looked at her and she had genuine worry in her eyes.

"She was here," he said to her. "I can feel it. She's still alive."

Jesamyn stared at him, opened her mouth like she was going to say something and then clamped it shut. They stared at each other for a second.

"If she was here, if she's still alive, we'll find her," she said, her voice soothing and sure.

"How?" he yelled, causing Jesamyn to jump a little in surprise. "There's *nothing* here. We're too late."

He looked at her a second, felt briefly bad for yelling at her, and then turned his back and walked away toward the breezeway. After a second, he heard her running after him.

"Maybe not," she said. "You have to talk to some of these people."

"Why," he said, turning. "You got something?"

"I don't know. They seem normal enough at first. But the longer you talk to them, the weirder they get. Mount, there's something wrong with these people. Something really wrong with them."

Usually when people woke up in a room with Dax, there was some kind of a powerful reaction. But Charley opened his eyes, registered Dax's presence, and was as placid as a lamb. He sat up on the cot they'd placed him on, taking the ice pack off his face, and asked politely for some water. Dax complied.

"How are you feeling, Charley?" Dax asked when he returned with a frosty bottle of water. He removed the lid and handed it to Charley.

"Not very well," he answered. He drank gingerly, as if the action pained him. "My head hurts."

Charley looked like a raccoon. His eyes were so purple and swollen that Dax was surprised he could even open his lids. The ridge on his nose told Dax that Charley's nose was broken and that he'd never be quite as pretty again.

"So let's have a little chat," said Dax, straddling a chair he'd placed beside the cot. Charley slid back on the cot, rested his back against the bare white wall and pulled his legs into a half-lotus position, as if nothing could please him more than having a little chat. He gave Dax a peaceful half-smile.

"Let's start with the fact that your name's not Charley," said Dax, softly. "It's James. James Rainer."

Charley blinked slowly. "You're mistaken," he said. "My name is Charley."

"Your name is James Rainer, known as Jamie to your friends. You're twenty-two years old and were reported missing by your parents eight months ago. You were last seen leaving a party at the Tribeca loft belonging to your girlfriend. You were angry, upset, drunk."

Two more long, slow blinks. He said calmly, "You're mistaken."

"Okay," said Dax. "You tell me then, friend. Where were you born?"

He shook his head quickly and answered without hesitation.

"My New Day dawned on April 3rd of this year. I am reborn as the Universe intended me, free of attachments and addictions."

Dax looked at him. Charley was calm, certain of his statement, his half-smile unwavering. He looked at Dax with clear blue eyes beneath the purple shiners. His skin had a milky quality to it and it was pulled taut over a jutting collarbone, shoulder knobs that pressed through the cotton on his tunic, pronounced cheekbones. His hands looked skeletal.

"And before that?"

"There is nothing before that." He lifted a bony hand and ran it through his silky blonde hair; it fell like sand through his fingers. Dax saw Charley's eyes shift down and to the right, as they tend to when a person is trying to remember something or to make sense of a confusing situation. There was something delicate, effeminate about him.

Dax smiled kindly, slid his chair in a little closer.

"Your girlfriend, Amanda Knight, told police that on the night you disappeared you admitted to her that you were gay. That the relationship you'd been carrying on with her was more of a sham for your parents than anything. And though you cared for her as a friend, you didn't love her in the way she loved you.

"You told her, James, in a room full of the friends you shared, that the only way you could become aroused with her was to imagine that she was another man. You were drunk at the time, James, terribly drunk and furious with her, with yourself, with your parents. Friends tried to stop you from leaving, but you fought them off. They never saw you again."

A slight quiver had started on Charley's bottom lip.

"Do you remember?"

"You are mistaken."

Dax waited a second and listened as Charley's breathing became labored.

"I don't know how you heard about The New Day," Dax said, keeping his voice measured and calm. "Maybe the Internet, maybe an ad on the subway. But to someone who was as lost, as headlong into personal crisis as you were, James, it must have seemed like a safe haven. Maybe you went to them. Maybe they came to you."

Charley didn't say anything right away. His eyes had taken on a kind of glazed-over look, like he had disappeared into himself.

"I was lost," he said. "I walked blindly for so long trying to make sense of all my pain. And then The New Day dawned. Everything that came before is darkness, like the time before birth."

His words had the practiced quality of a mantra. He knew them by rote, like he'd spoken them a thousand times. Dax let a few beats pass before talking again.

"About two weeks after you dropped out of your life, you showed up at the bank and withdrew all your money. Cashed in your CDs and money market accounts, cleared out your savings and checking. You had quite a bit of money for a young guy, between a trust from your wealthy uncle and the money you were raking in as a trader on Wall

Street. Nearly a quarter of a million dollars. You took a cashier's check when they couldn't give you cash."

"I have no need for money any longer. It's a drug, you only want more and more. There's never enough, there's nothing you won't do for it. We're junkies for the green stuff, all of us."

Dax took a picture from his pocket and handed it to Charley. It was a picture of Mickey with his girlfriend Mariah.

"Do you know these people?"

Charley laid his eyes on the photo briefly and shook his head. He tried to rub his eyes then pulled his hand away quickly and groaned at the pain he caused himself. He reached for the ice pack that lay beside him and put it back to his forehead. Dax thought it was notable that the kid never once asked where he was, who Dax was, or what the hell had happened to his head. He seemed to accept his surroundings and situation without question.

"How about this girl?" Dax asked, handing him another photo, this time of Lily Samuels. Another quick shake of his head, a shift of the eyes.

"I'm tired," he said.

"Okay, James. I'm going to give you a little time to think."

He walked over to the table that sat in the center of the room and took the article he'd printed off the Internet, complete with a picture of James Rainer. He placed it next to Charley on the cot.

"When you're feeling up to it, why don't you read this article? I'll be back in a little while."

He left the room then and locked the door behind him. He walked into an adjacent room where Lydia and Jeffrey were watching through a two-way mirror. They were in Dax's dungeon, as Lydia liked to call it, that mysterious maze of rooms in his basement that was an endless source of fascination for Lydia.

Dax saw as he entered the darkened room that Charley sat perfectly still and hadn't made a move for the article.

"We better take it easy on him," said Dax. "With that kind of conditioning, he could crack up, get lost forever in there." He tapped his temple.

"We might need a professional," said Lydia. It had taken her about a half an hour on the Internet searching stories on missing young men to come up with the website James Rainer's parents had posted, the articles that had run in the wake of his disappearance, the blogs from friends who recounted the night he'd disappeared, pleas from people who wanted him to know that they loved him and wanted him home no matter what. Jeffrey had recognized the picture from before his eyes had turned purple and swollen.

"Like a cult deprogrammer?" asked Jeffrey.

She nodded. "But first, we need to get in touch with his family."

"Well," said Dax, reluctantly. "Once we do that, we're going to lose him."

"Dax," said Lydia, looking at him incredulous. "You're implying that we keep him here and only let his family know when we're done with him?"

He shrugged. "He's been missing for eight months. Another day or two isn't going to kill them."

"Jesus, Dax," said Lydia. "Are you even human?"

Another shrug. "That kid's the only thing we got out of our botched visit to The New Day."

"Not quite," said Jeffrey. He took the blank visitor's page from his pocket and laid it on the table. Dax and Lydia leaned in.

"Oh, good. So we have this blank piece of paper, too," said Dax. "Congratulations, detective, you cracked the case."

Jeffrey gave him a look and sat down at the round metal table that stood in the corner of the room. He flattened the page out in front of him and turned on the halogen lamp, which shone a bright, direct beam onto the paper.

"You can see the indentation of writing from the page that was above this one on the clipboard. It's a visitor's log."

Dax opened a drawer in the table and took out a pencil. He sat down beside Jeffrey and slid the paper away from him.

"Let me have it," he said.

"Don't fuck it up," said Lydia, leaning over his shoulder.

Slowly, as Dax delicately shaded over the page, a list of names in a long scrawling hand started to appear in relief. Much of it was illegible, the impressions from the handwriting above uneven in the pressure applied. They could make out some common surnames, like Walsh, Smith, Jones.

Lydia looked away in frustration and noticed Charley reaching for the article beside him. She watched as his eyes scanned the page and his hand started to shake. She started to wonder if maybe they shouldn't have left that for him to read. Maybe it was too much for him, to see it in black and white. She was about to say something when Jeffrey said,

"Whoa, is that who I think it is?" He reached into his coat pocket and took out his glasses.

Lydia looked down at the page and saw what he had seen. Just then, Charley began to cry.

"You have no right to take these people into custody," said Jude Templar on the walkway. He'd jumped out of his Jag when he saw the van approaching and the members of The New Day began filing out of the building. He approached the van's back door as Matt and a couple of the uniformed officers led the New Day members out into the cold. Everyone was getting tired, the sun starting to make its debut over the horizon. Even Templar was starting to look a little wiped out, a little frayed.

Their search of The New Day buildings had yielded nothing immediate. But they'd spent the last couple of hours interviewing each of the few members they'd found on the premises. But talking to one of them was like talking to a radio. Their programming was *not* interactive. Finally, in frustration, Matt had called in for a van and told the members that they were going to the Fiftieth Precinct for further interviews. No one objected.

"I'm not taking them into custody," said Matt calmly. "I'm taking them in for questioning. There's a big difference."

At this point, Templar threw up his hands and walked toward his Jag.

"Don't say I didn't warn you, Detective," he said over his shoulder. "And you'll be seeing me again in a few hours with a court order to release these innocent people."

"Okay," said Mount with a friendly wave. "See you then."

Jesamyn had this low-level anxiety over the way Mount was antagonizing Templar. It was her opinion that when it came to snakes like Templar, it was always better to stay out of striking distance. Matt was poking him with a short stick.

She watched as the six members of The New Day filed into the van with a weird calm. Not one of them ever asked what was happening to them or where they were going. The sight of them made Jesamyn shudder; their vacancy and docility unsettled her.

At the unfamiliar Fiftieth Precinct, Jesamyn found some terrible coffee in the break room and then asked around for a computer. She wound up being escorted to the desk of one of the homicide detectives who would not be in for another few hours. Someone who knew him well, a young black detective in his twenties with broad shoulders and a shy smile, logged her onto the machine using Detective Winslow's password. As he did this, she stared at a picture sitting on the desk. It was one of those Sears family portraits featuring a big grizzly of a man Jesamyn assumed was Detective Charles Winslow, his petite and lovely red-headed wife and teenage twin daughters. The girls wore coordinating floral dresses, their hair swept up in matching French twists. Mrs. Detective wore a plain cream silk blouse open at the neck to reveal a strand of pearls. They all smiled brightly. They looked so normal to Jesamyn, so solid. She found herself envying them, wishing she and Dylan could have given normal and solid to Benjamin.

Oh, snap out of it, she was thinking to herself as she thanked the detective. Cute. Too young. She turned her attention to the computer and found the FBI's Missing Persons website. She didn't have any real names, so she'd have to sift through pictures and hope for a stroke of luck until Matt was able to get some real names to go on. If he was able to.

She scrolled through picture after picture of missing young men and women, sipping on the bitter, tepid coffee. A young Korean girl who'd left a Halloween party on her Pennsylvania college campus and was never seen again, a young man who'd gone to Argentina as an exchange student who was last seen walking the streets of Bariloche in Rio Negro, a young woman last seen jogging in her parents' Texas subdivision at 11:30 in the morning while home on Christmas vacation. The list went on, tiny thumbnail pictures of smiling faces that she clicked on to learn the details of each disappearance.

Jesamyn was getting that sick, hollow feeling she got when she searched this database. Where were these people, so many of them children and teenagers, so many of them young women? She thought of what would happen to her world if she went to pick up Benji one day and he wasn't there, the teacher saying, "Oh, his dad/uncle/cousin, picked him up." Or if she let him go to the store for her the way he always begged her to, and he never came home. She'd created a thousand scenarios like this, lived them a million times in her heart. She imagined seeing his face on a computer screen like this. Her throat was dry just at the thought of it. It was this job that made her overprotective of her son. Because she knew the worst could happen, saw it every day, no matter what the statistics said.

She was in the middle of her nightmare fantasy when she saw a face she recognized and her heart leapt . . . a girl with long dark hair, a round sweet face, and deep jet eyes. She'd told them her name was

Carla; she was twenty pounds thinner now, at least, her hair shaved tight to her head. But it was the eyes that gave her away, mournful, thickly lashed. Jessica Rawlins of Gatlinburg, Tennessee had been missing since January of that year. She'd told them that her "New Day dawned on January 30th" when they asked her date of birth. According to the FBI, she'd been born on May 10th, 1982. She'd left her college campus one evening, no one knew why. Friends said she'd been depressed since the death of her father not quite a year earlier, that she'd been drinking too much. But no one feared her to be suicidal; she never talked about walking away from her life. When she didn't return to her dorm that January night, her roommate called the police. There was a $75,000 reward for information leading to her return home. Jesamyn felt happy for a second; today was going to be a good day for Jessica Rawlin's family. A very good day.

Fifteen

Tim Samuels looked as if he had aged ten years since the last time they saw him. Their visit this time was a surprise; though it was well past noon he clearly hadn't showered or combed his hair. It was apparently a look he'd been cultivating for days by the smell of him. His face was a mask of stubble and deep lines. He wasn't happy to see them. No one was ever happy to see them the second time.

"I wasn't expecting you," he said when he came to the door.

"Can we talk, Mr. Samuels?" asked Lydia.

He narrowed his eyes at her. "That depends."

"On?"

"On what you have to say," he said nastily.

Gone was the hospitable, helpful, and concerned father. Tim Samuels looked like a man on the edge, someone who'd abandoned the petty civilities that help people to get along with others. He had an aura of unstable belligerence. This was Lydia's cue to step back and let Jeffrey do the talking. She didn't deal well with unpleasant people; they tended to make her behave unpleasantly, which never helped matters.

"Mr. Samuels," said Jeffrey quietly. "We know you visited The New Day building sometime in the past week. We need to ask you about that visit because when last we spoke you told us that you'd never heard of that organization."

He stared at them blankly.

"I don't know what you're talking about," he said.

"Are you sure, Mr. Samuels? Because so far we haven't gone to the police with this information. But we will."

"You can go to the police with whatever you want. I've never heard of The New Day," he said, and slammed the door so hard, the small glass panes along the top rattled.

"There's a videotape, Mr. Samuels," Jeffrey said loudly to the door. "It shows you entering a building in Riverdale owned and occupied by New Day members."

This was a lie but it seemed to have the desired effect. Samuels opened the door a crack.

"Do yourselves a favor and get out of here right now," he whispered desperately. "Don't make me talk to you about this. I guarantee you'll both be sorry."

"We're already in pretty deep," said Jeffrey. "We broke into the building last night, created some chaos, rescued one of their members. If these people have Lily, Mr. Samuels, she's in big, big trouble. Please. Talk to us."

Samuels closed his eyes and when he opened them again, two tears trailed down his face.

"Oh, God," he said. "What have I done?"

Before paying Tim Samuels another visit, Lydia and Jeffrey had returned James to his parents. Lydia had called the number on the website and asked to speak to Mr. Rainer.

"Mr. Rainer," she said when he came on the line. "My name is Lydia Strong. Do you know who I am?"

"Uh, yes," he said. "I do. You're the true crime writer." She heard the mingling of hope and dread in his German-accented English. It was a tone she recognized in the families of victims. They knew her involvement would generate publicity that might well bring justice or answers. But they also knew that tentatively healing wounds would be reopened, that reignited hopes might be shattered once again.

"I want you to know that in the commission of an investigation we've found your son, James Rainer."

She heard him make a sharp inhale and a long slow exhale. "Please," he said. "This is not a joke?"

She heard a woman's voice in the background.

"No," she said quickly. "We have reason to believe that your son joined an organization called The New Day to help himself with some of his problems."

"The New Day," Mr. Rainer repeated as if in a daze. The woman's voice in the background grew louder, more urgent.

"We infiltrated this group in the search for another missing person, a young woman. We encountered your son and removed him against his will from the premises."

"Against his will?"

"Yes, Mr. Rainer."

It took a while to make him understand what had happened to his son and that the road home was going to be more difficult than just arranging a place to meet. She tried to explain that he called himself Charley now and that he might not acknowledge them until he'd gotten some help, to undo the things that had been done to him at The New Day. But she wasn't quite sure he understood her. He just seemed dazed and a little confused as he shared the news with his wife, who started to weep.

"I've arranged to have him accepted to a psychiatric facility in New York City," she said when Mr. Rainer returned to the phone. "It's the best possible place for him right now."

"I—I can't afford that. I'm sorry. We'll have to help James here at home."

She'd already anticipated that.

"I've taken care of the expense, Mr. Rainer," said Lydia. "And I just want you to do one thing for me. When he's well, if we haven't found Lily Samuels, I'd just like to talk to him again."

She heard him sigh on the other end. "I can't," he said, his voice growing strained with tears, "express my gratitude."

Lydia had made a late-night call to Irma Fox, a child psychiatrist she had met through Ford McKirdy, a retired homicide detective whom she and Jeff had worked with on the Julian Ross case last year. Irma was unlucky enough to be the only shrink in Lydia's Palm Pilot and Lydia recalled her having mentioned doing cult deprogramming work with adolescents and young adults in their late teens. On hearing the situation, Irma was very quick to accommodate Lydia, calling back immediately to say that a bed could be arranged for James Rainer that night at a facility on the Upper West Side. The cost was exorbitant. But Lydia figured it was the least they could do, since Jeffrey had practically killed the kid and Dax had pumped him so full of Xanax to calm him that James was nearly catatonic.

Tim Samuels wasn't looking much better than James had when they dropped him off, beaten and drugged and about to undergo the worst few weeks of his life.

"This is what they do," said Samuels in his living room. The beautifully appointed space was a mess. The couch was being used as a bed. Half-empty glasses and cups with congealed liquid, dirty plates crusted with dried food, and empty fast food containers occupied most available spaces. The shades had been drawn against the view and the room had an unpleasant odor.

"Who?"

"The New Day. They ruin. What they can't possess, they destroy."

He put his head in his hands and started to weep. It sounded a little forced and pathetic to Lydia, but then she didn't have a lot of patience for sobbing men.

"Where's your wife?" she said. He looked up at her.

"She left." He sighed and hung his head. "She can't stand the sight of me."

Lydia bit back an impolite comment but he must have seen it on her face.

"Yeah, imagine that. Right?" he said.

Lydia raised her eyebrows at him but said nothing.

"Time for you to come clean with us, Mr. Samuels," said Jeffrey, sitting across from him. "For Lily's sake. And by the looks of it, for yours too."

"You don't understand," he said, looking up at them with red-rimmed eyes.

Jeffrey showed Samuels his palms. "Make me understand. Make me understand what's happening here."

Tim Samuels was desperately unhappy. So he had an affair with a twenty-two-year-old stripper and bought a Ferrari. When that didn't work, he went looking for God.

"I just started getting this feeling like everything worth doing was already behind me," he said quietly. He looked beaten as he sipped from the glass of ice water Lydia had fetched him from the kitchen.

"The kids were grown, living their lives. Much more fulfilling, exciting lives than I ever dreamed of, I might add. Monica and I, we love each other, you know. She's my best friend. But after twenty-five years, things were not exactly hot . . . if you know what I mean."

Lydia hoped he wasn't going to go into detail and she shifted in her seat on the couch across from him. Jeffrey stood by the hearth, watching Samuels in that way that he had. Listening carefully, critically. Looking for all the cues that Lydia looked for, the shifting eyes, the tapping foot. It was the furtive gesture, the uneasy glance, the unconscious tick that told you the most about a person. Words were chosen. But the body never lied. Tim Samuels gave her the impression of someone who'd been crushed. He slumped in his chair like he didn't even have the energy to sit upright anymore.

"When I retired a year and a half ago, sold my business, I made a killing. I mean like, more money than I ever dreamed of."

He let out a little laugh. "It was what I had worked for my entire life . . . to have enough money so that I didn't have to work. It took about a year of golfing and drinking, sleeping late, watching soaps, to realize that I didn't know anything about myself. All my life I had always done what I was told to do, the right thing, work hard, marry well, send your children to college. I was always so busy working, or working on the house, or raising the kids, or taking care of my marriage. I'd never had any time to really think about myself, my life. Do you know how scary that is? To realize that your life is more than half over and that you are a stranger to yourself? It scared the shit out of me."

He was looking at them both with pleading eyes. He wanted compassion, sympathy. Jeffrey nodded solemnly and sat on the hearth.

"I understand," he said. Lydia looked at him and back to Tim Samuels. She couldn't imagine two men more different.

It seemed like Samuels' generation of men, men in their late fifties, early sixties, had been robbed in a way, that they'd never really been given the tools to be happy. They'd been taught to work, to provide for their families, to accrue wealth. But no one had really taught them how to love, how to reflect, how to communicate. So many of them held onto sexism, racism, elitism as crutches to make themselves feel better, feel bigger. They seemed clueless to Lydia, lost and wandering with these outdated ideas in their heads and unexpressed emotions in their chests and no idea what to do with either of them.

"So I'm embarrassed to say I started acting like a typical jackass having a midlife crisis. I bought a 575M Maranello Ferrari, started staying out late or not coming home at all. I met this young girl at a strip club in the city; she made me feel like I was twenty-one again." A wide smile spread across his face as he thought of her. Lydia felt like smacking it off his face.

"Mariah," said Lydia, fishing the picture from her pocket.

He hung his head and didn't say anything for a second. "I didn't know her as Mariah. I knew her as Marilyn."

"But you recognized her when we showed you the picture?" asked Jeffrey.

He nodded. "Yes."

"Where was your wife during all of this?" asked Lydia.

"Here. She kicked me out; I stayed in the city. A friend of mine divides his year between New York and Paris. He has a nice place on Park Avenue South. For a few months, I was having a ball . . . hot car, hot woman, clubs every night. Then suddenly, it all started to seem a little hollow."

"Imagine that," said Lydia. Out of the corner of her eye, she saw Jeffrey shoot her a look. It wasn't a good idea to be judgmental when someone was spilling his guts. You might dam the flow. "Sorry," she said.

"No," said Samuels. "You're right. I walked away from this beautiful life that Monica and I had constructed over twenty-five years together, looking for whatever it was I imagined was missing. And then I realized that the only thing missing was gratitude. But it was too late. It's amazingly easy to walk away from your life; it's almost impossible to go back. When you tear the fabric of trust, it never feels the same again."

He released a heavy sigh, seemed to sink even deeper into his chair.

"So by then I was lower than when I started what I called my 'vision quest.' That's when Marilyn told me about The New Day."

Lydia leaned forward. "Did you join?"

"She took me up to Riverdale and I met some of the members at this old house off of Broadway behind the train yards."

Lydia nodded. "We've been there. Mariah or Marilyn—her real name was Michele LaForge—had that address on her driver's license. We received information that a black SUV was seen waiting outside the bank for Lily as she closed all of her accounts. That vehicle was registered to Michele LaForge."

He nodded. "I see," he said. He looked at some space on the wall behind Lydia. Maybe imagining Lily at the bank, with Michele waiting outside.

"So what happened at the house?" asked Jeffrey.

"I'll tell you what. It's a powerful message. They make a lot of sense. They tell you that everything you've been taught will make you happy is exactly the opposite of true. Possessions, the craving for more possessions, attachments to unhealthy relationships, media-generated low self-esteem, chronic busyness are elements of the deep sense of despair so many people feel. Most people are completely divorced from themselves. I really related to it, considering how I was feeling when I left Monica. And how none of the things I'd done to make myself feel better had helped."

Lydia nodded. The message *was* powerful, because it was so deeply true. But The New Day was only using that truth as a hook for desperate people . . . not to help them, to *own* them.

"After meeting with her friends a couple of times, Trevor Rhames sent for me. We talked for *hours*. I told him things about myself, about my life, that I had never told anyone else."

"Did you drink the tea they gave you?"

He looked at her, surprised. "Yes, I did."

"We had it analyzed," said Jeffrey. "It contains a very mild tranquilizer. Nothing that would knock you out and nothing that you would notice more than, say, if you'd taken a cold medicine. But it makes you very relaxed, very receptive to suggestion. A psychiatrist might prescribe it before a session of hypnosis."

He nodded. "That makes sense. Because, you know, they never force you to stay. You can always leave when you want to, at first. But the more often you go back, the more you talk to Rhames and the other members, the less you want to go each time, until finally you find yourself staying at the dorm."

"Is that what happened to you?"

"Yes," he nodded. "If you stayed, you were given a job the next day, something easy like dusting or emptying wastepaper baskets. They gave you a clean set of clothes, this cotton tunic and blue jeans, a pair of flip flops. You feel so peaceful, so relaxed . . . but it's more than that. It's like this low-grade euphoria. You've *found* the way. Then it was the next day and the next day."

A kind of a half-smile had spread across his face as he remembered the experience. He'd moved up in his chair and leaned into them. He looked back and forth between their faces.

"But you left eventually," said Lydia.

He nodded.

"I saw something that frightened me," he said, his brow wrinkling. "I saw horrible things. I was cleaning floors and I walked into a room filled with computers and closed-circuit monitors."

He put his head in his hands.

"I saw it, too," said Jeffrey. "The people in restraints, on feeding tubes."

"Their heads shaved, their eyes open in terror," he said, his voice low. The room had taken on a kind of hush and no one spoke for a moment.

"What did you do?" asked Lydia softly.

"I stopped drinking the tea," he said, giving her a small smile.

"Suddenly, the euphoria was gone and I felt like a prisoner, even though ostensibly I could leave at any time. I realized that I had told them virtually every intimate detail of my life. I had told them every mistake I ever made and, believe me, there were some big ones."

He released a shuddering sigh that seemed to come from deep inside of him.

"I was afraid then, afraid to leave. But when Rhames asked to see me, started talking about my turning assets over to The New Day and entering the 'cleansing' phase of my initiation, I realized that the whole thing was just a scam, just a way to steal people's money. I got mad. I flipped out."

"How did Rhames react?" asked Lydia.

"Very calmly," said Samuels. "I was ranting and screaming and he was just sitting. We were in this room with the door locked. It was dim, so he flipped on a light that sat on his desk and he slid this file over to me. I took it and opened it."

He didn't say anything, just stared at the blank space on the wall behind Lydia.

"What was in it?" she asked finally.

"Everything," he said. "Everything about me, about Monica, about Lily and Mickey. There were copies of my tax returns, medical records, account numbers. It was a complete dossier."

His breathing came quickly now, labored and slightly raspy. "He said to me, 'It's too late, my friend. You've shed this life. It belongs to me now.' I told him to go fuck himself and I walked out of there. No one stopped me. I went back to Monica. I didn't tell her about The New Day. I begged her to forgive me. She let me move back in and promised to work on our marriage but no guarantees. I changed all my bank accounts and was terrified for a few weeks. I called some of the guys that used to work for my security firm and I asked them to hang around me and Monica, Lily and Mickey. After a few days with no incident, I started to think everything was going to be all right. And for a while, it was."

He laughed a little at his own stupidity.

"I don't understand. Why didn't you just go to the police and tell them about The New Day?" asked Lydia.

He laughed again; it sounded hard and angry like the bark of a dog. "With what they knew about me? Not an option."

"What did they know about you?"

He shook his head. "Sorry. I'm not falling for that again."

Lydia looked at him and thought he had the aura of a kite with its line cut, as if there was nothing to hold him to this world.

"Then slowly," he said, "they started to take my world apart."

He sighed and rubbed his eyes. "First, I was notified that I was being audited by the IRS for the period of fifteen years during which I owned the security firm. My tax attorney who'd been with me since 1980 told me, 'Hey, buddy, don't worry about it. We'll handle it.' I was relieved. He was a powerful guy, had a way of making problems disappear, if you know what I mean. The next night, he was mugged and died from a gunshot wound to the heart. All my records disappeared from his office."

"So what happened?" asked Jeffrey when he didn't go on.

"Nothing yet. I had copies of everything here at my house. My meeting with them is scheduled for next week." He smiled quickly.

He slumped back down in his chair, as if he'd been drained of all his energy in the telling of his tale.

"Then Mickey committed suicide, and Lily disappeared. Monica was nearly psychotic with grief, medicated to the point of catatonia. I was alone, on the verge of losing everything. Still part of me refused to believe that The New Day was behind it. Part of me believed it was punishment for my selfishness, my foolishness, all the crimes and sins of my life."

"When did you come to believe differently?" asked Lydia.

"When you came to see me, started asking me about The New Day."

"Is that why you went there?"

"I went there to make a deal."

Lydia frowned at him. "What kind of a deal, Mr. Samuels?"

He shrugged. "I have something he wants. He has something I want. I proposed a trade." Again he fell into silence. Then, "You know what's brilliant about Rhames is that he doesn't break you completely. He took Mickey. How? I still don't quite know but I have an idea. But with the death of my son, he showed me what he was capable of doing. Everything else he just left dangling. He knows that once a man is without hope, once he has nothing to lose, there's no way to control him. Things might go all right with the IRS, Lily might come home, Monica might come back from her place of grief. Things might normalize a bit someday. He knew it was that hope that would bring me to him."

"What does he want?" asked Jeffrey, shaking his head. "It can't just be your money. All of this . . . there are easier ways to get a person's money."

"No. Not just my money."

"He wants you to say Uncle," said Lydia. "He wants to you to surrender."

Tim Samuels shrugged. "Something like that."

"So what kind of deal did you make, Mr. Samuels?" asked Lydia. "Whatever it was, please let us help you."

He shook his head slowly. "I don't need any help, Ms. Strong. I got my family into this and I'll get them out."

"How?"

"The less you know, the better. And now, I'm going to ask you to leave."

"Mr. Samuels, you know we're going to have to involve the police."

He rose and started walking toward the door. Lydia and Jeffrey exchanged a look and followed.

"You do what you have to do," he said in the foyer.

Lydia didn't like his calm. It was eerily incongruous with the things he was saying.

Samuels opened the door for them. His hand was pale with strawberry blond hair and a riot of freckles, nails bitten to the quick. He rested it on the brushed chrome door handle and turned tired eyes on them.

"Why are you telling us all of this now, Mr Samuels?" asked Jeffrey.

He didn't smile; he didn't open his mouth. He just looked at them and the answer was clear. That whatever arrangement he'd made, it was too late to stop it. Tim Samuels had wrangled with the devil and lost.

"What now?" asked Lydia as she climbed into the passenger seat of the Kompressor. Jeffrey didn't answer, just put the car in gear and headed up the drive.

"We can't just go," she said, looking back at the house. She felt the tension of helplessness in her hands, a deep frustration constricting her chest. She knew what Tim Samuels apparently did not; that there were no deals with people like Trevor Rhames.

"We're not going. We just need him to think we are."

Samuels stood in the doorway and watched them leave, face blank, hands hanging at his sides. Jeff turned off the drive as if they were headed back toward the highway and drove until the house was out of sight. After about a mile, he looped around on a winding back road that left them off on a scenic overlook where they had a clear view of Samuels' driveway. The house sat below them, a picture postcard of white and gray against a moody sea.

Lydia didn't have to ask what they were doing: watching Samuels to see what happened next. She played the conversation they'd had with him over in her mind.

"Anything bother you about that conversation?" asked Lydia.

Jeffrey blew a sharp breath out of his nose. "Where do I begin?"

"You know what's bothering me?" she asked.

"Hmm," said Jeffrey, his chin in his hand, his eyes on the house below them.

"Monica Samuels."

He nodded.

"I mean, where is she?"

"Catatonic with grief, doped up on tranquilizers."

"According to Samuels," she said, leaning against the door. "But she wasn't catatonic if she left him."

"Okay."

"So where is she?"

Jeffrey considered it. "Well, we can't ask Tim Samuels where his wife went. What about that girl you interviewed?"

"Jasmine."

"Maybe she knows."

They spent the next few hours in the Kompressor watching the property, hoping that Tim Samuels would leave so that they could follow him, or that someone from The New Day would show up at his house. Neither of those things happened.

Eventually Dax showed up in the Rover to relieve them. He pulled up behind them and didn't exit the vehicle. He had a friend with him, a guy Lydia and Jeffrey knew only as Claude. He was mute; he looked like Frankenstein's monster with a square jaw, bad hair, and assorted scars on his face and hands. Dax couldn't work alone yet, since he still couldn't run properly. He was slow and stiff, as they'd seen earlier at The New Day. And anything that didn't involve him pulling out his big gun and firing from a sitting position was going to be difficult for him. He'd brought Claude along for anything that required speed and finesse. Which was kind of like using a sledgehammer to etch glass.

"Maybe we should have asked one of the trainees at the firm to work with him," said Jeffrey, gazing at Dax and Claude in the rearview mirror. They looked like a pair of escapees from an asylum, brooding, drinking Mountain Dew from giant plastic cups.

Lydia gave him a look. "Dax doesn't play well with others. Anyway,

it'll be dark soon. There are no other houses for a mile or so, so hopefully the villagers won't see them and come after them with torches."

Lydia's cell phone rang and she looked in the rearview mirror as
she answered.

"Hey," she said.

"What are we looking for?" asked Dax.

"Anyone who comes in, follow when they leave. If he leaves, trail
him."

"How long do you want us to say?"

She shrugged. "I don't know, call us later."

She saw him nod in the rearview. She and Jeffrey took off and
headed back to the city.

Monica Samuels moved like she was made out of glass, as though the
slightest misstep or sudden noise would cause her to shatter into a
thousand pieces.

"I didn't have anyplace else to go," she told Lydia, placing a cup of
tea on the table before her. "I couldn't stand the thought of a hotel. So
impersonal. I feel disconnected enough as it is."

A call to Jasmine had revealed that Monica Samuels had moved
into her daughter's apartment. Now, Lydia and Monica sat at the small
round table in Lily's tiny kitchen. Monica had asked Lydia if she
wanted tea and Lydia had declined. But Monica didn't seem to hear,
boiled some water and made her a cup anyway. The bitter smell of
some herbal concoction drifted unpleasantly into Lydia's nostrils.

"I'll stay just until she comes home," she said with a sad, hopeful
smile. "A young woman doesn't need her mother hanging around."

Monica Samuels wasn't a beautiful woman, not in the classic sense.
Her nose was too long, her mouth too thin. Her long dark hair was
streaked with wiry grays and badly in need of a shaping. But there was a
fire to her, something wild that lived in the deep brown of her eyes. She
was dulled by grief and drugs but there was an unmistakable radiance to
her, a captivating mix of sexuality and vulnerability. She wore an oversized blue cardigan, which she wrapped protectively around herself.

"Timothy told me you were looking for Lily," she said softly, giving
Lydia a look she couldn't quite read. "The police have given up. You
can tell just by their tone, at first. Then they stop returning your calls."

She seemed to drift off then, her eyes focusing on a point somewhere above and behind Lydia. Her hand rested wearily on the cup of
tea she hadn't touched.

"I feel close to Lily here," said Monica. "Can't you feel her? Feel her energy?"

Lydia nodded carefully. She waited a beat before saying, "I need to ask you about The New Day, Mrs. Samuels."

She drew in a deep breath and then let it out slowly. "They're like a pestilence Tim let into our lives. They're eating us alive." She shook her head then, looked regretful. "But that's not entirely fair. I've made mistakes, too. Awful ones."

"What kind of mistakes?"

"The kind of mistakes that keep you hostage in your efforts to conceal them, to keep them buried in the past. The kind that make you prey to people like Trevor Rhames."

Lydia waited but Monica didn't go on. That frustration she'd felt with Tim Samuels rose up in her chest again. What was it with these people and their secrets?

"I can't help you and I can't help Lily," said Lydia more harshly than she'd intended, "if you and your husband continue to be secretive and dishonest. What does Rhames have on you? What could be so bad that you will sacrifice both of your children to hide it?"

Monica smiled patiently at Lydia and leaned into her.

"I know you're just trying to help, Ms. Strong," she said in a low, conspiratorial voice. "But what you don't understand is that you are just making things worse. I think it would be best if you just leave now."

Lydia looked at Monica Samuels and saw a surprising mettle. Lydia shook her head.

"I don't understand," she said.

"I know you don't," said Monica, suddenly looking tired. She got up and took the blue ceramic teacup she'd placed before Lydia and walked it over to the sink. Lydia had never touched it. "Believe me; it's better that way."

Lydia stood up from her place at the table. She could see that their conversation was over.

"Your husband thinks he's made some kind of deal with Rhames," she said to Monica's back. "Do you know what it is?"

Monica let go of a mirthless laugh. "That's Timothy for you. Always thinking he can make things right with the last-ditch heroic effort, never realizing that if he behaved properly in the first place there'd be nothing to *save*."

Out on the street, Lydia breathed in the cold air. Monica Samuels had asked her to leave and although she was no closer to Lily than she had been when she arrived, she respected the older woman's wishes and left her to her grief. She leaned against the brick wall beside the entrance to Lily's building and wished she had a cigarette, took a deep breath instead.

The avenue was packed with rush-hour traffic and busy New Yorkers raced by talking on cell phones or staring at the ground beneath their feet. A bicycle messenger barely avoided a nasty collision with a taxicab and the driver rolled down the window to shout something in Spanish. She felt Lily slipping away and she quashed the tide of anxiety that rose at the thought of it. She started walking, bag clutched tight to her side, heels connecting purposefully with the concrete. She became part of the wave of pedestrians on the city sidewalk, lost in her own head, trying to find a way to believe that she hadn't come to an absolute dead end.

Sixteen

Somehow the box she'd left in Jeffrey's office had made it into their living room and it stood there taunting her for her cowardice as she stepped off the elevator into her apartment. The pile of letters sat on top and snickered their agreement. She stared at it a second and then made her way through the room, up the stairs of their duplex and into the bedroom. It was empty. She dropped her bag and stripped off her coat, throwing both on the bed. She marched back down the stairs, through the living room to the other end of the foyer and down the few small steps into her office where Jeffrey sat at the computer. Hiding, from the look of him.

"Jeffrey," she said.

He swiveled in the chair to look at her. "Don't be mad," he said with a grimace. He held up his arms as if to ward off blows. She sighed and threw herself on the couch. He came and sat across from her.

"I just thought you'd be more comfortable opening it here," he said quietly. "If you decide that's what you want to do."

She nodded. He was right as usual and she wouldn't bother arguing. Anyway she wasn't really thinking about the box. She was thinking about Lily.

"I've got a bad feeling," she said.

"About the box."

"No, about Tim Samuels."

"Did you talk to Dax?" Jeffrey asked, sitting up.

"I just called and there was no answer. I left a message," she said.

"Okay," said Jeffrey, ever mellow. "He'll call."

"I just feel like we screwed everything up," she said, looking at him.

"I feel like when we went to The New Day we lost every chance we had at finding Lily. I feel like she's gone, Jeffrey."

She had pain in her neck and shoulder and she lifted a hand to rub the muscle there. Jeffrey came and stood beside her. She lifted her feet, he sat, and she dropped her legs on top of his.

"No," he said. "We did our best, what we thought was right. We'll find her."

He sounded so certain, she could almost believe he wasn't just saying it to make her feel better.

"I don't think Detective Stenopolis feels the same way."

She pulled her tiny phone from the pocket of her jeans and called in for the message she'd saved. She handed it to Jeffrey so he could listen.

He'd left her a scathing message about how The New Day had cleared out of the building, wiped their computers, and lawyered up by the time he'd arrived. He didn't say it outright but his tone implied that he blamed them. Which she thought was a little unfair considering that without them, he'd never have even known about The New Day in the first place. It wasn't like his brilliant detective work had led him there and they'd screwed it up for him.

"She was here, Lydia," the detective said in his message, sounding angry and desperate. "I can feel her. But she's gone now. I think gone for good."

Her heart had clenched at his words. Naturally, they hadn't intended to shoot their way out of there. They'd expected the whole thing to go a little more quietly but it just hadn't worked out that way.

"I hope you can use some of those resources you were talking about to find out where Rhames might have gone," he went on angrily. "Because, I'll tell you what. When my CO finds out how badly this went, I'm going to be doing traffic duty for the rest of my goddamn career."

"He was just frustrated," said Jeffrey, ending the call. "We all are."

"Besides," he went on when she said nothing. "When you talk to him again you'll be able to tell him that we have a good idea where to find Rhames."

"Oh, yeah?" she said, sitting up. "Where's that?"

He smiled, patted her on the thigh. "Detective Stenopolis told you that The New Day owned a good deal of real estate in Florida, that they've been buying up a lot of property in a town by the Gulf."

"Right."

"Well, I made some calls."

A contact of Jeffrey's at the Westchester Airport confirmed that a private jet belonging to The New Day had left the airport after midnight en route to Tampa with five passengers on board. But there was no passenger manifest.

"That's illegal, isn't it?" asked Jeffrey.

"It is," confirmed Jack Anderson, one of the Transportation Security Administration security directors of the Westchester Airport. Jeffrey had done a number of favors for him in the past, including running a in-depth background check on his daughter's fiancé about six months earlier, who it turned out was a pretty stand-up guy.

"But with the private jets, sometimes we seem to have this problem. People make a lot of 'mistakes' when money is involved, if you know what I mean."

"Seems like a pretty big security hole," said Jeffrey uneasily. He hated airplanes and this was just one more thing he could add to his list of reasons to stay on the ground.

"It is. And it has been. People flying privately are looking for the ultimate in security and secrecy. Passenger manifests are available only to customs and immigration. As long as other security precautions are met, that manifest is very rarely requested. So pilots are often, shall we say, 'lax' about obtaining the identities of all the passengers on board, particularly if that pilot works for the owner of the jet and not a charter company or one of those 'jet share' companies."

"Can we talk to that pilot?"

"I'll get in touch with him, see what I can find out. But he works for The New Day. Those guys are pretty slippery."

"What do you mean?"

"I mean I had some questions for one of their pilots awhile back and the guy just disappeared. They basically said that he left the organization and we were never able to find him."

"What kind of questions?"

"The same kind you're asking."

Some unformed thoughts were tumbling around in Jeffrey's head . . . Tim Samuels' private security agency, The New Day's private jet fleet, the dead jeweler and his missing cache of pink diamonds.

"When was this?"

"A couple of weeks ago actually."

"Did it have something to do with a murdered jewel dealer from South Africa?"

There was a pause on the other end of the phone. "I can't answer that, Jeff. Sorry."

An answer like that and he didn't really have to.

"So I guess we're going to Florida," said Lydia with a roll of her eyes.

"I guess."

Jeffrey whipped up some egg-white omelets with scallions and smoked salmon while Lydia brooded at the counter with a cup of coffee. She didn't cook, never had really. But she was a master with the 'one-button' machines, as Jeffrey called them. Coffee maker, mini–food processor, toaster . . . she could make espresso, chop garlic, and toast up a piece of sourdough bread like nobody's business.

She sat on one of the stools by the counter and turned her back to the box that sat on the floor between the loveseat and the fireplace hearth. As long as she had Lily Samuels to think about, she didn't have to think about Arthur Tavernier and his legacy or his letters. In fact, it would be selfish to worry about her issues when Lily Samuels could be somewhere fighting for her life.

"We should go tonight," she said, starting to feel the buzz of anxiety. She stood and turned toward the staircase.

"First we eat, then we rest a bit," he said sensibly. "Then we'll go."

He was always the one that made sure they took care of themselves, even when there was chaos all around them, even when the buzz could keep her running on empty for days.

"The worst mistakes are made when you're hungry or when you're tired," was his famous philosophy. "When we can, we need to avoid making decisions during those times."

"I can't believe we're going back there," she said, after a minute.

"Me neither."

They'd just sat down at the table when the phone rang. Lydia leapt up to grab it.

"Hello?"

The line was staticky, the cellular signal weak and slipping in and out. She thought she heard Dax say her name and the low wail of sirens in the background. Jeffrey got up from the table and picked up the extension in the living room.

"Dax?" she said, glancing at the caller ID and seeing that the number was unavailable.

"—gunshot—and then we—too late." That was all she got. She had no idea what he was saying but she was fairly certain it was bad news.

"Dax, I'm not getting you. The signal is bad."

"Lydia, can you hear me?"

"Okay, I got you. What's happening?"

More static. She was about to hang up and try to call him back but then his voice came over the line as clear as a gong.

"Tim Samuels killed himself," he said. "He's dead."

Part Two

The Burning

When the house has burned
And all that's left is ash and smoke
You can stand rooted in regret
Or forge ahead
But you can't go home again.
                                    —Anonymous

Seventeen

When Internal Affairs came to his doorstep, Matt Stenopolis was still in his boxers, eating a glazed chocolate donut and drinking a cup of coffee. He heard the Caprice pull into the driveway and pulled himself away from the Pokémon cartoon he was watching. He drew back the curtains and stood at the picture window, watching as two men, one paunchy and balding, one young with a body builder's physique, both of them wearing bad suits and cheap ties and matching wool coats, emerged from the car. There was an aura of cheesy self-importance about them and he recognized them immediately as IAD.

He didn't bother to put on pants before he answered the door.

"Gentlemen," said Matt through the screen door. The cold air of the morning was biting, made more brutal by the sharp wind that blew. He noticed the dead trees and the empty street, the streetlamp that still hadn't dimmed for the day.

"Detective Stenopolis," said the older man. He had thick lines and soft purple bags under his eyes, his moustache needed a trim, the wool coat he wore over his suit needed a good lint brush. But there was something steely about him, something really tough. A lead toe under a worn old boot.

"What can I do for you this morning?" Matt had an idea that this was about Jorge Alonzo, the Latin King he'd been rough with when he'd disrespected Jesamyn. Those punks all had lawyers; they were always screaming police brutality. Murderers, drug dealers, rapists every last one of them, but God forbid their civil rights were violated.

"Can we come in?"

Matt hesitated. IAD officers were like vampires: once you invited them in, they were hard to get rid of. He noticed then that they'd left the engine running and the backseat of the car stood open. White clouds of exhaust plumed around the vehicle in the frigid air.

"I was just being polite, Detective," said the older officer when Matt didn't answer right away. "Don't make this worse than it's going to be. Okay, buddy?"

That's when he felt his stomach clench. He saw his mother and father come out of their house next door, their coats on over their pajamas. They shuffled over the icy sidewalk, his father holding on tightly to his mother so that she wouldn't slip. The echo of a door shutting in the morning air told him that his brother had been called and was on his way up the street. He wanted to yell at them, tell them to go back into the house, but he didn't.

"Mateo," his mother called, looking at him worriedly. "What's wrong?"

Her short red hair hadn't been brushed and it stuck up amusingly in several places; his father's glasses fogged in the cold.

"Nothing, Ma," he said, holding the screen door open for the officers. He was starting to feel a flutter in his belly, a tingling in his hands.

"Ma'am, sir, I'm going to have to ask you to stand back," said the younger officer as he walked over to Matt's parents.

In the distance, he heard sirens sound and as they drew closer and closer Matt realized that they were for him.

"Look," he said to the older officer. "What's going on here?"

"Mateo Stenopolis," he said, removing two pairs of cuffs from his pockets. They were linked together because Matt was too big to have his arms cuffed behind him with just one set. They'd done it before they arrived. If he had known they were going to take him out in cuffs without letting him get dressed, he would have taken the time to do so before allowing them into his home.

"You're not going to let me put on my clothes?" said Matt, turning his back and putting his hands behind his back like he'd asked a thousand perps to do a thousand times.

"You are under arrest for the rape and murder of Katrina Silvana Aliti. You have the right to remain silent . . ."

But Matt didn't hear anything else as two squad cars pulled up, sirens screaming. His mother was crying, emitting a kind of low, despairing moan, standing between his father and brother, who looked on in shock.

"Don't worry, bro. We're going to call a lawyer and meet you down there," his brother said calmly. "Don't worry, Mateo."

But it sounded like he was talking behind a piece of thick glass. All

Matt could think, as they let him put on his sneakers that lay by the door and led him down the icy path to the waiting squad car, was that he'd never known her last name before this morning. He'd never asked Katrina her last name.

Jesamyn was in a kind of haze as she dropped Benjamin off at school, still tired from the all-nighter they'd pulled the day before yesterday. She kissed him on the forehead.

"See ya," he said, sliding from the car.

"See ya, little man. I love you." But he was already gone. She watched as he ran toward the wide double doors without a second glance back at her. She didn't have time to feel wistful about it as her cell phone started singing. She saw Dylan's number on the ID. She sighed and considered not answering. But they'd both made a promise to each other long ago to always take each other's calls out of respect for their mutual love for Benjamin. No matter what passed between them they were each parent to the same child; that meant something.

"What do you want?" she answered.

"Yeah, look, I know you don't want to talk to me right now. But I'm down here at 1 Police Plaza, answering more questions about my shooting. There's something you need to know."

"Spare me the drama and spit it out." She was so sick of him, she could barely stand the sound of his voice.

"They just brought Mount in."

"What? You've gotta be kidding me." She immediately remembered the incident with Jorge Alonzo. That little shit, she thought.

"In cuffs, still in his boxers."

"What?" she said again. That didn't sound right.

"They arrested him. Word is, Jez, they took him in for murdering a prostitute."

She sighed with relief. "Man, you will sink to any level to get an emotional response out of me. You're not just selfish; you're sick."

She took the phone away from her ear and was about to end the call, but she heard him raise his voice. She put the phone back to her ear.

"Listen to me, Jez," he was saying. "Please. This is not a joke. I am absolutely serious."

She felt her heart start to race. "Oh my God," she said.

Two days ago, the night of the raid on The New Day, once they'd identified Carla as Jessica Rawlins, it hadn't taken long for them to contact
her parents in Tennessee. It gave them a reason to put a warrant out for
the arrest of Trevor Rhames and to send squad cars to Jude Templar's
home and office. They could question him now on the whereabouts of
his client and charge him with aiding and abetting if he didn't cooperate. But Templar was gone. Not to be found at his office, his home, or at
the city courthouses, and by late that night, he still hadn't turned up.
Other than finding Jessica Rawlins, very little came from the search of
The New Day. They were no closer to finding Lily, and Trevor Rhames
and anything that might have incriminated him in Lily's disappearance
were gone from the premises before they arrived. And none of the people they interviewed, including Jessica Rawlins, had anything bad to say
about The New Day; they all claimed never to have seen Lily. It was a
big goose egg. They had nothing. And Kepler was angrier than Jesamyn
had ever seen him. Matt left after Kepler ripped him a new one and for
the first time since she'd known him, he didn't go into the precinct on
their day off the next day. She hadn't seen or talked to her partner in
almost forty-eight hours.

"Jesamyn, are you listening to me?" asked Dylan, still on the other
line.

"What?"

"I said, what do you know about this?"

"Know about it? I don't know anything about it. It's complete bullshit. Matt Stenopolis is the most upright guy I have ever known. Honest, reliable, mature," she said, turning the knife a little and hoping he
was picking up on it.

"But he's got a temper," said Dylan.

She paused a second.

"Yeah, he's got a temper but only when people act like assholes.
Anyway, what are you saying? You think he did this?"

He didn't say anything but she could hear him breathing on the
line. Then, "Jez, I hear they have pictures of him entering and leaving
her apartment. Fingerprint evidence at the scene, blood in his car. I
mean, they're not going to bring a cop in like that, humiliate him in
front of his family, unless they're real sure they're dealing with someone capable of what they say he did to that pro."

"What do you mean?"

"That girl was beaten to death. Someone beat her to death with his
fists. Someone big."

She squeezed her eyes shut tight and when she opened them, her vision had a white ring around it "You *know* him, Dylan. *I* know him. It's not possible. It's just not."

He sighed. "I hope you're right."

"I'm coming down there," she said. "I'll be there in an hour."

"They're not going to let you see him," he was saying as she ended the call. She started the engine of the Explorer and pulled out of the school drive.

A ghost of a thought was starting to form in her mind. She tried to push it down, but it wouldn't go.

Eighteen

It was a rage killing. A rage killing that was followed by deep remorse. They knew that by the way Katrina Silvana Aliti had been beaten with big heavy fists, beaten until she died. She was a tiny woman, not five-three, not even a hundred and ten pounds. She never had a chance against a man that size, was likely unconscious after the first blow to her head.

When she was dead, the killer must have come back to himself. Realized fully what he had done. Then he covered her face and body with the pink flowered sheet from her bed. The man that the killer found her with had run, not even bothering to retrieve his clothes. He had wrapped himself in a blanket he found on the couch and fled. His dick was still hard and would stay that way for hours, since he'd taken a double hit of Viagra in anticipation of his evening with Katrina.

The big man had allowed the john to leave, barely even registering his presence. From the street outside where he called the police from a pay phone, the john said he heard the giant wailing like an injured moose. He hid himself in a doorway as the man ran from the building, climbed into an SUV, and sped off.

"I've never seen anyone that tall outside a basketball court," he told the police when they arrived. "He came through that door like it was made out of cardboard. She called him 'Mateo.'"

The surveillance camera from the livery cab company outside captured Detective Mateo Stenopolis arriving at Katrina's apartment around midnight and leaving less than a half an hour later.

"He doesn't look upset," said Jesamyn after watching the tape for the fifth time. "He's not upset. He's not running."

"That's because he's a stone-cold killer, Detective Breslow."

"Bullshit. I don't care what kind of evidence you have. You'll never convince me of that."

"We have an eyewitness account, a videotape, blood evidence in his vehicle."

"What about his DNA at the scene? If he beat her to death, his DNA should be all over her body. His knuckles should be broken and bloodied. Or bruised."

"Evidence suggests that he wore gloves."

"Hair, then. Fibers."

"It'll take weeks for that to come back."

The interrogation room was too cold. She found herself wondering if they knew that she hated the cold, that it made her feel vulnerable somehow and small, that it opened a strange place of sadness within her that she couldn't explain. She folded her arms across her chest, tucked her hands under her arms.

"Just two days ago, we had a civilian complaint from a Jorge Alonzo. Alonzo claims that Stenopolis menaced and brutalized him, damaged his property."

Jesamyn looked at the old cop, pushed a disdainful breath out of her mouth. "Give me a break."

"Is it true?"

She remembered how mad Mount had gotten, how she'd turned her back so she wouldn't see him put his hands on the guy.

"The kid was a punk, he had an attitude, he made some shitty comment about me and Detective Stenopolis raised his voice."

Detective Ray Bloom looked at her with wise, moist eyes. She could see that he'd been handsome about a hundred years ago. She could see that he was smart and kind and a good cop. But she hated him anyway.

"He didn't put his hands on Alonzo?"

"No," she said. The lie stuck in her throat and she reached for the coffee they'd placed in front of her. It was bitter and cold.

"He didn't put his hands on Alonzo," repeated Detective Bloom. He knew she was lying, that it pained her, and he wanted to force her to say it again.

But Jesamyn didn't say anything, just turned her eyes on Bloom.

"I heard you didn't even let him put on his clothes," she said quietly. "How do you people live with yourselves?"

His partner pushed himself away from the wall behind her where he'd been standing for a while and moved into her field of vision. He was a big guy, with a body builder's physique. Square jaw in square head on square shoulders, very little neck, heavy brow. He didn't look very smart. Did he think he was intimidating her? Even the biggest of them fell and cried like little girls with a solid kick to the knee cap; hit hard and directly in just the right place it shattered like a china saucer beneath the wheels of a car.

"Let's try to stay focused, Detective Breslow," said Bloom. "Did you know he was seeing a prostitute?"

"No," she said. "If it's true, I didn't know that. You still haven't convinced me it's true."

"I don't have to convince you of anything, Detective," he said quietly.

She nodded. She'd been in with them for nearly two hours and she was getting tired. Dylan had been right. When she showed up at 1 PP, they wouldn't let her see Matt. He was being processed and it would be twelve hours at least before she could even talk to him. She'd spent a few minutes with Mount's family, his mother, father, and younger brother Theo. His mom had been crying and started again when Jesamyn approached them.

She'd embraced each of them and told them that it was all going to be fine, though she wasn't sure of that at all. It was just a misunderstanding. A mistake, she assured them. Theo looked the least freaked out of the three of them, so she took him aside.

"What you need to do," she told him, "is get in touch with Mateo's PBA rep. Call the desk sergeant at the Ninth Precinct, he'll know who it is and how to get in touch. They'll know what to do and they'll help you find a lawyer."

He put a hand on her arm. "Just tell me the truth. It's bad, isn't it?"

She hesitated a second. Then, "Yes, Theo. It's very bad. Get him a very good lawyer. The best you can afford."

Theo nodded, looking stunned. She could relate. She felt pretty stunned herself. That's when Detective Bloom approached her.

"You saved me a trip, Detective," he'd said, coming up behind her. "I have some questions about your partner."

They'd led her to an interrogation room, showed her the videotape. Once. Twice. Three times. As often as she asked them to rewind it and play it again.

"If he was seeing her regularly, that video could have been taken anytime," she said suddenly.

"It's date stamped."

"That can be tampered with."

"What are you saying?"

"I'm saying that this is all a little too easy. Don't you think?"

"I don't understand what that means," he said, leaning back in his chair. "We have a lot of good evidence against your partner, if that's what you mean by 'too easy.' What are you suggesting?"

She sighed. "We were threatened," she said. "The night before last we infiltrated this church group called The New Day. And their lawyer threatened Detective Stenopolis."

He frowned and his bushy eyebrows came together, looked like a long furry caterpillar on his head.

"So you're suggesting that this church is setting up your partner," said Bloom carefully, as a wide smile spread across his partner's face. She didn't say anything.

"How about this instead?" said Bloom, leaning into her. "Your partner became obsessed with the Lily Samuels case, started to develop inappropriate feelings for the missing girl. He ran into one dead end after another, enough so that your CO insisted that you both start working on another case. Your partner continued to follow up leads on his own time, looking for a girl who maybe didn't want to be found, eventually relying on the statement of an unreliable witness to obtain a search warrant in the middle of the night. When that turned into a huge clusterfuck that did nothing to further your case, he was angry and frustrated. Witnesses at the scene said that Matt lost his temper with an attorney, started making threats. Is that true, Detective?"

Again, she just stayed quiet and held his eyes.

"Maybe finding the prostitute whom he fantasized was his girlfriend with another man was just the last straw. He lost it."

She shook her head slowly, held herself tighter. "That's the biggest load of crap I've ever heard," she said.

"Really," said Bloom, tapping his pen twice, quickly, on the table. " Have you ever known Detective Stenopolis to be involved in a healthy relationship with a woman?"

She hesitated, then shook her head.

"While he doesn't live in the same house with his parents, doesn't he live just one door down and doesn't his mother continue to cook and clean for him as if he were still a child?"

She didn't answer because it didn't matter. Bloom already knew the answer.

"Didn't Detective Stenopolis lose his temper with Jorge Alonzo when he made a *sexual* comment toward you?"

"Well, I wouldn't say it was sexual exactly—"

"How would you characterize it then?"

She found herself stammering. "I—I—" she said stupidly.

Bloom glanced down at his notes and read. " 'Your shit is tight, girl.' That comment doesn't have a sexual connotation to you?"

Jesamyn shrugged and shook her head slowly. They were making him sound like some sexually frustrated psychopath, and pretty convincingly at that. If she didn't know Mount, really *know* him, they might be able to convince her. And that scared her. She was scared for the man who was her partner and her friend. She looked at the video on the screen in front of her, frozen as Matt climbed calmly into his Dodge.

"Didn't your eyewitness say that he *raced* from the building?"

Bloom looked at her. She nodded toward the screen and his eyes followed.

"He's not racing," she said. "He's calm. That's a discrepancy between the witness statement and the videotape. We're talking about a life here, not just a career. You owe it to him and to yourself as a cop to check out that discrepancy. And to check out what I'm telling you about The New Day." She leaned across the table and forced him to hold her eyes. "Because as sure as I'm sitting here, I will tell you that Mateo Stenopolis is no killer. The fact that he hasn't had a girlfriend in a while and that his mom still does his laundry doesn't prove a thing."

Bloom held her eyes for a second longer, then rose from his chair. He was a rumpled, tired-looking little man with messy gray hair and a funny moustache. His suit needed a trip to the dry cleaners. He wore a simple gold band on his left hand. He wasn't very tall, maybe five-six. He had a modest potbelly that strained the bottom button on his white oxford. But she was afraid of him, afraid of what he could do to Mount.

"Please, Detective Bloom," she said. "Just take a look at The New Day."

But he just gathered up his file and walked from the room.

"Don't go anywhere, Detective," said Bloom's partner. "We have a little more talking to do." They closed the door behind them.

A second later the door opened slowly and Dylan poked his head in. "You okay?" he asked.

She simultaneously was happy to see him and wanted to put her fist through his teeth. She shrugged, looked away from him. She didn't trust her voice at the moment. He entered the room and closed the door behind him, straddled the chair Bloom had just left. He held a gray fleece pullover in his hand, which he slid across the table to her. She took it gratefully and pulled it on. He always knew her so well; it was part of the reason he was able to manipulate her so easily.

"So, what's the deal?" he asked.

"They're trying to make him sound like some sexual freak."

"Is that the surveillance tape?" he asked, nodding toward the video monitor.

She nodded, reached over, and rewound it to where Mount exited the vehicle. She fast-forwarded it and they watched as a small, balding man with an earring came rushing out the front door wrapped in a blanket, looking stricken. He ran to a nearby pay phone. A few fast-forwarded seconds later, Mount walked calmly from the building and climbed into his car.

"He's calm. He doesn't have a drop of blood on him. He's not wearing gloves," she said, looking at Dylan.

He nodded. "But look how he has the jacket zipped all the way up to his neck. On the way in it wasn't even closed, you could see his shirt. The gloves could be in his pocket."

She turned her eyes to his. "Whose side are you on?"

"Yours, Jez. I just think it's better if you have an open mind."

"What? Like be open to the possibility that my partner is a psycho who could beat a woman to death with his own fists and then walk out of her place like nothing happened?"

He shrugged. Looked at the wall above her.

"Come on," she said with disdain. "Open *your* mind. Forget your history with him for one second and think about it."

He let out a long, slow sigh. "There is one thing weird about this tape."

"What?"

"If the guy came out just a minute or so after Stenopolis entered and called the cops, why did it take them twenty minutes to get there? I mean he had time to finish the job, wash his face, zip up his coat, and walk calmly to the car. They get a call that a woman is being beaten to death and it takes them that long? I doubt it. Someone will have to check the 911 tapes to get the timing."

She nodded. "That's true," she said, feeling a rush of excitement. She watched her ex-husband for a second and wondered if she could trust him with her thoughts. He stared back at her, like they were in some kind of standoff.

"What?" he said finally, showing her his palms.

"Dylan, I think Mount is being set up."

He smiled and shook his head. "Come on. Seriously, Jez?"

She told him about The New Day and the threats Templar had made. She told him about Jessica Rawlins. He didn't say anything for a second after she was finished talking.

"Just tell me you think it's possible," she said. He held her eyes for a second and then looked away.

"I guess it's possible," he said grudgingly. "Unlikely, Jez. But possible."

She sat back, relieved. That was all she needed: independent confirmation that her thoughts weren't totally insane.

Nineteen

Lydia sat, fidgety and anxious, the passenger seat of the Rover. They should have flown. But between Jeff's ever increasing phobia of flying and Dax's need to travel with a small armory, Lydia was outvoted. If they took turns and didn't stop except for gas and snacks, they could make it in seventeen hours. A big waste of time they didn't have. The sky was dusty pink and gray with the setting sun and a light rain fell. Lydia watched as the headlights of an eighteen-wheeler approached in the oncoming lane and then whipped past them in a wet, noisy blur. She shuddered at its speed and size, imagining vividly that it jackknifed and the Rover went crashing into its body, squealing tires, then metal on metal, killing all three of them instantly.

"Whatever the deal was," said Dax, "seems to me like Tim Samuels got the fuzzy end of the lollipop."

Lydia shook her head. "I didn't figure him for a suicide. He seemed too narcissistic."

In her experience people like Tim Samuels thought too much of themselves to ever put an end to their own lives. It didn't rest well with her that she was so wrong about him.

"Is it possible someone else shot him in the head?" asked Jeffrey from behind her, reading her mind.

Dax shook his head. "No one left or entered his place while we were there. And you say no one left or entered while you and Jeff watched. Unless someone came and went and we missed it, which I doubt, there was no one else there to do the job."

"Or unless there was someone in the house already," suggested Lydia.

"We saw the flash in the upstairs window and were in the house in less than five minutes. If there had been someone else in the house, we'd have seen him leave."

"They could have come from the water," suggested Lydia, thinking of the beach behind the house.

"We'd have heard the boat or seen the lights. Besides, the water was really rough. Too rough for a small craft."

"How did you get into the house?" asked Jeffrey.

"Through the front door. We were going to break it down but it wasn't locked."

"That seems weird. Who leaves their door unlocked?"

"Lots of people," said Dax. "Look, if you're planning on offing yourself why would you bother locking the door? What exactly at that point would you worry about protecting?"

"It's a habit," said Jeffrey. "You do it without thinking."

"They live out in the middle of nowhere," suggested Lydia. "Maybe it was his habit *not* to lock the door."

"Don't you remember seeing an alarm system in that house?" asked Jeffrey. "If I recall it was pretty high end. Not the kind of thing you would invest in if you were going to leave your doors unlocked." He always got very worked up about people who were careless about their personal security. Maybe it was their work, or the fact that they'd had to be so vigilant about their own personal security for so long.

"Maybe he was expecting someone," she said.

No one said anything for a minute, each lost in their thoughts about Tim Samuels.

"He was smart," said Dax finally. "He put the gun to his temple and fired. Most people think they should put it in their mouth. But you can really fuck yourself up like that. Make yourself a total vegetable. His face was okay, good enough for an open casket, but he was seriously dead."

"Where was he?" Lydia asked.

"It looked like a girl's bedroom. Must have been Lily's childhood room, lots of dolls and gymnastics trophies, pretty pale pink carpet and window seat looking out over the ocean."

Dax told Lydia and Jeffrey how he'd found Samuels slumped in the bed. The gun had fallen to the floor. It seemed that he'd positioned himself so that the blood and brain matter would splatter on a blank wall beside the bed. But maybe that hadn't been his intent. Maybe he'd just wanted to be in Lily's room when he ended his life, not caring what kind of damage his exit would do to it.

Lydia shook her head. There was something about that detail she didn't like. Something about it seemed wrong. Thinking about his wife, she wondered what it would be like to know your husband had killed himself in your missing daughter's bedroom.

"You sure it was him?" asked Lydia.

"Who else would it be?"

"You've never seen Tim Samuels before. How do you know it was him?"

He took his eyes off the road and gave her a look.

"What am I . . . an amateur? I checked. There were some pictures on the shelf in Lily's room. Him teaching her how to ride a bike, him at her graduation. It was him. Trust me."

They were all quiet for a second, as if out of respect. Each of them was thinking about Tim Samuels and his final moments.

"So what kind of deal would involve him killing himself?" asked Lydia.

"A really shitty one," said Dax.

"I mean, how could he be sure the other party was living up to his side of the bargain?" said Lydia.

"And if you were going to kill yourself, why would you bother to make a deal at all, in the same way that you wouldn't bother to lock the door," said Jeffrey.

"Unless the deal was his life for Lily's," suggested Lydia. "He could die knowing that she'd be safe."

"But he couldn't know that," said Jeffrey. "He would only have the word of a psychopath, assuming that he made the deal with Rhames."

Lydia sighed. "Maybe it was literally the last thing he could do. All of his other resources had been exhausted. Nothing else he could do would save her. He told us Rhames wanted him to surrender. Isn't suicide the ultimate surrender?"

Dax laughed without mirth. "No," he said gravely. "Suicide is the ultimate fuck-you. It's the ultimate act of control, of total selfishness. It tells everyone that *you* make the decisions about your life, no one else." He said it with conviction, as if he'd given it a lot of thought. A *lot* of thought. He went on, "You're a soldier and you get captured by the enemy? If you *surrender,* you've failed. If you kill yourself, you've robbed them of their control over you."

"What are you saying then?"

"I'm saying what if Tim Samuels *broke* the deal he made with Rhames or whoever? What if his suicide wasn't the deal at all but his way of taking back control of his life, even if only to end it."

It made a sick kind of sense to Lydia. She rubbed the fatigue from her eyes.

"So if he broke the deal with Rhames, then what happens to Lily?" she asked.

Dax stared at the road, his jaw tense. He didn't answer. Jeffrey caught her eyes in the rearview mirror and she turned to look at him. He reached for her shoulder.

A heavy rain started then and Lydia settled into her seat. They still had ten hours of driving ahead of them before they got to Florida, her least favorite place in the world. Or one of them anyway.

Twenty

The bodies of Rosario Mendez and her unborn son were spotted floating in the East River by a tour helicopter pilot. The Coast Guard and NYPD responded immediately and within an hour had retrieved the bodies from the frigid gray waters. It was grim work, unclear whether Rosario had given birth to her son prior to her death, or whether the gases of her decomposing body had expelled the fetus. The umbilical cord was intact.

The wind seemed to have a personal problem with Jesamyn as she stood beside Evelyn on the pier near the medical examiner's van. With the sun low in the sky and a damp rain to make things worse, the cold pulled at the bottom of her coat, snuck in through her cuffs, under her collar. She wrapped her arms around herself and watched as the Coast Guard officers lifted the bodies with as much care as the rocking waves would allow. Jesamyn turned away, walked back toward the FDR, and watched as the cars raced past. Some guy from the ME's office she'd never met before leaned against the back of the van smoking a cigarette like he was waiting for a bus. She nodded at him.

On the way down, she'd found herself hoping that it wasn't Rosario Mendez that they'd found. But then she thought, if it's not her . . . then who. Sometimes it seemed like there was nothing to hope for in this line of work. She watched Evelyn, who kept her eyes on the boat, trying to see the face of the corpse no doubt. She looked strained and exhausted; she paced the end of the pier with her hands in the pockets of her thick parka. Evelyn's partner, Wong, was on medical leave after knee surgery. And with Mount in trouble, they were assigned to each other.

"Can you keep your mind on the job?" asked Kepler when she'd returned to the station.

She nodded, not really sure if she could. But she didn't have the luxury of flaking; she had Benjamin. As much as she'd like to run off on a crusade to prove Mount's innocence, she needed to do her job and do it well for her son. Luckily, she had a repentant ex-husband with a lot of time on his hands.

"Good. Because there's nothing you can do for him right now," said Kepler, sitting down at his desk. He actually sounded human. She found herself examining him as he sifted through papers on his desk.

"You know he didn't do this, right?"

He looked up at her and gave her a quick shrug. "That's not for me to decide. Innocent until proven guilty, as far as I'm concerned," he said with no feeling at all.

"Right," she said.

He looked at her, seemed to be on the verge of saying something, but then the moment passed. Finally, he said, "Wong's out on leave. Work with Rosa until things are . . . resolved."

He didn't look up at her again, started scribbling something on the page in front of him. She wondered, not for the first time, what made this guy tick. He obviously didn't give a shit about the job or the people who worked with him. Why be a cop if you just didn't care at all? Nobody was in it for the money. She nodded, though he wasn't looking at her, and left his office. Fifteen minutes later the phone rang about a floater in the East River.

Jesamyn and Evelyn watched as the boat approached the pier, engines sputtering, smoke filling the air with the aroma of gasoline. One of the guys on board threw a line which Evelyn caught and tied off on a cleat. She jumped on board as another guy tied off the stern line. Jesamyn stayed on the dock and watched as Evelyn uncovered the body and stood staring for a second. She laid the sheet back down after a second, looked at Jesamyn, and nodded. She felt a dryness in her throat.

Jesamyn climbed on board and stood beside Evelyn, who lifted the sheet again. The wind whipped around them. Rosario's face was bloated and green, badly decomposed but not unrecognizable from the photos Jesamyn had seen. There was a tiny lump beside her on the gurney where they'd laid her, which Jesamyn was careful to keep covered. That was something she didn't want to see.

She lifted a hand to her nose against the wet, heavy stench that came off of the body. Something had been at her, probably more than one thing. Jesamyn pulled back the sheet farther. She wanted to see what Rosario had been wearing. A long gray knit cotton dress, like a nightgown. Not something you'd wear to the club. Something you'd wear if you were pregnant and tired and home for the evening.

"The guy that pulled her out says it looks like there was a blunt-force trauma to the back of her head. But it's hard to tell at this point," said Rosa.

"She didn't get dressed to go to the clubs," said Jesamyn.

"What?" asked Evelyn.

"Baby Boy said that Alonzo was hounding her that night to go out. When Baby Boy came home, he said that what she'd been wearing when he left was folded on the bed. That he figured she'd gotten dressed and gone out to avoid a fight."

Evelyn nodded. "But she didn't get dressed."

"It doesn't appear so," said Jesamyn lowering the sheet. Evelyn was quiet a moment, looked at the sky gray turning black over Jesamyn's head.

"So what are you thinking?" she asked. Her voice was smoky and deep, her eyes heavy and thoughtful.

"I'm not sure," Jesamyn said. The medical examiner came up behind her quickly and startled her.

"Sorry," he said, though he didn't sound sorry at all as he nudged her out of the way. She stepped aside and let him start taking pictures. As she stepped off the boat onto the dock, she saw an unmarked Caprice pull up, and two guys she recognized from Midtown North homicide stepped out. She couldn't remember their names, but she remembered Mount saying he didn't like the tall one with the bad skin and the strawberry blond hair. She hadn't heard anything too bad about his Latino partner, other than that he was a bit of a dog.

"Hey, Breslow," said the redhead as they approached. "I heard you got a floater."

"Yeah," she said, looking at him. She tried to remember his name but it wouldn't come to her.

He looked at her a second. "I heard some fucked-up shit about your partner today," he said, narrowing his eyes at her. There was a kind of malicious glee there that made her want to slap his pale white face.

"Don't believe everything you hear," she said, squaring off her shoulders at him.

"I don't," he said, raising his palms and giving her a condescending smile. "Seriously, though. What's the deal?"

Her cell phone sounded then and she'd never been so happy to hear its annoying little ring.

"You can talk to Evelyn over there. She's the principal on the Mendez case," she said, giving him a look and answering the phone.

"Breslow."

"You're my one phone call," said Mount.

"Jesus," she said, feeling her heart skip she was so happy to hear his voice. She walked away so that the others wouldn't hear her conversation.

"Get me the fuck out of here, Jez."

She sighed, looked at the cold gray waters of the East River. Two seagulls fought in the air over something one of them was holding in his mouth. They were screaming bloody murder.

"How would you like me to do that?" she said quietly. "You're envisioning a jailbreak maybe?"

She heard him breathing on the other end. "Tell me you know I didn't do this." He sounded tired, afraid.

"I know, Matt," she said without hesitation. "I know you couldn't do it."

"They're doing this . . . The New Day." She believed that, too. But something about the way he said it made him seem so desperate, a little unstable. She knew no one would believe him, unless they could prove it somehow.

She didn't say anything.

"You need to figure it out, Jesamyn," he said when she didn't answer. "How they got that videotape, planted the evidence in my car, how they got that witness to tell the story he told."

"What about the fingerprints? How did they get your fingerprints in there?"

He didn't say anything for a minute. "My fingerprints would have been in there already."

She sighed. "Oh, Matt. Christ."

"I was there that night, the night she was killed. They must have been waiting for me to come and go."

She exhaled through pursed lips in a soft whistle. That was very bad news. *Yeah, officer, I was there that night with the prostitute but she was fine when I left her. I swear.*

"I—cared about her. She was a good person," he said, his voice catching. "She didn't deserve this."

"Okay," she said, pushing any uncertainty from her voice. "We're going to figure out how they're doing this to you. We're going to prove that you're being set up."

"Start with that witness."

"We're already on it."

"Who's 'we'?"

"Dylan's got some time on his hands."

"Dylan." There was no love lost between the two men. "Why would he want to help me?"

"I think he wants to help *me*."

"Well," he said with a sigh, "beggars can't be choosers, I guess. Just do me a favor. Watch your back, Jesamyn. If they can get to me, they can get to you."

Her mind immediately went to Benjamin and she felt a pulse of fear. He started to say something else, but there was a heavy click on the line and an electronic voice told them that their time was up. The line went dead in her hand. The wind was whipping around her, pulling at her coat and flipping her blonde hair around.

She turned to see the two homicide detectives and Evelyn huddled around the covered bodies of Rosario Mendez and her child, whose life probably ended before it began at the bottom of the East River. She found herself thinking about Baby Boy Mendez and how he'd wavered between the past and present tense when referring to his sister. She thought about something Mount had said about Rosario practically being Baby Boy's mother. About how his mother hadn't cared enough about him to give him a proper name. Then she thought about Mount, accused of murdering a woman, beating her to death with his fists . . . a prostitute he might have loved or thought he loved. It was up to Jesamyn to prove he didn't kill her. And suddenly, it all just felt like too much. She walked toward the road, turning away from anyone who might see that tears she couldn't stop had welled in her eyes, threatened to spill down her face.

Twenty-One

Florida didn't seem like a real place with its pink birds and orange groves, mobile homes and hurricanes, the endless Jimmy Buffet soundtrack that played from the speakers of every restaurant and beachside souvenir shop. It seemed like someone's idea of a place. And not a very good idea at that. Furthermore, it was uncomfortable to wear black in Florida. And why would anyone want to go somewhere where it was difficult to wear black?

"And don't even get me started on Disney," Lydia said, peeling off her leather jacket and looking at the paper white skin on her arms.

Jeff and Dax both rolled their eyes. They'd heard the Florida rant before. They both knew after a couple of days down here, she'd shed all her clothes and turn into a total beach babe. You had to force her to put a tee-shirt on over her sunburn like a kid.

"If you ask me, this place is black at its core," she went on, not noticing as Jeffrey and Dax exchanged a look in the rearview mirror. "Anything this shiny and pretty and plastic has to have a rotten center. Pure evil."

In front of them, the gleaming white Gulf beach and the crystalline blue water beyond looked like an oasis between the heat waves that rose off the black concrete of the road. Of course, their last visit to Florida had been pretty frightening.

"You know, when we travel, we tend to see only the very worst a place has to offer . . . men with guns, back alleys," said Jeffrey. "Maybe you should give it a chance."

An ice cream truck jingled around the roundabout they were waiting to enter.

"They should outlaw those things," said Lydia.

"They should," said Dax. "That stupid goddamn music makes me want to pull out my rocket launcher."

"Man, this is a tough crowd," said Jeff. "You can't take New York anywhere. I kind of like it here. It's peaceful."

They pulled past a strip of outdoor bars and restaurants, tacky souvenir shops and real estate offices. To the right, white-capped water lapped lazily against a sugar-white beach. A median lined with tall, full palm trees that looked like giant pineapples divided the north- and south-heading lanes of the road. They stopped at a crosswalk and let a dumpy tourist family wearing tacky beach cover-ups and painful-looking sunburns cross in front of them. Dax ogled two bikini-clad rollerbladers with matching heads of bottle-blonde hair, huge fake tits, and impossibly slim bodies.

"Maybe it's not so bad down here after all, eh?" he observed absently.

They passed a row of gleaming high-rise hotels and crested a causeway that looked out over a marina lined with hundreds of boats in a canal that led to the Gulf. High cumulous clouds towered full and dramatic in a cerulean sky. Lydia rolled down the window to breathe in the salt and they all felt the swath of hot, humid air as it saturated the cool interior of the car.

The causeway ended in a lush explosion of green. The temperature dropped as they passed beneath a glade of trees that seemed to shelter the island in a dark canopy. From the road, they could no longer see the ocean because of the high walls that edged the magnificent homes lining the beaches. A thick cover of palms, oleander, and hibiscus bushes, fanning birds of paradise, and loblolly pine allowed only glimpses of tile roofs.

"I think this is it. Up here on the right," said Dax, scrolling down on his portable global positioning device.

They slowed as they passed a pair of heavy wrought-iron gates, the metal twisted and shaped to resemble thorned branches. Lydia saw the New Day logo on an unmarked plaque above an intercom speaker box. She felt the familiar buzz, an agitation to get behind those gates made her fidget in her seat. When she thought of Lily now, all she could see was that image, those sharp shoulder blades, the shaved head.

"Maybe we should call the police," said Lydia.

"Tell them what?" asked Jeffrey.

"That we think a missing girl is locked inside those gates," she said.

"And what do you think they'll do? Take a report and investigate, announcing to Trevor Rhames and company that we're here in Florida."

"And who knows?" added Dax. "They're as powerful in this town as the FBI seems to think, who's to say the chief of police is not a New Day devotee."

"Jeez, it was just a thought. Take it easy."

"We'll wait till dark," said Jeffrey, his eyes on the road, both hands on the wheel. "Then we'll try to find our way in."

"Since that's been working so well for us," she said, looking at him.

She heard Dax in the back tapping on the keys of his BlackBerry.

"What are you doing?" she asked, turning to watch as he typed furiously with his thumbs.

He looked up at her. "None of your beeswax," he said, sticking the device in his pocket. Lydia had a wave of technology lust and felt jealous.

"I need one of those," she said sullenly as she turned to watch the property pass. She could see the cupola on the roof peeking out through the trees and her thoughts turned, for some reason, to Shawna Fox, a girl she'd been far too late to help. She remembered the green eyes that stared out at her from a photograph handed to her by Shawna's desperate, sad boyfriend, Greg.

Lydia was a different person then, as sad and desperate as Greg, haunted by an unresolved grief for her mother that had become so much a part of her she barely even realized it. Old photos of people who were gone had angered Lydia then. They were cold, eerie reminders of how easily life was lost, of how vividly alive people remained in the memories of those who loved them, and how grief was the slick-walled, bottomless abyss between those places.

Her experiences since that time had taught her something about the nature of love and what it meant to lose it. She'd come to understand that though we may lose the people we love, the gift of their love remains. In the throes of grief, that was little comfort. But in time, that knowledge could bring a kind of peace, a tentative healing. She thought then of her father, whom she'd lost before she ever knew him, who she now realized had been trying to reach out to her for most of her life. She thought of the woman, the stranger, who might be her sister. She felt a wash of anxiety mingling with a strange feeling of hope. Shawna. Tatiana. Lily. The lost, grief-mangled girl Lydia herself had been once.

"Shit," she said aloud.

Jeffrey put a hand on her knee. "We'll find her," he said. "I promise."

She put her hand over his, looked at the wedding band on her finger, and nodded.

"We need to go inland," said Dax.

"Why?" asked Lydia, watching the house disappear from her view in the mirror.

"That compound you mentioned . . . organic produce or something, right?"

"Yeah."

"I found a listing for a New Day Farms."

She turned in the passenger seat to look at him; he turned his GPS out to her and showed her a little map on its screen.

"That must be the place Rusty Klautz claimed they were stockpiling weapons."

"It's interesting, isn't it?" said Jeffrey. "The waterfront property in an affluent area and a farm out in the-middle-of-nowhere Florida."

Dax nodded. "It's a good setup for trafficking."

"Trafficking what?" asked Lydia.

Dax shrugged. "Pretty much anything," he said. "Guns, drugs."

"Diamonds," said Jeffrey.

Dylan Breslow wouldn't walk a block to piss on Matt Stenopolis if he was on fire. The guy was an asshole, and if it weren't for old Mount, Dylan strongly suspected that he and Jesamyn would still be together. Maybe not. But it certainly hadn't helped their situation when Matt had stumbled upon Dylan making out with a female rookie from the Fifth Precinct at a bar on the Lower East Side. In fact, that was the incident that had led to Jesamyn asking Dylan to leave their home. Not that things had been great prior to that incident.

"I've dealt with the pain and humiliation your infidelity has caused me in our relationship. But I can't handle being humiliated in front of my co-workers," she told him. "You've just walked over the line. Don't even try to come back."

She'd meant it. He hadn't believed her at first but it wasn't even a month before he was served divorce papers. She had him served on the job during roll call, trying to get even with him, he figured, for hurting and humiliating her the way he had. He didn't blame her, really. He knew every shitty thing that had passed between them had been his fault; he even knew he didn't deserve her. But he loved her, loved her like a freight train through his heart. He just couldn't be faithful to her. He didn't have enough perspective on himself to understand why.

"Why am I trying to help this guy?" he asked himself aloud as he pulled the unmarked Caprice in front of the Brooklyn row house that belonged to Clifford Stern, the eyewitness who claimed to have seen Matt leave the scene of Katrina Aliti's murder. The day was bright and cold. An old lady in a black wool coat and a kerchief on her hair made her way slowly up the street with a walker and an air of determination. A young mother in tight jeans and a short, puffy white coat pushed a stroller, had a little rhythm to her step from whatever she was listening to on her headphones. In the schoolyard across the street, children about Ben's age played, bundled in thick parkas and little wool hats . . . jump rope, swing sets, jungle gyms. He smiled, thinking that no matter how the world changed, the schoolyard seemed always to maintain a comforting sameness. No video games, no Internet, just the simple physical games he had played when he was a kid. That's what kids needed, to run around, burn off some of that energy. They didn't need to be sitting in front of a screen somewhere, stimulating their developing brains with the worst possible garbage, growing physically inactive. It was a recipe for bad physical and mental health. He noticed teachers standing like sentries, arms crossed, eyes alert, by every possible exit or entrance from the yard, four in total. Someone had to keep the world and all its many terrible changes outside the perimeter of the last safe place.

He peeled back the tab on his coffee from the deli up the street and settled in. A door slammed somewhere close by and he started, spilling a little hot coffee on his jeans.

"Nice," he said, reaching for a napkin from the glove box. He dabbed the hot liquid and swore at the stain it left on his thigh. Since the shooting, he'd been really edgy. He dreamed about Jerome "Busta" White, the boy he'd killed. He'd wake up sweating, and more frightening, he'd had a couple of intense flashbacks during his waking hours. The shrink they made him see told him it was normal and that it would pass. And it *did* seem to be better, a little better every day. But he knew for a fact that he'd never forget that kid's eyes. How they were liquid and full of life and in a moment they'd turned cold and still as glass.

He'd never given a whole lot of thought to the concept of soul. But Dylan saw something *leave* that kid. How could it be that life just vanished that way? It was hard to understand in theory; it was harder to witness. They'd all wind up that way, abandoned by life. Him, Jesamyn, Ben, too, someday. The thought filled him with dread. He tried to push the dark thoughts away. They made him question everything about himself, everything about the way he'd lived his life so far. He got the terrible sense that everything he thought was cool and important was shit. That the things he thought were irrelevant, the things he had abused and taken for granted, were the only things that mattered. He'd been on the road for forty years, walking in the wrong direction, taking all the wrong turns. It made him feel sick inside. Worse, Jerome knew it, too. In those last seconds, he saw it. But it was too late for Jerome.

He closed his eyes a second and rested his head back against the seat. When he opened his eyes, he saw Clifford Stern come around the corner of Sixty-Sixth Street and walk up Fourteenth Avenue. He was a small, weaselly-looking man, with a shiny balding head and small, darting eyes. He walked quickly, looking around him nervously, then jogged up the stairs that led to his front door. Dylan noticed that he didn't turn his back completely to the street as he unlocked the door, but stood awkwardly sideways so that he could see behind him.

Jesamyn was right; there was something weird about all of this. He knew Stenopolis had a temper. He'd been on the receiving end of it. But having a temper and being the kind of soulless killer you had to be to beat a woman to death with your fists were not the same thing. He decided he'd give Clifford Stern a few minutes to relax; he seemed jumpy and afraid. Let him think he was home and safe for a few minutes. Then Dylan would have a few words with him, find out how well his story held up outside the safe environment of a police station.

This was not the best choice of activities for someone already being investigated by IAD for a shooting. But what could he do? The woman he loved, who currently hated his guts, needed him. He'd be crazy to pass up the opportunity to help her.

He dialed Jesamyn but got her voicemail and hung up. He thought about dialing Elena but thought better of it. After Jesamyn had wigged out that night, he'd broken it off with Elena, which pained him because of her outrageous ass, perfect tits, and silky blonde hair down to her waist. But she wasn't Jesamyn. He wanted to try to be faithful to Jez, even if there was no relationship at the moment. Maybe because he'd screwed up so many times, he'd have to be faithful to her *before* she took him back. That was his strategy anyway. He'd tell her about it after he helped her and she was feeling grateful. He knew he could make her listen. He could always make her listen; it was just getting her to *believe* that would be a challenge.

He turned the rearview mirror so that he could makes faces at himself for a second . . . sexy face, tough face, innocent face . . . and instead saw something behind him that caught his attention. He lowered himself in his seat and looked out the sideview mirror as a white van cruised slowly up Fourteenth Avenue. He slunk down further and closed his eyes to slits, feigning sleep, as the van passed by his parked car. The windows were darkly tinted, too dark to see the driver. This was illegal in New York City now, but older-model cars that were already tinted before the law was passed couldn't be ticketed. The van was well kept but definitely an earlier-model vehicle.

As the van passed by him slowly, he saw the New Day logo on its side.

"Huh," he said to himself. "How about that?"

Part of him had figured Jez was just being paranoid. She did have paranoid tendencies, especially where Ben was concerned. But there it was. The van made a U-turn and drove past Stern's house, pulled into a parking space, and came to a stop. Maybe Dylan was catching Jez's paranoia but he felt the hairs rise on his arms. There was something menacing about that van. He slunk down a little farther and waited.

"You shouldn't have done this," said Matt.

"My son is going to rot in prison? No," his mother said with an emphatic shake of her head. "No."

"Where'd you get the money?" he asked from the backseat of their 1990 Dodge Minivan.

"Don't worry about it," his father said sternly.

"Dad."

"They'll get it back," said Theo, putting a hand on his arm, which Matt promptly shook off and gave him a black look. How could he let them do this?

"After the trial," Theo said, like he needed to explain the law to Matt. Matt turned away from his brother's face; it was so earnest and young that he couldn't bear to see it. He would have rather stayed in jail than have his family risk their future to make the $500,000 bond. Even the ten percent they needed . . . where had they gotten that kind of money?

"They'd have killed you in there, bro," Theo whispered. "You're a cop."

Matt didn't look back at him or answer. He just stared at the river, at the other cars on the highway. The world seemed so changed. Grayer, colder. He envied the girl he saw singing along with whatever was playing on the radio of her sky blue convertible bug. He envied the kid talking into the wireless cell-phone headset, smiling. Their lives were blissfully intact. Maybe not perfect, but not shattered. They probably didn't even know how lucky they were.

"Your lawyer says that there are a lot of holes in their theory. He says he bets the charges will be dropped before this goes to trial." His brother was nervous, worried, filling silence.

"The truth will set you free, Mateo," said his father, raising a finger in the air. "The system works. They won't send an innocent man to jail."

He looked at the back of his father's balding head, his tearing eyes in the rearview mirror. Matt found himself, as always, simultaneously bolstered and enervated by the old man's optimism. Matt wanted to believe his father was right, but in his heart feared that his father was just hopelessly naïve about the way the world could grind you up if you got yourself caught in the wrong groove. Theo was more like their father, always facing the hard times with an outstretched chin, believing that the light was on their side. Matt was more like his mother. In the courtroom and in the sideview mirror now, he could see that her face was a mask of fear and sadness. In her brow resided the knowledge that something black had come for her son and it would likely as not succeed in taking him from her. She rested the side of her head in her palm, as if she didn't have the strength to sit upright.

"A prostitute," she said softly and then jumped as if she hadn't meant to say it out loud.

"That's not all she was, Ma," Matt said softly.

She released a noise that effectively communicated her disdain. He closed his eyes. His father turned on the radio, some oldies station where Bing Crosby was singing "White Christmas." They rode home in silence.

He was glad for the solitude when everyone stopped hovering and falling over themselves to feed him and comfort him, offering words of solace and encouragement. His aunts and uncles, a couple of his cousins had been waiting at his place when he returned, obviously cooking all day as a way to comfort themselves. The Greeks believed that there was no bad thing that could not be made bearable with enough food. He loved them all for what they were trying to do, but he'd never been so glad for the quiet of his own home. His mother urged him to come back and sleep in his old room, which they kept like a shrine to him and Theo. But he had refused. She'd looked at him with the hurt and angry expression that she'd had all day and eventually stopped insisting.

He lay on his bed in the dark and breathed in the heavy scent of oil and garlic that still hung in the air; in fact, he was comforted by it for a time. A heaviness, a terrible inertia had come over him. He should be out there, trying to find out who killed Katrina, trying to prove his innocence, trying to find Lily Samuels, but he felt like his legs were filled with sand, like there was lead in his belly. He knew fatigue on a level that he'd never experienced. Maybe it was all the *baklava,* but more likely it was the fact that no matter how he looked at it now, his life was over, or so changed as to be unrecognizable. They had taken his gun and shield; his career was over. Even if the charges were dropped or if he was acquitted, he'd never be a cop again. The thought of it was almost too much. He felt a heavy despair settle into his chest and his shoulders.

He was about to call Jesamyn and tell her he was out on bail when the phone rang.

"Hello?" he answered, rubbing his eyes and sitting up on the bed.

"You sound tired, Detective Stenopolis." It was a sweet female voice, young and mellifluous. "I'm not surprised with all that you've been through."

"Who's this?" he said.

He heard the sound of a car alarm somewhere off in the distance outside his window and realized he was also hearing it on the phone. He walked to the window and on the street across from his house, he saw a young woman dressed in blue jeans and a short leather jacket, holding a cell phone to her ear. She smiled at him and his heart thumped.

"Lily?"

She laughed and gave him a little wave. As he turned and bounded down the stairs with the cordless still in his hand, he heard the line go dead. He threw open the door and ran out onto his front stoop, wearing only a pair of navy blue sweatpants. The street was empty but he jogged down the steps and onto his drive, the frigid concrete burning his feet with its terrible cold.

"Lily!" he called hugging himself and running up the street. "Lily!" But she was gone. He turned the corner and saw no one. There was no way she could have disappeared so fast on foot. He walked a little farther up the block, then turned around. The excitement he'd felt turned to fear and embarrassment. Some neighbors had gathered at their windows and were looking at him with worried faces.

"Did anybody see her? Did anybody see a woman standing here?" he yelled, looking from window to window.

But no one answered him; they moved back from the windows and soon it was only him on the cold street, half naked. Theo was coming up the block hurriedly, carrying a coat for his brother.

"What's going on, man? Who was it? Who did you see?"

"Did you see her?" he asked urgently as he accepted the coat and wrapped it around his big shoulders.

"No, I didn't see anyone," said Theo, looking at him strangely. "I just heard you yelling. Shit, man. The whole neighborhood heard you yelling."

The younger, smaller man put his arm around his big brother and pushed him back toward the house. Theo glanced back over his shoulder and looked around him, glaring, as if daring anyone to still be staring at his brother.

Matt saw his parents coming out their door and suddenly realized how crazy he looked. He pulled the coat tighter and moved faster toward his house.

"Who did you see?" Theo asked again.

"Lily Samuels," he whispered. "I saw her."

Matt looked at his brother's face and saw something there that frightened him. Pity.

Twenty-Two

"Your boy's in trouble," said Dax.

Lydia was lying on one of the queen beds in the hotel room they'd taken to wait for nightfall. The place was a dump. Lydia had scanned the faux wood nightstands with their worn surfaces and nicked edges, initials carved on their sides, water-stained ceiling, and gritty stained bedspreads the most hideous shade of mauve. Then she closed her eyes. Outside, through glass doors that led to a small porch, the Gulf waters lapped the shore and the salt air almost covered the smell, some combination of cigarettes, stale booze, and puke. Jeffrey tapped away on his laptop on the rickety table by the window.

"What?" said Lydia, not opening her eyes. Dax turned up the volume on the set.

"Detective Mateo Stenopolis was released on bail today. Charged with the beating death of prostitute Katrina Aliti, Stenopolis left the courthouse after his family posted bond. The lawyers for the prosecution were outraged by the decision."

Lydia sat up quickly, shimmied to the end of the bed. The newscast continued.

"Obviously, special consideration was given to this man because he was a cop," a polished-looking young woman in a gray suit with dark hair pulled back severely from her face complained into the camera. "Anyone else charged with a crime of this viciousness would be held without bail until trial."

"The prosecution claims," the newscaster went on, "that they have overwhelming physical evidence as well as eyewitness testimony against Stenopolis and that their case against him is nothing less than airtight."

"No way," said Lydia. "Absolutely no way."

Dax turned down the volume on the set.

Jeff had come to sit beside her on the bed. "I was wondering why we hadn't heard from him after that message you left," he said.

"I thought he was just pissed at us because of the New Day break-in. Maybe trying to distance himself," said Lydia, standing up and walking over toward the glass doors.

They were all quiet for a second. "There's no way he is capable of something like that," Lydia said finally with an emphatic shake of her head.

"So what are you thinking?"

"He said that lawyer for The New Day threatened him," she said.

"So you think that he was set up for this?" asked Jeffrey. He sounded skeptical.

She looked at him. "It's easier to believe that than it is to believe he killed someone with his fists. He's a good man, a good cop. Do you know what kind of sociopath you have to be to do something like that? You have to be in a narcissistic rage, utterly without empathy."

"Lots of seemingly normal men are walking around with a terrible misogyny in their hearts, secretly believing themselves to be superior to women, hating them for the power of their sexuality," said Dax. He leaned back in the chair that groaned beneath his weight and gave her a smile, proud of himself.

Lydia looked at him; he had a point. He was a complete clod most of the time but every once in a while he came out with something pretty insightful. It always amazed her.

"Trust me, it's not as secret as they think," she said. "Any intelligent woman can spot a misogynist a mile away. It's in the way he looks at you, the tone in his voice. I got the sense of Stenopolis as very respectful, even when he was gruff."

Dax lifted his shoulders. "But you don't know."

"Overwhelming physical evidence and eyewitness testimony," said Jeffrey, repeating what they'd just heard on the screen.

"Can we find out what that means exactly?" asked Lydia.

"I'll call Striker and see what information he can gather," he said, reaching for the cell phone by the bed.

Lydia fished her own phone out of her bag and scrolled through the call log until she found Mart's cell phone number. His voicemail picked up before the first ring completed; he had his phone off. She hung up without leaving a message. She wasn't sure what to say. Chances are he wasn't thinking about Lily Samuels at the moment. She thought about Matt Stenopolis, how he'd looked on the street that day when she suggested he might think about a move to the private sector. Like he couldn't imagine himself as anything but a cop. She felt a strong twist of empathy and concern for him, even as she wondered if he was capable of murder—or if The New Day was doing this to get him off of Lily's trail.

She walked over to Jeffrey's laptop while he talked to Striker on the phone. She saw the satellite image of the New Day Farm that Craig had been able to obtain for them.

Lydia always called Craig "The Brain" behind his back. He stood a full head taller than Jeffrey but looked as thin as one of Jeffrey's thighs. Clad forever in hugely baggy jeans, a white tee-shirt under a flannel shirt, and a pair of Doc Martens, his pockets were always full of electronic devices . . . cell phone, pager, Palm Pilot, all manner of thin black beeping, ringing toys. A pair of round wire spectacles, nearly hidden by a shock of bleached blond hair, framed his blue-green eyes. Craig called himself a cybernavigator, though his title at Jeffrey's firm was Information Specialist. More or less plugged into the Internet twenty-four-seven, more or less legally, Craig could gather almost any piece of information needed at any time of the day or night.

The image just looked like a bunch of trees seen from above to Lydia but Jeffrey had been on the phone with Craig for nearly an hour talking about various elements of the image, Dax looking over his shoulder, chiming in. It annoyed her that they all seemed to be seeing something there that evaded her, like one of those stupid computer-generated images that revealed itself only after you stared at it for an hour. She opened another window and looked at the survey of the property. It showed three structures built on the fifteen-acre property. She looked back at the satellite image. Dax and Jeff claimed to be able to see at least six structures. She couldn't even see one through all the tree cover.

"Look for the unnatural lines," said Jeff, coming up beside her. "Nature doesn't like straight lines."

"Oh, there," she said after a moment, touching a finger to the screen where a hard edge showed through the tree cover. He nodded.

An anxiousness washed over her. As she traced the line of the building, the LCD screen turned black beneath the pressure of her finger.

"She's in there," she said. It was part declaration, part question. But something inside her told her they were close to Lily.

"If she is, we're going to bring her home."

She looked up at him. He had this way of sounding so confident she couldn't think of doubting him.

Jeff's phone rang then. He answered and sat on the bed. Lydia turned back to the screen. Another window revealed blueprints of one of the buildings at the New Day Farm. As far as Lydia was concerned, she might as well have been looking at hieroglyphics. Anything like that . . . maps, blueprints, forms . . . just shut her down mentally.

"Notice anything weird about this building?" whispered Dax who'd come to stand beside her.

She shook her head.

"No windows," he said.

"What does that mean?"

"Nothing good."

"Interesting," said Jeffrey, dropping the phone into the pocket of his shirt.

"What?"

"That was Chiam Bechim, the jeweler I saw. Someone tried to move some of those stolen stones. Apparently whoever was behind it paid the team in gems. Someone got anxious for his money and tried to sell a couple of small canary diamonds. Bechim's people were notified."

"Who are 'Bechim's people'?" asked Lydia.

Jeffrey looked at her and raised his eyebrows. "He didn't say."

"Okay," she said with a frown. "So who was it?"

"A guy named Manny Underwood. Started out in corrections. Lost his job and did some hard time for dealing drugs to inmates."

Dax winced. "Corrections officers don't usually do well in prison."

Jeff nodded. "He lived through it because he made some powerful friends inside. Later on, these same people gave him work in 'personal security.' Apparently, Manny's a big guy, total roid case. Good bodyguard material. Anyway, after he was released he went to work for a company called Body Armor. Ring a bell?"

"Body Armor," Lydia repeated, the name sounding familiar to her.

"Owned until about a year and a half ago by Tim Samuels."

Lydia let the information sink in. "Huh," she said, not having anything more intelligent to offer at the moment. The loose connections between people and events were not coalescing for her. Tim Samuels to Michele LeForge to The New Day, The New Day to Mickey, Mickey to Lily, Tim Samuels' former employee to a jewel robbery to a pink stone found in an abandoned building that LaForge once declared as her residence. It was a chain of evidence linked only to itself, circular and useless.

"Do we know who bought his company?" asked Dax.

"We don't know. But I'm starting to have my suspicions."

"The New Day," said Dax.

"I'd put money on it. That's probably how Samuels got tangled up with them in the first place. Maybe he didn't even know it."

"What would The New Day want with a personal security firm?" said Lydia.

Jeffrey shrugged. "Maybe they needed some trained muscle."

They were all quiet as they considered the reasons why a 'church' would need trained muscle. She thought of the men who'd chased her from the premises. She thought of Lily in restraints. She thought of the jewel heist and Detective Stenopolis accused of a terrible crime she was sure he couldn't have committed. Who are these people? she thought.

"Well, maybe Underwood has some answers," suggested Dax.

"Doesn't sound like he knows much of anything. At least nothing Bechim was willing to share."

"We can talk to him when we get back to New York. Tomorrow. With Lily," said Lydia. She was shooting for optimism but it sounded more like desperation even to her own ears.

"When are we going to leave?" asked Lydia. She'd managed her anxiety into a low-level buzz but the volume was coming up again.

"I just want to do a little more research on that building," said Dax, moving over to the computer.

There was an aggressive knock on the door to their room. All of them froze for a second, then Lydia moved to the wall beside the door. She felt her heart start to stutter and looked at the bag across the room that contained her gun.

"Room service," a gruff muffled voice said through the thin wood. Jeffrey and Dax exchanged a look.

"Ever see a dump like this offer room service?" whispered Dax.

"Especially when we didn't call for anything," said Jeff, kneeling behind the bed and taking his gun from his waist. Dax was about to follow suit, when the door busted in and three unpleasant-looking men in suits entered, guns drawn.

"Guns on the bed, please. Hands where we can see them," said a balding man with ice blue eyes and small but powerful-looking physique. He sounded tired, bored, like he'd said the words so many times that his jaw ached from it.

Jeff and Dax put their guns on the bed and their hands on their heads. Lydia felt the tension drain from her shoulders and her adrenaline stop pumping. Federal Agents; better than the New Day freaks.

"Ms. Strong, can you please stand over by your associates?"

Lydia complied and the man replaced his sidearm in its holster and withdrew identification from the lapel pocket of his jacket.

"I'm Special Agent John Grimm with the FBI and you are in my space." He glanced behind him. "Stand down, boys." The two younger agents, both thin and fresh faced with good haircuts, replaced their weapons.

"You can take your hands off your heads," said Grimm, moving toward the bed. Jeffrey and Dax got to their feet. Grimm leaned down and picked up the Desert Eagle.

"Jesus. That's nice. I've never seen one of those. Going moose hunting?"

Dax looked very stiff, his face drained of color. Grimm laid the gun back on the bed.

"I know who you are, Ms. Strong. And you, Mr. Mark, I believe we met when you were still with the Bureau. But I'm not sure I've been introduced to your colleague here."

"Ignatius Bond," said Dax, extending a hand.

Grimm looked at Dax and nodded. Dax withdrew his hand with a smile that was really more like a grimace. There was an energy between the two men that Lydia wasn't sure she understood.

"So what brings you all to Florida?" said Grimm, walking over to the laptop and touching the mouse pad.

"We're vacationing," said Lydia.

Grimm turned the laptop around so that they could see the satellite photo of the New Day Farms.

"I don't know what you're planning here, my friends. But let's sit down and have a little talk about what you think you know about The New Day."

Twenty-Three

"Is it her? How do you know it's her?"

Baby Boy Mendez kept asking the same two questions as they drove him from the Alphabet City apartment he'd shared with his sister to the morgue at Belleview Hospital. It was like he'd been caught in some kind of hysterical loop since they showed up at his apartment and gave him the news. He'd been eating a Whopper and watching SpongeBob SquarePants on Nickelodeon when they'd entered the apartment, told him the body of a woman and her child had been found in the East River.

"We'll need you to identify her, Baby Boy," Evelyn told him quietly. "We'll confirm her identity with dental records but that'll take time. It's going to be hard but you need to come and see if the woman we found is your sister."

He'd looked at them, eyes moving back and forth between the two women as if he was looking for an expression that would tell him it was a joke or a mistake. Then he ran from them. They waited patiently as they listened to him throw up in the bathroom.

"What if you're wrong?" Evelyn whispered to Jesamyn.

She put her hands in her pockets and rocked back on her heels, considering the question. Then, "He still needs to identify her."

"He could do it from a photograph or on a video monitor."

Jesamyn shook her head. She wanted Baby Boy Mendez to see his sister's body and the body of his nephew. She wanted him to see what she suspected he had done to them. If she was wrong, well, she was unnecessarily traumatizing an innocent family member. And that would suck for him and for her; she'd feel very badly about it. She just didn't think she was wrong.

Evelyn looked doubtful. She didn't see it in Mendez. But Jesamyn saw a kind of childish rage, a jealousy over the baby who would soon be the focus of his sister's life, leaving Baby Boy without a mother, in his mind anyway. The child who no one ever cared about enough to even name would be losing the only mother he'd ever known. He probably hadn't meant to kill her. Or maybe he had. It didn't much matter in the scheme of things.

In the car, she could still smell his vomit and the acrid odor of fear, sweat.

"Is it her? How do you know it's her?"

She'd be doubting herself if he was wailing, accusing Jorge Alonzo of his sister's murder. But he wasn't doing any of those things. He was pale, the features on his face slack, his eyes shifting back and forth almost imperceptibly. To Jesamyn all of these things said guilt and fear, not grief, not terror over the fate of a loved one, not hope that the police were mistaken in their tentative identification of the body.

"That's why we need you to make the positive ID, Baby Boy," said Evelyn. "We could be wrong."

Evelyn threw her a look and Jesamyn folded her arms. No one would ever ask a family member to ID a body as badly decomposed as Rosario Mendez's and Jesamyn could see that Evelyn was sick over it. They could wind up getting sued, especially since this was technically no longer their case. It was a homicide case now.

"She never changed to go out to the clubs that night," Jesamyn had said to Evelyn on the dock. "She stayed home."

"Which contradicts what Baby Boy told us," said Evelyn, watching the Medical Examiner's van pull away.

"He pointedly told us that she had changed. That he saw what she'd been wearing when he left folded on her bed."

Evelyn nodded.

"When Mount and I talked to him, he wavered back and forth between referring to her in the past and present tense," Jesamyn went on when the other woman didn't say anything.

"He did that with us, too. Wong thought it meant something."

"I don't think Alonzo cared enough about Rosario and their baby to bother killing them. I mean, what's his motive? What does he have to gain?"

"He claimed the baby wasn't his," said Evelyn.

"So?" she said with a shrug. "That's not a motive. She never asked him for anything, not even money, according to her friends."

"So what are you suggesting?" Evelyn had asked, putting her hands in her pocket and shrugging against the cold.

"Let's bring the brother in for the ID."

Baby Boy started to sniffle as the three of them walked up the cold gray hallway. Until then, there had only been the sound of her and Evelyn's heels, the squeaking of Baby Boy's sneakers on the linoleum floors. The smell of death and chemicals was already strong and the morgue was still a few doors down. The fluorescent lights above buzzed.

"I don't know if I can do this," he said, coming to a stop. Jesamyn took a hard look at him. There was only fear there in his liquid brown eyes. He'd wrapped his arms around himself, was shifting from foot to foot.

"There's no other way," said Jesamyn. "I'm sorry."

"One of her friends, maybe," he suggested. "One of them could do it."

Jesamyn shook her head. "You're her next of kin, Baby Boy. It's your job to do this for her. You're all she has, now. The only one. She took care of you all your life; now you have to do this for her." It was a bull's-eye; she saw it as his face fell to pieces. His liquid brown eyes ran over and the tears started to fall. He doubled over, gripping his stomach as if he were in terrible pain.

"Oh, God," he wailed. "I'm so sorry. Rosie, I'm so sorry. Oh, God. I miss her so much." He dropped to his knees and Jesamyn was beside him.

"You were so jealous of that baby, weren't you?" she whispered, putting her arm around him. He wailed harder. "You were so angry with her for betraying you, loving someone else as much as she loved you. More. He wasn't even born yet and she already loved him more, didn't she?"

He pushed Jesamyn away and leaned against the wall. "Get away from me," he shrieked.

"There's nothing like the love between a mother and her son," said Jesamyn, standing, her voice low and sure now. "It can't even compare to the love between a sister and her brother; it's not the same."

He released the most heartbreaking cry. "He was all she ever talked about," he screamed. "The baby, the baby, her baby boy. I just wanted her to shut the fuck up about him. *I* was her baby boy. That's *my* name."

Jesamyn felt a stab of pity for him. Pity and disgust.

"She was in labor, wasn't she, when you came home?" asked Evelyn, as if the thought had just occurred to her. "She needed you to take her to the hospital."

Jesamyn shot her a look, afraid the shaking judgment in Evelyn's voice would shut him down. Baby Boy was sobbing now, sliding down the wall until he was sitting on his haunches.

"She was in labor and you killed her," said Evelyn with a shake of her head. "How did you do it?"

He stopped crying then. He wiped his eyes and his nose with the sleeve of his Rangers jersey. He issued a couple of shuddering breaths. Jesamyn was sure he had realized that he was on the brink of confessing, that he'd come back to himself.

"I hit her in the back of the head with a bat," he said, quietly. "She never even saw it coming. She never knew."

Evelyn let go of a sigh and bowed her head. Baby Boy's face went blank then and he glanced up at the ceiling for a second.

When he looked down, he said quietly, "I want my lawyer."

The homicide guys tried to take the collar but Evelyn fought them for it. It was her case from the beginning and she wanted the arrest. She wasn't going to let someone stroll in during the last round and take the credit for all her weeks of late nights and dead ends. It didn't give Jesamyn any satisfaction to put the cuffs on Baby Boy and bring him in with Evelyn. Jorge Alonzo she would have liked to see in a cage. But Mendez was this damaged kid, acting out of his own abused spirit. He'd live with the hell of what he had done every day for the rest of his life.

Jesamyn left the precinct a few hours later after helping Evelyn get started with the paperwork, then leaving her to finish it up. It was Evelyn's collar, after all. She'd get the glory, which Jesamyn didn't mind, as long as she didn't have to do all the typing and waiting around that followed an arrest. Stepping onto the concrete, she saw Dylan across the street on the swing set in the park beside the lot. She crossed the street and laced her fingers through the chain-link fence.

"What's going on?" she asked.

"I've been trying to call you," he said, coming around the fence. "I have something to show you. You need to come with me."

"What do you need to show me?" she asked, suspicious. She

wondered if he was just dangling a line to get her to spend some time alone with him.

"I'll tell you on the way," he said, moving toward his GTO. She could see the fin and the white stripe that ran from the hood to the trunk just a few cars down. She didn't follow him right away.

"Where are we going?" she asked again, but the wind took her words away. He didn't appear to hear her question.

He turned around and extended a hand. "Come on. What are you waiting for?"

Though her feet felt like they were made out of lead all of a sudden, though something inside her resisted, she followed him. She always followed him.

The moon shone through his window and bathed his legs in its milky light. He was watching for her, the phone in his hand. He could hear the laugh track from whatever his brother was watching on the television downstairs; his family didn't want to leave him alone now. All he wanted was to be alone and wait for Lily in peace. If it was Lily he had seen at all. If there had been anyone there on the street outside his house. He wondered absently if he was losing his mind. He didn't think so; he still felt like himself, if a little numb, a little emptied out.

He'd tried to call Jesamyn but she hadn't picked up the phone and he hadn't left a message. He'd checked his messages and found three from Lydia Strong. The last one had been left just a few hours earlier.

"Don't worry," she'd said. "We're in Florida. We're going to find Lily and—" The cell phone connection had cut out before she'd finished her message. He wondered if she knew that he'd been accused of murder and arrested. He thought about calling her back but he didn't know what to say. The phone had sat limp in his hand for the better part of an hour while he scrolled through all his options, rejected each, and eventually wound up doing nothing except sitting by the window, waiting.

"What are you doing, bro?" asked Theo, who had appeared in the doorway. He looked worried. No, that wasn't right. He looked scared.

"Just sitting here."

Theo nodded in the solemn way he had. "Why don't you try to get some sleep?"

"I will," said Matt.

Theo nodded again and put his hands in the pockets of his jeans and pulled his shoulders up, took a deep breath. "It's going to be okay, you know?"

"I know."

Matt was older and bigger than Theo, but Theo had always been the one to take care of him. When Matt was taunted at school for his height and awkwardness, it was Theo who always took up the fight. When Matt was tortured by his shyness around girls, it was Theo who advised him. Matt felt guilty that Theo had to sit on his couch while his wife was home alone.

"Go home, man," said Matt. "You don't need to be here. I'm not going to do anything stupid."

"I don't want you to be alone, Mateo," his brother said sadly. He'd been a sensitive, compassionate kid who'd grown into a kind and caring adult. Matt was proud of Theo.

"I'm okay. Really. I'm just going to go to bed. Before? I was probably just dreaming. The stress of everything, maybe just got to me for a minute. But it's fine, you know. I'm fine."

He tried to make himself look normal by sitting up straight and smiling. But from the look on Theo's face he suspected that it wasn't successful. Theo walked over to him and put a hand on his shoulder, bent down and kissed him on the head.

"Just call me if you see anything else, you know, before you go running out into the street like that?"

"I promise," said Matt, inwardly breathing a sigh of relief.

Theo gave him a quick pat on the back and moved backward toward the door.

"You sure—?" he started to say, but Matt lifted a hand to stop him.

"I'm sure, Theo. Thanks."

When he heard the door close downstairs, he stood and quickly got dressed, pulling on a pair of jeans, a gray wool sweater and a pair of Timberlands. He took his wallet from the dresser and from a lock box in the back of his closet he removed his off-duty revolver, a five-shot Smith and Wesson. He moved quickly to his office and took out a file that contained all his banking records, his life insurance policy, of which his parents were the beneficiaries, and all of his investments. There was another file that contained his will. They were papers most cops had in order, someplace easy to find. He left them all on the kitchen table. There was enough, he thought, to cover his bond if he didn't make it back. He pulled on his leather jacket and walked out the back door of his house. He told himself not to look back and he didn't.

———

Too many bodies and a struggling old window air-conditioning unit made the hotel room too warm. Lydia shed the tailored black gabardine jacket she'd been wearing and laid it on the bed beside her. She pulled her hair back into a twist at the base of her neck as Special Agent John Grimm spoke. She liked him. He was sarcastic and tough, but not disrespectful of why they'd come to Florida.

"We first heard about Trevor Rhames in 1994," said Grimm, crossing his legs and tapping a finger on the tabletop. His eyes were on the satellite image of the New Day compound. "He was arrested in the former Yugoslavia for selling arms to the Bosnians after the UN had imposed the embargo that pretty much left them at the mercy of the Serbian nationalists."

"There are plenty of people who think the UN never should have imposed that embargo," said Dax, a little defensively, thought Lydia. John Grimm gave him a long, hard look.

"Anyway," said Grimm, looking away from him and turning his eyes to Jeffrey. "He was found to be working with a company called Kintex."

"The arms company owned by the Bulgarian government," said Jeffrey with a frown. "How did he wind up working with them?"

"It's a bit of a mystery," said Grimm. "Rhames, as you probably know, is an American. You might not know that he was a decorated Marine, honorably discharged from service after touring in Rwanda, Iraq, and the former Yugoslavia. For a couple of years, he kept a very low profile, worked in security systems in the private sector with the training he'd received in the Marines. He dropped off the radar for a while, then he turned up overseas in Bulgaria.

"Bulgaria has been notorious for decades as an anything-goes arms bazaar, selling things like assault rifles, mortars, antitank mines, ammunition, all kinds of explosives to anyone who has the money to buy, no matter what their agenda," said Grimm. "They've supplied—utterly without code or conscience—arms in Yugoslavia, Iraq, Sierra Leone, Libya, regions riven with conflict, rebel governments guilty of the most heinous civil-rights violations.

"The government keeps trying to get it under control because they want very badly to become part of NATO and the European Union," he continued. "But the arms business is so entrenched in that culture that it's almost impossible to be rid of it without bankrupting the economy. Then of course there's all the corruption."

"Okay," said Lydia, thinking this was the first she'd heard of Bulgaria's weapons activities. "So he wound up there doing what?"

"We're not sure exactly. But he was apprehended during an Interpol sting where Kintex was selling guns to the Bosnians in direct violation of the UN embargo. He was extradited to the United States. He was charged and indicted for illegal weapons sales and did two years in a military prison."

"That's all you get for something like that?" asked Lydia. "Two years?"

Grimm leaned back and crossed his arms. "His spotless military record and lack of criminal history helped. And he made a deal. He gave up some of the security codes he'd established for Kintex, some names and some upcoming deals, which allowed Interpol to intercept some illegal shipments. Anyway, after he was released he disappeared completely for a few years. Then he turned up working for a company called Sandline, a Privatized Military Company incorporated in the Bahamas but with bases of operation all over world."

"What's a Privatized Military Company?" said Lydia with a frown. "Like mercenaries?"

"In a sense," said Grimm. "More like companies that facilitate arms deals, consult with 'legitimate' or democratically elected governments being threatened by rebel factions, provide trained soldiers for 'conflict resolution,' usually elite former military men from around the world."

"For a price," said Lydia.

"For a *huge* price," said Grimm with a nod.

Her eyes fell on Dax, who was examining with great fascination the floor between his feet. He raised his eyes to her, saw her looking at him, and quickly looked away. Lydia held back a smile.

"They work best for small conflicts," said Jeffrey. "Where only a couple of thousand men are needed for a job. But if they operate without conscience or in violation of UN accords, then they can have a destabilizing effect. You know, like arming rebels against a democratically elected government. But at their best, PMCs are effective for hostage negotiations or rescue operations, disaster cleanup, monitoring elections, sort of small, dirty jobs."

Lydia nodded absently, the wheels already turning as she tried to connect this new information to what they already had.

"How do you go from being a mercenary to being a preacher?" Lydia asked.

"It's a good question. He joined The New Day in 1998 after injuries he sustained on an op for Sandline. He almost died from multiple gunshot wounds and broken bones. He took some bullets and got blasted out a third-floor window in Kosovo. There was no reason for him to survive but he did. And apparently, during a grueling convalescence at a rehab center in Florida, he found religion."

"Or it found him," said Jeffrey.

Grimm nodded. "He was ripe for recruitment. Injured, likely depressed, no family or personal connections. Rhames was orphaned at the age of ten when his parents died in a house fire that he escaped; he went to live on a working farm belonging to his uncle and aunt.

"By all accounts, he was happy enough there. With a genius-level IQ, he did well in school, but was a bit of loner. Unfortunately, a year after Rhames arrived, his aunt and uncle died in a house fire that the boy escaped."

Jeffrey and Lydia exchanged a look. They knew too well the childhood signs of psychosis. Arson was a big one.

"Suspicious? Yes," said Grimm, reading their faces. "But there was never any evidence that Rhames had started those fires. He had no other history of violent or aberrant behavior. He was sent to a state-run orphanage, the money and the land left to him by his parents and his uncle kept in a trust for him until he turned eighteen and was emancipated from the system. It was a fair amount of money for a young man, enough to go to college and start a life. But he chose to join the Marines.

"He excelled in the Corps. I mean, he was the best of the best. He became a part of an elite unit that doesn't officially have a name. And his activities, until his honorable discharge in 1981, are classified. There aren't many people who know what he did during that time."

"Okay, so he went into the Marines, was discharged in 1981. He was off the radar for a while, you have no idea what he was doing until he showed up selling arms in 1994. He was arrested and went to prison for two years. After which point he went to work for Sandline. He was injured and almost killed but somehow recovered and wound up running The New Day?" asked Jeffrey.

Grimm shook his head. "Well, I wouldn't say 'runs' it exactly," he said, leaning forward. "It's a big multinational organization, with tentacles reaching into a number of different business arenas, real estate, the entertainment industry, banking. Rhames isn't a businessman. He's a tactician, a security specialist, a soldier. We don't know enough about his military career but we do know that he's trained in what the military refers to as 'psych ops,' the ability to manipulate and control an enemy through brainwashing and mind games. What he does for the organization is unclear."

"So who shot him in Kosovo?" asked Jeffrey.

"Who shot him, how he survived and got back to Florida are all unknowns. The unofficial word was that Sandline wanted to be rid of Rhames," said Grimm. "He was unpredictable and becoming a liability; they doubted his loyalty. A couple of security breaches led the higher-ups to suspect someone was selling codes and information. But he knew too much to just serve him his walking papers."

"So they arranged for his termination, but he survived?" asked Jeff. Grimm nodded.

"Why haven't they come after him again?" asked Lydia.

"Who says they haven't? They just haven't succeeded in getting to him. In fact, you three got closer to him than anyone ever has. As you know, his security is very tight."

It was clear now why Rhames had spent so much money on his security system.

"I just walked in through the front door," said Lydia.

"What did you see in there?" asked Grimm.

"A guy with a lot of personal power giving desperate people some hope, some spaced-out looking people in tunics, and a couple of big bald guys in leather."

"On security monitors I saw people in five-point restraints, on feeding tubes, wide awake," said Jeffrey.

Grimm didn't seem surprised. "We've been on you since that night."

"Why?" asked Jeffrey. "What do you want from us?"

"I'm glad you asked," said Grimm.

"I was sitting out here, waiting to go in when the van pulled up. Look. It's still there."

They'd parked the GTO on Fourteenth Avenue and walked up Sixty-Sixth Street, stopping at the corner across from Clifford Stern's residence. Jesamyn looked at her watch.

"How long ago?" she asked.

Dylan shrugged. "Like five or six hours."

"Just sitting there all this time. Why?"

"Maybe they're trying to make sure he stays put. At first, I thought maybe they were going to head in there . . . kill him, take him, what-ever. But then I thought, why? If what you say is true and The New Day is trying to frame Stenopolis, they need his testimony."

"Right."

"I waited here for hours and then I came to find you."

"Why didn't you just call me?"

He looked down at his feet. "I tried; you didn't answer," he said.

"And I was afraid you wouldn't come if I just left a message for you to meet me here."

She looked at him, then back at the van. "You didn't go across the street to see what was going on in there?"

He shook his head, turned his eyes on her. "I didn't want to give myself up, in case they were looking to make some kind of a move."

"And you didn't see anyone exit the van?" Another shake of the head. She didn't see anyone in the driver's seat.

"You should have kept trying to call me and stayed with the van. Who knows what happened here in the hour or so you were gone?"

He didn't say anything, just pulled his sheepish face. He'd used this as an excuse to spend time with her. He brought her here not to help Mount but to hold her in his thrall, create a drama they could share. If he'd called, she would have come but she would have had her own car, could have come and gone as she pleased without him. He was such a child.

"So what are we doing here?" she said. "I mean what are we going to accomplish here?"

"Let's call it in, let's call the van into 911. Suspicious vehicle."

"What does that do?"

"It ties The New Day to Clifford Stern, gives some plausibility to the story you told Detective Bloom."

She held his eyes for a second. It wasn't a bad idea. It was effective and by the book. Or they could call Bloom directly; they weren't breaking any laws by being there. They were both off duty, just passing through the neighborhood that just happened to be where Clifford Stern, the man who'd implicated her friend and partner, was probably watching television like he hadn't just ruined somebody's life.

"Why didn't you do that before?"

He showed her his palms.

"Did you run the plate?"

He opened his mouth to answer when two flashes of light lit up Stern's bay window. Two sharp pops followed; then another blue flash. Another pop.

"Oh, shit," said Dylan, grabbing her arm hard and pulling her back from the corner. The sound of gunfire, even muffled, was unmistakable to both of them.

"Oh, my God," said Jesamyn, reaching for the Glock at her waist as she instinctively dropped to a crouch. But no one exited the front door of the row house; there was no movement from the van. The street remained quiet, no one popping their heads out windows, no new lights coming on.

"Call 911," said Dylan.

She hesitated, wanting to go up there herself. He put a hand on her arm.

"If you don't, and someone just killed Clifford Stern, you're the first person on the scene. Do you realize what that looks like?" he said, reaching into the pocket of her coat for her phone.

She looked at him. He was right. It would look like she shot him. She had no business being there, no legitimate reason for being in the vicinity. Something in her went stone cold.

"That's crazy," she said uncertainly. "My gun hasn't been fired. Ballistics test would prove I hadn't shot him."

He looked at her like she'd lost her mind. There was something she hadn't seen very often in his eyes. Fear. "Aren't you the one insisting that The New Day framed Stenopolis, that somehow they managed to plant blood and fingerprint evidence to implicate him?" he whispered fiercely. "Protect yourself, Jesamyn. Protect both of us. For Ben."

The sound of their son's name caused a tide of panic to rise within her. She grabbed the cell phone from him and put it back in her pocket.

"I can't use that. Are you nuts?" she said and moved away from him quickly toward the pay phone on the corner. She pulled on her gloves and dialed 911, made the report, keeping the receiver away from her mouth and ear. These days they could get prints and DNA off of anything. Chances were if there were no other witnesses, they'd be looking for the person who made the 911 call. Inwardly she cursed herself as they climbed into the GTO. Every instinct had told her not to come here with him. They pulled down Fourteenth Avenue as three police cars raced past them, sirens crying, lights spinning.

"What if someone saw us?" she asked him.

"No one saw us. Besides, even if they did, there's no way for them to identify us. I mean it's not like we're wearing name tags."

He was trying to be funny. But there was nothing funny about this. He pulled the car over in front of an espresso shop; she could smell the aroma of coffee and the sweet smell of pastry from inside the car. He leaned over her and turned on his police scanner; the chatter, sizzle of static, and beeping filled the car.

"Let's get a coffee and listen to the scanner. See what happened in there."

She nodded and he left the car. She listened to the crackle and hiss of his police scanner, the voices fuzzy and distant like they were coming from the moon. A robbery, two units responding. A suspicious man standing on the corner, one car on the way. She listened. A Medical Examiners van and CSI team summoned to 1604 Fourteenth Avenue.

"Dispatch, we got a DB, multiple gunshot wounds," said a deep male voice. "A witness describes the suspect as a Caucasian male, more than six feet tall, big build, over two hundred and fifty pounds, wearing a dark jacket, possibly leather, and blue jeans. He exited the back of the home and scaled the fence to the street. Witnesses say he headed east on foot."

"Units responding," said the dispatcher.

"Oh my God," said Jesamyn.

Dylan slid back into the car, handed her a coffee and a white bag that was already greasing through on the bottom with whatever pastry was inside.

"They've got a dead body at the scene. The suspect matches Mount's description," she said to him with a smile. "But Mount's in lockup. Maybe whoever killed Stern, killed Katrina Aliti. They said he was heading east on foot; let's go."

Dylan looked down at her with a frown. "Jesamyn, you didn't hear?"

"What?"

"Mount's out," he said. "He was released on bail earlier this afternoon."

She looked at him and thought she might throw up.

"No," she said, searching his face for dishonesty or uncertainty. "He would have called."

Dylan shook his head slowly. "His family posted bond. He went home this afternoon. Suspended without pay pending the outcome of the trial."

She kept staring at him, the full implication of his words sinking in. Dylan looked away uncomfortably after a moment, sipped on his coffee. Taking the phone from her pocket, she scrolled through the call log. A couple hours earlier there was a call from Mart's home phone but no message. She quickly dialed the number and waited as the phone just rang and rang. She tried his cell, but the voicemail picked up immediately, indicating to her that he had it off. Her throat felt tight; her hands cold.

"Listen," Dylan said gently. "Nobody who was guilty of Aliti's murder would kill the witness implicating someone else. If The New Day is trying to frame Mount, they're not going to kill their eyewitness. The only person who would want the witness dead is the person being implicated."

"Unless they just want Matt to look guilty for this, too."

Dylan sighed and rolled his eyes. "Come on Jez. Let's get real, here."

"You saw the van," she almost shouted. "What were they doing there? What's The New Day's connection to Clifford Stern?"

"Maybe it was a coincidence," he said with a shrug.

She looked at him, incredulous. "A coincidence?"

"Yeah," he said weakly. "It's not out of the realm of possibility, is it? That the van was parked there for some other reason not relating to Clifford Stern?"

She shook her head. "Just drive East on Sixty-Sixth Street."

"Why?"

"Just do it."

He put the car into gear and made a left on Sixty-Sixth Street.

"He could be anywhere by now. It's not like we're going to find him strolling up the street, taking in some air."

Jesamyn knew he was right but it made her feel better to be doing something. She scanned the few figures on the street, walking quickly, huddled against the cold. Matt or someone who looked like him would be easy to spot. Speaking of coincidences, she couldn't help but wonder how they wound up here for this. She thought about how they just happened to get there, minutes before the shooting, just in time to call 911. She looked at Dylan, who had his eyes on the road.

"Why did you bring me here?"

"What? I told you. So you could see the van." He glanced at her quickly, then put his eyes back on the road.

"How did you know it would still be here?"

"I didn't."

She didn't say anything, just scanned the streets, peering between buildings, glancing up on the el platform. Maybe she was getting paranoid. After all, what was she thinking? She'd asked him to help her and that's what he was doing, in his own self-serving way. Her head felt foggy; she was overtired, overwhelmed, and confused. She rested her head against the cool window, never taking her eyes off the street. Was it possible that Mount had killed Clifford Stern? She tried it on, toyed with accepting the idea. That he was terrified or had lost his mind, had shot the man out of some kind of desperation or temporary insanity. She shook her head. It just didn't fit; there was no way. But he might as well have shot Stern; a man matching Mount's description was seen leaving the scene after shots were fired. There weren't that many people who looked like Mount and he was already accused of another murder in which Stern was the witness. His fate was more or less sealed, wasn't it? Except that she had seen the New Day van parked outside the apartment.

"Go back," she said.

"Where?

"To Stern's street," she said. "I want to make sure that van doesn't go anywhere."

He nodded and made a U-turn, headed back toward Fourteenth Avenue.

There was a sea of police vehicles in front of the Stern residence. They arrived as the Medical Examiners van and the CSI team were approaching the row house. She saw Ray Bloom through the bay window over the porch as they parked the car and approached the corner where they'd heard the gunfire. She turned to see the van. But, of course, it was gone. A beat-up red Saturn had already taken its place.

"Shit," she said. "Shit." She put her head in her hands. She almost cried right there on the street.

Dylan put a hand on her shoulder. "Let's go talk to Bloom," he said softly. "Let's tell him what we saw. He's a smart guy; he'll know we're telling the truth."

She nodded. They had no choice. If they didn't, Mount didn't have a chance.

Matt sat against the concrete wall in the alley, barely noticing the stench of urine and garbage. His heart had just slowed to a normal rhythm but his lungs still ached from the exertion of effort and terror. He'd run nearly ten blocks through back alleys. His hands and thighs were still shaking. He put his head down in his hands and felt the warm, viscous liquid against his forehead.

"Oh, Christ," he said, surprised at the shaking fear he heard in his own voice. He drew his hands back and they were dark with blood. He thought of the backdoor handle where he'd exited the house, the fence that he'd grabbed and pulled himself over. He stood and stripped off his leather jacket, then the sweater he wore beneath it. If the police caught up with him, he didn't want to be wearing clothes soaked with Clifford Stern's blood. He threw the sweater in the trash Dumpster beside him. He inspected the leather jacket for blood in the dim glow of the streetlight and saw that it was clean; he put it back on and zipped it up to his throat. He leaned over and vomited, his whole body wracked with it.

A squad car raced past the alleyway, lights flashing but siren off. He jumped and crouched behind the Dumpster, hitting his head on its metal side. He was shivering now from fear and from the cold and from pain. He could barely believe that his life had come to this, that he was squatting in an alley hiding from the police. He tried to think of the moment, the pivot on which his life had turned. He could pinpoint it exactly: when he'd threatened Trevor Rhames and The New Day. But no. Maybe it was earlier than that. Maybe it was the day he fell in love with Lily Samuels, a girl he'd never seen in the flesh until tonight. If the girl he'd seen had been her at all. If he'd even seen a girl. He couldn't be sure now; the memory of her felt foggy and indistinct.

He tried to think about his options but the pain in his head was so bad he thought he might be having a stroke. He *wished* he were having a stroke, that he would drop dead right there—then at least he wouldn't have to deal with the disaster his life had become. What was he supposed to do now?

He'd just wanted to talk to Clifford Stern, wanted to understand why this stranger had implicated him in a crime he didn't commit. He'd believed he could convince the guy to go to the police with the truth: that The New Day had paid him or threatened him to be an eyewitness. There was no other explanation. But he should have known not to go there, should have known that they'd be waiting. Now the abyss he'd fallen into was deeper and darker than it had been hours earlier, and it had been pretty fucking deep and dark.

He had five hundred dollars in cash in his pocket and a five-shot Smith and Wesson. He was a fugitive, wanted now for two murders. Within hours, his face was going to be all over the television, in post offices, airports, bus and train stations. He looked at the cell phone in his pocket. Who could he call? Theo? Jesamyn? Lydia Strong? No. The first thing Bloom would do was subpoena his cell phone records; anyone he called could be accused of aiding and abetting. It struck him strangely, hard to the gut, that he was alone now. He'd been lonely before, maybe for most of his life; he was used to that. But he'd never been *alone* like this, never felt like every connection he had to his life had snapped and he was lofting away into the sky. He could feel himself getting farther and farther away from Earth.

He took a deep shuddering breath, stood. He figured there was only one thing left to do.

Twenty-Four

Basically, Grimm wanted to use them. Lydia had pretty much figured this the moment he pulled up a chair. Otherwise, rather than sitting and having a friendly little chat about Trevor Rhames and The New Day, he probably would have arrested them. He could easily do that and hold them for as long as he wanted under the Patriot Act.

"We can't go in there," Grimm told them. "They've got lawyers and political connections up the yin-yang. We've been in there before and found nothing."

"After Rusty Klautz escaped," said Lydia.

"That's right."

"So what makes you think there's anything there now?" asked Jeffrey.

"These satellite photos," he said, pointing to Jeffrey's laptop screen, "which I'm not even going to ask how you got your hands on, reveal buildings that don't exist on the property survey."

"They weren't there when you went in the first time?"

"No," said Grimm with a shake of his head. "We also have new information. Are any of you familiar with the topography of Florida?"

Jeffrey nodded. "It's karstic, meaning that it's basically a porous limestone bedrock over a high water table."

"Right. And beneath Florida is a system of caves formed by water running through the pores of that limestone, many of which are submerged. Cave-diving and spelunking heaven."

"Yeah, okay," said Lydia, not sure she liked where this was going.

"According to our source, they're using some of the dry caves to hide weapons. Not just guns."

"Who's your source?" asked Lydia.

"Well, that's the other thing," said Grimm, shifting in his seat and putting his eyes on Lydia. "We've lost contact. We lost contact weeks ago."

"You sent someone to infiltrate," said Jeffrey, with a frown. "Because the kid we pulled out of there? He was fried, totally divorced from reality and from his personality."

Grimm nodded. "In most cases, we train our people to resist those techniques."

"In most cases?" asked Lydia.

"In this case, there was no time. It was a matter of opportunity."

"So there's an agent in the compound somewhere? Doesn't that give you cause to go in?" asked Lydia.

"It's more complicated than that. Let's just say—" He paused as if searching for the right words. "*Rules* have been broken. It comes from on high that it's hands off The New Day. But some of us didn't think that was such a good idea."

"So now you've lost someone that you can't get out without admitting that you've been investigating a group that was supposed to be immune to investigation," said Jeffrey.

Grimm didn't answer, just glanced back at the computer screen. Lydia watched Jeffrey; there was a muscle working in the side of his jaw and he had leaned forward, his forearms resting on his thighs. He had turned a hard look on Grimm. He didn't believe what Grimm was telling them, or not all of it. Lydia felt the same edge of uncertainty. An uneasiness had burrowed its way into her gut. They both knew that with the new anti-terrorism laws the FBI didn't really need cause to raid the New Day Farm. There was some other reason they didn't want to go in there.

"You want us to find your agent and bring him out," said Dax.

"Since you're in the neighborhood and were planning a visit anyway." There was a blankness to Grimm's face and his voice, a strange nebulousness to his whole being, as if you might forget what he looked like shortly after you'd left him. Suddenly Lydia didn't like him or what he was asking them to do. It seemed *off*, crooked even for the FBI. "And in return, we won't arrest you for any of the variety of things we could arrest you for right now." He smiled. It wasn't pretty.

"So who's your man?" asked Jeffrey.

"Our man is a woman," said Grimm, looking down at his shoes. "I believe you all know her. Her name is Lily Samuels."

Lydia drew in a sharp breath of surprise. "Oh my God," she said, standing up with the shock of it; both Dax and Jeffrey turned their eyes to her. A thousand things that hadn't made sense suddenly did. "You used her," said Lydia. Her voice was quiet but her tone was white hot with anger. "She came to you for help, trying to understand what happened to her brother and you used her."

She thought of the message Lily had left her. *"I really need your help. I am out of my league. Big time. I—I just really need to talk to you,"* she'd said. Man, she wasn't kidding.

"It wasn't like that, Ms. Strong," said Grimm, holding up a hand. "Not at all. Lily Samuels came to us with a proposition. We took her up on it. Otherwise, she would have gone in on her own. We thought we could offer her some protection while pursuing our own agenda. We were wrong."

"What was her proposition?" asked Jeffrey.

"She was convinced that The New Day had something to gain through Mickey's death. She wanted to know what that was. In return for our support, she would provide evidence against The New Day and write an exposé that would tear the lid off the organization and send its political supporters scattering like roaches."

"Allowing you to go in and get Trevor Rhames," said Dax.

"And expose The New Day for what we believe them to be," said Grimm. "A criminal organization that robs people of their lives and their money. One that uses that money and the money earned through a variety of illegal activities to fund terrorist groups and supply weapons and men to rebel factions, destabilizing political situations around the world to create chaos."

"So your feeling is that The New Day is a Privatized Military Company masquerading as a religion," said Jeffrey. Lydia looked at him and could tell that the same things were flashing through his mind: the house on the water, the compound in the middle of nowhere, the pink diamond, the jewel heist, Tim Samuels' security company. All the pieces fell together, but something still didn't feel right.

"At least partially—the part that Trevor Rhames runs," said Grimm vaguely.

They were all quiet for a second. The sun had dropped below the horizon outside and the sky was deep blue-black with streaks of orange like the belly of tiger. Outside two pelicans dive-bombed into the dark, gold-tinged water, taking advantage of the last bit of light to fish by.

"What are the security specs?" asked Jeffrey.

"So that's what you do? You work for one of these Privatized Military Companies?"

Jeffrey had the wheel and Lydia sat beside him, turned to look at Dax who sat in the backseat, his legs up, his back against the door.

"I've done a lot of things."

Something in his face changed when he said it, as if the memory of some of those things pained him. He looked away from her, his eyes taking on that veiled look they got when she asked too many questions. He was shutting her out.

"You're a mercenary," she said. She'd leveled this accusation against him before but never with any seriousness. He turned his eyes on her then, seemed about to say something but didn't. Jeffrey hadn't said anything, she noticed. She settled into her seat and watched Dax out of her sideview mirror. She thought he looked a little sad.

"What difference does it make who else he works for or what he does?" Jeffrey said after a few minutes of riding in an uncomfortable silence. "You've saved our asses and sacrificed enough for us, Dax, that we could never doubt your loyalty or your friendship."

Dax nodded and Lydia didn't say anything. It was true, of course. But something in her still felt bruised. She folded her arms across her chest, rested her head against the back of her seat and closed her eyes for a minute. When she opened them, she saw Dax watching her in the mirror. She held his eyes for a second and looked away from him.

"Do you think Grimm can be trusted?" Jeffrey asked Dax.

"As much as anyone," he said with a shrug.

"Do you know him?" Lydia asked, suddenly turning around. "There was something between the two of you in that room."

Dax was silent, turned to look out the window. Lydia blew out a sharp breath, turned back around.

"The question is," said Jeffrey, looking at the headlights in his rearview mirror, "are we doing the right thing in helping them?"

"I don't see where we have a choice," said Dax. "We were going to go in anyway. Now we have better security specs. It doesn't matter whether Lily Samuels was working with them or not. We still need to bring her home. They're not going in after her. What do we have to lose?"

The question made Lydia flinch. It was like tempting the Universe; there was plenty to lose—Lily, for one. She didn't say anything.

The drive to the New Day Farm was long and mostly silent; nearly an hour and a half toward the center of the state. They took a small state highway that passed quickly through the pretty seaside town, then past a fairly large metropolis with tall gleaming buildings in its downtown center, creating a small but attractive skyline. The city was edged with million-dollar bayfront homes, all hosting boats bigger than some houses Lydia had seen. The scenery quickly turned to the projects and dilapidated houses of a depressed outer urban area. About an hour outside the city the dark, empty roadside was dotted by rundown houses and shacks. Shells of old cars lay in front yards like sleeping dogs, wash hung on lines, people gathered on porches, monster trucks rumbled in short gravel driveways. They passed a couple of seedy-looking bars, some barbeque joints, a Waffle House. Near the middle of the state everything turned green-black and they saw nothing for miles but lush, thick vegetation in the glow of the headlights.

Buried in the middle of nowhere, the New Day Farm kept only a high chain-link fence at the end of the drive that connected to the road. Lydia and Jeffrey scaled it easily; Dax took it a little harder and the landing looked like it caused him some pain. But all in all, he seemed to be getting back to form, still stiff but much stronger and more agile.

"Stop looking at me like that."

"Like what?"

"Like I'm some foreign specimen under a microscope."

"I just don't understand—" she started but Jeffrey held up a hand and looked at them both sternly.

"This is not the time."

"I'm the same person," he whispered to her as they walked along the edge of the drive. She nodded, looked into his eyes. "Nothing has changed," he said when she didn't answer him.

The air was so thick with humidity that Lydia felt like she was breathing gauze. Even in short sleeves, she was sweating as they made their way quietly but quickly in a light jog up the drive. The heavy foliage around them was so green it was black in the dark; it had a pulse, it moved. She felt like they were walking beside a living thing. She heard the flapping of giant wings in the leaves above them, something scurrying near their feet. There was a threatening aura to the exotic ferns, twisting vine–covered trucks, fanning palm leaves, so much they couldn't see. She kept close to Jeff and away from Dax.

"There won't be any security to speak of until you get to the end of the drive. Then it's going to get complicated," Grimm had told them.

But Lydia felt watched. She felt like the wall of living green to her right had eyes, that they were expected and someone was having a good laugh about it.

"I don't like a single thing about this," said Lydia to Jeffrey. "Me neither," said Jeffrey. "Just stay close and be careful."

———

"So what you're telling me is that you just happened to be in the neighborhood at the time of the shooting and spotted the New Day van on the side of the street."

Jesamyn shrugged, wondering if he'd let it fly. But he turned a hard look on her.

"Detective, if we're straight with each other things might go easier for everyone, including your partner."

She sighed and sat down at Clifford Stern's dining-room table, old, full of nicks and hairline scratches. It wobbled when she put her elbow on it. Bloom sat beside her. She looked at him and wondered: Was he a good cop just looking for the truth? Or was he an asshole who thought he already had it sewn up and any new evidence or information that proved otherwise would be an assault to his ego?

She looked up at Dylan, who nodded.

"I asked my ex-husband to come up here and watch Clifford Stern, see where he went, see who visited him."

"And you saw the van?" asked Bloom, turning to Dylan who stood behind him. Dylan nodded, told him how he'd seen it pull up and sit.

"But no one got out. No one went into the Stern residence."

"No," said Dylan, shaking his head and folding his arms across his chest. "I waited a few hours, there was no activity from the van. I went to get Jez—Detective Breslow, to show her the van, and while we were here deciding what to do, we saw three flashes in the window, heard the sound of gunfire. We called 911."

Bloom had his head cocked to Dylan, but his eyes were on the wall beside him, as if the scene were playing out for him there. "Then you took off?" asked Bloom with a frown that was somewhere between surprise and suspicion. "Why didn't you investigate?"

Dylan and Jez were silent, exchanged a look. "We weren't sure how it would look," Jez said finally. "I thought, if they could frame Mount the way they did, why not me?" She paused and looked down at the table. "I have a son."

Bloom looked at her carefully, with a slight narrowing of the eyes.

"But the van's gone now," he said after a minute of considering their story. They both nodded. "Seems like you could have called and told me what you were up to, Breslow."

"I told you about The New Day when you questioned me. You didn't seem to be taking me seriously."

He shrugged. "I was taking you seriously. But some crazy-sounding story about a cult framing your partner and actually seeing the van in front of the residence of the only eyewitness to his crime is a different matter. Don't you agree?"

She nodded, feeling like she'd let Matt down in a major way.

"Did you get the plate?" Bloom asked Dylan.

Dylan removed a slip of paper from his pocket and handed it to the Detective. Jesamyn looked at him. She'd asked him the same question right before the gunfire and he hadn't had a chance to answer.

"Did you run it?"

Dylan nodded. "The van is registered to The New Day. There are two outstanding parking tickets, one on the Upper West Side, and one in Riverdale."

Jesamyn started at the harsh ripping sound of a body bag being zipped. She felt despair at the sound of it. "Two .38 slugs to the head," said Bloom as the ME rolled the corpse out.

Jesamyn nodded. She knew Mount had a Smith and Wesson five-shot at home. His off-duty revolver, smaller and lighter than the Glock he carried on the job. From the look on Bloom's face, he knew it too.

"You said two shots?" asked Dylan. "You find a third slug?"

Bloom shook his head. "Not yet. We're not finished with the scene."

"We heard three shots," said Jesamyn.

Bloom shrugged. "If it's here, we'll find it."

Jesamyn held Bloom's eyes. She knew what he was thinking; she was thinking the same thing. If they'd come in here after the shots were fired, what would they have found? She pushed the thought away; there was no point in worrying about that now. But if she had to make the decision again, she'd do the same. Ben came first. He *always* came first. She fought the urge to put her head in her hands.

Since the slashing of his Achilles tendons, Dax Chicago had had a lot of time to think about the things he'd done. He'd managed to push so many days and moments from his memory that there were big black spaces in the narrative of his life. He liked it that way. Some things he wasn't supposed to remember, other things he just didn't want to re-member. The little game Lydia played, trying to tease him into telling her things he couldn't tell. She thought he was keeping things from her. And in some cases, that was true. There were things he couldn't tell her or anyone. But there were plenty more he'd succeeded in forgetting al-together. Most people didn't understand how that was possible. But then most people hadn't been the places he'd been.

Since the accident, memories had returned unbidden. It was the inactivity, the insomnia, the time that was filled only with the pain of his slowly healing legs that allowed his deeds to come marching back. Now people, too, it seemed. People like Grimm. He'd never thought they would see each other again, and that had been fine by him.

Lydia and Jeffrey were ahead of him on the path. She was just within his reach. He wanted to grab her shoulders and spin her around, force her to look into his eyes. Her new knowledge of his past—or what she thought was her new knowledge—didn't change their friendship. Jeffrey, Dax knew, was comfortable with the gray choices. He knew better than most that the just thing wasn't always the legal thing. He knew that some people had to die so that other people could live. And Jeff, like Dax, was willing to be the person who made choices like that. But Lydia had never shared those feelings . . . even when her own life was at stake.

"In our line of work, there's just a thin line that separates us from the monsters we chase. Once it has been crossed, you're Ahab, you've caught the disease, whether you know it or not," she'd said to him once. He'd never forgotten those words; they resonated with him. Maybe she was right. Maybe he had the disease and he just didn't real ize it. Maybe she thought she saw it in him now and would never be able to see him any other way. The thought pained him. Jeff and Lydia were the only true friends he'd ever known.

He reached for her but before his hand touched her shoulder, the ground fell out from beneath his feet and he was falling, falling into black. He heard Lydia screaming Jeffrey's name and then there was nothing.

Twenty-Five

Jesamyn stood on Mount's porch, ringing the bell and freezing her ass off. She knew it was pointless and stupid. He wasn't going to be there. But part of her was just hoping that he'd come to the door in his sweatpants, groggy from sleep.

"What are you talking about?" he'd say, giving her that look he gave when he thought she was acting crazy. "Arrested? On the run accused of murdering one, possibly two people? That's nuts."

But he didn't come and eventually she took the keys from her purse after a few more rings and let herself in. They'd exchanged keys a long time ago. It was in case something ever happened to either one of them and, for whatever reason, one of them needed entry into the other's residence. She promised that if he was ever hurt or killed on the job, she'd go and take his porn videos and throw them out so his mother wouldn't find them. Other than that they hadn't really thought it through. It had just seemed like a good idea. She was glad for it now.

She was immediately assailed by the smell of garlic and oil as she stepped inside. The heat was blasting and she was grateful for the warmth. She closed the door behind her and stood in the living room, listened to the silence of an empty old house. She wasn't sure why she'd come here, what she was looking for exactly. She guessed she'd know it when she saw it. She felt tired suddenly, the last few days catching up with her in a big way. She sat on his couch, threw her bag down beside her, put her feet on his coffee table and tried to think like Mateo Stenopolis.

He was a person that she *knew*. She knew her son Ben. She knew her mother. And she knew her partner. She had loved Dylan deeply once and maybe still did but she'd never really known him, at least not in the way she imagined she did. He kept secrets, told lies, wouldn't share big parts of himself. You can't know a person like that; you can love him, fill in the blanks with all your own dreams and desires. But, of course, he'll disappoint you again and again, until you wake up and realize you can't build a life with someone who won't give himself up to it. You can't live a life built on the romantic imagining of a person.

Mount never held anything back; he wasn't even capable of it. He was hopelessly open and honest, couldn't lie or be fake if he wanted to. That's why he didn't get along well with people; that's why he was always vulnerable to getting hurt. She let the fatigue take her, let a few tears drain from her eyes and spill down her face.

"Mount," she said. "Where did you go?"

She heard it before she saw it; it was a slight creaking of the wood on the porch where she'd been standing just a minute earlier. Then a large shadow drifted past the glass. She was grateful that he hadn't turned on the lights and then wondered if she'd locked the door behind her. She slid from her place on the couch, crouched behind the big overstuffed arm and took the Glock from the holster at her waist as the knob started to turn.

"Lydia."

The voice came from deep inside a long, dark tunnel; it was sweetly familiar and edged with worry.

"Lydia, come on."

She felt warm hands on her shoulders, a soft palm on her face. She woke then with a start, taking in a ragged, gasping breath. Her eyes were open but it was still pitch black; she kept still, unsure of where she was or how she had gotten there. Her mind raced, struggling to make sense of what was happening. She thought of the hotel room they'd been in, the walk along the dark drive.

"Are you okay? Lydia, say something." Jeffrey. She could feel him and hear him, she could smell his cologne but she couldn't see him at all. It was that dark where they were.

"I—" she began. "What happened?"

"Can you move? Are you hurt?"

She lay flat on her back on a cool, gritty surface. For a second, she didn't even want to try to move her limbs or lift her pounding head from the ground. She was afraid; she felt like someone had put her in a giant cocktail shaker and shaken mercilessly. What if she tried to move and she couldn't?

"I don't know," she said, lying still. "Are you okay? I can't see you."

"I'm okay," he said. "We fell. I don't know where we are now."

She tentatively moved her feet, then bent her legs. Same with her arms. Then she pushed herself up. There was a general feeling of physical trauma but nothing sharply or frighteningly painful anywhere as she came to a sitting position.

"Nothing broken?" he asked, putting his hands on her shoulders, her arms, then her legs, as if checking her for fractures he might be able to feel with his hands.

"No." She put her hands on his face, still unable to see him in the darkness. "You're fine?" she asked him again. "You're sure."

She felt him nod, then he took her into his arms. "A few bumps and bruises but okay for the fall we took."

"Where's Dax?" she said into his shoulder.

"I don't know," he said, moving away from her and then pulling her to her feet.

"You said we fell? Fell where?"

"We were walking and then we fell into some kind of a hole. Now we're here."

"At the bottom of the hole?"

"I don't think so. Our guns and our cell phones are gone." He took her hand and placed it on cold, smooth concrete; she felt the rough ridges and valleys of brick and mortar. "These are manmade walls. There's no light coming from up above."

"Is there a door?" she asked.

"Here," he said, pulling her over. She felt cool metal. Her hand drifted down to a locked knob. She yanked on it hard but it acted like a big, locked metal door. She let go of a sigh.

"So we fell down a hole. Someone then came, took our cell phones and guns, moved us from the hole and now we're trapped," she said.

"I'd say that's a fair guess."

She let herself slide down the door and come to a crouch near the floor. "How did we get here?" she asked. "Again?"

She was thinking of Jed McIntyre's lair beneath the city streets of New York, about the tunnels where he chased her and then she chased him.

Jeffrey sat beside her. "I've been thinking about that."

"Really? When? While I was lying here unconscious?"

"I've been sitting here beside you in the dark for a while. As long as you were still breathing, I figured I'd wait for you to come around."

She didn't say anything, knowing he'd go on.

"I think we've made some serious errors in judgment."

Given their current situation, she couldn't really argue with him. He slid down beside her and she leaned against him. Just his nearness quelled the low-grade panic she felt at being trapped, her fear for where Dax might be. She rested her head on his shoulder.

"We've been following Lily's steps, assuming that she was following Mickey," he said.

"Right. An assumption that Grimm more or less confirmed."

"Yeah, I'm not sure we can trust Grimm. He just wanted someone in here to find those weapons and give him a reason to come in guns blazing. Maybe he talked to Lily, maybe he didn't. Anyway, stay with me."

"Sorry."

"We assumed that Mickey, prone to depression anyway, was an easy target for the people looking to put a hurting on Tim Samuels."

"Right."

"But what if Mickey didn't get sucked in? What if he *walked* in?"

She thought about it a second. "Why?"

"I don't know. Maybe he was trying to help his stepfather?"

"But they didn't get along. Why would he go out of his way to help him?"

"It doesn't matter whether you get along or not—family is family. He loved Lily. He loved his mother. That was reason enough to help his stepfather."

"Okay," said Lydia. "But because he was prone to depression, they got to him?"

"Tim Samuels had a strong enough sense of self to break away from The New Day when he realized they were rotten."

"But maybe Mickey didn't?"

"Right," said Jeffrey.

"But wouldn't Tim Samuels have told us that? There was no way Mickey could know about his issues with The New Day unless Tim told him."

She felt him shift in the darkness. "He'd probably feel pretty guilty about it. Maybe he didn't want us to see him as responsible for Mickey's death."

Lydia was quiet for a second, turning the scenario around in her mind. "Okay. What if that's the case? Mickey left his job on Wall Street and moved up there, hooked up with his dad's ex-girlfriend and tried to infiltrate. He couldn't take the mind-control techniques of The New Day; they caused him to snap and he killed himself. What difference does it make? He's still dead and Lily was still trying to find out what happened to him when she disappeared."

"Right, but the whole basic assumption shifts," said Jeff.

"Huh? I'm not following."

"Well, Samuels made it sound like The New Day was systematically stalking his children in order to force him to surrender, tugging at the strings of his life to see which one he couldn't bear to lose."

"Which one would cause him to say 'Uncle.'"

"But what if, actually, it was Mickey and then Lily stalking The New Day?"

"Not doing such a great job of it, but giving it the old college try."

"But if *they* were chasing The New Day and not the other way around . . ."

"Then The New Day wasn't targeting Tim Samuels?" she said. "But what about the IRS and the murdered lawyer?"

"I don't know," said Jeffrey.

"He lost his children, his wife left him, and he had a meeting looming with the IRS, which could result in his losing everything and possibly doing time. Somebody was messing with his life."

"Yeah," said Jeffrey. "Just maybe not The New Day."

"But what about the 'deal' with Rhames? What about his name in the guest book?"

"I was thinking about that. Did he ever say the deal was with Rhames, exactly?"

"Yes," said Lydia emphatically. "I think so. I'm not sure."

"We made a lot of assumptions," said Jeffrey.

Lydia was silent as she tried to recast her thinking, see it in this new way. She had trouble getting her head around it. She'd cast Trevor Rhames and The New Day as the monsters and everyone else as their victims. It was hard to imagine another scenario.

"Remember what Dax said about suicide being the ultimate fuck-you?" said Jeffrey after a moment.

"Yeah. I'm not so sure about that," she answered.

"Me neither. But in this case, Samuels implied that all his assets were in jeopardy because of the IRS investigation. He stood to lose everything. But say he had a big life insurance policy and on his death, a settlement would be paid to whomever the beneficiaries were. He was still worth something."

Lydia thought about it. She saw where he was going suddenly. "Unless he killed himself."

"Most policies have a suicide clause," said Jeffrey.

"If he killed himself, no life insurance. If the IRS took everything else, he'd be leaving nothing behind for anyone."

"That *is* the ultimate."

"Isn't it, though?"

"So whoever is the beneficiary of that policy gets the big middle finger."

They were quiet again and the darkness seemed to swell around them. The buzz was deafening and Lydia's agitation at being trapped was starting to feel like something living in her chest. Her hands were tingling to get on a keyboard or a telephone pad to start finding answers to all her new questions.

"We're not in much of a position to figure out who that beneficiary might be," she said.

"No," said Jeffrey, squeezing her shoulder. "We're not."

She took a deep breath and leaned her head against the cold concrete wall.

"So, as long as we're questioning our assumptions," she said after a minute, "what about Mickey?"

Jeffrey exhaled sharply and shifted back further toward the wall, straightened out his legs.

"I guess I've been operating under the belief that he killed himself, maybe due to the maneuverings of The New Day in addition to the fact that he was depressed, feeling bad about the breakup and the failed business. Lily was grief-stricken, trying to hold onto her brother by proving that he didn't end his own life. Maybe in tangling with The New Day, making serious accusations, threatening an exposé of the organization, she got in over her head. If she was good at what she did, she probably found out everything that Detective Stenopolis told you about Rusty Klautz and the others. She was a threat to The New Day, at least an inconvenience. She thought she was protecting herself by involving the FBI, not realizing that they were just using her and wouldn't be any help in a jam."

"How does that all change if Mickey *didn't* kill himself, if Lily was right and he was actually murdered?"

She could hear him breathing. "I'm not sure," he said finally.

"What if she found proof that Mickey didn't commit suicide?" She heard Lily's voice again. *"I'm out of my league. Big time."*

"Then it would mean that whoever was threatened by that proof is a likely suspect in her disappearance."

"Right, so it would mean that there was another motivator in getting rid of Lily, not just another blow to Samuels."

They both knew there was a big piece missing, a hole that ran through their investigation which had been there all along. They had just been too blinded by their assumptions to realize it.

"You know what else is bothering me?" said Lydia.

"What's that?"

"Michele LaForge."

"How she seduced both father and son?"

"That was okay when we were assuming that The New Day was trying to take Tim Samuels' life apart. She seduced Tim as Marilyn and Mickey as Mariah, a siren luring them onto the rocks of The New Day."

"Very poetic."

"Thank you. But if we're thinking that Mickey and Lily were going after The New Day and not the other way around, where does Michele LaForge come into all of this?"

Jeffrey was quiet. She felt rather than saw him lift his head and sniff the air.

"What?" she said.

"Do you smell something?" he asked, standing up and pulling her to her feet.

She took some air in through her nose. She did smell something. Smoke.

She put her hand against the metal door and drew it back quickly. It was burning hot. She backed away from the door, wrapping her arms around herself.

"Jeffrey." Her throat suddenly went dry. Her heart started to pump in her chest. They were trapped and there was a fire raging outside the door.

"Come here," he said, pulling at her arm, dragging her to the far corner of the room and pulling her to the floor. She lay down on her stomach in the corner and Jeffrey lay in front of her, protecting her body with his, so that she was between him and the wall.

"It's okay. This room is made out of concrete and the door is metal. The heat will rise. We'll be okay."

It seemed wildly optimistic but she chose to be comforted by the sound of his voice and the feel of his body beside her, his arms around her. The smell of smoke was getting stronger and the temperature seemed to have risen twenty degrees.

"We're going to cook in here," she said, her voice tight with fear.

There was a pounding on the door then, and the muffled sound of a shouting voice.

"What was that?" asked Lydia.

More pounding and then the voice came again louder. Lydia couldn't understand what he was saying but she recognized the cadence of the voice. It was Dax.

"What the hell is he saying?" she yelled at Jeffrey.

"I think he said to stay away from the—" Jeffrey started. "Shit. Cover your head."

The explosion was so loud that Lydia wouldn't hear right for hours. The metal door that had seemed immovable crumpled like paper and they were blasted with a wave of heat and concussion that Lydia was sure was going to kill them both. The silence that followed felt like a vacuum to Lydia. Then there was a high-pitched ringing in her ears as her body wracked with coughing from the concrete dust. She could see Jeffrey coughing too, but she couldn't hear him. A bulky form emerged from the cloud. Dax. He was yelling something at them, then leaning in and dragging her to her feet, pulling on her arm. Jeffrey got up and stood behind her. She looked at Dax's face; he was scared, angry, something, still yelling. She tried to read his lips.

"It's on fire. We have to go," he was saying.

"What do you mean it's on fire?" she yelled. "What's on fire?"

"Everything. It's burning."

He pushed Lydia and Jeffrey in front of him and they all started to run down a long hallway, toward cool air they felt flowing from somewhere, the heat of flames at their backs.

For a second Jesamyn almost lowered her guard as the knob started to turn and then stopped; whoever stood outside started jiggling the knob lightly. She *had* locked the door behind her like a good New Yorker. She thought, what if it's Theo or Matt's dad. But then the dark form moved in closer to the door and blocked all the light coming in from the nine glass panes. He was huge; she felt her heart drop into her stomach. Tired apparently of messing around with locked knobs, the form put a gloved hand through one of the panes of glass as if it were made out of cellophane, reached in and unlocked the dead bolt and turned the simple lock on the knob itself. Then, as if thinking now he should be quiet, he opened the door slowly and stepped inside. He had to bend his head to avoid hitting it on the frame.

From her place behind the couch, she had a good look at him as he entered the foyer. Giant, with a buzz cut so close to the scalp that his hair looked like a five o'clock shadow. His face was grim and blank of expression, deep lines carved between protruding bones, a long hook of a nose. She checked his body for the bulge of a gun and saw something inside his jacket that could very well have been a big revolver or a semi-automatic. He stood and lifted his nose to the air for a second and turned his head toward the living room, moved toward her slowly. She felt the reverberations of his footfalls in the floor beneath her own feet. She crouched lower. She'd need the element of surprise to have the advantage over his size. She'd need him to come very close to her before she revealed herself. The blood was rushing in her ears as he approached the couch. When he was not a foot away from her, she moved from her spot and held the gun in front of her, aimed directly at his center mass.

"Freeze," she yelled, deepening her voice. "Get on the ground and put your hands behind your head."

She hated the way her heart was pounding, the way her chest was heaving with her fearful breathing. He smiled at her like she was a pretty child putting on a show and that made her angry as well as afraid. He put his hands up and mock shivered, started backing away from her.

"Oooh," he said.

"Get on the ground," she yelled, making her voice as loud and deep as possible. She didn't want to kill this guy; he might know something that could help Mount. But she *would* kill him if it came to that. He moved backward and she followed, her finger on the trigger of her gun. She could already hear the deafening boom it would release when she fired. He had his back against the wall now, knocking down a portrait of the Stenopolis family. She jumped when it crashed to the ground and shattered. In that instant she saw him glance down at the bulge in his jacket, saw his right hand twitch.

"Don't even think about it," she said, reaching behind for her cuffs. "How many times do I have to tell you? Get down on the fucking ground. *Right. Now.*"

He started to bend toward the ground, but telegraphed the lunge that followed by bringing his right knee up quickly. All her fear subsided now that the fight had begun. All her training from the academy and from the kung fu temple kicked in. She was pure action, no thought at all.

She sidestepped him easily and he crashed into the low coffee table, headfirst. She let a round go and felt the concussion in her chest, was temporarily deafened by the roar of the Glock, felt the sting of powder in her nose. She'd missed him, the bullet creating a valley in the end table and exploding the lamp on top of it. A piece of glass or some-thing ricocheted and hit Jesamyn below her left eye. But she barely felt it, seeing that the giant had managed to draw his weapon, a huge re-volver that looked like a Ruger with a big long barrel.

She dropped as he got to his feet, put her hands on the ground with the gun still in her grip and swept him hard, using her foot as a hook. Her ankle connected hard with his thick leather boots and it hurt like hell, but he fell right on his back, feet flipping up from beneath him like he was wearing roller skates. She heard his head connect with the floor and it sounded like a bowling ball dropping on a lane. The Ruger came loose from his hand and landed harmlessly on the velour couch. She was on him then, her knee in his solar plexus as the porch outside exploded with light and sound. He reached to pull her off him and she used her elbow to strike him hard on the side of his face. Once, he was still smiling. Twice, the smile faded and he started to get a dazy look in his eyes.

The front door slammed open and the room was full of voices and heavy footfalls. She knew the sound of her colleagues: radio static, booming voices, holsters unsnapping. She felt hands on her then and she got to her feet, still pointing her gun at the man dressed in leather. He looked stunned; two blows to the head and a knee to the solar plexus could do that to a guy, no matter how big he was. Still, it took two guys to flip him and two sets of cuffs linked together to bind his hands.

"We had to link the cuffs together for your partner like that," said Bloom, coming up behind her.

She turned to look at him. The adrenaline was draining, leaving her shaking in its wake, the wound on her face starting to throb. "You followed me?"

She wouldn't admit to it, but under the circumstances she was grateful. She'd been able to bring the guy down but she wasn't sure she would have been able to cuff him. She might have wound up cuffing one wrist to the couch leg and calling for backup.

He nodded, watching as two uniformed officers pulled the intruder to his feet. He was a little unsteady, dazed, and he hadn't said a word. One of the uniformed officers starting reading him his rights.

"I figured you'd lead us straight to Stenopolis."

"But instead I led you to this guy. He matches Mount's description. Don't you think?" she said, nodding toward the leather-clad freak.

"We'll see," he said, noncommittal. "Anyway, I'd go so far as to say things are looking a little better for Stenopolis, except that he's a fugitive on the run considered armed and dangerous." He sighed. "It's always a bad idea to run."

She shook her head at him. He'd made all his assumptions already; he'd have to wrestle his ego a little before he came to terms with the fact that she'd been right all along. But she could tell he was the kind of man who'd put the truth first and she respected him for it.

Dylan came through the door then, looking afraid and a little angry. He walked over to her, eyes scanning the room, then resting on the big man in cuffs. She'd split off from Dylan after he brought her back to the precinct to get her car, saying she wanted to get home and rest. Really, she hadn't wanted to drag Dylan into the gray area of entering Matt's house and looking for clues as to where he might have gone. It could be bad for his career, considering he was already on temporary suspension. And, maybe most of all, she'd just wanted some distance from him.

"I thought you were going home," he said to her.

"I thought *you* were going home," she said, looking at him. She fought the urge to wrap her arms around him until she could stop shaking.

"I was. I heard the call on my scanner and turned around."

He put a hand to her face and she winced at the pain. "You're gonna need stitches on that," he said as the two uniforms moved past them with the prisoner.

"Not before I talk to that guy."

"I'll be talking to him, Detective," said Bloom. "I don't need to re-mind you that this is not your case."

"The hell it isn't," she said, pushing past Bloom. "I would have been the one to put the cuffs on him if your boys hadn't come in. *I* would have had him for breaking and entering, assaulting an officer." He put a gentle but firm hand on her arm.

"I don't want to have to arrest you for obstructing an investiga-tion," he said quietly. "Which I could do, considering we both know why you came here."

She looked him up and down. He was half the size of her most re-cent assailant, but there was something tougher about him.

"If you'd listened to me in the first place, we wouldn't even be here. It never would have gone this far," she said, looking down at his arm and then turning her eyes on him.

He gave her a black look and she let out a sigh, looked at the ground.

"Let me come with you, at least," she said when he didn't an-swer her.

He nodded grudgingly and released her arm. "Paramedics are outside. Let them patch you up first. Meet me at HQ."

"What is happening?" yelled Lydia.

"They moved in. They're taking the compound."

Dax's sentence was punctuated by the sharp report of semi-automatic gun fire. In the distance she heard voices but they sounded faint and far away, yelling, as they stepped from the building they'd been in into the humid night. There was another sound, too, also faint and far away to Lydia's damaged ears: the crackle of flames. The thick, hazy air seemed to hold an orange glow and smelled strongly of burning wood. She felt like she was breathing in the color gray. She held a hand over her mouth.

"Who's moving in? The Feds? I thought they couldn't come in here," she said as they followed Dax at a run into the cover of a glade of trees.

She was feeling disoriented and her heart was still chugging. But something was bugging her, nudging at her consciousness. She could see the look on Jeffrey's face, too. Blank but eyes slightly narrowed, trained on Dax.

How did Dax know where they were? Was it her imagination or did he seem to know where they were going?

"About a half an acre west of here, there's a wall that we can get over and get out of here," said Dax.

"No," she said. "We're not leaving without Lily."

He looked at her. "Do you understand what's happening here?" he asked her. There was something cold in his tone she'd never heard before. She didn't like it.

"No, I don't, Dax. Why don't you tell me?" she said, turning to him, moving in closer.

She felt Jeffrey's hand on her arm. "We should do this later," he said. "We have to get out of here."

"We have to find Lily," said Lydia.

"Look at the reality here," said Dax. "The place is burning. Every building in this compound is on fire. FBI and ATF are all over the place."

The sky exploded with light and the chopping blades of a helicopter. Lydia felt her hair whip around her, and she covered her eyes, squinting against the brightness of the spotlight that shone through the trees directly on them.

"Drop your weapons and get down on the ground." It sounded like the voice of God coming down from the sky. But it was really just someone in full body armor with the big letters ATF printed on his chest. Still, Lydia figured it behooved them to listen. He had a gun trained on them—a very big scary-looking gun much like the one Dax was carrying. A moment later, four other men in body armor emerged from the trees around them, their faces obscured behind the Plexiglas masks of their helmets.

Jeffrey and Lydia exchanged looks and did what they were told.

"What? I can't hear you?" Lydia yelled. She wasn't trying to be obnoxious; she really couldn't hear very well. Maybe she was trying to be a *little* obnoxious, but given what the FBI was trying to pull she figured they deserved it.

The young agent who was questioning her looked annoyed. They sat together in the back of a van that was mercifully air-conditioned, just the two of them, on two metal chairs he had provided. She didn't know where Dax and Jeff were; she imagined they were in two other vans somewhere close by. The agent had given her an ice pack when she'd complained of a pain in her ribs and then he'd started questioning her. She wasn't worried until he started acting like he didn't know Agent Grimm.

"Did he show you any identification?" the kid yelled at her. He *was* a kid, maybe not even twenty-five. He had the fleshy, earnest face of the very young and wore the look that milk-fed people have before they've experienced the rest of the world, before they've realized that 95 percent of people are living in poverty and chaos, that hatred reigns and justice is in short supply. But maybe Lydia was just feeling bitter.

"Yes," she said more quietly. "He showed us his shield and identification." He'd flashed it, actually. She hadn't inspected it closely, mainly because they had guns that she recognized as Glocks, pretty standard law-enforcement equipment.

"You got a close look at it?"

She shrugged. "Close enough."

"Close enough?"

"Close enough to be convinced. He was out of shape and wore a bad suit. He had a crappy attitude and a kind of annoying self-righteousness to him that just screamed FBI."

Agent Gary Hunt ignored her comment, to his credit, and scribbled something in a black notebook.

The doors to the van were closed but through the rear windows she could see that the fire at the New Day Farm still raged; she could smell burning wood and hear the hiss of the chemical spray firefighters were using to quell the blaze. They were a safe distance from the scene now, but the occasional shout and bursts of gunfire carried through the air. The New Day compound was a war zone, another Waco in progress, and they were a part of that. Maybe the biggest part, since the Feds were using them as their reason for invading the compound. And for all Lydia knew, Lily Samuels was somewhere inside. Failure sat in her stomach like a piece of lead. Lydia still felt herself start to shiver slightly from a cold that seemed to come from deep inside her center and spread out through her veins to the rest of her body.

The kid ran a hand through a thick, silky shock of jet-black hair.

"Okay," he said. "You, Mr. Mark, and Mr. Bond are private investigators. You were following leads on the disappearance of a girl." He stopped and checked his notes. "Lily Samuels. You were planning on gaining entry to the New Day Farm to search for her when someone claiming to be an FBI agent named Grimm approached you and your associates. He told you that Lily Samuels was working for him when they lost contact with her. He wanted you to go in and try to retrieve Lily Samuels and provide proof that The New Day was stockpiling weapons so that the resultant publicity would make it possible for them to take down an illegal organization that was being protected by high-ranking members of the government."

"She could still be in there," said Lydia. "There could be an innocent girl in there."

Her desperation was making her loud but Agent Hunt didn't say anything; he just looked at her like he was trying to figure out what her angle might be.

"A *lot* of the people in there could be innocent. Brainwashed, trapped. Do you understand?" she said when he remained silent.

He shook his head, wrote something in his little notebook. She took a deep breath, tried to chill out a little, trying to quell the combination of anger and anxiety doing battle in her chest.

"Okay," she said, trying to sound calmer. "If he wasn't a federal agent the way you seem to be implying, then how did you know we were in there? Why did you come in after us?"

"We've had the compound under surveillance for about six months, gathering evidence in preparation for a raid scheduled next month," he said. "We heard gunfire and explosions, then a fire broke out. We had to move in tonight or never."

"How convenient. So you're claiming that the gunfire, explosions, and fire all started before you ever stepped foot onto the farm."

"You're saying different?" he asked, and something in his voice sounded cold as steel to her. He suddenly didn't seem so young.

She paused, looked at the ceiling above her.

"I fell down a hole, lost consciousness, and woke up in a concrete cell," she said, looking him straight in the eyes. "I don't know what happened."

"So you say," he said, returning her gaze.

Uh-oh, Lydia thought. Time to shut up.

"Lawyer," she said quietly. The kid gave her a look.

"Give me a break," he said, like she was asking him to fetch her a cup of coffee.

She pressed her mouth into a thin, tight line and crossed her arms in front of her chest, causing herself a surprisingly sharp pain in her ribs. She shook her head to indicate that she wouldn't be saying another word.

He held her eyes for a moment and was too young to hide his exasperation. He got up suddenly and marched away from her, exited the rear of the van and locked the doors behind him.

She leaned back in her chair and suddenly wished she had a better knowledge of the Patriot Act. How long *could* they hold them without evidence and without charge? She started to wonder if maybe "stubborn smart-ass" wasn't the best tack to take. She wondered what Dax and Jeffrey had said and how much trouble they were all in. What she needed to do, she figured, was to call Striker and have him send down one of the firm's lawyers. Or maybe more than one. Three lawyers. They were going to need three.

These were the things on her mind when the chrome handles on the rear door of the van started to turn and one of them opened, letting in a swath of humid air. Lydia sat up in her seat and was about to start getting loud about wanting to call her lawyer, when she saw a face she didn't expect step into view. All the words she had been planning to say deserted her, died between her throat and her mouth.

"Hi," said a painfully thin young girl with her hair shorn close to her head.

Something came alive in Lydia, something that was hope and elation, anger and confusion in one ugly tumble.

"Lily," she breathed. Her lost girl found.

Twenty-Six

Jesamyn climbed into the cold interior of her Ford Explorer, gunned the engine, and blasted the heat. She had three stitches on the side of her face, right beneath her eye. She turned down the rearview mirror so that she could take a look at them; she kind of liked them. Like the bruises she often got in kung fu, big purple and brown flowers of blood beneath her skin, she saw this as a badge of honor, the mark of a battle fought and survived. She was glad Dylan had agreed to leave and go to her mom's to help her get Ben ready for school in a few hours. Her mother hated Dylan with the passion only a mother can muster for the person who hurt her child. But she was able to stay civil for Benjamin's sake.

She felt fatigue tugging at the lids on her eyes as she backed the Explorer out of Matt's driveway. Matt's parents and Theo had come out in the commotion and she had had to tell them that Matt was on the run. Detective Bloom had found the files Matt had left on the kitchen table, and Matt's mother had wept inconsolably. Now she saw the living-room light glowing in the row house next to Mount's. She wanted more than anything to bring him back to that place, safe and sound, proven innocent.

She hoped Bloom wasn't just paying her lip service about talking to the suspect. But she suspected he was just trying to get her to shut up. She was going there anyway; she'd make a huge scene if she had to. She was about to merge onto the highway when she saw the darkness in the back seat shift. Her heart thumped as she pulled onto the shoulder suddenly with a screeching of her tires, ripped her gun from its holster and thrust it behind her, slamming the vehicle into park with her free hand.

"Hands where I can see them," she yelled, motivated by her own fear rather than a desire to intimidate.

"Take it easy," said the darkness. "I'm sorry. I fell asleep or I would have said something before you started driving."

Her fear drained away and she sank back into her seat, the adrenaline rush leaving her shaking at her core. "Jesus Christ," she sighed, leaning her head back against the upholstery. "Are you trying to give me a heart attack?"

"I'm sorry," said Mount.

"You are a major, major fuck-up, you know that?" she said, turning to look at him. "What were you thinking?"

"I wasn't thinking, I guess. I was acting. I saw her. I saw Lily."

"What? Where?" she said. He looked exhausted, pale with blue canyons of fatigue under his eyes, dark stubble on his jaw. There was something in his eyes that didn't thrill her. For a second she wondered, has he lost it?

"On my street, in front of my house. I went out after her but she was gone."

"Were you dreaming?"

"No. I saw a woman. I'm sure of that. I'm not sure it was Lily. But I was certain of one thing when I saw her: that someone was fucking with me and if I didn't do something about it, I was going to spend the rest of my life in jail."

"So you went to see Clifford Stern?" she said, guessing, because that's what she would have done.

"I didn't know where else to go. They cleared out the church in the Bronx. Jude Templar was gone. I knew Stern was lying. There was no other reason for him to lie or to be a part of that set-up unless he had a connection to The New Day. I figured I could scare him into telling me the truth."

He leaned back in the seat, put his feet up, and rested his head against the glass.

"They knew," he said. "That's the scariest thing. They knew enough about me to know that I'd show up there, trying to get the guy to come clean. They sent that girl, whoever she was, to make that call, and knew it would cause me to act. Don't you think that's frightening?"

Jesamyn watched her friend and partner. He met her eyes for a second and then closed them, fell silent. She was about to say something when he went on.

"They were waiting there for me. I came in through the back. The door was unlocked, that should have been my first clue. Stern was in a La-Z-Boy, half asleep in front of the game.

"I walked right through his dining room and stood twenty feet away from him before he turned to look at me. He smiled. 'Man, you *are* predictable,' he said. But he looked stoned, I mean high as a kite. It was more like he was talking to someone he thought was a figment of his imagination than me, standing by his recliner with a gun in my hand. But there was something crazy in his eyes; I think now it was a warning. I moved in close to him until I was standing right over him. He smiled again.

"There was this deafening sound and his chest kind of exploded and splattered all over me. He died immediately with that crazy, stoned expression still on his face. He never even knew what hit him. There were two shots and they came from behind me, so I spun around and found a man as big as I am, a little taller even, slightly wider. He held a thirty-eight identical to my own in a gloved hand. I drew on him when I heard something behind me. I turned and there was another one."

"Another what?"

"Another guy all in leather, bald, big. Like it was a uniform, some kind of look they were cultivating."

"He fired on me and I ran. I knew what they were trying to do. They wanted it to look like I broke into his house and that Stern and I shot each other. Case closed. They're rid of me and they don't have to worry about Stern either. Nice and neat."

"We arrested one of them," she said. "One of those men you saw."

"Just now?"

"Yeah, I came to your place to get your porn," she said with a smile. "And he came in after me."

"You took him to the mat?"

"You bet your ass."

"You're a tough bitch, Detective Breslow."

She smiled. "If I'd known he was such a bad shot, I wouldn't have been so scared."

"Bad shot?"

"Yeah, he fired at you and missed. You're like the proverbial side of the barn."

He coughed a little. "Who said he missed?"

"Oh, shit," she said, leaning over the seat. "You're shot?"

He nodded. "I was coming home to die like a wounded old grizzly," he said with a smile. "But it was too crowded at my place. I thought I'd do it in the back of your car."

"How bad is it?" she said, unzipping his jacket and seeing that the tee-shirt beneath was red with his blood.

"Not that bad, I don't think. I think it went straight through."

She looked at him more closely; he was fading, his lids lowering over eyes that seemed to be having trouble focusing. There was so much blood, she couldn't see where the wound was. She saw that the waistband of his jeans was black with his blood. She quashed the rise of panic down hard. No time for that.

"Mateo Stenopolis," she said loudly, pulling on his legs to get him to slide all the way down. She didn't want him falling over during the mad dash she was about to make for the nearest hospital. "You stay with me."

He looked at her and nodded weakly.

"Don't make me pull out the kung fu," she said when he said nothing. He raised his hands in a gesture of mock surrender, then winced at the movement.

"Jez," he said, as she turned and threw the car into drive, roared onto the highway. "Just be careful."

"Careful of what?" she said, pushing her foot heavily on the gas. "You worried about my driving?"

"The other one. You only got one of those guys. I think they travel in pairs."

She thought of her vacant-eyed leather-clad assailant and wasn't thrilled that he had a partner. Then she saw a pair of headlights behind her, square and bearing down quickly.

"Mount," she said.

He didn't answer and she looked up in her rearview mirror, saw only darkness in the backseat and the hot, high beams of the white van on her tail.

Lily felt like she could crumble to dust in Lydia's arms, she was so fragile. She clung to Lydia like she was a buoy in the violent water of Lily's life.

"Lily, my God," she said. Agent Hunt stood behind them.

"This is the girl you were looking for?" he said.

"Yes," she said. He nodded his acknowledgment and may have even smiled a little.

"She came wandering out of the New Day Farms about an hour before you. She's been talking about an Agent Grimm, too. For someone who doesn't exist, he sure does get around."

Lily was shivering in her arms and Lydia held onto her tight as the girl began to sob.

"Please," she said, appealing to the youthful humanity she saw in him. "Let me take her back to our hotel. I'll tell you anything you want to know, just let me get her comfortable and safe."

An hour later, Lydia, Jeffrey, and Lily were back in the hotel room with an escort waiting outside their door and Agent Hunt sitting at the table. Dax had not been released and no one would discuss his situation with either of them; Lydia was concerned . . . for a lot of reasons. She wasn't sure how he had found them and led them out, or what would happen to him now. But she knew he could take care of himself; she'd worry about him after they'd talked to Lily, made sure she was safe from The New Day and returned her to her mother where she belonged.

"I did what you taught me to do. Only it worked a little too well," she said with a slight laugh. She sat across from Agent Hunt, accepting a bottle of water from the minibar but nothing more.

Everything about her was changed. Where she'd been bright and exuberant, she was quiet and careful. Lily had always been the kind of girl who got excited by things, spoke quickly, moved her hands wildly, laughed easily. This girl was pale and thin as a slip of paper, speaking through lips that were cracked with dehydration, eyes that were dull and filled with grief. Her cloud of silky black curls that had always bounced around her face was gone; only the slightest stubble of her hair remained. She kept bringing a shaking hand up to it, feeling its texture. Lydia wanted to take her home so that she could be tucked in to bed and fed soup until she was feeling better. It was painful to watch her.

"So after your brother's funeral you went up to Riverdale," Lydia said. "To try to get into his head."

She nodded. Swallowing the water seemed to cause her pain and Lydia remembered what Jeffrey had told her about the tubes he'd seen in the throats of New Day guests.

"I had the keys to his apartment. It didn't take me long to figure out what he had been trying to do."

"Did you know about the problems your stepfather was having with The New Day?" asked Jeffrey. Lydia glanced at him, realizing that Lily probably didn't know Tim Samuels was dead. She figured that this wasn't the right time and they weren't the right people to tell her.

She shook her head. "No. I knew he and my mother were having problems. I suspected an affair, some asinine midlife crisis. But I didn't know anything about The New Day."

"Until?"

"Until after my brother's alleged suicide."

Lydia noticed Lily's use of the word *alleged,* as if she still didn't believe her brother had killed himself.

"So Mickey went there to try to help your stepfather?"

She shook her head slowly, like she still couldn't believe it. "That's the way it looked to me; like he'd gone up there for the express purpose of infiltrating The New Day, maybe hoping to expose them or find evidence that could get them to release their grip on Tim."

"What did you find in your brother's apartment that made you think that?" asked Jeffrey. His tone was kind and warm, but there was a slight wrinkle in his brow that Lydia recognized as the expression of his natural skepticism. She was with him; something felt off.

"When we were kids, Mickey lived in his imagination, you know? He had a rough time of it after our father's death. I was too young, really, to feel the impact the way he did. It altered him." She paused, and turned the bottle of water on the table, inspected it with intensity, as if the movie of her childhood were playing out on the sweating plastic. "It was like he was always looking for something to fill the empty space our father left."

The words hit Lydia hard, reminded her of her own childhood after her mother died. Her lonely hours filled with books and the stories she wrote. Even before her mother died her mind had worked that way; but afterward she practically disappeared into the mysteries she was forever trying to solve.

"He was different from other kids. He wore this loneliness, this sadness like a cape that somehow set him apart from everyone else, made him seem freakish and strange. So he was a target for bullies, he was awkward and never seemed to fit in anywhere. So he wrote. Notebook after notebook. Journals, poetry, short stories. He exorcised all his demons there. He cut the fabric on the bottom of his box spring and slipped them up inside there."

"That's where you found his journals in Riverdale?"

She nodded. "It was his current obsession, The New Day. But it was always something. He was always pouring himself heart and soul into something, trying to lose himself, trying to find himself. I'm not sure which."

"And you always followed," said Lydia, remembering the conversation when she'd told her as much.

"All my life I felt like I was chasing him up this path, and he was always just about to turn that one corner after which I'd never be able to find him again."

Rivers of tears fell from both her eyes and met at her chin, dripped onto the ATF sweatshirt Agent Hunt had given her. Lydia wanted to comfort her but wasn't sure how; she kept her distance.

"Your brother and your stepdad didn't always get along. Did it seem weird to you that Mickey would shift off his life to help him?" said Jeffrey.

"They didn't always get along, that's true. But Tim raised us both, you know. They had a relationship, even if it wasn't always an easy one." She sighed and rolled her head from side to side as if to release tension residing there. "But you're right. I don't really know why he did it. My suspicion is that he just *thought* he was helping Tim. That there was something about the message of The New Day that resonated with him and he was just using Tim's problems as an excuse."

She put an elbow on the table and leaned her head on her hand. Lydia noticed how frail and small her arms looked.

"So much made sense to me after I found his journals. He'd been so strange since the move, so distant, so wrapped up in Mariah. I just thought he was getting himself into another obsessive relationship that was going to end in disaster. Reading his journals I could see clearly how he lost his perspective, his advantage. He went in thinking he had the upper hand and they went to work on him."

"Maybe The New Day knew who he was all along," said Lydia.

"It's possible, I guess. They knew everything about my stepfather."

"How did your brother get involved with Mariah?"

"He met her at one of the New Day meetings. It was right at the point where his journal entries started to shift. He started out with nothing but disdain for them and slowly began to express a kind of grudging admiration."

"He didn't connect that Mariah was Marilyn."

She shook her head. "No. He never made that connection that I know of. We'd never met her while my father was dating her. So he would have had no way of knowing what she looked like. Maybe Tim never even told him about her. I only learned that they were the same person after Mickey died. When I found the journals, I confronted Tim. He admitted to me that he'd confided in Mickey but claimed he had no idea what Mickey was planning."

"At that point, Lily, why didn't you take what you knew to the police?" asked Jeffrey.

She looked at him. "My stepfather. He has made some terrible mistakes that he thought were dead and buried. Trevor Rhames knew those secrets, threatened to expose him."

Lydia shook her head. "What could be so bad that he would sacrifice his children to escape it?" It was the second time she'd asked that question in forty-eight hours.

Lily turned her eyes to Lydia. "I really don't know. But he said it involved my mother and that she would be hurt by the exposure, as well."

"You weren't curious to know what they might be, these secrets?" asked Lydia, knowing the heart of a journalist too well to let that slide.

"I pressed him, believe me. I did some digging on my own. The best I can figure is that it has something to do with Body Armor and possibly his military career before he married my mother."

She saw Jeff shift in his seat and Agent Hunt scribble in his book. She thought of the Privatized Military Companies Grimm talked about, she thought about the weapons, the pink diamond they'd found. Everything vague, their connections as delicate and translucent as a spider's silk.

"So you decided to follow Mickey's plan and get yourself into The New Day?" said Lydia.

Lily looked at her; there was a flash of something in the young woman's eyes. That fire they both had to *know,* no matter the cost.

"I wanted to free my stepfather from their grasp. I wanted to prove that they killed my brother. I wanted to expose them. I thought I was stronger than Mickey. That I had a more evolved sense of myself, too much so to fall prey to their brainwashing."

"But?"

"But their program is amazingly strong," she said with a long exhale. "I didn't *know* how tentative a hold we have on reality, how under the right conditions we lose ourselves and our ideas of right and wrong like a cheap pair of sunglasses. They take you away from everything that defines you, family, friends, your profession, your privacy. And then they create a new world for you. It's wild. I thought I could resist."

"And you did," said Lydia.

She laughed sadly. "Just barely. I took some precautions; I used my connections at the paper to get in touch with the FBI. I called around and got a lot of sidestepping, no one knew anything about The New Day, no one was available to speak to me, until finally Grimm contacted me. You met him?"

Lydia nodded.

"Grimm wanted The New Day but couldn't pursue them for political reasons . . . or that's what he told me. The deal was: I infiltrated, got all the info I needed to do a ripping exposé and gave him the juice he needed to bust them. In exchange, I kept in contact with him and if I didn't report he was supposed to come in after me."

"How did you keep in contact?"

"However I could. I wasn't a prisoner, ostensibly. I could come and go as I pleased. I called a couple times from my own cell phone, from payphones at coffee shops. Emailed from an Internet café. I just didn't count on the drugs and then the cleansing." She gave a visible shudder and then drank from the water bottle. The very act of talking seemed to drain her.

"I went to a Monday night meeting and I stayed. It was only a matter of days before I turned my money over to them. I figured I should go along with it, just to be convincing. Eventually, keeping in touch with Grimm started to seem like a smaller and smaller priority. By the time they started pushing the 'cleansing' on me, it seemed like a promotion, some kind of honor."

She paused here and looked at the floor. Then out the window into the blackness. They all stayed silent, waiting for her to go on.

"It was Halloween night. I was supposed to begin my cleansing the next day. They claim to wash you of all the negative thoughts and energies and messages that you accumulate throughout your life. When you're done, you're this new creature filled with light and positive thoughts, free of pain and addictions, able to go on to achieve everything the Universe intended for you. I was so happy, nearly euphoric. I just had the slightest memory, the tiniest nagging thought that maybe this wasn't the right thing, that it wasn't why I'd come.

"Then the weirdest thing happened. A car drove past on the road that ran outside my dorm room. The windows were open and the radio blaring. It was a song from the eighties, 'Shout' by Tears for Fears. And all of a sudden I was a kid again, walking through the hallways of my high school, the speckled linoleum floors and olive green lockers, the fluorescent lights, the smell from the chemistry lab, and that song playing on a tiny pink Sanyo boom box."

For a second, she seemed like the Lily Lydia remembered, animated, excited. Some of the color came back to her cheeks and she started to use her hands to express herself.

"And just like that, my life started to leak back, my job, my parents, my apartment. I realized that I was about twelve hours away from losing myself completely, becoming one of the zombies I'd seen hanging out in the common room."

"So you ran," said Lydia.

"Yes, I ran. I ran for my life. But they caught me."

She slumped in her chair.

"They shot me . . . not with bullets but with those hard rubber pellets riot police use to subdue crowds. It felt like bullets. I thought they'd killed me; I tasted my own blood. I lost consciousness. When I woke up, they had strapped me down, they forced a feeding tube down my throat, played these audio visual messages about shedding the old self, my new day dawning, shifting off the negative messages of a sick society and smothering family. But I don't remember much of it." She stopped and smiled here.

"I just kept hearing that song in my head. 'Shout, shout, let it all out.' You know it?"

Lydia nodded.

"I don't know why, but that song saved me. When I heard it in my head I just remembered who I was and where my life was. And I knew that no one could take my power; only I could give it away."

The tears fell again. She took a tissue from the box and wiped them dry, blew her nose.

"I'm not sure how much time passed but as soon as they removed the tube, I started acting like my New Day had dawned. I just did whatever they wanted, looked vacant and euphoric. But I started pouring out the tea they gave me; I realized whatever is in that just makes you really mellow and susceptible. And all this time I've been listening, observing, taking notes.

"I figured Grimm would come for me at some point but then after a couple of weeks I started to get worried. Maybe he couldn't come in after me; I knew he wasn't supposed to be dealing with me at all. I started figuring out how I could get away.

"Then there was some emergency in Riverdale. I thought, finally, it was the FBI coming but they moved us down here . . . just a few of us. They left some people behind; the ones that didn't have any more money I think, those whose families had cut them off, who couldn't be extorted."

"So that's the agenda?" said Jeffrey. "To draw people with problems into The New Day, take all their money, then extort more funds from the families?"

She nodded. "I mean, you tell Rhames *everything*. Between the way he is, his personal power and the drugs, he becomes like your confessor, your lover, the only true friend you ever had. You bare your soul and all your pain to him. And he *heals* you. Or anyway that's the way it feels in that controlled environment with the drugs and the audio visual messages they play."

There was something pleading to her tone. She wanted them to understand, and Lydia did.

"But you have to be in pain first, right? In order to be healed by him?"

Lily looked at her with wide, sad eyes. She nodded.

"And that's what you didn't count on. That your grief over the loss of your brother fractured you, that you were in terrible pain and seeking revenge. It made you vulnerable."

"That's right. And I think I had a sense of it before I went in that night. I'd read Mickey's journals and contacted the FBI. But I felt so overwhelmed, suddenly, unsure if I was doing the right thing. That's why I called you."

"I'm sorry, Lily," said Lydia, moving to sit beside her. "I'm sorry I wasn't there for you."

She held Lily for a minute and then released her.

"No," Lily said, shaking her head. "You couldn't have known. Besides, if I hadn't made that call, I might still be in there. Did it lead the police to you?"

Lydia nodded. "And then we came looking for you."

Lily smiled a real smile for the first time. "Thank you."

After a moment, the smile faded and worry clouded her features.

"I need to get in touch with my parents. They need to know I'm okay. And they need to be warned. They'll come after me. And they'll do that by trying to get to my parents."

Lydia looked down and took Lily's hands. "Your mom is staying at your apartment in New York. We can send someone to look out for her."

Lily nodded. "They're having problems again," she said, as if she suspected it was inevitable. "Where's my stepdad? At the house?"

"I'm so sorry, Lily," Lydia said. She hadn't wanted to tell Lily about Tim Samuels, but she didn't want to lie either. Lily deserved better than that.

"What?" said Lily, her eyes widening.

"He's dead," she said simply. There was no better choice of words.

Lily jerked as if Lydia had slapped her. And Lydia instantly regretted her decision to tell the truth. Lily wasn't strong enough to handle the news. Lydia reached for the younger woman.

"What?" she breathed into Lydia's ear. "How?"

Lydia shook her head, searching for what to say. Lily drew away from Lydia and looked her in the face. There was something hard and angry in her expression, a look Lydia had never seen on her. It turned her prettiness to granite. The girl was gone. In her place was a woman made hard by bitter experiences and crippling grief.

"It was suicide."

"Suicide?" she said, incredulous.

Lydia nodded slowly. "I'm sorry, Lily. Yes."

All the air seemed to suck out of the room as they waited for her to crumble beneath the weight of this new grief they'd delivered. But she didn't crumble. Her face went blank and her lids lowered in rage.

"That bastard," she hissed. "That coward."

She stood suddenly, then lost her legs and fell into a pile of skin and bones on the filthy carpet. Lydia knelt beside her. Lily put her head in her hands and started to sob, terrible wracking sobs that connected painfully to the grief in Lydia's own heart. Lydia pushed back tears, rested a hand on Lily's shoulder. She hadn't expected anger like that from Lily; it surprised her.

"He did this to us, to all of us," she managed, between sobs. "And then he just *bails*? How could he?"

She leaned into Lydia and started to wail. Lydia looked up at Jeffrey who was leaning into them, his hand on Lydia's shoulder. Agent Hunt stood back from the scene, looking uncomfortable and useless. On Jeffrey's face she saw concern but she saw something else, too. Suspicion.

The high beams of the van were blinding her in the rearview mirror and the roar of its engine told her that it was souped up. Her Explorer was all bark and no bite, its engine no match for whatever was humming beneath the hood of the white van. The van rammed her hard from behind and she jerked hard from the impact. She'd managed to get her seat belt on before she started driving and she was glad for it when it locked and held her tightly in place, though she felt the sting of the friction burn on the side of her neck. She pressed her foot to the gas and the Explorer and the headlights dropped behind her but kept following fast.

"Matt," she called. "Matt, please." But there was no answer from behind her and she felt panic rise up in her throat. Her heart was thumping hard and her arms and hands were tingling with adrenaline. A few cars flew past her on the other end of the highway in the opposite direction. Her Glock lay between her thighs. The van came up fast and rammed her again; this time so hard she involuntarily let go of the wheel for a moment and the car veered toward the shoulder. She caught the wheel and held the vehicle steady. The van was bigger and had a lower center of gravity; the driver was trying to get her to flip. Then when they were stunned or trapped in the vehicle, he'd walk up and kill them both. She could just barely see him in her rearview mirror, a large, dark, hairless form at the wheel. Terrified tears threatened then, but she held them back.

"No way," she said out loud, gripping the wheel hard. "No fucking way this guy's going to get us."

But there was only silence in the back of the Explorer.

"Please, God," she said, as she saw the van come at her again fast for another try. She sped up and veered into the righthand lane. The exit she needed was less than a mile away; if she could get to it, she figured he wouldn't follow her onto the streets. At nearly four A.M., the BQE was practically empty, with just a smattering of cars making their way through the dark morning. She hoped one of them had a cell phone and might call the police to report the van ramming her, two drivers racing out of control. Her own phone was out of reach in her bag on the floor, and she didn't dare take her eyes off the road.

He rammed her again, this time harder, and she lost control of the Explorer for a second, felt the left side of the car leave the ground. She caught the wheel and righted herself. Something in the engine was straining hard.

"Jez," said Mount from the back. "Slow down. Let him approach the vehicle and then blow his head off."

She practically wept with relief to hear his voice. "Slow down? Are you crazy?"

"We can't outrun him."

"We can make it to the hospital. Just one more exit. Once we're on the streets, he'll pull away. He's not going to follow us into a populated area where there'll be good witnesses."

"Just pull over. He'll never expect you to do that."

The van had dropped behind but was picking up speed again for another hit. Harder. It went against all her instincts screaming to drive as hard and as fast as she could. But she knew in her heart that Matt was right. They couldn't outrun the van. They had a better chance if they stood and fought.

She let the vehicle slow and pulled onto the shoulder as if she was in distress. She reached quickly for her bag and dialed 911.

"This is Detective Jesamyn Breslow with the Ninth Precinct," she said, watching the white van pull over hundred yards behind her and sit idle. "Officers in trouble. We need backup on the Eastbound BQE, just before exit 121. Assailant in white van, armed."

The dispatcher was saying something, but Jesamyn let the phone drop on the seat beside her. She turned around and used the back of her seat as a barricade, holding her gun over its edge. She looked down at Matt, who had his hand on his chest; his paper-white face seemed to float in the darkness.

"As soon as he starts to move on us, unload your weapon into him. Don't wait for him to fire first. They want us dead."

The door to the white van opened and a man identical in dress and hairstyle to the guy whose ass she'd kicked early, stepped out onto the road. An eighteen-wheeler whipped past them, horn blaring. Jesamyn felt the Explorer rock in its wake.

When he stepped into view, her heart did a flip from her chest to her stomach. He was taller than the other man, broader through the shoulders. She couldn't make out his face very well in the dark but she could see clearly that he had some kind of huge gun in his hand right hand. She couldn't tell what it was . . . a shotgun or an assault rifle; something big and nasty.

She breathed hard against the dread that was growing in her.

"Stay calm, make sure he's in range, and then just let it rip," Matt said weakly.

In the way far distance she heard the sound of sirens. They were far, maybe five or six minutes away. They won't get here in time, she thought, as the monster lifted the gun and started moving toward them slowly.

"Stay down," she yelled to Mount. She opened fire through her rear windshield and the air around them came alive with sound and light and a blizzard of glass.

Twenty-Seven

The Gulf slapped lazily against the white sand and a sliver of moon hung over palm tress that stood perfectly still in the windless night. Lydia lifted the beer to her lips. It wasn't as cold as it needed to be and there was no lime but it still tasted okay. Jeffrey grimaced as he drank it.

"It's warm," he complained.

"It's something."

Lily was finally sleeping in one of the queen beds and Lydia and Jeffrey sat outside on the cinderblock patio in white plastic chairs drinking Coronas. Agent Hunt had left to return to the scene, leaving behind two agents to ensure they made good on their promise to stick around. Lily had had a tearful conversation with her mother on the phone and then collapsed into bed after Jeffrey called Striker, asking him to send someone to protect Lily's mother and to send a lawyer down to Florida. Chances were the ATF would just let them go at a certain point, as long as things went their way. But you never could tell when federal agencies would be looking for a scapegoat; Lydia was glad Jeffrey took the precaution of getting a lawyer.

"What about Dax?" she asked.

"He'll be fine," Jeffrey said, turning to look at her.

"How did he know where we were?"

"Lydia," he said. "Over the years I've learned that, with Dax, the fewer questions you ask the better."

She frowned at him. "What kind of answer is that?"

"He saved our asses, right? He got us out of there. What more do you need to know?"

She looked at him, incredulous. "You're kidding, right?"

He didn't say anything, took a drink of his Corona and avoided her eyes.

Then, "It's none of our business."

She was quiet for a second. "So that's what he does? He works for one of those Privatized Military Companies? So was he working for them tonight or was he working with us?"

Dax had never really answered her and now Jeffrey was being equally tight-lipped. She got the idea that he knew more than he was telling her and the thought made her crazy.

"So we're going to start keeping things from each other now?" she asked.

Jeffrey turned his eyes on her.

"No, Lydia," he said, softly. He reached for her hand. "I know as much about what he does as you do. But I know *Dax*. I trust him. I trust his friendship. And I figure if he needs to hold certain things back from us, then maybe it's for our safety or for his. That's okay with me."

Her heart fluttered a little as a dark form emerged beside Jeffrey, stepping around from the side of the building. She stood quickly and then saw that it was Dax as he stepped into the light.

"But it's not okay with you, is it, Lydia?" he said quietly, holding her eyes.

She sat back down and looked away from him. She was glad to see him, glad they'd let him go, but there was something between them now that prevented her from being entirely comfortable with him in the way she'd always been.

Jeffrey handed Dax a beer. He pulled up one of the plastic chairs and straddled it like he was mounting a horse. He popped the lid with his hand even though it required a bottle opener.

"We got what we came for, right? What are we still doing here?" he said.

"Waiting for you, for one," said Jeffrey. "And we told the ATF we'd stick around for a while."

"Fuck the ATF," said Dax, taking a long swig of his beer and drinking nearly a third of it down. "Let's get that girl home where she belongs. It's done, right?"

Lydia looked at him. It *was* done. They'd come looking for Lily and they'd found her. She told them what had happened to her and now she was safe. The ATF and supposedly the FBI got what they wanted, the scene that allowed them to go into The New Day and the publicity that would follow would take care of the rest of the organization. This cult that had been stealing people's will and all their money was fin-ished . . . or at least mortally wounded. But it didn't *feel* finished, not to Lydia. There were giant holes, myriad unanswered questions. She could sense them, even if she couldn't exactly verbalize what was both-ering her.

"Dax, how did you find us? How did you get us out of there?"

"Someone wanted us out of the way," said Jeffrey. "Hence the fall down the hole and waking up in a cell."

"Same thing happened to me. Only when I woke up, the door was open and I was still armed."

"So what happened?" said Jeffrey, leaning forward in his chair.

"I left the cell and went looking for the caves Grimm mentioned. I found them, saw the weapons stored there. I mean, we're talking like an arsenal that would make the U.S. Army proud. Unreal.

"I heard an explosion then, some gunfire. I came to the surface and the Feds were running all over the place, buildings were burning. I fig-ured that there had been some kind of screw-up and I was out of luck. I came to get the two of you."

Lydia shook her head. "That doesn't make any sense. I thought the whole point was that the FBI *couldn't* go in after Rhames. That's why they secretly supported Lily; that's why they came to see us. Why was the ATF able to go in? Why didn't Grimm just piggyback on their in-vestigation? According to Hunt, they had the compound under surveil-lance in preparation for the raid."

"Maybe Grimm didn't know. Government agencies are notorious for not communicating with each other," said Dax, reaching for the last Corona from the six-pack by Jeffrey's feet.

"Right," said Jeff slowly. "But it makes more sense if Grimm *doesn't* actually work for the FBI, that he works for someone else with their own agenda for getting to Rhames."

Lydia thought about it for a second, looked at Dax.

"So we got duped?" she said.

"We were going in anyway," answered Jeffrey.

"What difference does it make?" asked Dax. "We got your girl. We're all alive and kicking. Let's go."

"I still don't understand how you found us and how you got us out."

"Not your problem. Just be glad I did."

Not my problem, thought Lydia. She looked at Dax but his face was blank. She took another sip of her warm beer and wondered if she'd ever know the whole story behind what happened to them tonight—or if she was going to have to add that to the list of unanswered questions in her life. She glanced behind her at the sleeping form on the hotel-room bed. Lily was the whole reason they'd come and she was safe now. It was over.

Twenty-Eight

She fired blind through the blizzard of glass and missed the guy completely. He kept coming. A shot fired from his weapon whipped past her so close and so fast that she thought it drew blood without touching her, blowing a cannon-sized hole in the windshield, then in the seat beside her. She looked down at Matt; he was pale and out cold but she could see his shallow breathing. But her mind was clear; panic had left her. As their assailant ratcheted the gun, bringing more ammunition to the chamber, she scrambled from the car and went around the hood. Inside the vehicle, she knew, she was a sitting duck. From outside, she could protect them both better.

"Put your gun on the ground and your hands in the air," she yelled ridiculously. "I'm a police officer and the sirens you hear are coming this way."

He answered her by putting another round into the car. The Explorer jerked with the impact and she held on tight to her Glock. She'd fired four rounds already, which meant she had thirteen left. She lay on the ground and saw his feet beside the Explorer, right beside the back driver's side where Mount lay wounded and helpless.

Then, "Stand where I can see you and I won't kill your partner," he said, his voice calm, hard and rough as the engine of a semi. "I'm standing over him with the barrel of my gun to his head."

Every nerve ending in her body felt like it had been electrified and all she could hear was the sound of her heart hammering in her ears.

"Okay," she said, her breathing so labored she was having trouble speaking. She fought to keep the fear out of her voice. "Put your gun on the ground and I'll move where you can see me."

"Yeah," he said with a laugh. "That's gonna happen."

She heard him ratchet the gun again as she moved onto her belly and held her Glock in front of her. She heard the sirens growing louder; they were still too far to help her. She was on her own. She fired at his ankles, a nearly impossible shot. But he had a big ankle and she had good aim and the night filled with the sound of him screaming, high pitched and girlish, frantic with agony. She fired again, clipping his other leg for good measure. She heard the gun go off as he fell and then landed on the concrete. She was on her feet before he hit the dirt and then she heard the sirens louder and closer. She felt something like relief pulse through her.

"Mount," she yelled as she came around behind him, her gun trained in front of her. The guy didn't look as big or as tough lying on the ground writhing in pain. She held the Glock in his direction as she came around his side and kicked his gun away. It slid across the gravel of the shoulder, out of his reach.

She made a mistake then. She looked away from the road and from the man lying there and into the window where Mount lay very still, too still. She yelled his name again and reached a hand in to feel his pulse.

She never even saw the other van come up from the other direction until shots fractured the night with sound and light. She felt an impossible impact and then a terrible burning in her shoulder, her leg, her arm. She opened fire with her own gun, putting holes in the side of the van. The man on the road reached for his gun and she put a round in his chest. He fell flat and motionless, eyes staring.

Then she was falling. The van was speeding off and the sirens were loud; she could see their red and blue glow. Before the van was out of sight, saw a beautiful young woman with long blonde hair at the wheel. And beside her was a young man. It was a face she recognized but could not place. Then there was black.

Part Three

Found

Stones and flowers on the ground,
We are lost and we are found,
But love is gonna save us . . .
        —Ben Benassi and The Biz

Twenty-Nine

The box sat waiting for her when they returned home from bringing Lily back to her mother. Dax drove the Range Rover back to New York. Lydia, Jeffrey, and Lily had boarded a plane in Tampa in the interest of getting Lily back to her mother as quickly as possible. It was mid-morning by the time they stepped from the elevator onto the bleached wood floor of their loft.

They'd been up all night. But Lydia didn't even take her coat off; she went straight to the kitchen for a box cutter, then strode over to the box and slashed at its taped center. Her eyes were heavy and her body ached with fatigue and from the fall she'd taken. She would have liked to climb into bed but now was the time; if she didn't look inside the box this morning, she never would. She had a gift for avoidance but she didn't want to do that this time. To turn her back on what could be inside those cardboard walls would be like turning her back on a part of herself.

"Do you want me to go?" asked Jeffrey, taking off his coat. She turned to look at him. There had been times in their past together when she would have pushed him away, asked him to leave so that she could experience her emotions the only way she knew how, alone. She saw the worried uncertainty in his face and she felt a wash of sadness; she'd often treated him badly and the memory of it hurt her.

"No," she said. "Stay with me."

He smiled at her and sank into the couch. She knelt on the floor near his legs, leaned into the box. Inside were stacks of large leather photo albums, color faded, edges frayed with age. On top rested a single letter. There were five albums in total. She lifted one out at a time and stacked them on the floor between her and Jeffrey. He leaned in, resting his forearms on his thighs.

She sat on the floor beside Jeffrey, her shoulder resting against his leg. She took the letter in her hand, and broke the seal, unfolded the single page inside. The handwriting was thick and uncertain, the author pressing so hard in places that the ink pooled and blotched. She read the words aloud so that Jeffrey could hear.

Dear Lydia,

You can probably guess the kind of man I am, if you don't already know from the letters I've sent you over the years. I have no reason to think you've ever read any of them. Maybe you just threw them in the trash unopened; or maybe they were kept from you. I know your grandparents aren't especially fond of me. Never were. Can't blame them really. There's a voice inside of me that tells me you've never seen them. You're a curious one, I know. I don't think you could have stayed away, had you known I'd been trying to reach you.

Anyway, if you're reading this, I guess I've taken leave of this place. I can't say I'm sorry to go. When you've spent most of your life making a mess of things, trying in your own pathetic way to clean up and then making even more mess, it starts to get a bit wearing. I don't imagine anyone will be shedding any tears. Not you, certainly. Not your half-sister, Estrellita or her mother Jaynie.

Some of the biggest mistakes I made involved your mother. I'd say, though you probably won't believe me, that she was the great love of my life. Life with Jaynie was a lot easier, don't get me wrong. Though I eventually screwed that up, too. But the love I felt for your mother . . . nothing ever came close to that again. Her death haunts me still today. I ask myself the question I know you must have asked yourself a thousand times. If I had stayed, would she still be with us? If I had been a different kind of husband and father, where would we all be? I think about her every night, remember her as she was when I married her. There are photos of the three of us enclosed that I know you've never seen. And I'm willing to bet that the woman there will be unrecognizable. When I met her, she was funny and full of passion, a prankster and a lover and there was this light inside her. I'll admit to you that I'm the one that snuffed out that light with my cruelty and irresponsibility. And then when it was gone, I couldn't bear to see her burned out and empty. I left her and you. But, Lydia, trust me, it was my loss. I truly believe you were better off without me.

I'm leaving these albums to you so that you can see that your mother and I shared happy times. That I held you in my arms and loved you like a father should. That as a family, we knew great joy for a short time. And most importantly, that I was always a part of your life whether you knew it or not.

I could tell you how sorry I am and try to convince you of how much I love you. I could tell you that I've lived my life in regret for all the mistakes I've made. But instead I'll tell you the only thing I've learned for sure about this life:

The past disappears into the air like smoke. We might catch its scent when the wind shifts but it is irretrievable, no matter how long we gaze after it wishing. The bad thing about this is that sometimes the consequences, the charred remains of our lives cannot be repaired. The good thing is, smoke can't bind you. It can't hold you prisoner. Only rage and regret can do that. You always can move forward, whether you deserve to or not.

Your father,
Arthur James Tavernier

The air in the apartment seemed heavy and silent when Lydia stopped reading. She waited for tears that didn't come, then she reached for one of the photo albums and moved up on the couch beside Jeffrey. She felt his eyes and turned to meet them.

"How are you doing?" he asked, putting an arm around her shoulder, pulling her in and putting his lips on her forehead.

She shook her head slowly, sank into him.

"I don't know," she said, feeling a little numb. "Sad, I suppose. But okay."

He nodded. She flipped the lid of the photo album, one side resting on her lap, the other resting on Jeffrey. The photos were black and white, darkened and yellowing with age. But there was something so beautiful about them, about the happy couple captured there.

Her mother laughed in the arms of a fair, handsome man with light eyes and a wide, generous smile. She leaned her head against his shoulder, her mouth open, her eyes moist with her happiness.

Marion Strong straddled a motorcycle, a young woman flirting with whomever held the camera, her hands on the grips, her eyes half-lidded. Sexy, mischievous, the light her father had mentioned blasting out of her like klieg.

There were others like this; her father had been right. The woman in the photographs was nothing like the woman Lydia knew. She was dancing, she was laughing with abandon, she was sexy and flirting with the man she loved. The woman Lydia had known had been exacting and sometimes cold, never cruel, always loving, but uncompromising and strict. Surely, she'd never been young the way the woman in the photo-graphs was young, she'd never known that kind of joy or abandon.

Tavernier held a dark-haired child with storm-cloud eyes. The little girl had her tiny arms wrapped around his neck, her head against his face. They both showed wide smiles for the camera. He was movie-star handsome with beautiful pronounced cheek bones and a strong ridge of a nose. In his eyes she saw a great capacity for humor.

She was glad to know her mother had been happy once and sad to never have witnessed it firsthand; she was glad that her mother had loved her father but sorry Marion had never shared the happy times with her. She flipped the page.

The later photos in the album showed Lydia from a distance: Lydia outside the church at her first communion, looking sweet and gazing up at her mother from beneath a veil; Lydia's high-school graduation, where she stood on the stage, looking too thin and not smiling at all. He'd been there for all those things, standing apart in the crowd, taking pictures for an album. The thought made her tired, sad, and a little an-gry that he'd always been within reach. That's when the frustrated feel-ing of regret came and settled in her bones.

Lydia flipped through a few more pages and then shut the cover. She gazed at the pile of letters on the table. It was too much, the pain in her chest, the ache in her head. Too much lost that could never be found. She placed the book on the table and turned to her husband. She put her hands on his face, and he wrapped his arms around her, pulling her into him. She put her lips to his and breathed him in.

"You can finish tomorrow," he said softly. He bent and lifted the al-bum from her lap and stacked it on top of the others.

"I love you," she whispered. He didn't answer; he didn't have to. He stood and pulled her to her feet. They walked upstairs to their bed-room and made love until the present drowned out the past and until Lydia remembered that she was not a lost girl, but a woman found and claimed by herself.

Thirty

He looked older and very tired in the dim blue light of the room. And she'd never seen him look so sad. He sat uncomfortably on a vinyl chair with metal arms, slouching, his chin resting on the knuckles of one hand and he stared out a window that looked out only into blackness that she could tell. She could see orange light coming in from under the doorjamb and she felt terrible pain in her arm, her head, her throat. She was aware then of a low beeping, distant voices, a peal of laughter somewhere outside.

Okay, she thought to herself, what's going on? She searched the room for something to orient herself but the only thing she recognized was her ex-husband and even he looked changed.

"What's wrong?" she managed. "What's happening?"

He jumped at the sound of her voice and looked at her, first with stunned disbelief and then with joy. He started to cry then, dropped from the chair beside her and knelt beside her bed, putting his lips to her hand.

"Jesamyn. Thank God." He just kept saying it over and over. She wanted to reach with her other hand to comfort him but it hurt too much. She'd never seen him cry, not like that. Never heard him sob. What could make him cry like that?

"Where's Ben?" she asked, suddenly feeling a deep dread.

"He's fine, honey. He's with your mom downstairs."

"Downstairs?"

He looked at her, seemed to be searching for words. But he didn't have to. It all came rushing back . . . the man in leather, the car chase, the showdown on the shoulder of the road. She had him. She had him down, she remembered. How did she wind up shot? She couldn't remember. She started to cry then. The act of it was painful.

"Dylan," she said after a moment when she'd struck up the courage. "Please tell me he's okay. Please."

"Mount?" he asked quietly.

She nodded.

"Jez."

"Please."

"He's alive," he said solemnly. "Barely, but he's alive."

She let relief wash over her and felt her sadness and fear start to fade a little. He'd make it; he didn't have a choice. He was her partner and she needed him. She'd tell him so as soon as she could. Then the darkness came and washed over her again.

Lily Samuels awoke with a start in her own bed, in her own apartment, and practically wept with relief at the sight of her Ikea furniture. The images from her nightmares still lingered, the white room, the restraints, the feeding tube, the sound of gunshots, the raging fire. But they weren't nightmares; they were memories. She wondered if this was how soldiers who'd survived combat felt when they woke up after their first night home from war. She wondered if they felt as cored out and empty, the fear and anger still raging in their blood.

The sun streamed in the tall windows and she could hear her mother moving about in the kitchen. She could hear the *Today* show on the television. Outside the song of New York City, the horns and sirens, the buzz of a million footfalls and voices. Normal sounds. But they seemed strange. She wondered if normal would ever seem normal again. Right now, it just felt like a veneer over the dark truth of her life.

She pushed herself upright on the bed, flipped the covers back. She looked at skinny arms and knobby knees she didn't recognize. She'd always considered herself to be a little fat; she'd dieted and exercised all her life like everyone else trying to get skinny, trying to fit the image the media plunged down her throat every day. Now she just wanted herself back, her healthy pink skin, her too-round bottom. She didn't want to be gray and sticklike, bony and strained-looking like the girl in the bathroom mirror last night. She couldn't wait to start eating real food again. In fact, did she smell bacon?

But there was another, much stronger urge than hunger. She looked around the room for her black case and remembered that she'd lost her computer somewhere along the line. And the notes she'd taken had to be abandoned when she fled the burning New Day compound. No matter; she remembered everything. Everything. Her fingers were itching, and her adrenaline was racing. Lydia Strong had always called this "the buzz." That tingle in your chest, that racing urge to get the words down, to get them out before they burst through your skin.

She slid off her bed and went over to the faux leather chair at her desk. She pulled a notebook and a pen from the drawer. And then she started to write.

Thirty-One

The headline read: NIGHT FALLS ON THE NEW DAY.

Hokey but effective, thought Matt. Gotta love the *Post*; they knew how to write headlines. It blared out at him from Jesamyn's hands as she read the article out loud from her wheelchair. They made quite a pair, him still in his hospital bed, the healing wound in his abdomen that nearly killed him still making it impossible to sit nearly a week after he'd taken the bullet. The shot that tore up his shoulder making it impossible for him to lift his right arm to hold the paper.

Jesamyn looked smaller than ever and was being wheeled around in a wheelchair until her bullet wound that had shattered her right thigh bone was healed enough to start rehab. Her shoulder and left calf were healing fine. Her memory of that night was still sketchy. She'd killed the shooter, who remained unidentified. The second van had not yet been found. But the important thing was that they'd both be okay, a hundred percent eventually. They both had a long road ahead of them, but neither of them was complaining. It definitely beat the alternative.

"I think your kid probably weighs more than you right now."

She peered over the paper at him. "You're pretty ballsy for someone who's totally defenseless."

"What are you gonna do—roll over me with your wheelchair?"

"Are you going to let me finish this?"

He nodded.

"Officials from The New Day have officially distanced themselves from what they refer to as the Rhames Division of their church. Officials claim that he joined as a member in 1998 and moved up the ranks of the organization until he was eventually awarded his own Initiation Center in Riverdale and control of one of their businesses, the New

Day Farms in Central Florida. At a certain point, The New Day asserts, Rhames broke contact and affiliation from the organization and that they have been on the verge of initiating legal action to stop him from using their name. The techniques of brainwashing and the usurping of member funds are neither employed nor condoned by The New Day, claimed one official. Likewise, they deny any involvement in what appears to be the framing of NYPD Detective Mateo Stenopolis in the beating death of Katrina Aliti and the shooting of witness Clifford Stern.

"In spite of their disassociation from Rhames, an official federal investigation has been opened into The New Day. Charges could include kidnapping, extortion, coercion, and fraud. And past complaints from former New Day members, including some that ended in the complainant's mysterious deaths, will be re-examined."

"So what does that mean?" asked Matt.

"It means that Trevor Rhames takes the fall in the public eye and for The New Day, it's probably business as usual. A couple of well-placed contributions and I bet that investigation goes away."

"We'll make sure that doesn't happen," said Lydia Strong, walking into the room with an armful of pink and white tulips in one hand and a large white take-out bag in the other. Jeffrey Mark was behind her.

"Hey," said Matt. "The nurse's station told me that you've been calling to check up on me." He tried to rise a bit on instinct and received a nasty reminder from his middle that it wasn't an option.

"I don't know what they're feeding you in here," she said. "But I brought you some take-out from the Greek place where we ate together."

He could smell it from where he lay. "You rock. I don't know if they'll let me eat it . . . but just the smell is making me feel better."

"We've never met," said Lydia, holding her hand out to Jesamyn. She took it and gave Lydia a smile. "But these are for you, Detective Breslow."

"Thank you," she said. "They're gorgeous."

"This is my husband, Jeffrey Mark," she said. Jesamyn nodded and took his hand.

"Good to meet you both. Thanks for bringing Lily Samuels home."

Matt thought he detected a note of sadness in her voice but when he looked at Jez's face, she was smiling. Maybe he was the one who was sad it hadn't been them to help Lily.

"You both look like you're on the mend," said Jeffrey, moving into the room and leaning against the windowsill.

"We're getting there," said Matt. "I've been dying to hear what happened that night in Florida."

Lydia told them about their visit from Grimm and their fall down the hole. She told him how Dax blasted them out and the ATF tried to hold them as scapegoats, then changed their minds and let them return home with Lily. She told him about their last visit with Tim Samuels and then about his suicide, and how a former employee from his company, Body Armor, was linked to the jewel robbery on the service road at JFK.

"So did you figure it out? What deal he made and with who?"

"The beneficiary on his policy was his wife, just as it should have been. Now she and Lily are left with nothing. The only one he screwed with his suicide was his family."

"Seems like he had a lot of practice at that," said Matt.

"And Rhames?" said Jesamyn.

"He disappeared that night. With his resources and connections . . . he's going to be hard to find."

"Is anybody looking?"

Lydia looked away and Matt could tell that there was more to say but that she wouldn't say it to him.

"So how is she?" asked Matt, trying and failing to seem casual. He was nursing a fantasy that she would come to see him, but that hadn't happened.

"Lily? Tough enough to write that article," said Lydia, nodding toward the newspaper in Jesamyn's hand. "But I think it's a long road back to normal."

His eyes traveled over to some pink roses that sat on the dresser across from his bed. "She sent those, thanking us for searching for her and not giving up."

"She's a good kid, stronger than I would have guessed. She'll be okay," said Lydia. She went on, saying how Lily and her mom were living together in Lily's apartment for the time being, trying to move forward together, but Matt stopped listening. He was watching Jesamyn who suddenly had gone pale; she had a dazed expression on her face, her head cocked to one side.

"Jez?"

"Oh, shit," she said. She held the paper in her hand and was looking at it closely. "This picture."

She handed the paper to Lydia. She saw the picture of Mickey and Michele LaForge that she'd taken from Lily's apartment early in the investigation. It was the only recent picture they had of the woman who remained at large, so Lydia had returned it to Lily for her article.

"What?" said Mount.

"The second van, the shooter that got me in the shoulder. There was a couple . . . a gorgeous woman with long blonde hair and a young guy. He shot me." She let her sentence trail off, shook her head, and they all looked at her. "I'm sorry. It's just that I've only had this really vague memory of that night. And this picture—it's shaken something loose."

Lydia felt her heart thump. "That man is Mickey Samuels," said Lydia. "He's dead, Detective Breslow."

Jesamyn nodded slowly. "I know," she said, rubbing her eyes. "But I'd almost swear to it. These are the people in the second van."

"Is it possible?" said Matt.

Jeffrey and Lydia exchanged a look, both afraid that it was entirely possible . . . and that they'd been wrong about everything all along.

"Where are we going?" asked Jeff, gripping the dashboard as Lydia quickly wove the Kompressor through the thick street traffic. She saw him pump his right leg, instinctively reaching for the breaks. He didn't like the way she drove. He said she was an "offensive" driver rather than a "defensive" driver. But Lydia believed that, even in driving, sometimes the best defense is a good offense.

"To Riverdale. To talk to Dax."

"Why? What does he have to do with this?"

She glanced at him and then put her eyes back on the road. "Think about it."

He stared ahead for a moment and then lifted his hands. "You lost me."

"Something Lily said in the motel. When I asked her what secrets her stepfather could be keeping that were bad enough to sacrifice his children. Something her mother would go along with."

"She said she didn't know. She said something possibly to do with Body Armor or with his military career before he met her mother."

She nodded but didn't say anything.

"You think Dax might know something about that?" he said.

She cut across two lanes, leaving an angry cabby leaning on his horn. "Remember what Grimm said about Sandline?"

"What about it?"

"How you don't get fired from a company like that; you get eliminated."

"So?"

"Okay, so what if Samuels worked for Sandline, too? What if he and Rhames knew each other from way back then? And what if that's the reason he couldn't say anything to help himself. All the mistakes he supposedly made, like his wife and Lily said, this dark past. He was willing to sacrifice Lily and Mickey. Maybe he didn't reveal it because he *couldn't,* not because he just didn't want to."

"Out of some kind of loyalty to Sandline?"

"Or fear of what they would do to him."

"But his life was already in shambles. The New Day killed his stepson—or so he believed—took his daughter, his wife had left him. He stood to lose all his money. What else could they take from him?"

"His life; until he took it himself."

Jeffrey tapped his finger on the door handle, was silent for a moment. "Maybe Dax was right after all; suicide as the ultimate act of control."

"Or surrender."

"Okay, say any of this is true. What does Dax have to do with it?"

"I just think he knows more than he's saying."

Jeffrey shook his head. "If he knew something that would help us, he would have told us."

"Not if he thought he was endangering us by doing so."

More silence. Then, "Where does Mickey fall into this?" asked Jeffrey.

"If Detective Breslow truly did see him that night and he's still alive, then we have to assume that he's in partnership with The New Day and not a victim," said Lydia.

Jeffrey shook his head. "Since Florida we've been thinking that he infiltrated The New Day to help Tim Samuels and either they fucked him up so badly that he killed himself, or he got too close and they took care of the job for him."

"But maybe Mickey was working with them," said Lydia, thinking aloud.

"But why? And how would they even have come in contact with one another?"

"Maybe Rhames sought him out. You know, the enemy of my enemy is my friend."

"Did Mickey really consider Tim Samuels his enemy?"

"I guess it depends on what those dark secrets are, on what Trevor Rhames may have told Mickey about his stepfather's past."

When they got to Dax's house, the windows were dark and the gate was locked. Lydia rolled down the car window and pressed the buzzer near the gate but the box was silent. She stared at it worriedly, as if doing so would cause him to answer. But it didn't work. She felt a rise of dread in her chest.

"He's not here," she said pointlessly. She turned anxious eyes on him.

He released a breath. "Oh no," he said raising his hand. "You don't want to break in."

She looked at him.

"Bad idea," he said. "Very bad idea."

She had to agree with him. She took her cell phone from the center console and dialed Dax's number. The voicemail picked up before the first ring.

"Leave a message. No names, no numbers. If I don't know who you are, you shouldn't be calling." A long tone.

"I need to talk to you," she said. "It's urgent. Seriously."

She ended the call and looked with dark frustration at the windows of his house. She fought the urge to pound the dashboard with her fist.

"What now?" she asked, as much of herself as of Jeffrey.

He was quiet a second. Then, "I think I know where we can get some information."

He got out of the car and walked around to the driver's side. "I'm driving."

She rolled her eyes and slid over to the passenger seat.

"Control freak," she said.

Manny Underwood looked as if he'd been on the losing end of an argument with a jackhammer. He lay on a thin cot in the center of a stone room beneath the streets of the diamond district. He turned swollen eyes on them when they entered the room.

"You can't keep him here forever," Jeffrey said to Chiam Bechim.

"We're very patient people. But, no," the old man said solemnly, "we can't."

"So what are you going to do with him?"

"All we want to know is where the rest of the stones are," he said vaguely.

"And who he was working for."

Chiam shifted on his feet, his eyes on Lydia. He leaned into Jeffrey and whispered. "This is not a place to bring a woman, Mr. Mark."

"She's no ordinary woman," said Jeffrey with a smile. "She's my wife."

Chiam made some kind of uncomfortable throat-clearing noise and looked over at Underwood. "He has been wholly uncooperative. But I have the sense that under the right circumstances, he might begin to loosen up."

Jeffrey looked at him.

"We're employing a program of gradual escalation," Chiam said softly, as if he were a doctor discussing the treatment of a terminally ill patient.

The man on the cot released a low groan. He didn't sound healthy and Jeffrey felt a wash of compassion for him.

"Don't feel too badly for him, Mr. Mark," said Bechim, reading his expression. "This is a very bad man, guilty of some heinous acts. When we enter this business and conduct ourselves poorly, we all know where we might wind up."

The old man's words were a warning and Jeffrey felt them in his bones. He felt Lydia stiffen at his side. He turned a cold stare on Chiam.

"All I'm saying is that you might just 'escalate' yourself out of what you want to know."

"If you think you can do better, be my guest," he said. He turned and left, leaving Lydia and Jeffrey alone in the cellar with Underwood. Jeffrey didn't hear the door at the top of the staircase open or close so he knew Chiam was nearby, listening.

"Mr. Underwood," Jeffrey said softly. "If you talk to us, we might be able to help you out of this mess."

Underwood jumped at the sound of his name, struggled to sit up and couldn't. Another low groan accompanied by a gurgling sound in his chest.

"You're thinking if you tell them what you know then they're going to kill you. And you might be right. But if you cooperate with me, I'll do my best to see that doesn't happen."

Manny turned to look at Jeffrey, moving his head slowly to the side. His face was purple and swollen and Jeffrey doubted that he'd recognize the man before the beating he'd received.

"Did Trevor Rhames hire you to steal those diamonds?"

He jumped at the sound of Rhames's name but didn't say anything. Jeffrey waited a minute for him to speak.

"We found a pink diamond in an abandoned house in Riverdale that we know is connected to The New Day. We believe that diamond was in the cache stolen from the dealer who was killed at the JFK airport. Who hired you to do that job?"

Still nothing from Underwood. Jeffrey waited a beat and then released a low sigh.

"Okay, this is what we're thinking, Mr. Underwood. We're thinking that Rhames had an issue with Tim Samuels, your former employer. That he bought Body Armor when Samuels put it up for sale and has been using it as a front to launder stolen money and gems. We think that you went to work for Rhames when he bought the company, just like the mercenary that you are and shifted easily from doing legitimate bodyguard work to being a thug for hire. You were unlucky enough to get caught by the people whose diamonds you helped to nab; now you're stuck. No one's going to help you because you're a mercenary. If you give up your employer, you're going to die. If you don't, you're going to die. So what are you doing—just buying time?"

Underwood started to shake a bit and make a low, horrible noise. "You don't understand," he said.

"Make me understand," said Jeffrey

More shaking from Underwood. It was disturbing, making Jeff uncomfortable. He looked over at Lydia who was leaning against the wall with her arms crossed, eyes narrowed on Underwood.

"He gets *in* you. Whatever they do to me here can't compare to what he can do."

Jeffrey heard Lydia draw in a breath and release it slowly.

"Rhames?" he asked.

Underwood nodded. Jeffrey noticed that a pool of blood was collecting beneath him, thick and black in the dim light.

"Manny, he can't do anything more to you."

"You saw what he did to Samuels and his family. And they were friends once. Imagine what he'd do to my kids."

Jeffrey watched as tears mingled with blood and traveled down Manny's face. He reached for Jeffrey's arm and gripped his wrist hard. "He knows everything. They'll never be free. No matter where they go or how they try to hide. And he'll wait until they think they're safe, until they think he's forgotten them or that he's dead. And then he'll move in and lay waste to their lives. That's what he does."

Jeffrey looked at Underwood's eyes and saw that he was starting to get a dazed look. He wasn't sure what to ask next.

"How did they know each other?"

"I don't know. It was a long time ago; that was the rumor anyway. There was bad blood. No one knew what." He was using all his strength to force the words out; it was painful to hear the horrible croaking of his voice.

"They worked together at Sandline?" asked Lydia.

Underwood didn't say anything. He turned his eyes back to Jeff; his face was too ruined to read his expression.

"Do yourself a favor," he said softly. "Stay out of it."

Jeff nodded. Underwood's eyes went blank then and he didn't say anything else. Ever.

Thirty-Two

They brought the Kompressor to a stop in front of Lily Samuels' apartment building and idled.

"We shouldn't be here. What if we're wrong?" said Lydia anxiously.

"Well, then. We're wrong."

"We need more evidence before we bring this to them. Right now we just have our hunches, the damaged memory of an injured police officer and the word of a man who was being slowly tortured to death," said Lydia. "Lily's fragile, just barely able to accept that her brother is gone. If we bring this to her and then it turns out that we've made another wrong assumption, we'll be hurting someone who doesn't need anymore hurt in her life."

"So what are you suggesting?"

"Let's go home, regroup, and try to corroborate some of this info."

"How?"

"I don't know," she said with a sigh.

"Why would Underwood lie? He knew he was dying; that's why he told us as much as he did."

"Why does anyone lie, Jeffrey? Because they can."

"Awfully cynical."

"Just drive. Please."

Before the elevator doors opened into their loft, they heard the television on inside. Jeffrey reached for his gun and Lydia quickly put her hand on his.

"Dax has a key, remember?"

Jeffrey rested his hand on the Glock at his waist but didn't draw the weapon. He'd given Dax a key when he was charged with protecting Lydia from Jed McIntyre and never asked for it back. Dax hadn't been up and around without their help much in the last year so he hadn't had the need to let himself in recently. Still, it wasn't good to make assumptions.

The doors opened but the apartment was dark except for the large flat-screen television in the living room. A huge dark form sat on the edge of the couch, feet up on the coffee table. An episode of South Park was turned up too loud. An arm the size of a jackhammer reached out and the light on the end table came up. Dax turned to look at them.

"What are you two looking so tense about? You said it was urgent, yeah?"

Lydia started to breathe again and wondered when she'd become so jumpy.

"Yeah," she said, dropping her leather coat over one of the chairs and stepping down into the sunken living room. "It's urgent."

"Great," he said. "Can we talk over pizza? I'm starved."

She sat on the coffee table and looked at him, reached for the remote, and flipped the television off.

"This is what I'm thinking. I'm thinking all of this started a long time ago. I'm thinking Rhames and Samuels both worked for Sandline."

The smile dropped from Dax's face and he got that granite look, those flat eyes he got when she pushed too hard into his past.

"I think Rhames and not The New Day was trying to ruin Tim Samuels' life. And I think he convinced Mickey to help him."

Dax sat silent and Jeffrey came up behind him.

"What I don't understand is what Tim Samuels did that could cause Rhames to hate him so much for so long, what could cause Mickey Samuels, the boy Tim raised like his own, to join forces with a psychopath and do all the awful things he's done."

"And you think I know the answer to that?"

"I think you know something about Sandline. And if you do, maybe you know something about what might have happened between those two."

Dax got up and walked toward the window on the other side of the television. He drew in and released a breath.

"If I knew something that would help you, do you think I would keep it from you?"

"If you had to or thought you had to, yes," she said to his back. "There are huge parts of your life we know nothing about."

He nodded but kept his back to her. "And that's probably not going to change. But I'm telling you the truth when I say that I don't know anything about this situation."

Lydia sighed and leaned back on the couch. She looked at the familiar form of their friend and thought he seemed like a stranger. She didn't think he would lie to her but she realized she didn't know for sure. And she wondered what that meant about their relationship. Can you trust someone who chooses what he reveals about himself? Can there be a true friendship with someone who hides huge parts of his life? Lydia didn't know. She felt a strange sadness, an odd distance from him as he came to sit across from her on the low, stout cocktail table.

"What I can tell you is that no one talks about Sandline. Everything about them, including whatever you've done for them, is classified. You violate that agreement and they burn your life down—not just your life, but the life of anyone you've told."

"If that's true, then I don't know where to go from here."

He shook his head and looked at the floor. "I don't know what to tell you."

"There's only one place we can go, I think," said Jeffrey.

"Grimm, right?" said Lydia, leaning forward looking at Dax. "How do we find him?"

Dax smiled. But the smile was cool and didn't reach his eyes. "You'll never see Grimm again."

"There's only one person who knows what links Rhames and Tim Samuels," said Jeffrey, coming to sit beside her. "There's only one person who might know the secret that would cause Mickey to turn against his stepfather like this, destroying his whole family in the process."

Lydia rubbed the tension from her neck. "Monica Samuels," she said. "She wouldn't tell us before."

"Let's try again," said Jeffrey.

Thirty-Three

They found Monica Samuels at Lily's apartment, looking pale and shaken.

"The police were just here," she told them as she held the door open for them. "They say Mickey may be alive, that he tried to kill a police officer. Can that be true?"

She looked at them with wide eyes and her skin was gray and papery. She seemed fragile, barely solid, as though the news the police had brought her might carry her away like a tornado.

"Where's Lily?" asked Lydia, looking around the small apartment.

"She left," said Monica, looking at the door.

"To find Mickey?" asked Jeffrey.

"Mostly to get away from me, I think," said Monica, sinking into the couch and curling her legs up beneath her.

"You fought?" asked Lydia sitting beside her. Jeffrey leaned against the granite countertop. Lydia released a breath when Monica didn't answer.

"Let us help you," Lydia said. "This has to end. Whatever you're hiding has destroyed your life."

Her face stayed blank, her eyes glazed over. "It's too late, I think. The family is shattered, just like he wanted. Just like he's wanted since he was a little boy."

"Why would he want that?"

She rested her forehead in her bony, well-manicured hand. "Because he thinks we killed his father."

"Simon Graves?"

Monica nodded. "They're so alike, that same dark place inside of them. They disappear in there. It swallows them . . . the anger, the sadness."

Lydia didn't say anything, waited for her to go on.

"Simon had Mickey with him that day when he walked in on Tim and me making love. We were at Tim's house on the island, you've been there. Simon and Mickey came strolling in. We were by the fire."

"They knew each other?"

"They were close friends," she said, looking at Lydia. "And they worked together."

"At Sandline," said Lydia.

Monica startled, like the sound of the word frightened her. She lowered her voice to a whisper. "How do you know that? We're *never* to talk about that."

"So all of them, Rhames, Samuels, and Graves worked together?" Jeffrey said from the counter.

Monica gave the slightest nod. But that's not what she wanted to talk about. There were other things she wanted to lay down before Lydia. "Mickey was too young to really understand what he was seeing. And because he was there, Simon just picked him up and left us without a word." She laughed a little. "Part of me was glad he found us. All the lies and sneaking around were finished. I figured he'd leave me; we'd all pick up the pieces and move on. I could finally be free of that darkness that leaked out of him like a fog. It was killing me."

"But he killed himself instead."

"Several weeks later, yes," she said, her hand flying to her mouth, the tears starting to fall.

"And Mickey blamed you and Tim."

"At first, yes," she said with a quick nod, wrapping her arms around herself.

"What changed?"

She seemed to shrink a little here, want to make herself as small as possible. "He was young, too young to really understand what he saw. Simon tried to spare Mickey by hiding his anger that day. But you can't really hide things from children. 'You made Daddy so sad and now he's gone,' he'd say to me afterward. 'Why was he so sad?'"

She paused here, released a shuddering sigh. Then, "We couldn't take it. We didn't want Mickey growing up with that memory."

"And you didn't want him reminding you."

She looked at Lydia and shook her head. "Over a period of

months, we were able to convince Mickey that he hadn't seen what he thought he saw, that it was a dream."

Lydia shook her head, not understanding. "How?"

"Using the psych ops Samuels learned in the military?" asked Jeffrey.

She looked at him as if she had forgotten he was there. Then she nodded. "With the help of Trevor Rhames. It was his area of specialty, tampering with people's minds, their memories, creating or erasing the events of their lives to comfort or torture them depending on his agenda. We thought we were helping him.

"But you can only calm the surface. The depths of him were teeming with these repressed memories. The depression that Lily never knew about, the medication, that's why?" Lydia tried to keep the judgment out of her voice but she wasn't sure she'd succeeded.

Monica shook her head. "He was prone to depression to begin with, just like his father."

"But this didn't help, tampering with his memories."

She shook her head again, more slowly. "No. It didn't help."

"So Rhames and Tim Samuels were friends once," said Jeffrey. "If he helped you to erase Mickey's memory, there must have been a relationship. What happened?"

"I can't talk about these things," she whispered, pleading to Lydia with her eyes.

Lydia leaned into her. "It's time. All of this—don't you see that it's toxic, it's poisoning your life? There's not much left to lose."

Monica looked at Lydia and wrapped her arms tighter around herself. She shook her head and pulled her mouth into a straight line. Then she seemed to soften, to change her mind about something. When Monica spoke again it was little more than a whisper.

"They knew each other long before Sandline. This all happened before we even knew Sandline existed. But that's all I can tell you."

Lydia wanted to grab Monica Samuels and shake some sense into her but she was surprised by a voice behind them.

"Tell her, Mom. Tell her everything. She's the only one we can trust now. Sandline's gone; they don't even exist anymore. It's Rhames we have to worry about."

Lydia turned to see Lily standing in the doorway. She wore jeans and leather boots, a long black coat. Without her hair, her face gaunt and still, she looked haunted. And Lydia guessed she was and would be—maybe forever.

Monica looked at her daughter with sad, frightened eyes. She seemed to steel herself.

"I don't know if Tim would have called Rhames a friend, even then. They'd served together in the Marines. Tim consulted with him in the private sector over the years. They were colleagues, I suppose, more than anything. I guess Rhames might have thought they were friends. But I was always a little nervous around him and so was Tim. Rhames had tremendous skills in certain areas."

"And you used those skills to erase Mickey's memories," said Jeffrey.

She nodded, her head hung.

"So at some point they went to work together at Sandline?" asked Lydia.

"Rhames went to work for Sandline. Tim only operated as a consultant. He had his own security firm by then, though it wasn't called Body Armor yet. But he had a team of people who worked for him; sometimes the whole team would go to work for Sandline, but only on a job-by-job basis."

"So what happened?" asked Lydia. "Why did Rhames grow to hate your husband so much?"

She sighed. "Rhames was reckless, dangerous. He was brilliant with the psych ops but on the field he was a kamikaze. During a Sandline op he made a tactical error and about ten men were killed. He led them into an ambush that most soldiers would have seen coming a mile away. That represents a big loss to a company like Sandline, loss of manpower, plus big payouts to the families."

"So they wanted to get rid of him," said Jeffrey.

Monica nodded.

"And they commissioned Tim Samuels to do that?" asked Jeffrey. "Because they were friends, because Rhames trusted him."

Monica smiled sadly. "No."

She sat up then, put her feet on the floor. She straightened her shoulders and seemed to come alive a bit. "Not Tim," she said. "Me. I shot Trevor Rhames and thought I'd killed him. I emptied my gun into his chest and he fell three stories."

"You worked for Sandline," said Lydia, incredulous. The waif before her looked as if she could barely support her own body weight.

Monica nodded. "Not for Sandline, per se. I was one of the people on Tim's team. I wasn't always the emotional mess you see today."

"No," said Lily. "Once you were a killer just like my father." The vitriol in her voice was palpable. Monica looked at her daughter with blank eyes.

"I was a *soldier.* I was one of three women; they needed us. We could go where men sometimes couldn't. We aroused less suspicion. But you're right, they chose me for the job because they knew Rhames trusted me."

"And how did you feel about him? Killing a man who'd helped you in friendship."

"I didn't feel anything. We weren't trained to feel; not in that context. It was a job and I completed it—or so I thought."

"But part of you was glad, right?" asked Lily. "That the only person who wasn't personally invested in keeping your secrets was dead?"

"No," said Monica, shaking her head vigorously. "No. It never entered my mind."

"Must be nice to operate without a conscience, Mom," said Lily, keeping cold eyes on her mother. Monica just sat there, taking her hits. She deserved Lily's anger and her judgment, and Monica knew it.

"Oh, and there's more," said Lily, moving into the room from the doorway where she'd been standing. "Did she get to the best part?"

Lydia shook her head. She wanted to reach for Lily but she was a bottle rocket, fuse sizzling; Lydia wasn't sure when she was going to blow.

"Simon Graves was *not* my father; Tim Samuels was. But I was never allowed to know that because to reveal it would be to undermine the memory altering they did on Mickey. So because of all their lies and all the black, terrible things they did, I never knew he was my father. Isn't that sick?"

They were all silent for a second, the air electric with Lily's rage.

"This is what happens to you when you fuck with Trevor Rhames," said Monica, to no one in particular. "He cores you, destroys you from the inside out."

Lily looked at her mother with undisguised hatred. "But he can only do that if there's an empty space inside you, someplace dark where he can get his hooks in."

Monica nodded, looked away from her daughter, to Lydia, and then into the space above her head. She leaned back into the couch. "I thought he was dead," she said pointlessly.

Lily released a disgusted breath but didn't say anything.

"So what kind of deal did Tim make with Rhames?" Lydia asked Monica.

"I really don't know. He called me that night," said Monica, tearing.

"He told me that he'd made everything right and that Lily would be home soon. That was the last time I spoke to him."

"I don't think he made his deal with Rhames," said Lily, leaning against the wall. She seemed cool, dispassionate suddenly, and Lydia thought she was in some kind of shock. "I think he made the deal with Mickey."

"Why do you say that?" asked Lydia.

"Because it's so perfect. It's like poetic justice. My parents' infidelity so wrecked Simon Graves that he ended his life; Mickey wanted Tim's life to end the same way. It's childish, like a child's tantrum. Only this child is grown and gone mad, with the help of my parents and Trevor Rhames."

They'd created a honeycomb of lies and deceptions, Tim and Monica Samuels, and tried to build their life upon it, thought Lydia. And all these years, Trevor Rhames had just been waiting to put his boot through it.

Thirty-Four

The water was painfully cold but she stood ankle deep in it, her jeans rolled up, her feet bare, and looked back at the house just as she'd done a hundred, a thousand times. The sea was moody gray with high, forceful waves and thick whitecaps; it just barely seemed to be containing its anger. Or maybe she was just projecting.

She tried to imagine other people living in that house, other people laughing, crying, fighting, putting their keys in the door and turning the lock to come home. She tried to imagine another little girl sleeping in her room, getting ready for her first day of school, her first slumber party, her prom. She'd always hoped to get married at this house. But she guessed it was a little dream to lose compared to everything else she'd lost. Her brother, her father, even her mother through her various betrayals now just seemed like a stranger to Lily, someone she could not understand and was not sure whether she could forgive.

When her mother delivered the news that Tim Samuels was her father, it didn't even come as a surprise. Hadn't she always known it on a cellular level? She might have been able to forgive them for that. After all, she'd always thought of him as her father; he'd loved her and raised her well. Biology didn't matter all that much, did it?

It was all the rest of it. Her parents' awful past, what they did to Mickey, what Mickey became as a result of that. That Trevor Rhames was free. Those were the things that were killing her inside. Angry tears spilled down her face and she felt like she had a rock in her throat where the injustice sat, impossible to swallow and digest.

Her mother stepped out through the French doors and leaned

against the railing, gave her a wave that meant, "Come in. It's too cold out here." But Lily turned her back. Her mother was collecting photographs and knickknacks, the detritus of their ruined lives, putting them in boxes. Lily wanted no part of anything like that. She'd only come to say good-bye to her home, her father, and the little girl who used to love them both. She would cut it all loose, let the ocean take it and start again.

She turned around again to look at her mother. But she was gone. On the balcony, there was a man. He had close-cropped, bleached-blond hair, wore a pair of black jeans and a hooded gray sweatshirt. She frowned, felt her heart lurch. Then she started to run toward the house as the man turned and walked inside. The sand slowed her progress as she ran with all her strength. Finally, she reached the wooded walkway and pounded toward the balcony. She flew up the stairs.

Inside her mother sat on the chintz couch weeping, and beside her stood her brother, changed in every way, his appearance, his aura, but still her brother. She didn't know whether to punch him or embrace him. She threw herself at him in some combination of those things, screaming at him in a voice she barely recognized.

"You bastard," she yelled. "You fucker."

He held onto her and let her pound on him with her fists. "I hate you, I hate you, I hate you." She just kept saying it over and over, like the words could hurt him the way he'd hurt her, like they were blades she could throw at him. Finally, exhausted, she slumped against him, felt his arms around her. She heard Lydia Strong's words in her head.

"Lily, I think he'll come to you. He loves you and he won't be able to live with himself without trying to make you understand why he did what he did. He'll come for your forgiveness."

She'd thought about it and knew Lydia was right.

"And when he does?" she'd asked.

"What makes you think he'll come today?" Jeffrey asked.

Where they sat in the Kompressor on the bluff, they could see Lily Samuels standing on the beach.

"The closing on the house is tomorrow; they have personal items they want to retrieve," said Lydia, staring at the ocean. "It seems like a good day for contrition."

Christian Striker sat in the backseat. "He'd be crazy to come back."

"I think it's safe to assume he's crazy, Striker," said Lydia. She caught his ice blue eyes in the rearview mirror and smiled.

"Look," said Jeffrey. "She's running. She's running toward the house."

Just then Lydia's cell phone rang.

"They killed my father," Mickey said to Lily while she was still in his arms.

"And you killed mine," she whispered.

"I didn't kill him. He killed himself."

The irony of his own words was completely lost on him. She pulled away from him and looked into his eyes. He looked a little unhinged, a little vacant.

"Mickey," she said softly. "Your father committed suicide. No one killed him."

"Their actions, their betrayal killed him," he said, waving a disgusted hand at their mother.

"You father was unwell, Mickey," Monica said softly. "He abused me. He abused you—"

"Don't do that," Mickey screamed. "Don't tell lies to make what you did okay. You betrayed him, you tampered with my mind—my *mind*."

Monica stood and reached for him. "We wanted you to forget, to move on and live a happy life. We didn't want the ghost of that day haunting you."

He pushed her away and she landed on the couch, put her head in her hands. "Get away from me," he yelled. "Stay away."

"You're acting like a child, Mickey," said Lily. "Grow up."

He looked at her in surprise. The wind wailed outside and the smell of salt was strong in the air. The door stood open and the room was growing cold.

"You burned the house down, okay," she said, spreading her arms. "Figuratively speaking, anyway. You've avenged your father; you've ruined your mother. You got everything you wanted, right? What I don't get is—why *me*? I've never done anything but love you."

He looked as his feet, then up into her eyes. She saw shame and a pouty, childish anger there. She wanted to slap his face.

"You were the only thing they really loved," he said with a shrug. "Their marriage went to shit. They thought *I* was dead, and they were about to lose all their money; Tim thought he might possibly go to jail, and they were still *standing*. It was only when Tim thought he'd lost *you* that he started to unravel, that he started bargaining with his life."

She thought about it a second.

"So that was the deal you made. He ended his life and you spared mine."

"He came to see us; he wanted to deal. He said if we killed him and made it look like an accident, that there would be insurance money. His cash and assets would cover his debt to the IRS and he knew he could get Mom to hand over the insurance money if it meant your life. He wanted to buy you back."

"But it was never about money," said Lily.

He shook his head. "I *have* money, Lily. I always have. I just wanted him to look down the barrel of that gun and see what my father saw: hopelessness, despair, the end of a life badly lived. I wanted him to die with all his sins and failings staring back at him from that cold metal eye. Just like my father. And I wanted *her* to be left with nothing. *That* was the deal, not some paltry insurance payout."

"And he agreed."

"As long as I promised to let you go when the deed was done."

"How did he know you'd keep your word?"

"He knew I loved you. That was the only thing we ever had in common. We both loved you so much."

Lily sank to the couch, feeling suddenly like her own legs couldn't hold her. Monica wept quietly beside her.

"How did Rhames find you?"

"He always knew where we were. He was watching for years, waiting."

He sighed, paced the room for a second.

"He came to see me when Body Armor went on the market. He was just in my apartment one night when I came home. I was terrified, thought he was some kind of maniac. But he knew things about us, about our life, about Monica and Tim. He knew *everything*. And then he helped me to retrieve my memories. Memories he had helped to erase."

"That's when you quit your job and moved to Riverdale, opened No Doze."

He nodded. "I wanted to tell you but I knew you wouldn't understand."

She let out a little laugh. "You're right about that."

"That's why I distanced myself from you."

"You staged everything: the suicide, the journals."

"I knew you wouldn't believe I could kill myself. And I knew you'd come looking for answers. And you did. We always have known each other so well." He came to kneel beside her but she stood and walked away.

"Who was that in the car? Who died there that night?"

Mickey closed his eyes. "I don't know who," he said, looking away from her. He walked over beside her and they both stared out at the surf. "Rhames took care of that. He made sure the face was unrecognizable, put him in some of my clothes, and staged the scene to look just like my father's suicide. My fingerprints weren't on record anywhere. There was no sign of foul play, so there was no investigation to be worried about DNA evidence. Just to be sure, they scrubbed my apartment clean and left traces of his DNA—hair in the brush, saliva on the toothbrush. Unless the police got creative and cross-referenced the DNA with Monica's, the police would assume what was in the apartment belonged to me and if it matched the corpse, they'd consider that a positive ID. It never came to that. I left instructions in my will that I wanted to be cremated right away, my ashes scattered out there." He nodded toward the shore and Lily remembered the day vividly as one of the worst of her life. "Whoever it was, he's gone," he said.

She felt a black hole open in her chest, a supernova that sucked all the hope and happiness out of her spirit. She'd never felt so angry and alone. Her mother wept on the couch, but Lily felt nothing but a kind of distant pity for her. She wondered if she'd ever feel anything else again. She was about to tell him what he'd done to her. She opened her mouth but he raised a finger and put it to his lips. He cocked his head, lifting an ear to the air. After a second, he smiled. She heard it, too, and held his eyes.

"Oh, Lily," he said, with a sad shake of his head. "You didn't."

She removed the cell phone from her pocket and held it up for him to see.

"I love you, Mickey. I really do. But you have to answer for the things you've done. I'm sorry."

He backed away from her slowly, shaking his head. The front door burst open and police officers entered clad in Kevlar vests, guns drawn. She saw Lydia and Jeffrey behind them, followed by another lean man with light blond hair who Lily thought she remembered as Striker. The air was still and they stood silent for a second; the moment seemed frozen where any outcome was possible. Then Mickey took a revolver from the pocket of his baggy jeans and smiled at his sister.

"Drop it, Samuels. Right now," yelled one of the plainclothes officers, edging closer.

But Mickey lifted the gun to his temple quickly and pulled the trigger. Lily wasn't sure what was louder, the blast of the gun or the sound of her wailing her brother's name.

Thirty-Five

He reclined on the pool chaise, a nice fruity Merlot in one hand, a fat Cuban in the other. The sun was red and bloated, low in the sky. He waited for the cheers that would rise up from the bar overlooking the ocean when the sun dipped below the horizon. He'd never understood this, why the tourists cheered for the setting sun. To cheer the end of a day, the inevitable approach of death seemed so stupid to him. But then people *were* stupid. He'd made a fortune off that stupidity and he figured he shouldn't knock it but be grateful for it instead.

The bar was far below his balcony on the edge of the cliff and by the time the cheers reached him, they'd be almost indistinguishable from the cries of the gulls floating over the blue-green waters of the Caribbean. He closed his eyes and lifted the cigar to his lips, let the last rays of the day touch the skin on his face. In the palm tree across the bluff some wild parrots bickered with each other. The smell of his cigar and the salt air mingled oddly but not unpleasantly. Then it grew dark too quickly.

He opened his eyes and a bulky shadow stood before him, muscle clad in black. The sun behind him, his face was shaded in darkness. But Trevor Rhames didn't need to see his face to recognize the man before him.

"Hello, mate." The thick Australian accent drew out the last syllable and Rhames could hear the smile in his voice. "Grimm sends his regards."

The sun sunk below the horizon line then and the cheering of the crowd below rose up into the air.

Thirty-Six

Lydia knew from her father's letters that Estrellita Tavernier, called Este by her family and friends, thought about being a writer when she was young but decided that she wanted to teach elementary school instead. She had the same blue-black hair that Lydia had—which was odd since their father had been fair. But her dark hair was the only thing she and Lydia shared. Este's face was soft and round, a light happiness and mischief dancing in her dark brown eyes. Her skin was a soft café au lait; she was petite but round about the bottom and chest. The effect was a robust and feminine prettiness, a youthful aura. There was none of the hardness to her features or to her aura that Lydia knew herself to possess. All her hardness, she guessed, had come from her mother.

Lydia watched her like a stalker from the corner, as Este corralled a group of bundled-up little munchkins on an East Village schoolyard. Lydia wore black jeans and a three-quarter-length leather jacket, belted at the waist, a newspaper tucked under arms. She leaned against a lamppost and felt the cold metal seep through the thin layers she wore. Her bare hands and cheeks were pink and painful from the cold. She thought about leaving. She wasn't sure what she could say to Este; she wasn't sure if she had anything to say at all.

For three years, Lydia's half-sister had been teaching second grade about ten minutes from the Great Jones Street loft. The thought of this filled her with a kind of longing regret. It was a feeling that had settled in her bloodstream since the opening of the box left to her by her father and the letters her grandmother had kept shut in a drawer for most of Lydia's life.

Lydia walked up to the chain-link fence and laced her fingers through the links. She stood waiting for Este to notice her and finally she did. She looked at Lydia lightly, with an uncertain half-smile. Lydia had the idea that Este would know her and after a moment of blankness, recognition warmed her features. She walked slowly toward the fence, then did something that made Lydia's heart jump. She laced her fingers over Lydia's through the fence. Lydia could smell the peppermint on her breath, the light floral scent of her perfume.

It was in that moment that Lydia felt a wave of grief for Arthur James Tavernier and the little girl who'd grown up without him. She felt grief, too, for the smiling, joyous woman Lydia saw in the photographs her father had left her, a woman Lydia recognized as her mother but whom she'd never known.

"I'm sorry," Lydia said, looking down at the sidewalk. She wasn't sure why she'd said it. It wasn't an apology; more an expression of regret for the way things were.

"No," said Este, softly. "Let's not be sorry for all the things neither of us can change. We'll just go forward from here."

She looked into the warmth of Este's eyes. In the bright, cold day with the sound of children and the promise of snow in the air, Lydia believed they could.

Epilogue

"Come on, Mom. Let's go."

She rested her hand on Ben's head for a second and then put the last of her stuff in the suitcase. "Get your dad," she said. "I can't close this with one arm."

"I can do it," he said. He reached up onto the bed, closed the top and easily closed the zipper, pulled it down onto the floor. "Let's go."

She smiled at him; he seemed to have grown two inches in the three weeks she'd been in the hospital. "You're such a big boy."

He rolled his eyes. "Mom."

"Sorry."

He pulled the suitcase toward the door where Dylan appeared. He reached for the suitcase and Ben reluctantly handed it over.

"I can get it," he said sullenly.

"No doubt, champ. But I want to help Mom, too."

"I'll meet you guys downstairs," she said. "I want to spend a few minutes with Mount."

Dylan looked at her uncertainly, then nodded and took Ben by the hand.

"Hurry, Mom," he threw over his shoulder. "You said we could have pizza. And I'm hungry."

"I'm right behind you."

Mount was sitting up in bed reading one of Lydia Strong's true crime books, *With a Vengeance,* about the man who murdered her mother. He was very thin, gaunt about the face, his collarbone protruding through his gown. He had charcoal circles beneath his eyes. But there was more color to his cheeks than there had been in weeks. And he was sitting up. So that was something.

"She's had a hard life," said Jesamyn, entering the room and pulling up a chair beside him, nodding toward the paperback in his hands.

"It just made her tougher."

"And sadder."

"You think she's sad?"

"Yeah, I think she's a little sad inside."

"Hey. Who isn't?"

She nodded and gave him a smile. "You a little sad, Mount?"

He gave her a wide warm smile that she didn't expect. "Not today," he said. "Looks like you're going home. So I won't have you breathing down my neck every minute, nagging me during rehab, 'That all you got, girly man?'" He finished the sentence with an unflattering mimic of her taunts in the hospital gym.

"I'll be back for rehab, Princess. Don't you worry."

He reached for her hand. "Seriously, partner, I wouldn't have wanted to be laid up here with anyone else."

"Don't get all mushy," she said, giving his big hand a squeeze. "We'll be back on the job in six months tops."

She wasn't sure of that and she could tell by the look on his face that he wasn't either but somehow he looked happier than she'd seen him . . . well, ever.

"What's going on?" she asked with a smile and a cock of her head.

He shook his head. "Nothing," he said. Then he changed the subject.

"Hey, did you hear they picked up Michele LaForge in Vegas? Speeding in a brand-new Testarosa."

"I heard," she said. "I guess she didn't spend too much time grieving for Mickey Samuels."

"We all handle our grief differently, Jez. Don't judge," he said with mock sternness.

There was a light knock on the door then and she turned to see a face that was too familiar to her, a face she'd only seen in photographs and in her dreams. She stood up.

"Lily," she said.

The young girl approached her and held out her hand. She looked older than her pictures or Jesamyn's imagining of her; she looked fatigued. The youthful prettiness, the joyful innocence of her photographs was all but gone from her face. But there was a graceful beauty to her still.

"You must be Jesamyn Breslow," Lily said. "I recognize you from your pictures in the newspaper."

Jesamyn nodded, not sure of her voice.

"Thank you," Lily said, embracing Jesamyn carefully. "Thank you for all you did for me. I can't express my gratitude. And I'm so sorry—for everything."

Jesamyn looked over at Mount, who had the biggest smile on his face she'd ever seen. He looked beautiful—*goofy*—but beautiful.

"You have nothing to apologize for, Lily. And you're welcome," Jesamyn said, putting a hand to the girl's face. "But Detective Stenopolis really deserves all the credit. He never gave up."

Lily walked over to Matt then and took his hand, sat in the chair beside him. Matt looked like he was going to float away. Jesamyn felt something in her chest lighten and shift.

"I'm so sorry for everything you had to go through," she said to him.

"Seeing you here, Ms. Samuels, it was worth it," he said softly.

"Please," she said. "Call me Lily."

Jesamyn slipped from the room, looked back at Matt for a second, then looked down the hall. She saw Dylan and Ben sitting on the benches over by the elevator. Dylan stood as she approached.

"You guys didn't have to wait. I could have met you downstairs."

"We couldn't let you walk out of here alone," Dylan said.

She smiled up at him and let him put his arm around her as she waited for the elevator. She turned around a second and saw the door to Mount's room close. She felt a little joy and a little pain. That was life, she guessed.

"I'm not sure it counts if you have it catered," said Jeffrey with a teasing smile.

"Trust me. Nobody needs me to be cooking a turkey."

He held his stomach and nodded his agreement.

"Just help me set the table," she said, smacking him on the shoulder.

The kitchen around her was littered with white and orange bags from her favorite gourmet shop and the air was rich with the aromas of ham, turkey, stuffing, gravy, mashed potatoes, sweet potato pie, and everything else she could order. There was enough food for twenty people, though they were only expecting five: Lydia's grandparents, her half-sister Este and Este's boyfriend Jones, as well as Este's mother. Dax was incommunicado; Lydia hoped he might retrieve her messages and show up at the last minute. It was going to be an odd grouping of people linked only by their connection to Lydia and her father. Lydia couldn't begin to imagine how it was going to go.

"Hey," he said, putting his hands on her shoulders. "Are you nervous?"

"Jeffrey."

He let out a whooping laugh. "You *are* nervous. I don't believe it," he said. "I can honestly say that this is the first time I've seen you nervous."

She breathed against the flock of butterflies in her middle and smiled at her husband.

"Remind me again why I married you," she said.

He took her into her arms and held her tight. "Because you adore me," he told her. "Couldn't make it a day without me."

She laughed. "It's true," she said, looking up at him and kissing him quickly. He tasted like the pumpkin pie he'd been eating.

"I don't know," she said into his shoulder. "It's like we have a— family."

He pulled her back and looked at her. She was half frowning, half smiling.

"That's a good thing, right?" he asked with a light laugh.

"I guess we'll see," she said.

He kneeled before her and rested his head on her belly. It was still flat and firm. But she figured not for very long, if all went well this time.

"What do you think, little guy?" he asked.

"How do you know it's a boy?" she said.

"I can tell," he said, rising. "Very masculine energy."

As if in agreement, the buzzer rang announcing visitors downstairs.

"Ready, my love?" he asked.

She gave him a bright, full smile that belied the flutter in her heart.

"Bring it on," she said. And they walked toward the elevator doors together.

DATE DUE

JAN 2 1 2006	JUN 0 1 2006
FEB 0 9 2006	JUN 1 3 2006
FEB 2 1 2006	DEC 0 4 2007
MAR 1 5 2006	MAY 2 1 2012
APR 0 7 2006	6/4/12
APR 2 4 2006	
MAY 0 6 2006	
MAY 3 0 2006	

DEMCO 128-5046

ce	
b,a,	